THE IMMORTALISTS

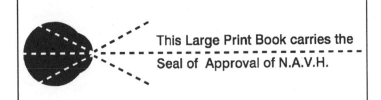

THE IMMORTALISTS

CHLOE BENJAMIN

THORNDIKE PRESS
A part of Gale, a Cengage Company

GALE
A Cengage Company

Farmington Hills, Mich • San Francisco • New York • Waterville, Maine
Meriden, Conn • Mason, Ohio • Chicago

Copyright © 2018 by Chloe Benjamin.
Thorndike Press, a part of Gale, a Cengage Company.

Thorndike Press® Large Print Basic.
The text of this Large Print edition is unabridged.
Other aspects of the book may vary from the original edition.
Set in 16 pt. Plantin.

LIBRARY OF CONGRESS CIP DATA ON FILE.
CATALOGUING IN PUBLICATION FOR THIS BOOK
IS AVAILABLE FROM THE LIBRARY OF CONGRESS

ISBN-13: 978-1-4328-4891-0 (hardcover)

Published in 2018 by arrangement with G.P. Putnam's Sons, an imprint of Penguin Publishing Group, a division of Penguin Random House LLC

Printed in Mexico
4 5 6 7 8 9 22 21 20 19 18

For my grandmother, Lee Krug

PROLOGUE:
THE WOMAN ON
HESTER STREET

1969
Varya

Varya is thirteen.

New to her are three more inches of height and the dark patch of fur between her legs. Her breasts are palm sized, her nipples pink dimes. Her hair is waist length and medium brown — not the black of her brother Daniel's or Simon's lemon curls, not Klara's glint of bronze. In the morning, she plaits it in two French braids; she likes the way they whisk her waist, like horses' tails. Her tiny nose is no one's, or so she thinks. By twenty, it will have risen to assume its full, hawkish majesty: her mother's nose. But not yet.

They wind through the neighborhood, all four of them: Varya, the eldest; Daniel, eleven; Klara, nine; and Simon, seven. Daniel leads the way, taking them down Clinton to Delancey, turning left at Forsyth. They walk the perimeter of Sara D. Roosevelt Park, keeping to the shade beneath the trees. At night, the park turns rowdy, but on this Tuesday morning there are only a few clumps of young people sleeping off the previous weekend's protests, their cheeks pressed to the grass.

At Hester, the siblings become quiet. Here they must pass Gold's Tailor and Dressmaking, which their father owns, and though it is not likely he'll see them — Saul works with total absorption, as if what he is sewing is not the hem of a men's pant leg but the fabric of the universe — he is still a threat to the magic of this muggy July day and its precarious, trembling object, which they have come to Hester Street to find.

Though Simon is the youngest, he's quick. He wears a pair of handed-down jean shorts from Daniel, which fit Daniel at the same age but sag around Simon's narrow waist. In one hand, he carries a drawstring bag made of a chinoiserie fabric. Inside, dollar bills rustle and coins shimmy their tin music.

"Where is this place?" he asks.

"I think it's right here," Daniel says.

They look up at the old building — at the zigzag of the fire escapes and the dark, rectangular windows of the fifth floor, where

8

the person they have come to see is said to reside.

"How do we get inside?" Varya asks.

It looks remarkably like their apartment building, except that it's cream instead of brown, with five floors instead of seven.

"I guess we ring the buzzer," Daniel says. "The buzzer for the fifth floor."

"Yeah," says Klara, "but which number?"

Daniel pulls a crumpled receipt out of his back pocket. When he looks up, his face is pink. "I'm not sure."

"Daniel!" Varya leans against the wall of the building and flaps a hand in front of her face. It's nearly ninety degrees, hot enough for her hairline to itch with sweat and her skirt to stick to her thighs.

"Wait," Daniel says. "Let me think for a second."

Simon sits down on the asphalt; the drawstring purse sags, like a jellyfish, between his legs. Klara pulls a piece of taffy from her pocket. Before she can unwrap it, the door to the building opens, and a young man walks out. He wears purple-tinged glasses and an unbuttoned paisley shirt.

He nods at the Golds. "You want in?"

"Yes," says Daniel. "We do," and he is scrambling to his feet as the others follow him, he is walking inside and thanking the man with the purple glasses before the door shuts — Daniel, their fearless, half-inept leader whose idea this was.

He heard two boys talking last week while in line for the kosher Chinese at Shmulke Bernstein's, where he intended to get one of the warm egg custard tarts he loves to eat even in the heat. The line was long, the fans whirring at top speed, so he had to lean forward to listen to the boys and what they said about the woman who had taken up temporary residence at the top of a building on Hester Street.

As he walked back to 72 Clinton, Daniel's heart skipped in his chest. In the bedroom, Klara and Simon were playing Chutes and Ladders on the floor while Varya read a book in her top bunk. Zoya, the black-and-white cat, lay on the radiator in a square frame of sun.

Daniel laid it out for them, his plan.

"I don't understand." Varya propped a dirty foot up on the ceiling. "What exactly does this woman *do*?"

"I told you." Daniel was hyper, impatient. "She has powers."

"Like what?" asked Klara, moving her game piece. She'd spent the first part of the summer teaching herself Houdini's rubber-band card trick, with limited success.

"What I heard," said Daniel, "is she can tell fortunes. What'll happen in your life — whether you'll have a good one or a bad one. And there's something else." He braced his hands in the door frame and leaned in. "She can say when you'll die."

Klara looked up.

"That's ridiculous," said Varya. "Nobody can say that."

"And what if they could?" asked Daniel.

"Then I wouldn't want to know."

"Why not?"

"Because." Varya put her book down and sat up, swinging her legs over the side of the bunk. "What if it's bad news? What if she says you'll die before you're even a grown-up?"

"Then it'd be better to know," said Daniel. "So you could get everything done before."

There was a beat of silence. Then Simon began to laugh, his bird's body fluttering. Daniel's face deepened in color.

"I'm serious," he said. "I'm going. I can't take another day in this apartment. I refuse. So who the hell is coming with me?"

Perhaps nothing would have happened were it not the pit of summer, with a month and a half of humid boredom behind them and a month and a half ahead. There is no air-conditioning in the apartment, and this year — the summer of 1969 — it seems something is happening to everyone but them. People are getting wasted at Woodstock and singing "Pinball Wizard" and watching *Midnight Cowboy,* which none of the Gold children are allowed to see. They're rioting outside Stonewall, ramming the doors with uprooted parking meters, smashing windows and jukeboxes. They're being murdered in the most gruesome way imaginable, with chemical explosives and guns that can fire five hundred and fifty bullets in succession, their faces transmitted with horrifying immediacy to the television in the Golds' kitchen. "They're walking on the motherfucking *moon,*" said Daniel, who has begun to use this sort of language, but only at a safe remove from their mother. James Earl Ray is sentenced, and so is Sirhan Sirhan, and all the while the Golds play jacks or darts or rescue Zoya from an open pipe behind the oven, which she seems convinced is her rightful home.

But something else created the atmosphere required for this pilgrimage: they are siblings, this summer, in a way they will never be again. Next year, Varya will go to the Catskills with her friend Aviva. Daniel will be immersed in the private rituals of the neighborhood boys, leaving Klara and Simon to their own devices. In 1969, though, they are still a unit, yoked as if it isn't possible to be anything but.

"I'll do it," said Klara.

"Me, too," Simon said.

"So how do we get an appointment with her?" asked Varya, who knew, by thirteen, that nothing comes for free. "What does she charge?"

Daniel frowned. "I'll find out."

So this is how it started: as a secret, a challenge, a fire escape they used to dodge the hulking mass of their mother, who demanded that they hang laundry or get the goddamn cat out of the stovepipe whenever she found them lounging in the bunk room. The Gold children asked around. The owner of a magic shop in Chinatown had heard of the woman on Hester Street. She was a nomad, he told Klara, traveling around the country, doing her work. Before Klara left, the owner held up one finger, disappeared into a back aisle, and returned with a large, square tome called *The Book of Divination*. Its cover showed twelve open eyes surrounded by symbols. Klara paid sixty-five cents and hugged it on the walk home.

Some of the other residents at 72 Clinton Street knew of the woman, too. Mrs. Blumenstein had met her in the fifties at a fabulous party, she told Simon. She let her schnauzer out to the front stoop, where Simon sat, and where the dog promptly produced a pellet-sized turd of which Mrs. Blumenstein did not dispose.

"She read my palm. She said I would have a very long life," Mrs. Blumenstein said, leaning forward for emphasis. Simon held his breath: Mrs. Blumenstein's own breath smelled stale, as if she were exhaling the same ninety-year-old air she had inhaled as a baby. "And do you know, my dear, she was right."

The Hindu family on the sixth floor called the woman a *rishika,* a seer. Varya wrapped a piece of Gertie's kugel in foil and brought it to Ruby Singh, her classmate at PS 42, in return for a plate of spiced butter chicken. They ate on the fire escape as the sun went down, their bare legs swinging beneath the grates.

Ruby knew all about the woman. "Two years ago," she said, "I was eleven, and my grandmother was sick. The first doctor said it was her heart. He told us she'd die in three months. But the second doctor said she was strong enough to recover. He thought she could live for two years."

Below them, a taxi squealed across Rivington. Ruby turned her head to squint at the East River, green-brown with muck and sewage.

"A Hindu dies at home," she said. "They should be surrounded by family. Even Papa's relatives in India wanted to come, but what could we tell them? Stay for two years? Then Papa heard of the rishika. He went to see her, and she gave him a date — the date Dadi was to die. We put Dadi's bed in the front room, with her head facing east. We lit a lamp and kept vigil: praying, singing hymns. Papa's brothers flew from Chandigarh. I sat on the floor with my cousins. There were twenty of us, maybe more. When Dadi died on May sixteenth, just like the rishika said, we cried with relief."

"You weren't mad?"

"Why would we be mad?"

"That the woman didn't save your grandma," Varya said. "That she didn't make her better."

"The rishika gave us a chance to say goodbye. We can never repay her for that." Ruby ate her last bite of kugel, then folded the foil in half. "Anyway, she couldn't make

15

Dadi better. She knows things, the rishika, but she can't stop them. She isn't God."

"Where is she now?" asked Varya. "Daniel heard she's staying in a building on Hester Street, but he doesn't know which."

"I wouldn't know, either. She stays in a different place every time. For her safety."

Inside the Singhs' apartment, there was a high-pitched crash and the sound of someone shouting in Hindi.

Ruby stood, brushing the crumbs off her skirt.

"What do you mean, her safety?" asked Varya, standing, too.

"There are always people going after a woman like that," Ruby said. "Who knows what she knows."

"Rubina!" called Ruby's mother.

"I gotta go." Ruby hopped through the window and pushed it shut behind her, leaving Varya to take the fire escape down to the fourth floor.

Varya was surprised that word of the woman had spread so far, but not everyone had heard of her. When she mentioned the seer to the men who worked the counter at Katz's, their arms tattooed with numbers, they stared at her with fear.

"Kids," said one of them. "Why would you

wanna get mixed up with something like that?"

His voice was sharp, as though Varya had personally insulted him. She left with her sandwich, flustered, and did not bring the subject up again.

In the end, the same boys Daniel originally overheard gave him the woman's address. He saw them that weekend on the walking path of the Williamsburg Bridge, smoking dope while they leaned against the railing. They were older than he — fourteen, maybe — and Daniel forced himself to confess his eavesdropping before he asked if they knew anything else.

The boys didn't seem to be bothered. They readily offered the number of the apartment building where the woman was said to be staying, though they didn't know how to make an appointment. The rumor, they told Daniel, was that you had to bring an offering. Some claimed it was cash, but others said the woman already had all the money she needed and that you had to get creative. One boy brought a bloody squirrel he found on the side of the road, picked up with tongs and delivered in a tied-off plastic bag. But Varya argued that nobody would want that, even a fortune teller, so in the end they collected their allowances in the drawstring bag and hoped that would be enough.

When Klara wasn't home, Varya retrieved *The Book of Divination* from beneath Klara's bed and climbed into her own. She lay on her stomach to sound out the words: *haruspicy* (by the livers of sacrificed animals), *ceromancy* (by patterns in wax), *rhabdomancy* (by rods). On cool days, breeze from the window ruffled the family trees and old photos she keeps taped to the wall beside her bed. Through these documents, she tracks the mysterious, underground brokering of traits: genes flicking on and off and on again, her grandfather Lev's rangy legs skipping Saul for Daniel.

Lev came to New York on a steamship with his father, a cloth merchant, after his mother was killed in the pogroms of 1905. At Ellis Island, they were tested for disease and interrogated in English while they stared at the fist of the iron woman who watched, impassive, from the sea they had just crossed. Lev's father repaired sewing machines; Lev worked in a garment factory run by a German Jew who allowed him to observe the Sabbath. Lev became an assistant manager, then a manager. In 1930, he opened his own business — Gold's Tailor and Dressmaking — in a basement apartment on Hester Street.

Varya was named for her father's mother, who worked as Lev's bookkeeper until their retirement. She knows less about her maternal grandparents — only that her grandmother was named Klara, like Varya's younger sister, and that she arrived from Hungary in 1913. But she died when Varya's mother, Gertie, was only six, and Gertie rarely speaks of her. Once, Klara and Varya snuck into Gertie's bedroom and scoured it for traces of their grandparents. Like dogs, they smelled the mystery that surrounded this pair, the whiff of intrigue and shame, and they nosed their way to the chest of drawers where Gertie keeps her underclothes. In the top drawer, they found a small wooden box, lacquered and gold hinged. Inside was a yellowed stack of photographs that showed a small, puckish woman with short black hair and heavy-lidded eyes. In the first photo, she stood in a skirted leotard with one hip cocked to the side, holding a cane above her head. In another, she rode a horse, bent over backward with her midriff showing. In the photo Varya and Klara liked best, the woman was suspended in midair, hanging from a rope that she held in her teeth.

Two things told them this woman was their grandmother. The first was a wrinkled old photo, greased with fingerprints, in which the same woman stood with a tall man and a small child. Varya and Klara knew the child was their mother, even at this reduced size: she held her parents' hands in her small, fat fists, and her face was squeezed into an expression of consternation that Gertie still frequently wore.

Klara claimed the box and its contents.

"It belongs to me," she said. "I got her name. Ma never looks at it, anyway."

But they soon found that was not true. The morning after Klara secreted the lacquered box back to the bedroom and tucked it beneath her bottom bunk, a caw came from their parents' room, followed by Gertie's heated interrogations and Saul's muffled denial. Moments later, Gertie burst into the bunk room.

"Who took it?" she cried. "Who?"

Her nostrils flared, and her wide hips blocked the light that usually spilled in from the hallway. Klara was hot with fear, nearly crying. When Saul left for work and Gertie stalked into the kitchen, Klara snuck into her parents' room and put the box exactly where she'd found it. But when the apartment was empty, Varya knew that Klara returned to the photos and the tiny woman inside them. She stared at the woman's intensity, her glamour, and vowed she'd live up to her namesake.

"Don't look around like that," Daniel hisses. "Act like you belong."

The Golds hurry up the stairs. The walls are covered in chipped beige paint, and the halls are dark. When they reach the fifth floor, Daniel pauses.

"What do you suggest we do now?" whispers Varya. She likes it when Daniel is stumped.

"We wait," says Daniel. "For someone to come out."

But Varya doesn't want to wait. She's jittery, filled with unexpected dread, and she starts down the hallway alone.

She thought that magic would be detectable, but the doors on this floor look exactly the same, with their scratched brass knobs and numbers. The *four* in number *fifty-four* has fallen sideways. When Varya walks toward the door, she hears the sound of a television or a radio: a baseball game. Assuming that a rishika would not care about baseball, she steps back again.

Her siblings have floated apart. Daniel stands near the stairwell with his hands in his pockets, watching the doors. Simon joins Varya at number fifty-four, rises onto his tiptoes and pushes the *four* back into place with his index finger. Klara has been wandering in the opposite direction, but now she comes to stand with them. She is followed by the scent of Breck Gold Formula, a product Klara bought with weeks of allowance; the rest of the family uses Prell, which comes in a plastic tube like toothpaste and squirts jelly the color of kelp. Though Varya scoffs outwardly — *she* would never spend so much on shampoo — she is envious of Klara, who smells like rosemary and oranges, and who now raises her hand to knock.

"What are you doing?" whispers Daniel. "That could be anyone. It could be —"

"Yeah?"

The voice that comes from behind the door is low in pitch and gruff.

"We're here to see the woman," Klara tries.

Silence. Varya holds her breath. There is a peephole in the door, smaller than a pencil eraser.

On the other side of the door, a throat is cleared.

"One at a time," the voice says.

Varya catches Daniel's eye. They have not

prepared to separate. But before they can negotiate, a bolt is pushed to one side, and Klara — what is she thinking? — steps through.

Nobody is sure how long Klara is inside. To Varya, it feels like hours. She sits against the wall with her knees to her chest. She is thinking of fairy tales: witches who take children, witches who eat them. A tree of panic sprouts in her stomach and grows until the door cracks open.

Varya scrambles to her feet, but Daniel is faster. It's impossible to see inside the apartment, though Varya hears music — a mariachi band? — and the clang of a pot on a burner.

Before Daniel enters, he looks at Varya and Simon. "Don't worry," he says.

But they do.

"Where's Klara?" asks Simon, once Daniel is gone. "Why didn't she come back out?"

"She's still inside," says Varya, though the same question has occurred to her. "They'll be there when we go in, Klara and Daniel both. They're probably just . . . . waiting for us."

"This was a bad idea," Simon says. His blond curls are matted with sweat. Because Varya is the oldest and Simon the youngest, she feels that she should be able to mother him, but Simon is an enigma to her; only Klara seems to understand him. He talks less than the others. At dinner, he sits with his brow furrowed and his eyes glazed. But he has a rabbit's speed and agility. Sometimes, while walking beside him to synagogue, Varya finds herself alone. She knows that Simon has only run ahead or dropped behind, but each time, it feels as though he's vanished.

When the door opens again, that same fraction of an inch, Varya puts a hand on his shoulder. "It's all right, Sy. You go ahead, and I'll stand lookout. Okay?"

For what or whom, she isn't sure — the hallway is just as empty as it was when they arrived. Really, Varya is timid: despite being the oldest, she'd rather let the others go first. But Simon seems comforted. He brushes a curl out of his eyes before he leaves her.

Alone, Varya's panic swells. She feels cut off from her siblings, as if she is standing on the shore, watching their ships float away. She should have stopped them from coming. By the time the door opens again, sweat has pooled above her upper lip and in the waistband of her skirt. But it's too late to leave the way she came in, and the others are waiting. Varya pushes the door open.

She finds herself in a tiny efficiency filled with so many belongings that at first she sees no person at all. Books are stacked on the floor like model skyscrapers. The kitchen shelves have been stuffed with newspapers instead of food, and nonperishables are clumped along the counter: crackers, cereal, canned soups, a dozen bright varieties of tea. There are tarot cards and playing cards, astrological charts and calendars — Varya recognizes one in Chinese, another with Roman numerals, and a third that shows the phases of the moon. There is a yellowed poster of the I Ching, whose hexagrams she remembers from Klara's *Book of Divination;* a vase filled with sand; gongs and copper bowls; a laurel wreath; a pile of twiglike wooden sticks, carved with horizontal lines; and a bowl of stones, some of which have been tied to long pieces of string.

Only a nook by the door has been cleared. There, a folding table sits between two folding chairs. Beside it, a smaller table has been set with red cloth roses and an open bible. Two white plaster elephants are arranged around the bible, along with a prayer candle, a wooden cross, and three statues: one of the Buddha, one of the Virgin Mary, and

25

one of Nefertiti, which Varya knows because of a small, handwritten sign that reads *NEFERTITI*.

Varya feels a pang of guilt. In Hebrew school, she heard the case against idols, listening solemnly as Rabbi Chaim read from the tractate Avodah Zarah. Her parents wouldn't want her to be here. But didn't God make the fortune teller, just as He made Varya's parents? In synagogue, Varya tries to pray, but God never seems to respond. The rishika, at least, will talk back.

The woman stands at the sink, shaking loose tea into a delicate metal ball. She wears a wide cotton dress, a pair of leather sandals, and a navy blue headscarf; her long, brown hair hangs in two slender braids. Though she is large, her movements are elegant and precise.

"Where are my siblings?" Varya's voice is throaty, and she is embarrassed by the desperation she hears in it.

The blinds are drawn. The woman pulls a mug from the top shelf and places the metal ball inside it.

"I want to know," Varya says, more loudly, "where my siblings are."

A kettle whistles on the stove top. The woman turns off the burner and lifts the kettle above the mug. Water pours out in a thick, clear cord, and the room fills with the smell of grass.

"Outside," she says.

"No, they're not. I waited in the hall, and they never came out."

The woman steps toward Varya. Her cheeks are doughy and her nose bulbous, her lips puckered. Her skin is golden brown, like Ruby Singh's.

"I can't do nothing if you don't trust me," she says. "Take off your shoes. Then you can sit down."

Varya slips off her saddle shoes and places them next to the door, chastised. Perhaps the woman is right. If Varya refuses to trust her, this trip will be for nothing, along with all they've risked for it: their father's gaze, their mother's displeasure, four sets of saved-up allowance. She sits at the folding table. The woman sets the mug of tea before her. Varya thinks of tinctures and poisons, of Rip Van Winkle and his twenty-year sleep. Then she thinks of Ruby. *She knows things, the rishika,* Ruby said. *We can never repay her for that.* Varya lifts the mug and sips.

The rishika sits in the opposite folding chair. She scans Varya's rigid shoulders, her damp hands, her face.

"You haven't been feeling so good, have you, honey?"

Varya swallows in surprise. She shakes her head.

"You been waitin' to feel better?"

Varya is still, though her pulse runs.

"You worry," says the woman, nodding. "You got troubles. You smile on your face, you laugh, but in your heart, you're not happy; you're alone. Am I right?"

Varya's mouth trembles its assent. Her heart is so full she feels it might crack.

"That's a shame," says the woman. "We got work to do." She snaps her fingers and gestures to Varya's left hand. "Your palm."

Varya scoots to the edge of her chair and offers her hand to the rishika, whose own hands are nimble and cool. Varya's breath is shallow. She can't remember the last time she touched a stranger; she prefers to keep a membrane, like a raincoat, between herself and other people. When she returns from school, where the desks are oily with finger-prints and the playground contaminated by kindergartners, she washes her hands until they're nearly raw.

"Can you really do it?" she asks. "Do you know when I'll die?"

She is frightened by the capriciousness of luck: the plain-colored tablets that can expand your mind or turn it upside down; the men randomly chosen and shipped to

28

Cam Ranh Bay and the mountain Dong Ap Bia, in whose bamboo thickets and twelve-foot elephant grass a thousand men were found dead. She has a classmate at PS 42, Eugene Bogopolski, whose three brothers were sent to Vietnam when Varya and Eugene were only nine. All three of them returned, and the Bogopolskis threw a party in their Broome Street apartment. The next year, Eugene dived into a swimming pool, hit his head on the concrete, and died. Varya's date of death would be one thing — perhaps the most important thing — she could know for sure.

The woman looks at Varya. Her eyes are bright, black marbles.

"I can help you," she says. "I can do you good."

She turns to Varya's palm, looking first at its general shape, then at the blunt, square fingers. Gently, she tugs Varya's thumb backward; it doesn't bend far before resisting. She examines the space between Varya's fourth and fifth fingers. She squeezes the tip of Varya's pinky.

"What are you looking for?" Varya asks.

"Your character. Ever heard of Heraclitus?" Varya shakes her head. "Greek philosopher. *Character is fate* — that's what he said. They're bound up, those two, like

29

brothers and sisters. You wanna know the future?" She points at Varya with her free hand. "Look in the mirror."

"And what if I change?" It seems impossible that Varya's future is already inside her like an actress just offstage, waiting decades to leave the wings.

"Then you'd be special. 'Cause most people don't."

The rishika turns Varya's hand over and sets it down on the table.

"January 21st, 2044." Her voice is matter-of-fact, as if she is stating the temperature, or the winner of the ballgame. "You got plenty of time."

For a moment, Varya's heart unlatches and lifts. Two thousand forty-four would make her eighty-eight, an altogether decent age to die. Then she pauses.

"How do you know?"

"What did I say about you trusting me?" The rishika raises a furry eyebrow and frowns. "Now, I want you to go home and think about what I said. If you do that, you're gonna feel better. But don't tell anybody, all right? What it shows in your hand, what I told you — that's between you and me."

The woman stares at Varya, and Varya stares back. Now that Varya is the appraiser and not the person appraised, something curious happens. The woman's eyes lose their luster, her movements their elegance. It is too good, the fortune Varya has been given, and her good fortune becomes proof of the seer's fraudulence: probably, she gives the same prediction to everyone. Varya thinks of the wizard of Oz. Like him, this woman is no mage and no seer. She is a swindler, a con artist. Varya stands.

"My brother should have paid you," she says, putting her shoes back on.

The woman rises, too. She walks toward what Varya thought was the door to a closet — a bra hangs from the handle, its mesh cups long as the nets Varya uses to catch monarchs in summer — but no: it's an exit. The woman cracks the door, and Varya sees a strip of red brick, a thatch of fire escape. When she hears the voices of her siblings drift up from below, her heart balloons.

But the rishika stands before her like a barrier. She pinches Varya's arm.

"Everything is gonna come out okay for you, honey." There is something threatening in her tone, as if it is urgent that Varya hear this, urgent that she believe it. "Everything is gonna work out okay."

Between the woman's fingers, Varya's skin turns white.

"Let me go," she says.

She is surprised by the coldness in her voice. In the woman's face, a curtain yanks shut. She releases Varya and steps aside.

Varya clangs down the stairs of the fire escape in her saddle shoes. A breeze strokes her arms and ruffles the downy, light brown hair that has begun to appear on her legs. When she reaches the alley, she sees that Klara's cheeks are streaked with salt water, her nose bright pink.

"What's wrong?"

Klara whirls. "What do you think?"

"Oh, but you can't actually believe . . ." Varya looks to Daniel for help, but he is stony. "Whatever she said to you — it doesn't mean anything. She made it up. Right, Daniel?"

"Right." Daniel turns and begins to walk toward the street. "Let's go."

Klara pulls Simon up by one arm. He still holds the drawstring bag, which is as full as it was when they came.

"You were supposed to pay her," Varya says.

"I forgot," says Simon.

"She doesn't deserve our money." Daniel stands on the sidewalk with his hands on his hips. "Come on!"

They are quiet on the walk home. Varya has never felt further from the others. At dinner, she picks at her brisket, but Simon doesn't eat at all.

"What is it, my sweet?" asks Gertie.

"Not hungry."

"Why not?"

Simon shrugs. His blond curls are white beneath the overhead light.

"Eat the food your mother has prepared," says Saul.

But Simon refuses. He sits on his hands.

"What is it, hm?" clucks Gertie, one eyebrow raised. "Not good enough for you?"

"Leave him alone." Klara reaches over to ruffle Simon's hair, but he jerks away and pushes his chair back with a screech.

"I hate you!" he cries, standing. "I! Hate! *All of you!*"

"Simon," says Saul, standing, too. He still wears the suit he wore to work. His hair is thinning and lighter than Gertie's, an unusual coppery blond. "You do not speak to your family that way."

He is wooden in this role. Gertie has always been the disciplinarian. Now, she only gapes.

"But I do," says Simon. There is wonder in his face.

■ ■ ■ ■

PART ONE:
YOU'D DANCE, KID

■ ■ ■ ■

1978–1982
Simon

1.

When Saul dies, Simon is in physics class, drawing concentric circles meant to represent the rings of an electron shell but which to Simon mean nothing at all. With his daydreaming and his dyslexia, he has never been a good student, and the purpose of the electron shell — the orbit of electrons around an atom's nucleus — escapes him. In this moment, his father bends over in the crosswalk on Broome Street while walking back from lunch. A taxi honks to a stop; Saul sinks to his knees; the blood drains from his heart. His death makes no more sense to Simon than the transfer of electrons from one atom to another: both are there one moment, and gone the next.

Varya drives down from college at Vassar, Daniel from SUNY Binghamton. None of them understand it. Yes, Saul was stressed, but the city's worst moments — the fiscal crisis, the blackout — are finally behind them. The unions saved the city from bankruptcy, and New York is looking up. At the hospital, Varya asks about her father's last moments. Had he been in any pain? Only briefly, says the nurse. Did he speak? No one can say that he did. This should not surprise his wife and children, who are used to his long silences — and yet Simon feels cheated, robbed of a final memory of his father, who remains as close-lipped in death as he was in life.

Because the next day is Shabbat, the funeral takes place on Sunday. They meet at Congregation Tifereth Israel, the conservative synagogue of which Saul was a member and patron. In the entryway, Rabbi Chaim gives each Gold a pair of scissors for the *kriah*.

"No. I won't do it," says Gertie, who must be walked through each step of the funeral as if through the customs process of a country she never meant to visit. She wears a sheath dress that Saul made for her in 1962: sturdy black cotton, with a fitted waistline, front button closure, and detachable belt. "You can't make me," she adds, her eyes darting between Rabbi Chaim and her children, who have all obediently slit their clothes above the heart, and though Rabbi Chaim explains that it is not *he* who can make her but God, it seems that God can't, either. In the end, the rabbi gives Gertie a black ribbon to cut, and she takes her seat with wounded victory.

Simon has never liked coming here. As a child, he thought the synagogue was haunted, with its rough, dark stone and dank interior. Worse were the services: the unending silent devotion, the fervent pleas for the restoration of Zion. Now Simon stands before the closed casket, air circulating through the slit in his shirt, and realizes he'll never see his father's face again. He pictures Saul's distant eyes and demure, almost feminine smile. Rabbi Chaim calls Saul magnanimous, a person of character and fortitude, but to Simon he was a decorous, timid man who skirted conflict and trouble — a man who seemed to do so little out of passion that it was a wonder he had ever married Gertie, for no one would have viewed Simon's mother, with her ambition and pendulum moods, as a pragmatic choice.

After the service, they follow the pallbearers to Mount Hebron Cemetery, where Saul's parents were buried. Both girls are weeping — Varya silently, Klara as loudly as her mother — and Daniel seems to be holding himself together out of nothing more than stunned obligation. But Simon finds himself unable to cry, even as the casket is lowered into the earth. He feels only loss, not of the father he knew but of the person that Saul might have been. At dinner, they sat at opposite ends of the table, lost in private thought. The shock came when one of them glanced up, and their eyes caught — an accident, but one that joined their separate worlds like a hinge before someone looked away again.

Now, there is no hinge. Distant though he was, Saul had allowed each Gold to assume their separate roles: he the breadwinner, Gertie the general, Varya the obedient oldest, Simon the unburdened youngest. If their father's body — his cholesterol lower than Gertie's, his heart nothing if not steady — had simply *stopped,* what else could go wrong? Which other laws might warp? Varya hides in her bunk. Daniel is twenty, barely a man, but he greets guests and lays out food, leads prayers in Hebrew. Klara, whose portion of the bedroom is messier than everyone else's, scrubs the kitchen until her biceps hurt. And Simon takes care of Gertie.

This is not their usual arrangement, for Gertie has always babied Simon more than the others. She wanted, once, to be an intellectual; she lay beside the fountain in Washington Square Park reading Kafka and Nietzsche and Proust. But at nineteen, she met Saul, who had joined his father's business after high school, and she was pregnant by twenty. Soon Gertie withdrew from New York University, where she was on scholarship, and moved into an apartment mere blocks from Gold's Tailor and Dressmaking, which Saul would inherit when his parents retired to Kew Gardens Hills.

Shortly after Varya was born — far sooner than Saul thought necessary, and to his embarrassment — Gertie became the receptionist at a law firm. At night, she was still their formidable captain. But in the morning, she put on a dress and applied rouge from a little round box before depositing the children at Mrs. Almendinger's, after which she exited the building with as much lightness as she had ever been capable. When Simon was born, though, Gertie stayed home for nine months instead of five, which turned into eighteen. She carried him everywhere. When he cried, she did not respond with bullish frustration but nuzzled him and sang, as if nostalgic for an experience she had always resented because she knew she would not repeat it. Shortly after Simon's birth, while Saul was at work, she went to the doctor's office and returned with a small glass pill bottle — *Enovid,* it read — that she kept in the back of her underwear drawer.

"Si-*mon!*" she calls now, in a rich long blast like a foghorn's. "Hand me that," she might say, lying in bed and pointing to a pillow just past her feet. Or, in a low, ominous tone: "I have a sore; I've been lying too long in this bed," and though Simon internally recoils, he examines the thick wedge of her heel. "That isn't a *sore,* Ma," he replies. "It's a blister." But by then she has moved on, asking him to bring her the Kaddish, or fish and chocolate from the shiva platter delivered by Rabbi Chaim.

Simon might think Gertie takes pleasure in commanding him, if not for the way she weeps at night — snuffled, so her children don't hear, though Simon does — or the times he sees her curled fetal on the bed she shared with Saul for two decades, looking like the teenager she was when she met him. She sits shiva with a devoutness Simon did not know she could muster, for Gertie has always believed in superstition more than any God. She spits three times when a funeral goes by, throws salt if the shaker falls over, and never passed a cemetery while pregnant, which required the family to endure constant rerouting between 1956 and 1962. Each Friday, she observes the Sabbath with effortful patience, as if the Sabbath is a guest she can't wait to get rid of. But this week, she wears no makeup. She avoids jewelry and leather shoes. As if in penitence for the failed *kriah,* she wears her black sheath day and night, ignoring the crust of brisket drippings on one thigh. Because the Golds own no wooden stools, she sits on the floor to recite the Kaddish and even tries to read the book of Job, squinting as she holds the *Tanakh* up to her face. When she sets it down, she appears wild-eyed and lost, like a child in search of her own parents, and then comes the call — "Si-*mon!*" — for something tangible: fresh fruit or pound cake, a window opened for air or closed against draft, a blanket, a washcloth, a candle.

When enough guests have assembled for a minyan, Simon helps her into a new dress and house slippers, and she emerges to pray. They're joined by Saul's longtime employees: the bookkeepers; the seamstresses; the pattern makers; the salesmen; and Saul's junior partner, Arthur Milavetz, a reedy, beakish man of thirty-two.

As a child, Simon loved to visit his father's shop. The bookkeepers gave him paper clips

43

to play with, or pieces of scrap fabric, and Simon was proud to be Saul's son — it was clear, by the reverence with which the staff treated him and by his large windowed office, that he was someone important. He bounced Simon on one knee as he demonstrated how to cut patterns and sew samples. Later, Simon accompanied him to fabric houses, where Saul selected the silks and tweeds that would be fashionable next season, and to Saks Fifth Avenue, whose latest styles he purchased to make knockoffs at the shop. After work, Simon was allowed to stay while the men played hearts or sat in Saul's office with a box of cigars, debating the teachers' strike and the sanitation strike, the Suez Canal and the Yom Kippur War.

All the while, something loomed larger, closer, until Simon was forced to see it in all its terrible majesty: his future. Daniel had always planned to be a doctor, which left one son — Simon, impatient and uncomfortable in his skin, let alone in a double-breasted suit. By the time he was a teenager, the women's clothing bored him and the wools made him itch. He resented the tenuousness of Saul's attention, which he sensed would not last his departure from the business, if such a thing were even possible. He bristled at Arthur, who was always at his father's side, and who treated Simon like a helpful little dog. Most of all, he felt something far more confusing: that the shop was Saul's true home, and that his employees knew him better than his children ever did.

Today, Arthur brings three deli platters and a tray of smoked fish. He bends his long, swanlike neck to kiss Gertie's cheek.

"What will we do, Arthur?" she asks, her mouth in his coat.

"It's terrible," he says. "It's horrific."

Tiny droplets of spring rain perch on Arthur's shoulders and on the lenses of his horn-rimmed glasses, but his eyes are sharp.

"Thank God for you. And for Simon," Gertie says.

On the last night of shiva, while Gertie sleeps, the siblings take to the attic. They're worn down, washed out, with bleary, baggy eyes and curdled stomachs. The shock hasn't faded; Simon cannot imagine it ever fading. Daniel and Varya sit on an orange velvet couch, stuffing spurting from the armrests. Klara takes the patchwork ottoman that once belonged to now-dead Mrs. Blumenstein. She pours bourbon into four chipped teacups. Simon hunches cross-legged on the floor, swirling the amber

45

liquid with his finger.

"So, what's the plan?" he asks, glancing at Daniel and Varya. "You're heading out tomorrow?"

Daniel nods. He and Varya will catch early trains back to school. They've already said goodbye to Gertie and promised to return in a month, when their exams are finished.

"I can't take any more time off if I'm going to pass," Daniel says. "Some of us" — he nudges Klara with his foot — "worry about that sort of thing."

Klara's senior year ends in two weeks, but she's already told her family she won't walk at graduation. ("All those penguins, shuffling around in unison? It's not me.") Varya is studying biology and Daniel hopes to be a military doctor, but Klara doesn't want to go to college. She wants to do magic.

She's spent the past nine years under the tutelage of Ilya Hlavacek, an aging vaudevillian and sleight-of-hand magician who is also her boss at Ilya's Magic & Co. Klara first learned of the shop at the age of nine, when she purchased *The Book of Divination* from Ilya; now, he is as much a father to her as Saul was. A Czech immigrant who came of age between the World Wars, Ilya — seventy-nine, stooped and arthritic, with a troll's tuft of white hair — tells fantastic

46

tales of his stage years: one he spent touring the Midwest's grimiest dime museums, his card table mere feet from rows of pickled human heads; the Pennsylvania circus tent in which he successfully vanished a brown Sicilian donkey named Antonio as one thousand onlookers burst with applause.

But over a century has passed since the Davenport brothers invoked spirits in the salons of the wealthy and John Nevil Maskelyne made a woman levitate in London's Egyptian Theatre. Today, the luckiest of America's magicians manage theatrical special effects or work elaborate shows in Las Vegas. Almost all of them are men. When Klara visited Marinka's, the oldest magic shop in the country, the young man at the register glanced up with disdain before directing her to a bookshelf marked *Witchcraft*. ("Bastard," Klara muttered, though she did buy *Demonology: The Blood Summonings* just to watch him squirm.)

Besides, Klara is drawn less to stage magicians — the bright lights and evening clothes, the wire-rigged levitations — than to those who perform in more modest venues, where magic is handed from person to person like a crumpled dollar bill. On Sundays, she watches the street magician Jeff Sheridan at his usual post by the Sir

Walter Scott statue in Central Park. But could she really make a living that way? New York is changing. In her neighborhood, the hippies have been replaced by hard-core kids, the drugs by harder drugs. Puerto Rican gangs hold court at Twelfth and Avenue A. Once, Klara was held up by men who probably would have done worse if Daniel had not happened to walk by at exactly that moment.

Varya ashes into an empty teacup. "I can't believe you're still going to leave. With Ma like this."

"That was always the plan, Varya. I was always going to leave."

"Well, sometimes plans change. Sometimes they have to."

Klara raises an eyebrow. "So why don't you change yours?"

"I can't. I have exams."

Varya's hands are rigid, her back straight. She has always been uncompromising, sanctimonious, someone who walks between the lines as if on a balance beam. On her fourteenth birthday, she blew out all but three candles, and Simon, just eight, stood on his tiptoes to do the rest. Varya yelled at him and cried so intensely that even Saul and Gertie were puzzled. She has none of Klara's beauty, no interest in clothing or makeup. Her one indulgence is her hair. It is waist length and has never been colored or dyed, not because Varya's natural color — the dusty, light brown of dirt in summer — is in any way remarkable; she simply prefers it as it has always been. Klara dyes her hair a vivid, drugstore red. Whenever she does her roots, the sink looks bloody for days.

"Exams," Klara says, waving a hand, as if exams are a hobby that Varya should have outgrown.

"And where do you plan to go?" asks Daniel.

"I haven't decided." Klara speaks coolly, but her features are tense.

"Good lord." Varya drops her head back. "You don't even have a plan?"

"I'm waiting," says Klara. "For it to be revealed to me."

Simon looks at his sister. He knows she's terrified about her future. He also knows she hides it effectively.

"And once it's revealed to you," says Daniel, "this place you're going. How will you get there? Are you waiting for that to be revealed to you, too? You don't have the money for a car. You don't have the money for a plane ticket."

"There's this new thing called hitchhiking, Danny." Klara is the only one who calls Daniel by his childhood nickname, knowing it calls up memories of bed-wetting and buck teeth and, most of all, a family trip to Lavallette, New Jersey, during which he could not help but shit his corduroys, ruining the first day of the Golds' vacation and the backseat of their rented Chevy. "All the cool kids are doing it."

"Klara, please." Varya's head snaps forward. "Promise me you aren't going to hitchhike. Across the country? You'll be killed."

"I won't be *killed.*" Klara takes a drag and blows smoke to the left, away from Varya. "But if it means that much to you, I'll take a Greyhound."

"That'll take days," says Daniel.

"Cheaper than the train. And besides. Do you really think Ma needs me? She's happier when I'm not around." The revelation that Klara would not be applying to college was followed by long screaming matches between her and Gertie, which gave way to bitter silence. "Anyway, she won't be alone. Sy'll be here."

She reaches for Simon, gives his knee a squeeze.

"That doesn't bother you, Simon?" Daniel asks.

It does. He can already see how it will be when everyone else is gone, he and Gertie trapped alone inside a never-ending shiva — "Si-*mon*!" — his father nowhere and everywhere at once. Nights when he'll sneak out to run, needing to be anywhere but home. And the business — of course, the business — which is now rightfully his. Equally bad is the thought of losing Klara, his ally, but for her sake, he shrugs.

"Nah. Klara should do what she wants. We got one life, right?"

"Far as we know." Klara snuffs out her cigarette. "Don't you guys ever think about it?"

Daniel raises his eyebrows. "About the afterlife?"

"No," says Klara. "About how long yours'll be."

Now that the box has been opened, quiet falls in the attic.

"Not that old bitch again," Daniel says.

Klara flinches, as if it's she who's been insulted. They have not discussed the woman on Hester Street in years. Tonight, though, she's drunk. Simon sees it in the glaze of her eyes, the way her *s*'s slosh together.

"You guys are cowards," she says. "You can't even admit it."

51

"Admit what?" asks Daniel.

"What she told you." Klara points a finger at him, the nail painted with chipping red polish. "Come on, Daniel. I dare you."

"No."

"Coward." Klara grins crookedly, closing her eyes.

"I couldn't tell you if I wanted to," says Daniel. "It was years ago — it was a *decade* ago. Do you honestly think I committed it to memory?"

"I did," says Varya. "January 21st, 2044. So there."

She takes a swig of her drink, then another, and puts the empty teacup on the ground. Klara looks at her sister with surprise. Then she grabs the bottle of bourbon by the neck with one hand and refills Varya's cup before her own.

"What's that?" asks Simon. "Eighty-eight years old?"

Varya nods.

"Congratulations." Klara closes her eyes. "She told me I'd die at thirty-one."

Daniel clears his throat. "Well, that's bullshit."

Klara raises her glass. "Here's hoping."

"Fine." Daniel drains his own. "November 24th, 2006. You beat me, V."

"Forty-eight," Klara says. "You worried?"

"Not at all. I'm sure that hag said the first thing that came to mind. I'd be a fool to put any stock in it." He puts his cup down; it rattles on the wood plank. "What about you, Sy?"

Simon is on his seventh cigarette. He takes a drag and exhales the smoke, keeping his eyes on the wall. "Young."

"How young?" Klara asks.

"My business."

"Oh, come on," says Varya. "This is ridiculous. She only has power over us if we give it to her — and it's obvious she was a fraud. Eighty-eight? Please. With a prophecy like that, I'll probably be hit by a truck when I'm forty."

"Then how come all the rest of ours were so bad?" asks Simon.

"I don't know. Variety? She can't tell everyone the same thing." Varya's face is flushed. "I'm sorry we ever went to see her. The only thing she did was lodge the idea in our heads."

"It's Daniel's fault," says Klara. "He made us go."

"Don't you think I know that?" hisses Daniel. "Besides, you were the first to agree."

Fury blooms in Simon's chest. For a moment, he resents them all: Varya, rational and distant, a lifetime ahead; Daniel, who staked his claim to medicine years ago, forcing Simon to carry Gold's; Klara, abandoning him now. He hates that they get to escape.

"Guys!" he says. "Stop it! Just shut up, okay? Dad is dead. So can you fucking shut up?"

He's surprised by the authority in his voice. Even Daniel seems to shrink.

"Simon says," says Daniel.

Varya and Daniel go downstairs to sleep in their beds, but Klara and Simon climb up to the roof. They bring pillows and blankets and fall asleep on the concrete beneath the glow of the smog-veiled moon. They're shaken awake before dawn. At first, they think it's Gertie, but then Varya's thin, drawn face comes into focus.

"We're leaving," she whispers. "The taxi's downstairs."

Daniel looms behind her, his eyes distant behind glasses. The skin below them has a silver-blue, piscine tinge, and the past week has carved deep parentheses around his mouth — or have they always been there?

Klara throws an arm over her face. "No."

Varya lifts it, smooths Klara's hair. "Say goodbye."

Her voice is gentle, and Klara sits up. She wraps her arms around Varya's neck so tightly she can touch her own elbows.

"Goodbye," she whispers.

After Varya and Daniel leave, the sky glows red, then amber. Simon presses his face to Klara's hair. It smells like smoke.

"Don't go," he says.

"I have to, Sy."

"What's out there for you, anyway?"

"Who knows?" Klara's eyes are watery with fatigue, and her pupils seem to shine. "That's the whole point."

They stand and fold the blankets together.

"You could come, too," Klara adds, eyeing him.

Simon laughs. "Yeah, right. Skip out on two more years of school? Ma'd kill me."

"Not if you got far enough away."

"I couldn't."

Klara walks to the railing and leans against it, still in her blue, fuzzy sweater and cut-off shorts. She isn't looking at him, but Simon can feel the force of her attention, how she vibrates with it, as if she knows that only by feigning nonchalance can she say what she does next.

"We could go to San Francisco."

Simon's breath catches. "Don't talk like that."

He crouches to pick up their pillows, then stuffs one under each arm. He's five-eight, like Saul was, with swift, muscular legs and a lean chest. His plump, reddish lips and dark blond curls — the contribution of some long-buried Aryan ancestor — have won him the admiration of the girls in his sophomore class, but this isn't the audience he wants.

Vaginas have never appealed to him: their cabbage-like folds, their long, hidden corridor. He craves the long thrust of the cock, its heady insistence, and the challenge of a body like his. Only Klara has ever known. After their parents fell asleep, she and Simon climbed out of the window, mace in Klara's fake leather purse, and took the fire escape down to the street. They went to Le Jardin to hear Bobby Guttadaro play, or rode the subway to 12 West, a flower warehouse turned discotheque where Simon met the go-go dancer who told him about San Francisco. They sat in the rooftop garden while the dancer said that San Francisco has a gay city commissioner and a gay newspaper, that gay people can work anywhere and have sex anytime because there are no laws against sodomy. "You can't imagine it," he said, and from then on Simon could do nothing else.

"Why not?" asks Klara, turning now. "Yeah, Ma would be angry. But I see what your life would be like here, Sy, and I don't want that for you. You don't want it, either. Sure, Ma wants me to go to college, but she got that with Danny and V. She has to understand that I'm not her. And you aren't Dad. Jesus — you aren't meant to be a tailor. A tailor!" She paused, as if to let the word sink all the way in. "It's all wrong. And it isn't fair. So give me one reason. Give me one good reason why you shouldn't start your life."

As soon as Simon allows himself to picture it, he is nearly overcome. Manhattan should be an oasis — there are gay clubs, even bathhouses — but he's afraid to reinvent himself in a place that has always been home. *"Faygelehs,"* Saul muttered once, glaring as a trio of slender men unloaded a panoply of instruments into the unit the Singhs could no longer afford. That Yiddish slur was also adopted by Gertie, and though Simon pretended not to hear it, he always felt they were talking about him.

In New York, he would live for them, but in San Francisco, he could live for himself. And though he does not like to think about it, though he in fact avoids the subject pathologically, he allows himself to think it now: What if the woman on Hester Street is right? The mere thought turns his life a different color; it makes everything feel urgent, glittering, precious.

"Jesus, Klara." Simon joins her at the railing. "But what's in it for you?"

The sun rises a rich, bloody red, and Klara squints at it.

"You can go one place," she says. "I can go anywhere."

She still has the last of her baby fat, and her face is round. Her teeth, when she smiles, are slightly crooked: half-feral, half-charming. His sister.

"Will I ever find someone I love as much as you?" he asks.

"Please." Klara laughs. "You'll find someone you love much more."

Six stories below, a young man runs down Clinton Street. He wears a thin white T-shirt and blue nylon shorts. Simon watches the muscles of his chest undulate beneath the shirt, watches the powerful trunks of his legs do their work. Klara follows his eyes.

"Let's get out of here," she says.

2.

May arrives in a blur of sunshine and color. Crocus shoots thumb the grass of Roosevelt Park. After her last high school class, Klara bursts through the door with her empty diploma frame. The diploma will be sent once the calligraphy is finished, but by then she will be gone. Gertie knows that Klara is leaving, so her suitcase sits in the hallway. What she doesn't know is that Simon — whose suitcase is jammed beneath his bed — is coming with her.

He is leaving behind most of his belongings, bringing only those that are utilitarian or precious. Two collared, striped velour T-shirts. The red drawstring bag. The brown corduroy flares he was wearing when a young Puerto Rican man caught his eye on the train and winked: his most romantic experience yet. His leather-banded gold watch, a gift from Saul. And his New Balance 320s: blue suede, the lightest running shoes he's worn.

Klara's bag is larger, as it includes something that Ilya Hlavacek gave Klara during her last day of work. The night before they leave, she tells Simon the story of the gift.

"Bring me that box over there," Ilya told her, pointing.

The box, made of wood and painted black, accompanied Ilya from sideshows to circuses until he contracted polio in 1931 — "Good timing," he often joked, "because by then the pictures had killed vaudeville anyway." He always referred to it as *that box,* though Klara knew it was his most precious possession. She did as he directed, hoisting it up onto the counter so Ilya wouldn't have to get up from his chair.

"Now, I want you to have this," he said. "All right? It's yours. I want you to use it and I want you to enjoy it. It's meant to be on the road, my dear, not stuck indoors with an old cripple like me. You know how to take it apart? Here, I'll show you." Klara watched as he stood with the help of his cane and turned the box into a table as he had so many times before. "Here's where you put your cards. You stand behind it like so."

Klara tried it out. "There you go," he said, smiling his old man's leprechaun smile. "It looks marvelous on you."

"Ilya." Klara was embarrassed to realize she was crying. "I don't know how to thank you."

"Just use it." Ilya waved a hand and hobbled to the back room with his cane — ostensibly to restock the shelves, though Klara suspected he wished to mourn in private. Klara carried the box home in her arms and filled it with her tools: a trio of silk scarves; a set of solid silver rings; a coin purse full of quarters; three brass cups with an equal number of strawberry-sized red balls; and a deck of cards so worn that the paper is flexible as fabric.

Simon knows that Klara is talented, but her interest in magic unsettles him. When she was a child, it was charming; now, it's just strange. He hopes it'll fade once they arrive in San Francisco, where the real world will surely be more exciting than whatever's in her black box.

That night, he lies awake for hours. With Saul's passing, an old prohibition has lifted: Arthur can run the business, and Saul won't have known the truth about Simon. How, though, to account for his mother? Simon builds his case. He tells himself that this is the way of the world, the child leaving the parent for adulthood — if anything, humans are pitifully slow. Frog tadpoles hatch in their fathers' mouths, but they hop out as soon as they lose their tails. (At least, Simon thinks this is so; his mind always drifts in biology class.) Pacific salmon are born in freshwater before they migrate to oceans. When it is time to spawn and die, they journey hundreds of miles, returning to the waters where they themselves were born. Like them, he could always come back.

When he finally sleeps, he dreams he's one of them. He floats through semen, a glowing coral egg, and lands in his mother's nest on the streambed. Then he bursts from his shell and hides in dark pools, eating what matter comes his way. His scales darken; he travels thousands of miles. At first, he is surrounded by masses of other fish, so close they brush sleekly together, but as he swims farther away, the pack thins. By the time he realizes they started home, he can't remember the way to the old, forgotten stream where he was born. He has gone too far to turn back.

They wake in early morning. Klara rustles Gertie awake to say goodbye, then soothes her back to sleep. She tiptoes down the stairs with both suitcases while Simon ties his sneakers. He steps into the hallway, avoiding the plank that always squeaks, and carefully makes his way toward the door.

"Going somewhere?"

He turns, his pulse leaping. His mother stands in the doorway of her bedroom. She is swaddled in the large, pink bathrobe she's worn since Varya's birth, and her hair — usually set in curlers at this time of day — is loose.

"I was just . . ." Simon shifts from one foot to the other. "Going to get a sandwich."

"It's six in the morning. Funny time for a sandwich."

Gertie's cheeks are pink, her eyes wide. A glint of light illuminates her pupils: small knots of dread, shining like black pearls.

A shock of tears springs to Simon's eyes. Gertie's feet — pink slabs, thick as pork chops — are squared beneath her shoulders, her body taut as a boxer's. When Simon was a toddler, and his siblings were in school, he and Gertie played a game they called the Dancing Balloon. Gertie set the radio to Motown — something she never listened to when Saul was home — and blew up a red balloon halfway. They boogied through the apartment, bopping the balloon from the bathroom to the kitchen, their only mission to make sure it didn't fall. Simon was nimble, Gertie thunderous: together, they could keep the balloon in the air for whole radio programs. Now, Simon remembers Gertie lunging through the dining room, a candlestick clattering to the floor — "Nothing broke!" she bellowed — and stifles a hiccup of inappropriate laughter that, if released, would surely have morphed into a sob.

"Ma," he says. "I gotta live my life."

He hates the way it comes out, like he's pleading. Suddenly, his body longs for his mother's, but Gertie looks out at Clinton Street. When her gaze returns to Simon, there's a surrender in her expression that he's never seen before.

"All right. Go get your sandwich." She inhales. "But go to the shop after school. Arthur'll show you how things are done. You should be going there every day, now that your father —"

But she doesn't finish.

"Okay, Ma," says Simon. His throat burns.

Gertie nods gratefully. Before he can stop himself, Simon flies down the stairs.

Simon imagined the bus ride in romantic terms, but he spends most of the first leg asleep. He cannot bear to think any more about what happened between him and his mother, so he rests his head on Klara's shoulder as she plays with a deck of cards and a pair of miniature steel rings: every so often, he wakes to faint clinking, or to the flapping noise of shuffling. At 6:10 the next morning, they get off at a transfer station in Missouri, where they wait for the bus that will take them to Arizona, and in Arizona they catch a bus to Los Angeles. The final leg takes nine hours. By the time they arrive in San Francisco, Simon feels like the most disgusting creature on earth. His blond hair is an oily brown, and his clothes are three days old. But when he sees the gaping blue skies and leather-clad men of Folsom Street, something inside him leaps like a dog into water, and he cannot help but laugh, just once: a bark of delight.

For three days, they stay with Teddy Winkleman, a boy from their high school who moved to San Francisco after graduation. Now Teddy hangs with a group of Sikhs and calls himself Baksheesh Khalsa. He has two roommates: Susie, who sells flowers outside Candlestick Park, and Raj, brown skinned with shoulder-length black hair, who spends weekends reading Garcia Marquez on the living room couch. The apartment is not the cobwebby Victorian Simon pictured but a dank, narrow series of rooms not unlike 72 Clinton. The décor, though, is different: tie-dyed fabric is pinned to the wall belly-up, like animal hide, and chili pepper lights wind around the perimeter of each doorway. The floor is strewn with records and empty beer bottles, and the smell of incense is so dense that Simon coughs whenever he comes inside.

On Saturday, Klara circles an apartment listing in red pen. *2 BD/1 BA,* it reads. *$389/ mo. Sunny/spacious/hardwood fl. Historic building!! MUST LIKE NOISE.* They take the J to Seventeenth and Market, and here it is: the Castro, that two-block heaven of which he has dreamed for years. Simon stares at the Castro Theatre, the brown awning of Toad Hall, and the men, sitting on fire escapes and smoking on stoops, wearing tight jeans and flannel shirts or no shirts at all. To have wanted this for so long — to have it both at last and so early — makes him feel as though he is glimpsing his future life. *This is present,* he tells himself, dizzy. *This is now.* He follows Klara to Collingwood, a quiet block lined by bulbous trees and candy-colored Edwardians. They stop in front of a wide, rectangular building. The first floor is a club, closed at this hour, with windows that stretch to the ceiling. Through the glass, Simon sees purple couches and disco balls and tall platforms like pedestals.

The name of the club is painted across the glass: *PURP.*

The apartment sits above the club. It isn't spacious, nor is it a two-bedroom: the first bedroom is the living room, and the second bedroom is a walk-in closet. But it is sunny, with golden wood floors and bay windows, and they can just afford the first month's rent. Klara spreads her arms. Her ruched, orange halter top rides up, exposing the soft pink of her belly. She spins once, then twice — his sister, a teacup, a dervish in the living room of their new apartment.

They buy mismatched kitchenware from a thrift store on Church Street and furniture from a garage sale on Diamond. Klara finds two twin mattresses on Douglass, still in their plastic packaging, which they wrestle upstairs.

They go dancing to celebrate. Before they leave, Baksheesh Khalsa supplies hash and tabs. Raj strums a ukulele with Susie on his knee; Klara sits against the wall and stares at a fortune-telling fish she found in the novelty aisle at Ilya's. Baksheesh Khalsa leans toward Simon and tries to engage him in a conversation about Anwar el-Sadat, but the windows are waving hello to Simon and he thinks he would rather kiss Baksheesh

Khalsa instead. There's not enough time: now they're at a club, dancing in a mass of people painted blue and red by flashing lights. Baksheesh Khalsa yanks off his turban, and his hair whips through the air like a rope. One man, tall and broad and covered in beautiful green glitter, trails light like a fireball. Simon plunges through the crowd, reaching for him, and their faces crash together with startling intensity: the first kiss Simon's ever had.

Soon they're flying through the night in a cab, bodies straining in the backseat. The other man pays. Outside, the moon flaps like a number come loose on a door; the sidewalk unrolls for them, a carpet. They enter a tall, silver apartment building and ride an elevator to some high-up floor.

"Where are we?" asks Simon, following him into a unit at the end of the hall.

The man strides into the kitchen but leaves the lights off, so that the apartment is illuminated only by the street lamps outside. When Simon's eyes adjust, he finds himself in a clean, modern living room, with a white leather couch and a chrome-legged glass table. A splattered, neon painting hangs on the opposite wall.

"Financial district. New to town?"

Simon nods. He walks to the living room

window and looks at the gleaming office buildings. Many stories down, the streets are mostly empty, save for a couple of bums and the same number of cabs.

"Want anything?" the man calls, his hand on the refrigerator handle. The tabs are rapidly wearing off, but he doesn't look any less attractive: he is muscular but lean, with the tidy features of a catalog model.

"What's your name?" Simon asks.

The man retrieves a bottle of white wine. "This all right?"

"Sure." Simon pauses. "You don't want to tell me your name?"

The man joins him on the couch with two glasses. "I try not to, in these situations. But you can call me Ian."

"Okay." Simon forces a smile, though he feels mildly sickened — sickened to be grouped with others (how many?) in *these situations,* and by the man's caginess. Isn't disclosure the reason gay men come to San Francisco? But perhaps Simon has to be patient. He imagines dating Ian: lying on a blanket in Golden Gate Park or eating sandwiches at Ocean Beach, the sky streaked orange-gray with seagulls.

Ian smiles. He is at least ten years older than Simon, maybe fifteen.

"I'm hard as shit," he says.

Simon startles, and a wave of desire builds inside him. Ian is already taking his pants off, now his underwear, and there it is: boldly red, its head proudly lifted — a king of a cock. Simon's own erection presses against his jeans; he stands to pull them down, yanking when one leg snags on his ankle. Ian kneels on the ground, facing him. There, in the narrow space between the couch and the glass table, Ian pulls Simon forward by the ass, and suddenly — shockingly — Simon's penis is in Ian's mouth.

Simon cries out, and his upper body bucks forward. Ian holds his chest up with one hand and sucks as Simon gasps in amazement and exquisite, long-dreamed-of pleasure. It is better than he imagined it would be — it is agonizing, mindless bliss, this mouth on him, it is as concentrated and intense as the sun. He swells. When he's at the brink of an orgasm, Ian pulls back and grins, slick.

"You wanna see this nice floor with cum all over it? You wanna come all over this nice hardwood floor?"

Simon pants in confusion, this being so far from any objective he had in mind. "Do you?"

"Yeah," says Ian. "Yeah, I do," and now he is crawling on his knees, his penis — so red it's nearly purple — extending toward Simon like a scepter. A large, meandering vein snakes along the shaft.

"Hey," says Simon. "Let's just slow down for a second, okay? Just really quick, for a second?"

"Sure, man. We can do that." Ian turns him around to face the windows and takes Simon's penis in one hand, pumping. Simon moans until a dull pain in his knees brings him back to the room and to Ian, whose own penis is persistently nudging Simon's ass cheeks apart.

"Can we just . . ." Simon gasps, so close it takes effort to speak at all. "Can we, you know . . ."

Ian sits back on his heels. "What? You want lube?"

"Lube." Simon swallows. "Yeah."

Lube isn't what he wants, but at least it buys him time. As Ian springs to his feet and disappears down a hallway, Simon catches his breath. *Remember this,* he tells himself, *the right-before.* He hears the light slap of footsteps, a bony thunk as Ian takes his place and sets a bright orange bottle to one side. There is a gloppy squirt as the lube is dispensed, then the slick sound of Ian rubbing it between his hands.

"All good?" asks Ian.

Simon braces himself, pressing his palms into the floor.

"All good," he says.

Sun slices through the blinds. There is the sound of a shower running and the bodily, other-person smell of unfamiliar sheets. Simon is naked in a king bed beneath thick white covers. When he sits up, his legs ache, and he feels he might be sick. He squints at the room: a closed side door, which must lead to the bathroom; stock photos of urban architecture in sleek black frames; a small walk-in closet, inside which Simon sees color-coordinated rows of suit jackets and collared shirts.

He climbs out of bed and scans the ground for his clothes before he realizes that he must have left them in the living room — he remembers it vaguely, the night before, though it feels less like reality than the most intense dream he's ever had. His jeans and polo shirt are crumpled under the coffee table, his beloved 320s by the door. He scrambles into them and looks outside. Hordes of people stride down the sidewalk with briefcases and coffee. In some alternate reality, it's Monday morning.

The shower stops. Simon walks back into the bedroom just as Ian comes out of the bathroom, a towel slung low around his waist.

"Hey." He smiles at Simon, takes the towel off and rubs it vigorously over his hair. "Can I get you anything? Coffee?"

"Um," says Simon. "That's okay." He stares as Ian walks to the closet and pulls on a pair of black underwear, then thin black socks. "Where do you work?"

"Martel and McRae." Ian buttons an expensive-looking white shirt and reaches for a tie.

"What's that?"

"Financial advising." Ian frowns into a mirror. "You really don't know much of anything, do you?"

"Hey. I told you I was new here."

"Relax." Ian has a suspiciously handsome smile, as might belong to a personal injury lawyer.

"The people at your work," says Simon. "Do they know you like guys?"

"Hell no." Ian laughs shortly. "And I'd like to keep it that way."

He strides out of the closet, and Simon steps away from the doorway.

"Listen, I gotta run. But make yourself at home, okay? Just be sure the door shuts behind you when you leave. It should lock automatically." Ian grabs a jacket from the hall closet and pauses at the door. "It's been fun."

Alone, Simon stands very still. Klara doesn't know where he is. Worse, Gertie must be hysterical. It's eight in the morning, which means it's nearly eleven in New York — six days since he left. What kind of person is he, to do this to his mother? He finds a phone on the kitchen counter. While it rings, he pictures the one at home, a cream-colored push button. He imagines Gertie walking over to it — his mother, his dear; he must make her understand — and grasping the receiver in her strong right hand.

"Hello?"

Simon is startled. It's Daniel.

"Hello?" Daniel repeats. "Anybody there?"

Simon clears his throat. "Hey."

"Simon." Daniel releases a long, ragged breath. "Jesus Christ. Jesus *fucking* Christ, Simon. Where the hell are you?"

"I'm in San Francisco."

"And Klara's with you?"

"Yeah, she's here."

"Okay." Daniel speaks slowly and with control, as if to a volatile toddler. "What are you doing in San Francisco?"

"Hang on." Simon rubs his forehead, which pounds with pain. "Aren't you supposed to be at school?"

"Yes," says Daniel, with the same eerie calm. "Yes, Simon, I *am* supposed to be at school. Would you like to know why I'm not at school? I'm not at school because Ma called me in a *fit* on Friday night when you hadn't come *home,* and being the good fucking son that I am, the only fucking *reasonable* person in this family, I left school to be with her. I'll be taking incompletes this semester."

Simon's brain spins. He feels unable to respond to all of this at once, and so he says, "Varya's reasonable."

Daniel ignores this. "I'll repeat myself. What the hell are you doing in San Francisco?"

"We decided to leave."

"Yeah, I got that far. I'm sure it's been *groovy.* And now that you've had your fun, let's talk about what you're going to do next."

What is he going to do next? Outside, the sky is a clear, endless blue.

"I'm looking at the Greyhound schedule for tomorrow," Daniel says. "There's a train leaving from Folsom at one in the afternoon. You'll have to transfer in Salt Lake City and again in Omaha. It'll cost you a hundred and twenty bucks, which I hope to God you didn't travel across the country without, but if you're stupider than I'm giving you credit for, I'll wire it to Klara's bank account. In that case, you'll have to wait and leave on Thursday. All right? Simon? Are you with me?"

"I'm not coming back." Simon is crying, for he realizes that what he's said is true: there now exists a pane of glass between him and his former home, a pane he can see through but not cross.

Daniel's voice softens. "Come on, big guy. You're dealing with a lot, I understand that. We all are. Dad's gone — I can see why you'd get impulsive. But you have to do what's right. Ma needs you. Gold's needs you. We need Klara, too, but she's more of a . . . a lost cause, you know what I mean? Listen, I get how it goes with her. She doesn't like to take no for an answer; I'm guessing she talked you into it. But she had no right to rope you into her bullshit. I mean, Jesus — you haven't even finished high school. You're a kid."

Simon is silent. He hears Gertie's voice in the background.

"Daniel? Who are you talking to?"

"Hang on, Ma!" Daniel shouts.

"I'm staying here, Dan. I am."

"Simon." Daniel's voice hardens. "Do you

76

know what it's been like around here? Ma has lost her godforsaken mind. She's talking about calling the cops. I'm doing my best, I'm promising her you'll come to your senses, but I can't hold her off for much longer. You're only sixteen — a minor. And technically, that makes you a runaway."

Simon is still crying. He leans against the counter.

"Sy?"

Simon wipes his cheeks with his palms. Gently, he hangs up.

3.

By the end of May, Klara has filled out dozens of job applications, but she gets no interviews. The city is changing, and she missed the very best parts: the hippies, the Diggers, the psychedelic gatherings in Golden Gate Park. She wants to play a tambourine and listen to Gary Snyder read in the Polo Fields, but now the park is filled with gay cruisers and drug dealers, and the hippies are just homeless. Corporate San Francisco won't have her, not that she would have it. She targets the feminist bookstores in the Mission, but the clerks glance at her flimsy dresses with disdain; the coffee shops are owned by lesbians who laid the cement floors themselves and certainly don't need help now. Grudgingly, she submits an application to a temp agency.

"We just need something to tide us over," she says. "Something easy, something that makes fast money. It doesn't have to mean anything about us."

Simon thinks of the club downstairs. He's passed it at night, when it's full of young men and dizzying purple light. The next afternoon, he smokes out front until a middle-aged man — barely five feet, with bright orange hair — walks up to the door carrying a jumble of keys.

"Hey!" Simon crushes his cigarette beneath his shoe. "I'm Simon. I live upstairs."

He sticks out his hand. The other man squints at him, shakes it.

"Benny. What can I do for you?"

Simon wonders who Benny was before he came to San Francisco. He looks like a theater kid with his black sneakers and black jeans, a black T-shirt tucked into the waistband.

"I'd like a job," Simon says.

Benny nudges the glass door with one shoulder, then holds it open with his foot to allow Simon through.

"You do, huh? How old are you?"

He strides through the space: flicking on the house lights, checking the smoke machines.

"Twenty-two. I could tend bar."

Simon thought it would sound more mature than *bartend,* but now he sees he was wrong. Benny smirks and walks to the bar, where he heaves down the stools that wait in stacks.

"Firstly," he says, "don't lie to me. You're what — seventeen, eighteen? Secondly, I don't know where you're from, but you gotta be twenty-one to *tend bar* in California, and I'm not losing my liquor license over some cute new hire. Thirdly —"

"Please." Simon is desperate: if he can't get a job and Gertie keeps after him, he'll have no choice but to go home. "I'm new here, and I need money. I'll do anything — wipe your floors, stamp hands. I'll —"

Benny holds up a palm. "Thirdly. If I *were* to hire you, I wouldn't put you at the bar."

"Where would you put me?"

Benny pauses, one foot propped up on the rung of a stool. He points at one of the tall purple platforms spaced evenly throughout the club. "There."

"Oh yeah?" Simon looks at the platforms. They're at least four feet high and perhaps two and a half wide. "What would I do up there?"

"You'd *dance,* kid. Think you can handle that?"

Simon grins. "Sure, I can dance. That's all I have to do?"

"That's all you gotta do. You're lucky Mikey quit last week. Otherwise, I wouldn't have anything for you. But you're pretty, and with the makeup . . ." Benny cocks his head. "With the makeup, yeah — you'll look older."

"What makeup?"

"What do you think? Purple paint. Head to toe." Benny drags a broom out of a side room and begins to collect the previous night's debris: bent straws, receipts, a purple condom wrapper. "Get here by seven tonight. The guys'll show you how."

There are five of them, each with their own pillar. Richie — a forty-five-year-old veteran with bulky muscles and a military haircut — has earned pillar number one, by the front windows. Across from him, at number two, is Lance, a transplant from Wisconsin whose ready smile and round, Canadian o's are playfully mocked. Pillar number three is Lady, six foot four and dressed in drag; number four is Colin, skinny as a poet and sad-eyed, so Lady calls him Jesus Boy. Adrian — devilishly beautiful, his golden-brown body entirely hairless — takes pillar number five.

"Number six," calls Lady, when Simon enters the dressing room. "How do you do?"

Lady is black, with high cheekbones and warm eyes rimmed by long lashes. The rest of the men wear nothing except flimsy purple thongs, but Benny lets Lady wear a tight pleather minidress — purple, of course — and chunky platform heels.

She shakes her can of purple paint. "Turn around, honey. I'll do you."

Adrian hoots, and Simon turns obediently, grinning. He's already drunk. He bends toward the ground, ass up, and shakes it in Lady's direction, who screams with delight. Lance turns on the radio — Chic's *"Le Freak"* — as Adrian takes a tube of purple makeup from his toiletries case. He does Simon's face, smoothing dyed foundation around his nostrils and hairline, then the lobes of his ears. They finish moments before nine o'clock, when it is time to line up and parade into the club.

Even at this early hour, Purp is well populated, and for a moment, Simon's vision goes dark. Not in his wildest San Francisco fantasies did he imagine doing something like this. If it weren't for Klara's bottle of Smirnoff, he would have already turned around, dashing out of the club and into his apartment like a runaway extra in a sci-fi gay porn. Instead, as the men split and take their places, Simon positions himself behind pillar number six. Because Lady is the tallest, she hoists each man up onto his pedestal. Richie is athletic and energized: he hops up and down with one fist in the air and occasionally whips an invisible rope over his head. Lance is goofy, sweet; already, an appreciative mass stands below his pedestal, cheering as he does the bus stop and the funky chicken. Colin sways listlessly, high on Quaaludes. Occasionally, he extends his arms and moves his palms through the air like a mime. Adrian humps the air and runs his hands over his crotch. Simon wills himself not to grow hard as he watches.

Lady appears behind him. "Ready for a lift?" she whispers.

"Ready," says Simon, and suddenly, he rises. Lady deposits him on top of the pedestal, her hands sure on his waist. When she lets go, he pauses. The men in the audience stare at him curiously.

"Give it up for the new boy!" Richie calls from across the room.

There are a few scattered claps, a whoop. The music swells: ABBA's "Dancing Queen." Simon gulps. He shifts his hips left, then right, but the movement isn't fluid like it is on Adrian; he feels jerky and awkward, like a good girl at a school dance. He tries again, jumping like Richie, which feels more natural, but perhaps too much like Richie.

He points at the audience with one hand and rolls the other shoulder behind his back.

"Come on, baby!" shouts a black man in a white tank top and jean shorts. "I know you can come better than that!"

Simon's mouth turns dry. "Relax," says Lady from behind him; she hasn't yet left for her own pillar. "Drop your shoulders." He hadn't realized they'd risen to his ears. When he lets them go, his neck releases, too, and his legs feel more limber. Gently, he sways his hips. He tosses his head. When he listens to the music instead of copying the other men, his body sinks into a rhythm, as it does when he's running. His heartbeat is vigorous but steady. Electricity circuits from his scalp to his toes, urging him on.

When he reports for his shift the next day, he finds Benny wiping down the bar.

"How'd I do?"

Benny raises his eyebrows, though he doesn't look up. "You did."

"What do you mean?"

Simon still feels high, remembering how it felt to dance with those beautiful, sculpted men, how it felt to be adored. For a moment, in the dressing room, he had friends. He wasn't thinking about home, about his mother, or what his father would think of the crowd.

Benny takes a sponge from behind the bar and begins to scrub at a crust of simple syrup. "You ever danced before?"

"Yeah, I've danced. Of course I've danced."

"Where at?"

"Clubs."

"Clubs. Where no one was watching you, right? Where you were just another face in the crowd? Well, they're watching you now. And my guys? They can dance. They're good. I need you" — he points the sponge at Simon — "to keep up."

Simon's pride stings. Sure, he might have been a little stiff, but by the end of the night, he was jiving like the rest of them — wasn't he?

"What about Colin?" he asks, boldly imitating Colin's limpid sway, his mime act. "Is he keeping up?"

"Colin," says Benny, "has a shtick. The art fags are into him. You need a shtick, too. Whatever you were doing last night? Shuffling around the pedestal like you had bugs in your pants? That wasn't it."

"Hey, man. It's not like I'm in bad shape. I'm a runner."

"So what? Anyone can run. Baryshnikov, Nureyev — you look at those guys, they don't run. They fly. And that's 'cause they're artists. You're a good-looking guy, no doubt about that, but the guys who come here have standards, and you'll need more than your looks to keep up."

"Like what?"

Benny exhales. "Like presence. *Charisma.*"

Simon watches as Benny opens the cash register and counts the previous night's earnings. "So you're firing me?"

"No, I'm not firing you. But I'd like you to take a class. Learn to move. There's a dance school at the corner of Church and Market — ballet. They get a lot of guys in there, so you wouldn't be hanging around with a bunch of chicks."

"Ballet?" Simon laughs. "Come on, man. That's not my scene."

"And you think this is?" Benny takes out two thick stacks of bills and wraps them in rubber bands. "You're out of your comfort zone, kid — that's a fact. What's one more step?"

4.

From the outside, the Ballet Academy of San Francisco is nothing but a narrow, white door. Simon climbs a tall staircase, turns right at the landing, and finds himself in a small reception area: creaking wooden floors, a chandelier furry with dust. He didn't think ballet dancers would be so loud, but women chatter in groups as they stretch against the wall and men in black tights shout at one another, kneading their quads. The receptionist signs him up for the twelve thirty mixed level — "Trial class is free" — and hands him a pair of black canvas slippers from the lost and found bin. Simon sits to pull them on. Seconds later, the French doors behind him bang open. Teenage girls in navy leotards stream out, hair pulled back so tightly their eyebrows lift. Behind them, the studio is as large as a school cafeteria. Simon presses against the wall to let the girls pass. It takes all of his resolve not to bolt down the stairs.

The other dancers gather their bags and water bottles and begin to amble into the studio. It's an old, dignified room, with high ceilings, worn floors, and a raised platform for the piano. Students carry heavy-looking metal barres from the perimeter to the center as an older man enters the studio. Later, Simon will learn that this is the Academy's director, Gali, an Israeli émigré who danced with the San Francisco Ballet before a back injury ended his career. He looks to be in his late forties, with a powerful stride and the dense body of a gymnast. His head is shaved, and so are his legs: he wears a maroon unitard that ends in shorts, revealing smooth thighs striated with muscle.

When he places a hand on the barre, the room becomes silent.

"First position," Gali says, turning his feet out with the heels touching. "We prepare both arms and we have: plié one, straighten two. Lift the arm three, lower into grand plié four, five — arms *en bas* — rise seven. *Tendu* to second position on eight."

He might as well have been speaking Dutch. Before they've finished with plies, Simon's knees are burning and his toes cramp. The exercises become more baffling as class continues: there are *dégagés* and *ronds de jambe,* the toes making wide circles on the floor and then above it; *pirouettes* and *frappés; développés* — the leg unfurling from the body, then enveloped back in — and *grand battements* to prepare the hips and hamstrings for large jumps. After the warm-up, forty-five minutes so excruciating that Simon can't imagine continuing for the same amount of time, the dancers clear the barres and process to what Gali calls the center, where they move across the floor in fleets. Mostly, Gali walks through the room shouting rhythmic nonsense — "Ba-dee-da-DUM! Da-pee-pah-PUM!" — but during pirouettes, he appears at Simon's side.

"Goodness." His eyes are dark and sunken, but they dance. "What, it's laundry day?"

Simon is wearing the same striped, collared shirt he wore on the bus to San Francisco, along with a pair of running shorts. When class finishes, he runs to the men's bathroom, takes off the black slippers — the pads of his feet are already swollen — and retches into the toilet.

He wipes his mouth with toilet paper and leans against the wall, panting. He didn't have time to close the door of the stall, and another dancer, entering the bathroom, stops short. He is easily the most beautiful man Simon has seen in person: sculpted as if from onyx, his skin a rich black. His face is round, with wide cheekbones that curve like wings. A tiny, silver hoop hangs from one earlobe.

"Hey." Sweat drips from the man's forehead. "You okay?"

Simon nods and fumbles past him. After the long flight of stairs, he wanders dazedly down Market Street. It's sixty-five degrees and windy. On an impulse, he takes his shirt off and reaches his arms above his head. When he feels the breeze on his chest, he's filled with unexpected euphoria.

It is beautiful masochism, what he just did, more difficult even than the half marathon he won at fifteen: hills, thunder of feet and Simon in the midst of it, gasping down the Hudson River waterfront. He fingers the black slippers, which he shoved in his back pocket. They seem to taunt him. He must become like the other male dancers: expert, majestic, invincibly strong.

In June, the Castro blooms. Prop 6 pamphlets drift through the street like leaves; flowers keel over the sides of boxes with such bounty they're almost a nuisance. On June 25th, Simon goes to the Freedom

Parade with the dancers from Purp. He didn't know that so many gay people existed in the country, let alone in one city, but there are two hundred and forty thousand of them, watching the kickoff by Dykes on Bikes and cheering as the first rainbow flag is hoisted into the air. Harvey Milk's upper body emerges from the sunroof of a moving Volvo.

"Jimmy Carter!" Milk bellows, his red bullhorn held high, as the sea of men roars. "You talk about human rights! There are fifteen million to twenty million gay people in this nation. When are you going to talk about their rights?"

Simon kisses Lance, then Richie, wrapping his legs around Richie's thick, muscular waist. For the first time in his life, he's dating — he calls it that, though usually, it's just sex. There is the go-go dancer from the I-Beam and the barista at Café Flore, a mild-mannered Taiwanese man who spanks Simon so hard that his ass cheeks blush for hours. He falls hard for a Mexican runaway with whom he spends four blissful days in Dolores Park; on the fourth day, Simon wakes up alone beside Sebastian's floppy, green-and-pink hat and never sees the boy again. But there are so many others: the recovering addict from Alapaha, Georgia;

the forty-something *Chronicle* reporter who is always on speed; the Australian flight attendant in possession of the largest cock Simon's seen.

On weekdays, Klara wakes before seven and dresses in one of two dull, beige skirt suits from Goodwill. She temps first at an insurance company, then at a dentist's office, and returns so moody that Simon avoids her until she's had her first drink. She hates the dentist, she says, but that doesn't explain the exasperation with which she looks at Simon when he primps in the mirror or returns from a shift at Purp — drowsy, ecstatic, purple paint running down his legs in rivulets. He wonders if it's the voice messages. They arrive daily: emotional missives from Gertie, lawyerly arguments from Daniel, and increasingly desperate appeals from Varya, who moved home after her final exams.

"If you don't come back, Simon, I'll have to put off graduate school," Varya says, her voice wavering. "*Someone* needs to stay with Ma. And I don't understand why it always has to be me."

Sometimes, he comes upon Klara with the cord wrapped around her wrist, pleading for one of them to understand.

"They're your family," she tells Simon

afterward. "You have to talk to them eventually."

Not now, Simon thinks. *Not yet.* If he speaks to them, their voices will reach into the warm, blissful ocean in which he's been floating and yank him — gasping, dripping wet — onto dry land.

One Monday afternoon in July, he returns from Academy to find Klara sitting on her mattress, playing with silk scarves. Taped to the window frame behind her is a picture of Gertie's mother, a curious woman whose diminutive size and fierce gaze has always made Simon uncomfortable. She reminds him of witches from fairy tales, not because there is anything sinister about her but because she seems to be neither child nor adult, woman or man: she's something between.

"What are you doing here?" he asks. "Shouldn't you be at work?"

"I'm quitting."

"You're quitting," says Simon, slowly. "Why?"

"Because I hate it." Klara packs one of the scarves down into her left fist. When she pulls it out the other end, it's turned from black to yellow. "Obviously."

"Well, you need to get another job. I can't make rent on my own."

93

"I'm aware of that. And I will. Why do you think I'm practicing?" She waves a scarf at Simon.

"Don't be ridiculous."

"Screw you." She grabs both of her scarves and stuffs them in the black box. "You think you're the only one who's entitled to do what you want? You're fucking the whole city. You're stripping and dancing *ballet,* and I haven't said a thing. If anyone has the right to discourage me, Simon, it isn't you."

"I'm making money, aren't I? I'm holding up my end of the bargain."

"You Castro gays." Klara sticks a finger at him. "You don't think of anyone but your-selves."

"What?" he says, stung; Klara never speaks to him this way.

"Think about it, Simon — how sexist the Castro is! I mean, where are the women? Where are the lesbians?"

"What's it to you? You're a lesbian now?"

"No," says Klara, and when she shakes her head, she looks almost sad. "I'm not a lesbian. But I'm not a gay guy, either. I'm not even a straight one. So where do I fit in here?"

When their eyes meet, Simon looks away. "How am I supposed to know?"

"How am I? At least, if I start my own

show, I can say that I tried."

"Your own *show*?"

"Yes," Klara snaps. "My own show. I don't expect you to understand, Simon. I don't expect you to worry about anything but yourself."

"You're the one who convinced me to come here! Did you really think they'd let us go without a fight? You thought they'd just let us stay?"

Klara's jaw is tight. "I wasn't thinking about those things."

"Then what the hell were you thinking about?"

Klara's cheeks have turned a sunburnt coral that only Daniel usually provokes, but she keeps quiet, as if indulging Simon. It's not like her to censor herself. It certainly isn't like her to avoid eye contact, which she does now, latching her black box with more focus than the task requires. Simon thinks of their conversation on the rooftop in May. *We could go to San Francisco,* she said, as if the idea only just occurred to her, as if she didn't know exactly what she was doing.

"That's the problem," Simon says. "You never think. You know exactly how to get into something and you know how to bring me with you, but you never think about what the consequences will be — or maybe you think about them and you just don't care, not until it's too late. And now you're blaming me? If you feel so bad, why don't you go back?"

Klara stands and strides into the kitchen. The sink is full of so many unwashed dishes that they've begun to stack more across the counter. She turns the water on and grabs a sponge and scrubs.

"I know why," Simon says, following her. "Because it would mean that Daniel was right. It would mean you have no plans — that you can't make a life for yourself, away from them. It would mean you've failed."

He's trying to trigger her — his sister's restraint disturbs him more than any of her outbursts — but Klara's mouth remains set, her knuckles white around the sponge.

Simon has been selfish, he knows. But thoughts of the family hum throughout his days. In some way, he continues at Academy for them: to prove that his life is not all excess, that it also contains discipline and self-betterment. He takes his guilt and turns it into a leap, a lift, one perfect turn.

The irony, of course, is that Saul would have been appalled to learn that Simon is dancing ballet. But Simon is convinced that if he were alive and came to watch, his father would see how hard it really is. It took six weeks to figure out how to point his feet, even longer to grasp the concept of turnout. By the end of the summer, though, his body has stopped hurting so much, and he's earned a larger dividend of Gali's attention. He likes the rhythm of the studio, likes having somewhere to go. In fleeting moments, it feels to him like home, or like *a* home, as it does to so many of them: Tommy, seventeen and breathtaking, a former student at the Royal Ballet in London; Missourian Beau, able to pirouette eight times in a row; and Eduardo and Fauzi, twins from Venezuela, who hitchhiked their way north on a soybean truck.

These four are all in Academy's company, Corps. In most ballet companies, male dancers act as bland fairy-tale princes or offer furniture-like support — but Gali's choreography is modern and acrobatic, and seven of Corps's twelve members are men. Among them is Robert, the man Simon saw while retching and with whom he hasn't made eye contact since. Not that Robert seems to have noticed: before class, the other men stretch together, but he warms up alone by the window.

"Snob," drawls Beau.

Late August: a cold front has brought the

Sunset's fog to the Castro, and Simon wears a sweatshirt over his white tee and black tights. He rolls his right ankle, wincing as it cracks. "What's his deal?"

"Is he a fag, you mean?" asks Tommy, pounding his fists up and down both thighs.

"That's the million-dollar question," purrs Beau. "Would that I knew."

Robert does not stand out only because he is solitary. His leaps are miles higher than anyone else's, his turns matched only by Beau's ("Cocksucker," mutters Beau, when Robert spins eight times to his six) — and, of course, he is black. But Robert is not only a black man in the white Castro. He is a black ballet dancer, even rarer.

Simon stays after class to watch him rehearse *Birth of Man*, Gali's newest creation. Five men use their bodies to create a tube: their bent knees touch and their backs curve, arms interlocked above their heads. Robert is Man. He threads through the tube, guided by Beau, the Midwife. At the end of the piece, Robert emerges from the front of the tube and dances a tremulous solo, nude except for a dark brown thong.

Corps performs in a black box theater at Fort Mason, a group of renovated military buildings on the San Francisco Bay. When they begin to rehearse there, Simon comes to assist, taking notes for Gali or taping marks on the stage. One afternoon, he wanders outside to see Robert smoking on the dock. Robert hears Simon behind him, turns, and nods affably enough. It isn't exactly an invitation, but Simon finds himself walking to the edge of the dock and sitting down.

"Smoke?" asks Robert, offering Simon the pack.

"Sure." Simon is surprised; Robert has a reputation for being a health nut. "Thanks."

Seagulls wheel overhead, calling; the smell of the water, brackish and salty, fills Simon's nose. He clears his throat. "You looked great in there."

Robert shakes his head. "Those *tours* are really giving me trouble."

"The *tour jetés*?" asks Simon, relieved that he has managed to remember this piece of terminology. "They seemed awesome to me."

Robert smiles. "You're going easy on me."

"I'm not. It's true."

Immediately, he wishes he hadn't said it. He sounds cloying, like some dumb fan.

"Okay." Robert's eyes gleam. "What's one thing I can do better?"

Simon is desperate to come up with something — it would be a kind of flirtation

— but to him, Robert's dancing is flawless. Instead, he says, "You could be friendlier."

Robert frowns. "You don't think I'm friendly."

"Not really, no. You warm up on your own. You've never said anything to me. Though I guess," Simon adds, "I've never said anything to you."

"That's fair," says Robert. They sit in companionable silence. Freestanding wood piers rise from the water like tree trunks. Every so often, a bird lands on one, screeches dictatorially, and departs with a thick flapping noise. Simon is watching this happen when Robert turns, dips his head, and kisses him on the mouth.

Simon is stunned. He keeps very still, as if Robert might otherwise fly away like the gull. Robert's lips are deliciously full; he tastes of sweat and smoke and very slightly of salt. Simon closes his eyes. If the dock were not beneath him, he would swoon straight into the water. When Robert pulls back, Simon leans forward, as if to find him again, and nearly loses his balance. Robert puts a hand on Simon's shoulder to steady him, laughing.

"I didn't know . . ." says Simon, shaking his head. "I didn't know you — liked me."

He had been about to say *liked guys*. Robert shrugs, but not flippantly; he is thinking, for his eyes are distant but focused, they are somewhere in the middle of the bay. Then they return to Simon.

"Neither did I," he says.

5.

Simon rides the train home that evening. Thinking about Robert's mouth makes him so turned on that all he can think about is getting through the door, getting his hands on himself, pumping while he calls up the unbelievable potency of that kiss. It isn't until he's halfway down the block that he sees the cop car parked outside his apartment.

A policeman leans against the hood. He's rangy, a redhead, and looks barely older than Simon. "Simon Gold?"

"Yeah," says Simon, slowing.

The cop opens the back door of the car and bows with a flourish. "After you."

"What? Why?"

"Answers at the station."

Simon wants to ask more, but he is afraid of giving the cop new information — if he doesn't know Simon is working at Purp underage, Simon won't be the one to tell him — and he can barely swallow: something fist sized and firm, like a fig, is stuck in his throat. The backseat is made of hard, black plastic. Up front, the redhead turns around, looks beadily at Simon, and shoves the soundproof barrier shut. When they pull up in front of the Mission Street station, Simon follows him indoors, then through a maze of rooms and uniformed men. They emerge in a small interview room with a plastic table and two chairs.

"Sit," says the cop.

On the table is a scuffed black phone. The cop takes a crumpled piece of paper from his shirt pocket and jabs at the buttons with one hand. Then he holds the receiver out to Simon, who looks at the phone with apprehension.

"What are you, thick?" asks the cop.

"Screw you," mutters Simon.

"What'd you say?"

The man shoves him by the shoulders. Simon's chair skids back, and he scrambles for his footing. When he scoots back to the table and reaches for the receiver, his left shoulder throbs.

"Hello?"

"Simon."

Who else would it be? Simon could kick himself for being so stupid. Immediately, the cop seems to disappear, and so does the pain in his shoulder.

"Ma," he says.

It is terrible: Gertie is crying the way she did at Saul's service, guttural and heavy like the sobs are something in her stomach she can physically expel.

"How could you?" she asks. "How could you do it?"

He winces. "I'm sorry."

"You're *sorry.* Then I expect you'll be on your way home."

There is a bitterness in her voice that he has heard before but which has never been directed at him. His first memory: lying on his mother's lap at two as she ran her hands through his curls. *Like an angel,* she clucked. *Like a cherub.* Yes, he left them — all of them — but he left her most of all.

And yet.

"I *am* sorry. I'm sorry for what I did — for leaving you. But I can't — I won't . . ." He trails off, tries again. "You picked your life, Ma. I want to pick mine."

"Nobody picks their life. I sure didn't." Gertie laughs, a scrape. "Here's what happens: you make choices, and then *they* make choices. Your choices make choices. You go to college — my God, you finish high school — that's one way of tipping the odds in your

104

favor. What you're doing right now, I don't know what the hell will happen to you. And neither do you."

"But that's the thing. I'm fine with not knowing. I'd rather not know."

"I've given you time," Gertie says. "I said to myself, *Just wait;* I thought, if I waited, you'd come to your senses. But you haven't."

"I have come to my senses. My senses are here."

"Have you ever once thought about the business?"

Simon grows hot. "That's what you care about?"

"The name," says Gertie, faltering. "It's changed. *Gold's* is *Milavetz's* now. It's Arthur's."

Simon feels a wash of shame. But Arthur always encouraged Saul to be forward thinking. The styles Saul specialized in — worsted gabardine slacks, suits with wide lapels and legs — were on their way out by the time Simon was born, and it gives him some relief to think that, in Arthur's hands, the business will continue.

"Arthur'll be good," he says. "He'll keep the shop up-to-date."

"I don't care about relevance. I care about family. There are things you do for the people who did them for you."

"And there's things you do for yourself."

He's never spoken to his mother like this before, but he is dying to convince her; he imagines her coming to see him at Academy, Gertie clapping from a folding chair as he leaps and turns.

"Oh, yes. There are plenty of things you do for yourself. Klara told me you're a dancer."

Her disdain comes through the receiver so loudly that the cop begins to laugh. "Yeah, I am," says Simon, glaring at him. "So what?"

"I don't understand it. You've never danced a day in your life."

What can Simon tell her? It's mysterious to him, too, how something he thought nothing of before, something that makes him feel pain and exhaustion and quite frequently embarrassment, has turned out to be a gateway to another thing entirely. When he points his foot, his leg grows by inches. During leaps, he hovers midair for minutes, as if he's sprouted wings.

"Well," he says. "I'm dancing now."

Gertie releases a long, ragged sigh; then she goes quiet. And in that gap — a gap she would typically fill with more argument, even threats — Simon recognizes his free-dom. If it's illegal to be a runaway in

California, he would already be in handcuffs.

"If you've made your decision," she says, "I don't want you coming back."

"You don't — what?"

"I don't want you," says Gertie, enunciating, "coming back. You made your choice — you left us. So live with it, then. Stay."

"Jesus, Ma," Simon mutters, pressing the phone to his ear. "Don't be so dramatic."

"I'm being very realistic, Simon." There is a pause as she inhales. Then Simon hears a quiet click, and the line goes dead.

He holds the receiver in one hand, dazed. Is this not what he wanted? His mother has relinquished him, given him to the world of which he's longed to be a part. And yet he feels a spike of fear: the filter has been taken off the lens, the safety net ripped from beneath his feet, and he is dizzy with dreadful independence.

The cop walks him to the exit. Outside, on the landing, he grabs the neck of Simon's T-shirt and yanks upward so forcefully that Simon rises onto the balls of his feet.

He says, "You runaways make me sick, d'you know that?"

Simon gasps. His toes search for purchase on the concrete. The cop's eyes are whiskey colored and sparsely lashed, his cheeks covered in freckles. On his forehead, near the hairline, is a cluster of round scars.

"When I was a kid," he says, "you people arrived by the truckload every goddamned day. I thought you'd've learned we didn't want you, but you're still here, clogging up the system like fat. You don't do anything useful with your lives, just live off the city like parasites. I was born in the Sunset, and so were my parents, and so were *their* parents, all the way back to our relatives who came here from Ireland, and that's excluding the ones who died 'cause they couldn't get fed. In my mind?" He leans in close; his mouth is a pink knot. "You deserve whatever you get."

Simon yanks out of his grip, coughing. In his peripheral vision, he sees a flash of bright red, a flash that becomes his sister. Klara stands at the foot of the stairs in a puff-shouldered black minidress and maroon Doc Martens, her hair blowing behind her like a cape. She looks like a superhero, radiant and vengeful. She looks like their mother.

"What are you doing here?" asks Simon, panting.

"Benny told me he saw cop cars. This was the nearest station." Klara runs up the granite steps and stops in front of the cop.

"What the fuck are you doing with my brother?"

The cop blinks, stopped short. Something flies between him and Klara that Simon can't quite see, something he can only feel: sparks, heat, a sour fury like metal. When Klara puts an arm around Simon's shoulders, the young cop shrinks. He looks so straight, so out of place in this new city, that Simon almost feels sorry for him.

"What's your name?" Klara asks, squinting at the little pin on the cop's blue shirt.

"Eddie," says the man, lifting his chin. "Eddie O'Donoghue."

Klara's arm around Simon is firm, their recent wounds forgiven. The comfort of her protection makes Simon think of Gertie, and his throat swells. But Eddie is still looking at Klara, his cheeks pink and slightly slack, as if Simon's sister is a mirage.

"I'll remember that," she says. Then she walks Simon down the steps of the station and into the heart of the Mission. It's eighty-five degrees, the sidewalk fruit stands full as Eden, and no one tries to stop them.

6.

"What'll it be?" asks Simon.

He rummages around in the tiny pantry, which is really a closet on whose jutting beams they keep an assortment of nonperishables: boxed cereal, cans of soup, alcohol. "I can do a vodka tonic, Jack and Coke . . ."

October: brisk silver-gray days, pumpkins on Academy's front steps. Someone put a men's dance belt on a fake skeleton and propped it up in the reception area. Simon and Robert have hooked up at Academy — kissing in the men's bathroom or the empty dressing room before class — but this is the first time Robert has come to Simon's apartment.

Robert leans back in the turquoise armchair. "I don't drink."

"No?" Simon pokes his head out of the closet and grins, one hand on the door. "I know I've got some dope around here, if that's your trip."

"Don't smoke, either. Not that stuff."

"No vices?"

"No vices."

"Except men," Simon says.

A tree branch waves in front of the living room window, blocking the sun, and Robert's face goes out like a lamp. "That's not a vice."

He gets up and brushes past Simon to the sink, where he pours himself a glass of water from the tap.

"Hey, man," says Simon. "You're the one who likes to keep this shit quiet."

In class, Robert still warms up alone. Once, Beau saw Robert and Simon leaving the bathroom and whistled with both pinkies in his mouth, but when he asked Simon about it, Simon feigned innocence. He senses that Robert would disapprove of any disclosure, and his moments with Robert — Robert's low, murmured laughter, his palms on Simon's face — are too good to give up.

Now Robert leans against the sink. "Just because I don't talk about it doesn't mean I keep it quiet."

"What's the difference?" Simon puts his index fingers through Robert's belt loops. He never dreamed he'd have the confidence to do such a thing, but San Francisco is a drug. Though he's only been here five months, it feels like he's aged by a decade.

"When I'm at the studio," says Robert, "I'm at work. I stay quiet out of respect — for the workplace, and for you."

Simon pulls him close, until their hips are pressed together. He puts his mouth to Robert's ear. "Disrespect me."

Robert laughs. "You don't want that."

"I do." Simon unfastens Robert's jeans and shoves his hand inside. He grabs Robert's cock and pumps. They still haven't had sex.

Robert steps back. "Come on, man. Don't be like that."

"Like what?"

"Cheap."

"Fun," Simon says, correcting him. "You're hard."

"So?"

"So?" repeats Simon. *So everything,* he wants to say. *So please.* But what comes out is different. "So fuck me like an animal."

It's something the *Chronicle* reporter once said to Simon. Robert looks as though he might laugh again, but then his mouth twists.

"What we're doing here, you and me?" he says. "Ain't nothing wrong with it. Nothing."

Simon's neck grows hot. "Yeah, I know that."

Robert grabs his jacket from the back of the turquoise chair and slips it on. "Do you? Sometimes I really don't know."

"Hey," says Simon, panicked. "I'm not ashamed, if that's what you're getting at."

Robert pauses by the door. "Good," he says. Then he pulls the door shut behind him and disappears down the stairwell.

When Harvey Milk is shot, Simon is in the dressing room at Purp, waiting for a staff meeting to begin. It's eleven thirty in the morning, a Monday, and the men are resentful of coming in during their off-hours, even more resentful that Benny is late. They have the TV on while they wait. Lady lies on a bench with cold tea bags on her eyes; Simon is missing men's class at Academy. The mood is somber, done in: one week before, Jim Jones led a thousand followers to death in Guyana.

When Dianne Feinstein's face fills the TV, her voice wavering — "It's my duty to make this announcement: Both Mayor Moscone and Supervisor Harvey Milk have been shot and killed" — Richie cries out so loudly that Simon jumps up from his chair. Colin and Lance are silent with shock, but Adrian and

Lady are crying thick tears, and when Benny arrives — harried, pale; traffic is stopped for blocks around Civic Center — his eyes are swollen pink. They close Purp for the day, hanging a black scarf of Lady's across the front door, and that night, they join the rest of the Castro to march.

It's late November, but the streets are warm with bodies. The crowd is so large that Simon has to take a back route to Cliff's to buy candles. The clerk gives him twelve for the price of two, and paper cups to cut the wind. Within hours, fifty thousand people have joined them. The march to City Hall is led by the sound of a single drum, and those who weep do so quietly. Simon's cheeks are slick. It is Harvey, but it is more than Harvey. This mass, grieving like father-less children, makes Simon think of his parents, both gone from him now. When the San Francisco Gay Men's Chorus sings a hymn by Mendelssohn — *Thou, Lord, Hast Been Our Refuge* — Simon hangs his head.

Who is his Lord, his refuge? Simon doesn't think he believes in God, but then again, he's never thought God believed in him. According to the Book of Leviticus, he's an abomination. What kind of God would create a person of which He so disapproved? Simon can only think of two explanations:

114

either there's no God at all, or Simon was a mistake, a fuck-up. He's never been sure which option scares him more.

By the time he wipes his cheeks, the other Purp dancers have been carried along in the swell. Simon scans the crowd and snags on a familiar face: warm, dark eyes; a glint of silver in one earlobe, bobbing above a bright white candle. Robert.

They've barely spoken since that October evening in Simon's apartment, but now they push against the crowd, reaching for each other, and meet somewhere in the middle of that sea.

Robert's studio is nestled in the steep, winding streets by Randall Park. By the time he unlocks the door and they stumble into the hallway, they're pulling at each other's shirts and fumbling with belt buckles. On a double bed beside the window, Simon fucks Robert, and Robert fucks him. Soon, though, it doesn't feel like fucking; once the initial frenzy gives way, Robert is tender and attentive, pushing into Simon with such emotion — emotion for whom? For Simon? For Harvey? — that Simon feels unusually shy. Robert takes Simon's cock in his mouth and sucks. When the pressure inside Simon builds to the point of bursting, Robert looks up from below, and their eyes meet with such startling intensity that Simon keels forward to cradle Robert's head as he comes.

Afterward, Robert turns on a bedside lamp. His apartment is not spartan, as Simon expected, but curated with objects Robert found during Corps's first international tour: painted Russian bowls, two strands of Japanese cranes. A wooden shelf across from the bed is filled with books — *Sula; The Football Man* — and the galley kitchen is hung with an assortment of pans. A cardboard cutout guards the entrance to the bedroom, the life-sized image of a football player mid-catch.

They sit propped up against pillows to smoke.

"I met him once," Robert says.

"Who? Milk?"

Robert nods. "It was after he lost his second campaign — '75? I saw him at a bar down the street from the camera shop. He was being propped up in the air by all these guys, and he was laughing, and I thought: That's the kind of person we need. Someone who doesn't stay down. Not a bitter old man, like me."

"Harvey was older than you." Simon smiles, though he stops when he realizes he's used the past tense.

"Yeah, he was. He didn't act like it, though." Robert shrugs. "Look, I don't go to the parades. I don't go to the clubs. I sure as hell don't go to the bathhouses."

"Why not?"

Robert eyes him. "How many people do you see around here that look like me?"

"There are black guys here." Simon flushes. "Not a lot, I guess."

"Yeah. Not a lot," says Robert. "Try and find me one that does ballet." He stubs out his cigarette. "That cop who picked you up? Think about what he'd have done if you looked like me."

"Worse," says Simon. "I know."

He likes Robert so much that he is reluctant to face the obvious difference between them. He wants their sexuality to be an equalizer; he wants to focus on the discrimination they face in common. But Simon can conceal his sexuality. Robert can't conceal his blackness, and almost everyone in the Castro is white.

Robert lights a new cigarette. "Why don't you go to the bathhouses?"

"Who says I don't?" asks Simon. But Robert snorts, and Simon laughs. "Honestly? They scare me a little. I don't know if I could take it."

Is there such a thing as too much pleasure? When Simon imagines the bathhouses, he thinks of a carnival of gluttony, an underworld so endless it seems possible to stay there forever. What he's said to Robert isn't a lie — he *is* afraid he wouldn't be able to take it — but he's also afraid he would, that his greed would have no edges and no end.

"I hear that." Robert wrinkles his nose. "Nasty."

Simon props himself up on one arm. "So why did you come to San Francisco?"

Robert raises an eyebrow. "I came to San Francisco because I didn't have a choice. I'm from Los Angeles. South Central — neighborhood called Watts. You ever heard of it?"

Simon nods. "That's where the riots were."

In 1965, when he was four, Simon went to the movies with Gertie and Klara while the older siblings were in school. Though he does not remember the film, he does remember the newsreel shown directly before it. There was the cheerful tootle of Universal City Studios and the familiar, rhythmic voice of Ed Herlihy, both of which were markedly unlike the black-and-white footage that appeared next: dim streets clouded by smoke and buildings billowing with fire.

The music turned foreboding as Ed Herlihy described brick-throwing Negro hoodlums — snipers shooting firefighters from rooftops, looters who stole liquor and playpens — but Simon only saw police officers with flak jackets and guns walking through empty streets. Finally, two blacks appeared, but these could not be the hoodlums Ed Herlihy mentioned: handcuffed and flanked by white officers, they walked with stoic nonresistance.

"Right." Robert stubs his cigarette out on a small blue dish. "I did okay in school — my mom was a teacher — but what I really had was physical power. Football was my game. In tenth grade, I was starting for the varsity team as a safety. My mom thought I'd get a scholarship to college. And when a scout came out from Mississippi, I started to think that way, too."

Other guys haven't talked to Simon like this. Actually, with other guys, Simon hasn't talked much at all, and certainly not about his family. But this is how it is with most of the men in the Castro — men suspended in time as if in amber, men who don't want to look back.

"So did you get the scholarship?" he asks.

Robert pauses. He seems to be gauging Simon.

"I was real close with this other guy on the team," he says. "Dante. I was on defense. Dante was our wide receiver. I could tell there was something different about him. And he could tell there was something different about me. Nothing happened until my junior year, last practice of the off-season. Dante was supposed to leave that summer; he had a scholarship from Alabama. I figured it was the last time we'd see each other. We waited till everyone else had left the locker room, took our time putting our street clothes on. And then we took them off again."

Robert takes a drag and exhales. Outside, Simon can still see the light of the march. Each candle marks one person. They flicker, white, like grounded stars.

"I swear to God I never heard anyone come in. But I guess somebody did. Next day, I get kicked off the team, and Dante loses his scholarship. They didn't even let us clean our shit out of the locker room. Last time I saw him, he was standing at the bus stop. He had his hat pulled down low. His jaw, it was shaking. And he looked at me like he wanted to kill me."

"Jesus." Simon shifts on the bed. "What happened to him?"

"A group of guys on the team caught up

with him. They caught up with me, too, but they didn't get me so bad. I was taller, stronger. Defense — that was my job, you know? But it wasn't Dante's. They bashed his face in, broke his back with a bat. Then they took him to the field and tied him to the fence. They said they left him breathing, but what kind of dumb-ass motherfucker would have believed that?"

Simon shakes his head. He is nauseous with fear.

"The judge. That's who," Robert says. "I knew I'd go crazy if I stayed down there. That's why I came to San Francisco. I started taking dance classes 'cause I knew that was one place they wouldn't kick me out for being queer. Nothing gayer than ballet, man. But there's a reason Lynn Swann does dance training. It's tough as shit. It makes you strong."

Robert scoots down to rest his face on Simon's chest, and Simon holds him. He wonders what he can do to protect Robert, to soothe him — whether to squeeze Robert's hand or to speak, whether to stroke his newly shaved head. This responsibility, newly gifted, is nothing like fucking: more intimidating, grown-up, so much wider margin for failure.

In April, Gali calls Simon and tells him to come to the theater, fast. Simon splurges on a cab, his dance bag in his arms. Gali meets him outside the stage door.

"Eduardo went down in rehearsal," Gali says. "He rolled his ankle on a *saut de basque.* A freak accident — terrible. We hope it is only a sprain. Even so, he's out for the month." He nods at Simon. "You know the choreography."

It isn't a question; it's a job offer for *Birth of Man.* Simon's heart clenches. "I mean — yeah, I know it. But I . . ."

What he wants to say is, *I'm not good enough.*

"You'll be at the end of the line," Gali says. "We have no choice."

Simon follows him down the long corridor to the dressing rooms. Eduardo sits on the floor with his leg propped up on a crate, a bag of ice on one ankle. His eyes are pink, but he cracks a smile for Simon.

"At least," he says, "you won't need to be fitted for a costume."

In *Birth of Man,* the men wear nothing but dance belts. Even their ass cheeks are exposed. In this regard, Purp has been good training: onstage, Simon feels little self-consciousness and can instead focus only on his movements. The lights are so bright that he can't see the audience, so he pretends they don't exist: there are only Simon and Fauzi, Tommy and Beau, all of them straining to support Robert as he navigates their manmade canal. They bow as a group, and Simon squeezes their hands until his own hurt. Afterward, they cab to the QT on Polk in their stage makeup. In a surge of ecstasy, Simon grabs Robert and kisses him in front of everyone. The other men cheer, and Robert grins with such bashful indulgence that Simon does it again.

That fall, Simon is given his own role in *The Naughty Nut,* Corps's *Nutcracker.* A write-up in the *Chronicle* doubles ticket sales, and Gali throws a party at his house in the Upper Haight to celebrate. The rooms are filled with brown leather furniture, and everything smells like the clove-pricked oranges that sit in a gold bowl on the mantel. Academy's pianist plays Tchaikovsky on Gali's Steinway. The doorways have been hung with mistletoe, and the party's hum is periodically interrupted by shrieks of delight as odd pairs are forced to kiss. Simon arrives with Robert, who wears a maroon button-down with black dress pants; he's replaced his silver hoop earring with a diamond the size of a peppercorn. They mingle with donors by the hors d'oeuvres before Robert pulls Simon down the hall and through a glass door that leads to the garden.

They sit on the deck. Even in December, the garden is lush. There are jade and nasturtiums and California poppies, all hearty enough to grow amidst fog. It occurs to Simon that he would like to have a life like this: a career, a house, a partner. He's always assumed that these things are not for him — that he's designed for something less lucky, less straight. In truth, it is not only Simon's gayness that makes him feel this way. It's the prophecy, too, something he would very much like to forget but has instead dragged behind him all these years. He hates the woman for giving it to him, and he hates himself for believing her. If the prophecy is a ball, his belief is its chain; it is the voice in his head that says *Hurry,* says *Faster,* says *Run.*

Robert says, "I got the place."

Last week, he applied for an apartment on Eureka Street. It's rent controlled, with a kitchen and a backyard. Simon went to the showing with Robert and marveled at the dishwasher, the washing machine, the bay windows.

"You get a roommate?" he asks.

The nasturtiums wave their festive red and yellow hands. Robert leans back on his forearms, grinning. "You want to room with me?"

The thought is bewitching: a tingle runs across Simon's scalp. "We'd be close to the studio. We could get a used car and drive to the theater together on performance days. We'd save gas."

Robert looks at Simon like he's just said he's straight. "You want to live together to save gas."

"No! — No. It's not the gas. Of course it isn't the gas."

Robert shakes his head. He's still smiling when he looks at Simon. "You can't admit it."

"Admit what?"

"How you feel about me."

"Sure I can."

"Okay. How do you feel about me?"

"I like you," says Simon, but it comes out a little too fast.

Robert throws his head back and laughs. "You are a bad fucking liar," he says.

7.

They are unpacking the apartment, Simon and Robert and Klara, who didn't mind the move; she seemed relieved to have the Collingwood apartment to herself. After a balmy December, temperatures have dipped into the forties. This would be nothing in New York, but California has made Simon soft: he wears legwarmers under his tracksuit as he runs between the apartment and the U-Haul. When Klara leaves, Simon and Robert kiss pressed up against the dishwasher: Robert's hands sure on Simon's waist, Simon groping for Robert's ass, his dick, his magnificent face.

It is 1980, the beginning of a new decade as well as a new year. In San Francisco, Simon is insulated from the global recession and the Soviet invasion of Afghanistan. He and Robert pool their money to buy a TV, and though the evening news makes them uneasy, the Castro is like a fallout shelter: there, Simon feels powerful and safe. He rises through the ranks at Corps, and by spring, he is a full company member instead of an understudy.

Klara has returned to the dentist's office, working days as a receptionist and nights as a restaurant hostess in Union Square. She spends weekends scripting her show and puts each month's sliver of leftover income into savings. On Sundays, Simon meets her for dinner at an Indian restaurant on Eighteenth Street. One evening, she brings a manila folder, rubber-banded twice and stuffed with photocopies: grainy black-and-white photos, old newspapers, vintage programs and ads. She uses the full length of their table to lay everything out.

"This," she says, "is Gran."

Simon leans over the table. He recognizes Gertie's mother from the photo tacked above Klara's bed. In one image, she stands with a tall, dark-haired man on top of a galloping horse, stocky in her shorts and tied-off Western blouse. In another, the cover of a program, she is tiny-waisted and teeny-footed. She lifts the lip of her skirt with one hand; with the other, she walks six men on leashes. Below the men are the words, "The QUEEN of BURLESQUE! Come see Miss KLARA KLINE'S muscles shake and shiver like a BOWL of JELLY in a GALE of WIND — the DANCE that John the Baptist LOST HIS HEAD over!"

Simon snorts. "That's Ma's mom?"

"Yup. And that," says Klara, pointing to the man on the horse, "is her dad."

"No shit." The man isn't quite handsome — he has thick, mustache-like eyebrows and Gertie's large nose — but he has a glowering sort of charisma. He looks like Daniel. "How do you know?"

"I've been researching. I couldn't find her birth certificate, but I know she arrived at Ellis Island in 1913 on a ship called the *Ultonia.* She was Hungarian; I'm pretty sure she was an orphan. Aunt Helga arrived later. So Gran came with a girl's dance troupe and lived in a boarding house: the De Hirsch Home for Working Girls."

Klara picks up a piece of paper on which several pictures have been photocopied: a large stone building, a dining hall full of seated, brown-haired girls, and the portrait of a severe-looking woman — the Baroness de Hirsch, reads the caption — in a high-necked blouse, gloves, and square hat, all of them black.

"I mean, God knows — Gran was Jewish, and she had no family. If it weren't for the home, she'd've probably been on the street.

But this place was really proper. It taught all the girls to sew, get married young, and Gran wasn't like that. At some point, she left, and that's when she started doing this." Klara fingers the burlesque program. "She got her start in vaudeville. She performed in dance halls, dime museums, amusement parks — nickel dumps, too, which is what they called movie theaters. And then she met him."

Carefully, she lifts a page hidden under the program and passes it to Simon. It's a marriage certificate.

"Klara Kline and Otto Gorski," says Klara. "He was a Wild West rider with Barnum & Bailey, a world champion. So here's my theory: Gran met Otto on the way to a gig, fell in love and joined the circus."

Klara pulls a folded piece of paper out of her wallet. It's another picture, but this one shows Klara Sr. sliding from the top of the circus tent to the bottom, suspended only from a rope that she holds in her teeth. Below the photo is a caption: *Klara Kline and her Jaws of Life!*

"Why are you showing me all this?" asks Simon.

Klara's cheeks are pink. "I want to do a combination show: mostly magic, plus one death-defying feat. I'm teaching myself the

Jaws of Life."

Simon stops chewing his vegetable korma. "That's nuts. You don't know how she did it. There must have been some trick."

Klara shakes her head. "No trick — it was real. Otto, Gran's husband? He was killed in a riding accident in 1936. After that, Gran moved back to New York with Ma. In 1941, she did the Jaws of Life across Times Square, from the Edison Hotel to the roof of the Palace Theater. Halfway through, she fell. She died."

"Jesus Christ. Why didn't we know about this?"

"Because Ma never talked about it. It was a pretty big story back then, but I think she's always been ashamed of Gran. She wasn't normal," says Klara, nodding at the photo of Gertie's mother on the horse, a denim shirt hiked up to reveal her muscular stomach. "Besides, it was such a long time ago — Ma was only six when she died. After that, Ma went to live with Aunt Helga."

Simon knows Gertie was raised by her mother's sister, a hawkish older woman who spoke mostly Hungarian and never married. She came to 72 Clinton on Jewish holidays, bringing hard candies wrapped in colored foil. But her nails were long and pointed, her smell was that of a box unopened for decades, and Simon was always afraid of her.

Now he watches Klara put the photocopies back in her folder. "Klara, you can't do this. It's insane."

"I'm not going to die, Simon."

"How the hell do you know that?"

"Because I do." Klara opens her bag, puts the folder inside, and zips it shut. "I refuse to."

"Right," says Simon. "You and every other person who's ever lived."

Klara doesn't respond. Simon knows this is how she gets when she has an idea. *Like a dog with a bone,* Gertie used to say, but that isn't quite true; it's more that Klara becomes impermeable, unreachable. She exists somewhere else.

"Hey." Simon flicks her arm. "What'll you call it? Your act?"

Klara smiles in her feline way: the sharp little canines, a shake of glitter in her eyes.

"The Immortalist," she says.

Robert holds Simon's face in his hands. Simon has woken in a panic from another bad dream.

"What are you so afraid of?" Robert asks.

Simon shakes his head. It's four in the afternoon, a Sunday, and they've spent the entire day in bed, save for the half hour when they made poached eggs and bread slathered in cherry jam.

It's too good, this feeling, is what he wants to say. *It can't last.* By next summer, he'll have lived for two decades — a long life for a cat or a bird, but not for a man. He's told no one of his visit to the woman on Hester Street or the sentence she gave him, which seems to be drawing toward him in double time. In August, he takes the 38 Geary bus to the edge of Golden Gate Park and walks the steep, jutting trail at Land's End. There, he sees cypress and wildflowers and what's left of the Sutro Baths. A century ago, the baths were a human aquarium, but now the concrete is in ruins. Still, had it not been a luxury once? Even Eden — especially Eden — didn't last forever.

When winter comes, he begins to rehearse for Corps's spring program, *Myth.* Tommy and Eduardo will open the show as Narcissus and his Shadow, their movements mirrored. Next is *The Myth of Sisyphus,* in which the women perform a series of motions at intervals, like a song in a round. In the final piece, *The Myth of Icarus,* Simon will perform his first starring role: he is Icarus, and Robert is the Sun.

On opening night, he soars around Robert. He orbits closer. He wears a pair of large wings, made of wax and feathers, like those Daedalus fashioned for Icarus. The physics of dancing with twenty pounds on his back compounds his dizziness, so he is grateful when Robert removes them, even though this means that they have melted, and that Simon, as Icarus, will die.

When the music — Addinsell's "Warsaw Concerto" — climbs its final summit, Simon's soul feels like a body lifted above ground, its feet hovering midair. He yearns for his family. *If you could see me now,* he thinks. Instead, he clings to Robert, who carries him to center stage. The light around Robert is so bright that Simon can see nothing else: not the members of the audience or the other company members, who crowd in the wings to watch them.

"I love you," he whispers.

"I know," Robert says.

The music is loud; no one can hear them. Robert lays him on the ground. Simon arranges his body the way Gali showed him, with his legs curled and his arms reaching for Robert. Robert uses the wings to cover Simon before he backs away.

They spend two years like this. Simon makes the coffee; Robert makes the bed.

Everything is new until it isn't anymore: Robert's frayed sweatpants, his groan of pleasure. How he trims his nails weekly — perfect, translucent half-moons in the sink. The feeling of possession, foreign and heady: *My man. Mine.* When Simon looks back, this period of time feels impossibly short. Moments come to him like film slides: Robert making guacamole at the counter. Robert stretching by the window. Robert going outside to snip rosemary or thyme from the clay pots in their garden. At night, the street lamps shine so brightly, the garden is visible in the dark.

8.

"Your movements," says Gali. "They must. Have. Integrity."

December 1981. In men's class, they are practicing *fouetté* turns, in which the body spins, balanced on the ball of one foot, with the other leg extended sideways. Simon has fallen twice, and now Gali stands behind him — one palm against Simon's stomach, the other against his back — while the rest of the men look on.

"Lift the right leg. Keep the tightness in the core. Keep the alignment." It's easy to keep the alignment when both feet are on the ground, but as Simon's leg lifts, his lower back arches and his chest drops back. Gali claps in disapproval. "You see? This is the problem. You lift the leg, the ego takes over. You must start with the foundation."

He strides to the center to demonstrate. Simon crosses his arms.

"Everything," says Gali, looking at the

men. "Everything is connected. Watch." He places his feet in fourth position and pliés. "*This* is when I prepare. This is when it matters. I feel the connection between my chest and my hips. I feel the connection between my knees and the balls of my feet. The structure of the body has alignment and it has integrity, you see? So when I push off" — he lifts his back leg and turns — "there is unity. It is effortless."

Tommy, the British wunderkind, catches Simon's eye. *Effortless?* he mouths, and Simon grins. Tommy is a jumper, not a turner, and he likes to commiserate with Simon.

Gali is still turning. "From control," he says, "comes freedom. From restraint comes flexibility. From the trunk" — he puts one hand to his core, then gestures, with his free hand, to his raised leg — "come the branches."

He returns to the ground down in a deep plié, then lifts a palm as if to say, *See?*

Simon sees, but doing is a different matter. When class ends, Tommy slings an arm over Simon's shoulder and groans as they walk toward the dressing room. Robert glances at them. Rain batters the windows, but the room is steamy with sweat and most of the men are bare chested. When Simon leaves with Beau and Tommy for lunch, Robert doesn't join them.

They walk to Orphan Andy's on Seventeenth. Simon tells himself that he isn't doing anything wrong: most of the men at Academy are flirtatious, and it isn't his fault if Robert doesn't join in. He loves Robert — he does. Robert is intelligent and mature and surprising. He likes classical music as much as he likes football, and though he's not yet thirty, he'd prefer to read in bed than go to Purp with Simon. "He's *classy,*" said Klara, the first time she met him, and Simon beamed with pride. But this is also part of the problem: Simon likes raunch, likes being spanked and ogled and sucked off, and he has some appetite for depravity — or at least, what his parents would have called depravity — that he is finally beginning to acknowledge.

After lunch, they head to Star Pharmacy for rolling papers. Simon pays while the other two wait outside. They're both staring at the pharmacy's glass window when he comes back.

"Oh my God, you guys," Tommy says. "Have you seen this?"

He points at a homemade flier taped to the window. *THE GAY CANCER,* it reads. Below are three Polaroid photos of a young man. In the first photo, he holds up his shirt to reveal purple splotches, raised and rippling like burns. In the second, his mouth is open wide. There's a splotch in there, too.

"Shut up, Tommy." Tommy is a notorious hypochondriac — he's always complaining of aches in muscle groups no one else has ever heard of — but Beau's voice is sharper than usual.

They huddle under the awning at Toad Hall to smoke. Simon inhales, sweetness and damp, and it should calm him but it doesn't: he feels like he could jump out of his skin. For the rest of the day, he can't erase the images from his mind — those terrible lesions, dark as plums — or the words that someone else scrawled at the bottom of the flier in red pen: *Watch out, guys. There's something out there.*

Richie wakes up with a red dot on the white of his left eye. Simon covers his shift so Richie can go to the doctor; he wants to make sure it's gone by Christmas Eve, the night of Purp's annual Jingle Bell Cock. Few of Purp's patrons visit family over the holidays, so the dancers paint themselves red and green, hang bells from the waists of their G-strings. The doctor sends Richie home with an antibiotic. "They're like,

'Maybe it's pink eye,' " Richie says the next day, spraying Adrian's backside purple. "This sweet little lab tech, she's probably nineteen, she goes, 'Any chance you came into contact with fecal matter?' I'm like" — hand to heart — " 'Oh no, honey, I wouldn't touch the stuff,' " and the men are laughing, and Simon will remember Richie like this later, his guffaw, his military buzz cut with the slightest hint of gray, because by the twentieth of December, Richie is dead.

How to describe the shock? The splotches appear on the flower seller in Dolores Park and on the beautiful feet of Beau, who once spun eight times without stopping and is now taken to San Francisco General in Eduardo's car, seizing. These are Simon's earliest memories of Ward 86, though it will not be named for another year: the squeak of meal carts; the nurses at the phone desk, their remarkable calm (*No, we don't know how it's transmitted. Is your lover with you now? Does he know you're coming to the hospital?*); and the men, men in their twenties and thirties sitting wide-eyed on cots and in wheelchairs as if hallucinating. *Rare Cancer Seen in 41 Homosexuals,* says the *Chronicle,* but nobody knows how you get it. Still, when the lymph nodes in Lance's armpits begin to swell, he finishes his shift at Purp and cabs to the hospital with the article in his backpack. Ten days later, the lumps are large as oranges.

Robert paces the apartment. "We need to stay here," he says. They have enough food for two weeks. Neither of them has slept in days.

But Simon is panicked by the thought of quarantine. He already feels cut off from the world, and he refuses to hide, refuses to believe this is the end. He's not dead yet. And yet he knows, of course he knows, or at least he fears — the thin line between fear and intuition; how one so easily masquerades as the other — that the woman is right, and that by June 21st, the first day of summer, he'll be gone, too.

Robert doesn't want him working at Purp. "It isn't safe," he says.

"Nothing is safe." Simon takes his bag of makeup and walks to the door. "I need the money."

"Bullshit. Corps pays you." Robert follows him and grabs his arm, hard. "Admit it, Simon. You like what you get there. You need it."

"Come on, Rob." Simon forces a laugh. "Don't be such a drag."

"Me? I'm a drag?"

There is a blaze in Robert's eyes that

makes Simon feel both intimidated and turned on. He reaches for Robert's cock.

Robert yanks back. "Don't play me like that. Don't touch me."

"Come with me," Simon slurs. He's been drinking, which Robert dislikes almost as much as his work at Purp. "Why don't you ever come anywhere?"

"I don't *fit* anywhere, Simon. Not with you white guys. Not with the black guys. Not in ballet or in football. Not back home, and not here." Robert speaks slowly, as though to a child. "So I stay home. I keep myself small. Except when I'm dancing. And even then — every time I get onstage, I know there's people in that audience who have never seen somebody like me dance like I dance. I know that some of them won't like it. I'm scared, Simon. Every day. And now you know what that's like. 'Cause you're scared, too."

"I don't know what you're talking about," says Simon, hoarse.

"I think you know exactly what I'm talking about. This is the first time you've felt like me — like there's nowhere that's safe. And you don't like it."

Simon feels his pulse in his skull. He is staked by the truth of what Robert has said like an insect to a board, his wings flapping.

"You're jealous," he hisses. "That's all. You could try harder, Rob, but you don't. And you're jealous — you're *jealous* — that I do."

Robert holds his ground but swings his face, abruptly, to one side. When he looks at Simon again, the whites of his eyes are pink.

"You're just like the rest of them," he says, "all the twinks and the art fags and the motherfucking bears. You guys, you go on about your rights and your freedoms, you cheer at all the parades, but all you really want's the right to fuck some leatherman in a den on Folsom or spew your shit all over a bathhouse. You want the right to be as careless as any other white guy — any straight one. But you're not any other white guy. And that's why this place is so dangerous: because it lets you forget that."

Simon burns with humiliation. *Fuck you,* he thinks. *Fuck you, fuck you, fuck you.* But Robert's speech has stricken him silent, in anger and in shame — why is it that those feelings are so inextricable? He turns and pushes out of the door, toward the dark blur of Castro Street, the lights and the men that always seem to be waiting for him.

Purp's new hires are terrible — they're sixteen and freaked, they can't even dance

— and the audience is thin, a couple of guys huddled in the corners and a few more grinding feverishly near the platforms. After their shift, Adrian is jumpy. "I need to get the fuck out of here," he mutters, toweling off. So does Simon. He gets in Adrian's car to cruise the Castro, but the owner of Alfie's is sick, and the scene at the QT's as depressing as it is at Purp, so Adrian takes a sharp turn and heads downtown.

Cornholes and Liberty Baths aren't open. They stop in Folsom Gulch Books — *Committed to Pleasure,* the tagline reads — but the movie booths are occupied and nobody's in the arcade. Boot Camp Baths on Bryant is empty. They wind up at Animals, a leather den, and neither Adrian nor Simon are wearing leather but thank God, at least there are people here, so they dump their clothes in the lockers before Adrian leads them through a dark maze of rooms. Men in chaps and dog collars ride each other in the shadows. Adrian disappears into a corner with a kid in a harness, but Simon can't bring himself to touch anyone. He waits by the entrance for Adrian, who returns in an hour with wide pupils and a slick red mouth.

Adrian drives him home. Simon breathes. He hasn't messed up, not irrevocably, not yet. They park a block away from Simon and Robert's apartment and stare at each other for seconds before Simon reaches for Adrian, and this is how it begins.

Klara stands onstage beneath a pool of blue light. The stage is a small platform designed for musicians. A scattering of audience members sits at round tables or on stools at the bar, though Simon can't tell how many of them are there to see her and how many are just regulars. Klara wears a men's tuxedo jacket with her pinstriped pants and Doc Martens. Her tricks are skillful, but they aren't big magic, they're quippy and clever, and her script has an air of studied perfectionism, like a graduate student at a dissertation defense. Simon swirls his martini with a straw and wonders what he'll tell her afterward. Over a year of planning and this is the result: scarf tricks in the only place that would take her, a jazz club on Fillmore whose patrons are already drifting into the cold spring night.

Only a handful are still there when Klara uncoils a rope from a nearby music stand and puts a small brown mouthpiece between her teeth. The rope hangs from a cable that hangs from a pipe on the ceiling, controlled by a pulley Klara rigged herself and which is now held, at her direction, by the bar manager.

"You trust him with that?" Simon asked last week, when Klara explained the procedure. "Do you want me to do it?"

"I don't mix business with pleasure."

"I'm pleasure?"

"Well, no," she said. "You're family."

Now he watches her rise to the second-story windows. During a brief intermission, she changed into a sleeveless dress, nude-colored and covered with gold sequins; its fringed skirt hits mid-thigh. Klara drifts in ghostly circles before pulling her arms and legs close to her body. Suddenly, she's a blur: red and gold, hair and glitter, a vortex of light. As she slows, she becomes his sister again — sweat gleams at her hairline, and her jaw is beginning to shake. Her feet stretch toward the stage, knees buckling once she's low enough to reach it. She spits the bit into her palm and bows.

There is the clink of ice, the screech of chairs being adjusted, before the applause begins to surge. It isn't magic, what Klara has done. There's no trick — just a curious combination of strength and strange, inhuman lightness. Simon can't tell whether it reminds him of a levitation or a hanging.

While the next act sets up, Simon finds

Klara in the greenroom. He waits outside as she talks to the manager, a broad man in a tracksuit who looks to be in his fifties. When he shakes her hand and wraps his other one around her back, resting it on the curve of her bottom, Klara becomes rigid. After he leaves, she glances at the door before walking to the chair on which the manager left his leather jacket. A wallet bulges from one pocket. She takes a wad of bills and stuffs them down the side of her dress.

"Seriously?" asks Simon, stepping inside.

Klara whirls. The shame in her face turns to righteousness. "He was an asshole. And they paid me like shit."

"So?"

"So what?" She pulls on her tuxedo coat. "He had hundreds. I took fifty."

"How noble of you."

"Really, Simon?" Klara is stiff-backed, packing supplies into Ilya's black box. "I do my first show, the show I've been working on for years, and this is all you have to say to me? You want to talk about being noble?"

"What's that supposed to mean?"

"It means word gets around." Klara closes the box and holds it between her arms like a shield. "My coworker is Adrian's cousin. Last week, she said, 'I think my cousin's dating your brother.' "

Simon blanches. "Well, that's bullshit."

"Don't lie to me." Klara leans toward him, her hair brushing his chest. "Robert is the best fucking thing that ever happened to you. You want to throw it away, that's your choice, but at least have the decency to break up with him."

"Don't tell me what to do," says Simon, but the worst part is that Klara doesn't know half of it. Cruising Golden Gate Park in the early hours of the morning, fucking strangers in Speedway Meadows or the public restrooms at Forty-First and JFK. Hand jobs in the back row of the Castro Theatre while Little Orphan Annie sings onscreen. Hordes of men at the Wasteland at Ocean Beach, warming one another.

And the worst night: May, the Tenderloin. A drag queen in a spangled silver dress and chunky heels leads him to a single-occupancy hotel on Hyde. Someone's pimp grabs Simon by the collar and searches for his wallet, but Simon knees him in the crotch and stumbles upstairs. They take a room and flick on a bedside lamp, and it is then that Simon sees his partner is Lady. She hasn't been at Purp in weeks; they all assumed the worst, that the gay cancer got her, and for seconds, Simon feels a gust of relief. But Lady doesn't recognize him. She takes a miniature vodka bottle out of her dress pocket. It's empty, with an aluminum foil screen. She stuffs a rock into the chamber and inhales.

On the first day of June, Simon stands in the shower. Last night's *Myth* performance was the first time that Simon touched Robert in days, the first time they stood together without arguing. Now, Simon tries to masturbate, thinking of Robert, but he can't come until he remembers Lady crouched over her homemade pipe.

He picks up the shampoo bottle and throws it at the shower caddy with all his strength. The caddy jolts upward to smack the showerhead, which jumps out of its setting and swings wildly, wetting the ceiling, until Simon is able to turn the goddamned thing off. He slides down to sit against the tub's cool porcelain and sobs. The dark mark still leers from his abdomen, though when he leans in, it looks more like a mole than it did the day before. Yes: it could definitely be a mole. He stands and adjusts the shower caddy, then steps onto the bath mat. Sunlight glazes the bathroom. Simon doesn't notice that Robert is standing in the doorway until he speaks.

"What is that?" He stares at Simon's stomach.

Simon grabs a towel. "Nothing."

"Like hell it's nothing." Robert puts one hand on Simon's shoulder and pulls the towel off. "Oh my God."

They stare at it together for seconds. Then Simon hangs his head.

"Rob," he whispers. "I'm so sorry. I'm so sorry for what I've done to us." Then, madly: "There's a show tonight. We have to get to the theater."

"No, baby," says Robert. "That's not where we need to go," and in minutes, he's called them a cab.

9.

There are twelve beds in Simon's ward at San Francisco General. The swinging door that leads inside has a laminated sign — *MASK GOWN GLOVES PUNCTURE PROOF NEEDLE BOX IN ROOM NO PREGNANT WOMEN* — and a smaller sign that reads *No Flowers*.

Klara and Robert stay overnight in Simon's room, sleeping in chairs. His bed is separated from another by a thin white curtain. Simon doesn't like to look at his roommate, a former chef whose bones now protrude; he can't keep anything down. Within days, the bed is empty again, the partition drifting in the breeze.

Robert says, "You have to tell your family."

Simon shakes his head. "They can't know I went like this."

"But you haven't gone," says Klara. Her lap is covered with pamphlets — *When a*

— and her eyes are slick. "You're right here, with us."

"Yeah." Simon's throat feels tight: the glands in his neck are swollen. One night, when Robert and Klara leave to get takeout, Simon scoots to the edge of the bed and reaches for the phone. He's ashamed to realize he doesn't even have Daniel's number, but Klara left a pile of belongings on her chair, including a slender red address book. Daniel picks up on the fifth ring.

"Dan," says Simon. His voice is raspy and his left foot twitches, but he floods with gratitude.

There is a long pause before Daniel speaks. "Who is this?"

"It's me, Daniel." He clears his throat. "It's Simon."

"Simon."

Another pause, which stretches so long Simon knows it won't end unless he fills it.

"I'm sick," he says.

"You're sick." A beat. "I'm sorry to hear that."

Daniel speaks stiffly, as if to a stranger. How long has it been since they've talked? Simon tries to imagine how Daniel's face might look. He's twenty-four years old.

"What are you doing?" Simon asks —

anything to keep his brother on the phone.

"I'm in medical school. I just got home from class."

Simon pictures it: doors whooshing open and shut, young people walking with backpacks. The thought comforts him so deeply that he feels almost able to fall asleep. With his nerve pain and his twitching, he spends most nights awake.

"Simon?" Daniel asks, softening. "Is there anything I can do?"

"No," Simon says, "there's nothing." He wonders if Daniel is relieved when he hangs up.

June 13th. Two of the men on Simon's hall died in the night. His new roommate — a Hmong boy in glasses who keeps asking for his mother — can't be older than seventeen.

"There was a woman," Simon tells Robert, perched beside him as always. "She told me when I'd die."

"A woman?" Robert scoots closer. "What woman, baby? A nurse?"

Simon is light-headed. They've been giving him morphine for the nerve pain. "No, not a nurse — a woman. She came to New York. When I was a kid."

"Sy." Klara looks up from her chair, where

she is stirring a yogurt for him. "Please don't."

Robert keeps his eyes on Simon. "And she told you — what? What do you remember?"

What does he remember? A narrow door. A bronze number swinging on its hinge. He remembers the filthiness of the apartment, which surprised him; he had imagined a scene of tranquility, as might appear around the Buddha. He remembers a stack of playing cards from which the woman asked him to pick four. He remembers the cards he chose — four spades, all of them black — and the hideous shock of the date she gave him. He remembers stumbling down the fire escape, his palm clammy on the railing. He remembers that she never asked for money.

"I always knew it," he says. "I always knew I'd die young. That's why I did what I did."

"Why you did what?" asks Robert.

Simon lifts a finger. "Why I left Ma. For one thing."

He puts a second finger out but loses his train of thought. Talking feels like trying to reach the surface of an ocean. More and more, it's like he's drifting toward the bottom, like he knows what's down there, though he can't explain it to anyone on land.

"Hush," says Robert, smoothing the hair

off his forehead. "It doesn't matter anymore. Nothing matters."

"No. You don't understand." Simon dog-paddles; he gulps. It is urgent, that he say this. "Everything does."

When Robert leaves to use the bathroom, Klara comes to Simon's cot. The skin beneath her eyes is swollen.

She says, "Will I ever find someone I love as much as you?"

She scoots into bed beside him. He's become so thin that they both fit easily in the hospital's twin.

"Please," says Simon: her words, when they stood on the roof as the sun rose, when they stood at the very beginning. "You'll find someone you love much more."

"No," gasps Klara. "I won't." She lays her head on Simon's pillow. When she turns to look at him, her hair falls over his collarbone. "What did she tell you?"

What does it matter, now? "Sunday," Simon says.

"Oh, Sy." There is a strangled cry, like something that would come from a chained dog. Klara puts a palm over her mouth when she realizes it's hers. "I wish — I wish . . ."

"Don't wish it. Look what she gave me."

"This!" says Klara, looking at the lesions

on his arms, his sharp ribs. Even his blond mane has thinned: after an aide helps him bathe, the drain is matted with curls.

"No," says Simon, "this," and he points at the window. "I would never have come to San Francisco if it weren't for her. I wouldn't have met Robert. I'd never have learned how to dance. I'd probably still be home, waiting for my life to begin."

He's angry with the disease. He rages at the disease. For so long, he hated the woman, too. How, he wondered, could she give such a terrible fortune to a child? But now he thinks of her differently, like a second mother or a god, she who showed him the door and said: *Go.*

Klara looks paralyzed. Simon remembers the expression he saw on her face after they moved to San Francisco, that eerie combination of irritation and indulgence, and he realizes why it disturbed him. She reminded him of the woman: counting down, watching him. Inside him a bud of love for his sister breaks open. He thinks of her on the rooftop — how she stood at the edge and spoke without looking at him. *Give me one good reason why you shouldn't start your life.*

"You aren't surprised that it's Sunday," Simon says. "You knew all along."

"Your date," Klara whispers. "You said it

was young. I wanted you to have everything you've ever wanted."

Simon squeezes Klara's hand. Her palm is fleshy, a healthy pink. "But I do," he says.

Sometimes, Klara leaves to let Simon and Robert be alone. When they're too tired to do anything else, they watch videos, rented from the San Francisco Public Library, of the great male dancers: Nureyev, Baryshnikov, Nijinsky. One of the Shanti Project volunteers wheels the television in from the community room, and Robert lies with Simon in his cot.

Simon stares at him. *How lucky I was to know you.* He fears for Robert's future.

"If he gets it," Simon tells Klara, "he has to get into the trial. Promise me, Klara — promise me you'll make sure."

Word has spread throughout the corridor about an experimental medication that showed promise in Africa.

"Okay, Sy," Klara whispers. "I promise. I'll try."

Why, in his years with Robert, has he had such trouble expressing love? As the days become longer, Simon says it over and over: *I love you, I love you,* that call and response, as essential to the body as food or breath. It is only when he hears Robert's reply that his pulse slows, his eyes close, and he is able, at last, to sleep.

■ ■ ■ ■

PART TWO:
PROTEUS

■ ■ ■ ■

1982–1991
Klara

10.

Klara can turn a black scarf into a single red rose and an ace into a queen. She can produce dimes from pennies and quarters from dimes and dollars from nothing but air. She can do the Hermann pass, the Thurston throw, the rising-card illusion, and the Back Palm. She is expert in the classic cup-and-ball routine, passed from the Canadian master Dai Vernon to Ilya Hlavacek and then to her: a dizzying, dazzling optical illusion in which an empty silver cup is filled with balls and dice and then, finally, one full, perfect lemon.

What she cannot do — what she will never stop trying to do — is bring her brother back.

When Klara arrives for a gig, her first task is to rig the space for the Jaws of Life. It isn't easy to find nightclubs with high ceilings, so she also performs in dinner theaters and concert halls, and occasionally, as an independent contractor with a small circus in Berkeley. Still, she prefers clubs for their smokiness and dark moods, for the fact that she can work them alone, and because they are populated by adults, the people for whom she prefers to perform. Most adults claim not to believe in magic, but Klara knows better. Why else would anyone play at permanence — fall in love, have children, buy a house — in the face of all evidence there's no such thing? The trick is not to convert them. The trick is to get them to admit it.

She brings her tools in a bulging duffel bag: drop line and ascension rope, wrench and clamps, swivel mouthpiece, sash cord. Ilya taught her that every rig is different, so Klara assesses the height of the ceiling, the width of the stage, the style and strength of the battens. There is no gap between failure and success — the timing is perfect or it is disastrous — and her pulse trills as she lashes the ascension rope to the batten from a ladder, as she wraps it thrice with sash cord and puts a safety break on the reverse rope. On stage, she measures sixty-nine inches up from the floor: her own five feet six inches, plus seven for her feet when pointed, and a two-inch clearance to the ground.

She started performing the Breakaway two years ago. An assistant pulls the rope until Klara hovers at the ceiling with the bit in her mouth. But instead of floating back down, as she did in her early shows, she plunges when the rope is released. The audience always believes it's an accident, and there are gasps, sometimes screams, until she jerks to a stop. By now, she's almost used to the way her jaw jolts as it absorbs the weight of her body, to the whiplash snap of her neck and the sting in her eyes, nose, and ears. All she can see is the hot white of the lights until the rope is lowered inches more and her feet touch down. When she lifts her head and spits the bit into her palm, she sees the audience for the first time, their faces slack with wonder.

"I love you all," she whispers, bowing — these words inspired by Howard Thurston, who repeated them before each show, standing behind the curtain as the overture swelled. "I love you all, I love you all, I love you all."

11.

On an unusually cold night in February, 1988, Klara stands onstage at the Committee, a Cabaret theater on Broadway that is typically populated by a comedy troupe of the same name. This Monday, they've rented it to Klara, who paid more to perform there than she'll ever make back. She's put a business card on every table — *The Immortalist,* the cards read — but the audience is sparse, guys who filtered over from the Condor and the Lusty Lady or are headed there afterward. Klara is witty in the cup-and-ball act, but nobody's interested in anything but the Breakaway, and even that has lost its novelty. "Enough magic, sweetheart," someone shouts. "Lemme see your tits!" When her act is over and a burlesque troupe begins to set up, Klara puts on the long, black duster she wears on performance nights and walks to the bar. She lifts a leather wallet from the heckler's pocket on her way to the ladies' room and slips it back, empty of cash, on her return.

"Hey."

Her stomach drops. She spins, expecting to see a freckled face and whiskey-colored eyes, a uniform and a badge, but instead she's faced with a tall man in a T-shirt, loose jeans, and work boots, a man who puts up his hands in surrender.

"Didn't mean to startle you," he says, but now Klara is staring at his light brown skin and shiny, shoulder-length black hair, both of which she's sure she's seen before.

"You're familiar."

"I'm Raj."

"Raj." And the light bulb. "Raj! My God — Teddy's roommate. Baksheesh Khalsa's, I mean," she adds, remembering Baksheesh Khalsa's long hair and steel bracelet.

Raj laughs. "I never liked that kid. What kind of white guy up and starts wearing a turban?"

"The kind who hangs in the Haight, I guess."

"They're all gone now. They work in Silicon Valley, or they're lawyers. With very short hair."

Klara laughs. She likes Raj's quickness and his eyes, which search her. People are filtering out of the theater; when the front door opens, she sees black night, speckled with stars and the neon marquees of the strip clubs. Ordinarily, after gigs, she rides the 30 Stockton to the Chinatown apartment where she lives alone.

"What are you doing right now?" she asks.

"Doing?" Raj's mouth is thin lipped but expressive, with a sly curl. "Right now, I'm doing nothing. I have no plans at all."

"Ten years have passed. Can you believe it? Ten years! And you're one of the first people I met in San Francisco."

They sit in Vesuvio's, an Italian café across the alley from City Lights. Klara likes it because it was once frequented by Ferlinghetti and Ginsberg, though it's now occupied by a rowdy group of Australian tourists.

"And we're still here," says Raj.

"And we're still here." Klara has hazy images of Raj in the apartment where she and Simon stayed during their first days in the city: Raj reading *One Hundred Years of Solitude* on the couch or making pancakes in the kitchen with blond, long-limbed Susie, who sold flowers near the ballpark. "What happened to Susie?"

"Ran off with a Christian Spiritualist. I haven't seen her since seventy-nine. You came with your brother, didn't you? How's he?"

Klara has been fingering her martini glass, squeezing the narrow stem, but now she looks up. "He's dead."

Raj coughs on his drink. "Dead? Fuck, Klara. I'm sorry. What of?"

"AIDS," says Klara, and she is grateful, at least, to have a reason for it, a name, which did not exist until three months after Simon's death. "He was twenty."

"Fucking shit." Raj shakes his head again. "It's a bastard, AIDS. Took one of my friends last year."

"What do you do?" asks Klara. Anything to change the subject.

"I'm a mechanic. I do car repair, mostly, but I've done construction, too. My dad wanted me to be a surgeon. Fat chance of that, I always told him, but he sent me here anyway. He stayed in Dharavi — slum of Bombay — half a million people in a mile, shit in the river, but it's home."

"That must have been hard, coming here without your dad," Klara says, looking at him. He has thick eyebrows, but his features are delicate — high cheekbones that taper into a slender jaw and pointed chin. "How old were you?"

"Ten. I moved in with my dad's cousin

Amit. He was the smartest person in our family — got a scholarship to college and moved to California for med school in the sixties on a student visa. My dad wanted me to be just like him. I was never good at science, I don't like fixing people, but I do like fixing *things,* so my dad, he was half-right about me; though half isn't enough, I suppose." He has a nervous laugh, the trace of an accent, though Klara has to listen hard to hear it. "And you? How long've you been doing this?"

"Mm," says Klara. "Six years?"

In the beginning, the grind was electrifying, but now it exhausts her: rigging and striking on her own, riding BART to Berkeley in her duster while hip-hop blasts from somebody's boom box. Home at one in the morning or three if she's coming from the East Bay, soaking in the tub as the Chinese bakery on the first floor whirs to life. Nights spent sewing the goddamn sequins back onto her dress with the junky machine she's too poor to replace — there are sequins between the couch cushions, sequins on the stairs, sequins in the shower drain.

One year ago, she was badly injured during the Breakaway. A girl she hired through the *Chronicle* let go of the rope without checking the safety break, and it slipped three feet on the batten. Klara didn't clear the floor. When she came to, she was on her hands and knees, her skull throbbing as if she'd taken a punch and her feet puffing up like dark balloons. She didn't have insurance, and the hospital fees nearly cleaned out the money she inherited from Saul. She spent six weeks in a boot, raging. For the past year, she's only worked with a nineteen-year-old boy from the circus, but he's leaving in March to join Barnum.

"It makes you happy, I see," says Raj. He's grinning.

"Oh." Klara smiles. "It did. It does. But I'm tired. It's hard to do it alone. And it's hard to get bookings. There are only so many venues that'll hire me, and there's only so many times they'll do it — you perform in the same place for years, word gets around, the hype swells and then it dies and you're still there, you know, hanging from a rope by your teeth."

"I liked that part, the rope trick. What's your secret?"

"There's no secret." Klara shrugs. "You just hold on."

"Impressive." Raj raises his eyebrows. "You get nervous?"

"Less than I used to, and only before. It's the anticipation; I'm backstage and I feel . . .

stage fright, I suppose, but it's more than that, it's excitement — the knowledge that I'm about to show people something they've never seen before. That I might change the way they see the world, if only for an hour." She frowns. "I don't feel nervous before the scarf tricks, or the cup and ball. That's what I was raised on, but nobody likes it as much as the Breakaway."

"Why don't you change the act, then? Cut the small stuff, go big time?"

"It'd be complicated. I'd need equipment and a real, full-time assistant. I'd have to find a way to maneuver bigger props. Plus, my favorite acts, the ones I've only read about in books? Well, I'd have to figure them out. As a species, magicians are pretty tight-lipped."

"Pretend, then: You can do anything. What do you do?"

"Anything? God." Klara grins. "DeKolta's Vanishing Birdcage, for one. He raised a cage in the air with a parrot inside it and then — boom! — it disappeared. I know it must have gone up his sleeve, but I've never been able to figure out how."

"It must have been collapsible. The bars — were they jointed? Thicker at the middle than they were at the ends?"

"I don't know," says Klara, but now she's

flushing, talking fast. "Then there's the Proteus cabinet. It's a small closet, upright with tall legs on casters, so the audience knows you can't come and go through a trapdoor. An assistant turns the cabinet around, opens the doors and closes them, and that's when a knock comes from inside. The doors open, and there you are."

"Mirrors," says Raj. "Viewers don't see the surface. They look through it, to whatever object's being reflected."

"Sure, I know that much. But it's all angles; the geometry has to be perfect, and that's the trick of it — the math." She's finished her drink, but for once, she doesn't notice. "The act I'd really want to do, though, my all-time favorite, is called Second Sight. It was invented by a magician named Charles Morritt. Audience members gave him certain objects — a gold watch, say, or a cigarette case — and his assistant, who was blindfolded, identified them. Other magicians have done it since, with patter — you know, 'Yes, here's an interesting object, please hand it over,' which was obviously some sort of code — but all Morritt said was 'Yes, thank you,' every time. He kept the secret till he died."

"The blindfold was see-through."

"His assistant was facing the wall."

"The audience members were plants."

Klara shakes her head. "No way. The act would never have become so famous — people have tried to crack it for over a century."

Raj laughs. "Dammit."

"I told you. I've thought about it for years."

"Then I suppose," says Raj, "we'll just have to think harder."

12.

Once, during the Golds' annual trip to Lavellette, New Jersey, Saul woke the family at dawn. Gertie groaned, the last to rise, as Saul led them through the rented beach house, with its blue and yellow shutters, and down the path that led to the sea. Everyone was barefoot; there was no time for shoes, and when they reached the water, Klara saw why.

"It looks like ketchup," Simon said, though it turned a watermelon fuchsia at the horizon.

"No," said Saul, "like the Nile," and stared at the ocean with such perfect belief that Klara was apt to agree with him.

Years later, in school, Klara learned of a phenomenon called red tide: algae blooms multiply, making coastal waters toxic and discolored. This knowledge made her feel curiously empty. She no longer had reason to wonder about the red sea or marvel at its mystery. She recognized that something had been given to her, but something else — the magic of transformation — had been taken away.

When Klara plucks a coin from inside someone's ear or turns a ball into a lemon, she hopes not to deceive but to impart a different kind of knowledge, an expanded sense of possibility. The point is not to negate reality but to peel back its scrim, revealing reality's peculiarities and contradictions. The very best magic tricks, the kind Klara wants to perform, do not subtract from reality. They add.

In the eighth century BC, Homer wrote of Proteus, sea god and seal herder, who could assume any form. He could tell the future, but he'd change shape to avoid it, answering only if seized. Three thousand years later, inventor John Henry Pepper presented a new illusion at London's Polytechnic Institution titled "Proteus, or We are Here but not Here." One century after that, in a construction dumpster at Fisherman's Wharf, Klara and Raj scavenge for wood scraps. At this late hour, the site is abandoned — even the sea lions are asleep, only their noses above water — and they haul nine planks back in Raj's truck. In the basement of the Sunset house he shares with four other men, Raj builds a cabinet three feet wide by six feet tall. Klara covers the interior with white and gold wallpaper, like John Henry Pepper's. Raj hinges two glass mirrors to the inside of the cabinet, wallpapered, too, so that they look like the cabinet walls when lying flat. When opened toward the center of the cabinet with their edges touching, they hide a wedge of open space inside which Klara fits perfectly. Now, the mirrors reflect a side wall instead of the back.

"It's beautiful," she breathes.

The illusion is flawless. Klara has disappeared in plain sight. There, in the midst of reality, is another one nobody can see.

Raj's past is anything but magical. His mother died of diphtheria when he was three; his father was a rag picker, wading through mountains of trash to find glass and metal and plastic to sell to scrap dealers. He brought the scraps of the scraps home to Raj, who turned them into tiny, delicate robots and lined them up on the floor of their one-room apartment.

"He had tuberculosis," Raj says. "That's why he sent me here. He knew he was dying, and he knew I had no one else. If he was going to get me out, it had to be soon."

They're lying on Klara's bed, only an inch of space between their noses. "How did he do it?"

Raj pauses. "He paid somebody off. Someone who faked papers for me, saying I was Amit's brother. It was the only way to get me in, and it took everything he had." There is a vulnerability in his face that she hasn't seen before, or an anxiety. "I'm legal now, if that's what you're wondering."

"It wasn't." Klara laces her hands with his and squeezes. "Did your dad ever make it here?"

Raj shakes his head. "He lived for another two years. But he didn't tell me he was sick, so I didn't get to see him before he died. I think he was afraid that if I visited, I wouldn't leave him. I was his only kid."

Klara pictures their fathers. In her mind, they're friends, wherever they are: they play chess in ghostly public parks and debate theism in heaven's smoky bars. She knows she's not supposed to believe in the Christian heaven, but she does. The Jewish version — the Sheol, Land of Forgetfulness — is too hopeless.

"What would they think of us?" she asks. "A Jew and a Hindu?"

"A barely Hindu." Raj pinches her nose.

"And a barely Jew."

Raj crafts his personal mythology anew. He is the son of the son of the legendary fakir who taught India's greatest magic tricks to Howard Thurston: how to grow a mango tree from a seed in seconds, how to sit on spikes, how to throw a loose rope in the air and then climb it. This is what he'll tell managers and booking agents, what he'll print on the inside of their programs, and each time, he feels a satisfaction bit by guilt. He isn't sure whether he feels more like the fakir's imaginary grandson, taking back something that belongs to him, or like the hustler Howard Thurston, sneaking from East to West with a stolen trick in his pocket.

"I don't get it," Raj says. "The Immortalist."

They sit on Klara's couch. It's April, four o'clock and drizzling, but heat rises from the bakery downstairs and they've propped a window open.

"What's not to get?" Klara wears a loose T-shirt and a pair of Raj's boxers; her bare feet rest on his thighs. "I'll never die."

"Big talker." He squeezes her calf. "I get what it means. I just don't get why you think that's what you're playing at."

"What am I playing at?"

"Transformation." He props himself up on one elbow. "A scarf becomes a flower. A ball becomes a lemon. A Hungarian dancer" — he wiggles his eyebrows; Klara's told him about Gran — "becomes an American star."

Raj has big plans: new costumes, new business cards, bigger venues. He's teaching himself the East Indian Needle Trick, in which a magician swallows loose needles and thread and pulls apart his cheeks for audience inspection before regurgitating them perfectly strung. He's even booked them a run at Teatro ZinZanni, a dinner theater owned by one of his clients at the repair shop.

Klara can't remember exactly when they decided to go into business together, or when they started to think of it as business. Then again, she can't remember a lot of things. But she loves Raj: the jolt of his energy, his genius in animating objects. She loves the straight dark hair he is always pushing out of his eyes, and she loves his name, Rajanikant Chapal. He builds a mechanical canary for the Vanishing Birdcage — hollow plaster to which he glues real feathers — and uses a rod to manipulate its head and wings. She loves that the bird comes alive in his hands.

Klara's greatest trick is not the Jaws of Life, but the force of will it takes to ignore her audience's pagers and stonewashed jeans. In performing, she rewinds the clock to a time when people marveled at illusion and spiritualists talked to the dead, when they believed the dead had something to say. William and Ira Davenport — brothers from Rochester, New York, who conjured ghosts while roped to plank seats inside a large wooden cabinet — are the most well-known Victorian mediums, but they were inspired by sisters. In 1848, seven years before the Davenports' first performance, Kate and Margaret Fox heard rapping sounds in the bedroom of their Hydesville farmhouse. Soon the Fox home was called the spook house, and the girls began a national tour. In Rochester, their first stop, physicians who examined the sisters claimed they were causing the noises by clicking bones in their knees. But a larger team of investigators could find no earthly reason for the raps, nor for the communication system — a code based on counting — that the sisters used to translate them.

In May, Klara bursts into the bathroom

while Raj is showering. "Time!"

Raj cracks the foggy shower door. "What?"

"Second Sight. Morritt's trick — it's time, time is how you do it," and she's laughing, it's so obvious, so simple.

"The mind-reading trick?" Raj shakes his head like a dog. Water splatters the walls. "How?"

"Synchronized counting," says Klara, thinking as she speaks. "He knew the audience was listening for a secret code, a code based on words. How could he get around it? By creating a code based on silence — the amount of silence *between* his words."

"And the silence corresponds to what — letters? Do you have any idea how long it would take to make whole words?"

"No, it couldn't be letters. But maybe they had a list, a list of common objects — you know, wallets and purses and, I don't know, hats — and if Morritt said 'thank you' after twelve seconds, his assistant knew it was a hat. And for the *type* of hat, they could have had another list — materials, let's say — one second for leather, two for wool, three for knits . . . We could do it, Raj. I know we could."

He's looking at her like she's crazy, and she is, of course, but that's never stopped her. Even years later, when they've done the act hundreds of times — even when Klara is pregnant with Ruby, even after Ruby is born — Klara never feels closer to Raj than she does during Second Sight. Together, they balance on the edge of failure, Raj holding an object and Klara straining, straining to hear his cue before racing through their numbered lists. A Reebok sneaker. A pack of Lifesavers. The sharp intake of breath from the audience when she gets it right. No wonder it takes a drink or three to calm her down after the show, hours before she's dull enough to sleep.

Two days before their opening at Teatro ZinZanni, Raj returns to Klara's apartment after his shift at the repair shop. They'll have to work through the night on the Vanishing Birdcage.

"You get the wire?" he calls, throwing his coat on a chair.

"I'm not sure." Klara swallows. Yesterday, she was supposed to get a pack of thick brass wire from the art supply store on Market, which Raj will use to finish the birdcage. "I think I forgot."

Raj comes toward her. "What do you mean, you forgot? Either you went to the store or you didn't."

She hasn't told Raj about the blackouts.

She's gone months without one, but yesterday, Raj worked an extra shift and she had no distraction from the thoughts that swarm her when she's alone: her father's absence, her mother's disappointment. She thought of how badly she wished Simon could see her now, not on the little blue-lit stage on Fillmore but at a real dinner theater, with real props and a real partner. So she left her apartment for a bar on Kearny and drank until the thoughts stopped.

"Well, I did forget," says Klara, bristling, because this is what Raj does — he never lets anything go. "But the wire isn't here, so I must not have gotten it. I'll go tomorrow."

She walks into the bedroom and pretends to adjust the string lights around the window. Raj follows her. He grabs her arm.

"Don't lie to me, Klara. If you didn't do it, say so. We have a show to run. And sometimes, it feels like I care about it more than you."

Raj designed their business cards — *The Immortalist,* they read, *with Raj Chapal* — and Klara's new costumes. He got a tuxedo jacket from a suiting outlet and paid a seamstress to tailor it to Klara's body. For the Jaws of Life, he ordered a gold sequined dress from an ice-skating catalog. Klara resisted — she thinks it's cheesy, that it doesn't look like vaudeville — but Raj says it'll sparkle under the lights.

"I care about this more than anything," she hisses. "And I wouldn't lie to you. That's insulting."

"Okay." Raj squints. "Tomorrow."

13.

In June 1982, days after Simon's death,
Klara arrived at 72 Clinton for his burial.
After a red-eye flight from San Francisco,
she stood outside the gate of the apartment
building, trembling. How had she become a
person who hadn't seen her family in years?
Walking up the long staircase, she thought
she might be sick. But when Varya opened
the door and reached for her — "Klara,"
she heaved, her thin body enveloped in
Klara's fuller one — the time apart did not
matter, not yet. They were sisters. That mat-
tered, nothing else.

Daniel was twenty-four. He had been
working out at the gym at the University of
Chicago, where he was preparing for medical school. Now, when he pulled a sweatshirt
off and Klara glimpsed his pale, muscled
chest, its twin puffs of dark hair, she reddened. Acne dotted his chin, but his teenage solemnity had been replaced by a strong

brow and jaw, a large Roman nose. He looked like Otto, their grandfather.

Gertie insisted on a Jewish ceremony for the burial. When Klara was a child, Saul explained the Jewish laws with dignity and persistence, as Josephus did to the Romans. Judaism is not superstition, he said, but a way of living lawfully: to be Jewish is to observe the laws that Moses brought down from Sinai. But Klara was not interested in rules. In Hebrew school, she loved the stories. Miriam, embittered prophet, whose rolling rock provided water during forty years of wandering! Daniel, unharmed in the lions' den! They suggested that she could do anything — so why would she want to sit in the basement of the synagogue for six hours every week, studying the Talmud?

Besides, it was a boys' club. When Klara was ten, twenty thousand women left their typewriters and babies to Strike for Equality on Fifth Avenue. Gertie watched on television with a sponge in her hand, her eyes shiny as spoons, though she turned the old Zenith off as soon as Saul came home. Klara's bat mitzvah took place not individually on the Sabbath, as had her brothers' ceremonies, but in a group of ten girls — none of whom were allowed to recite from the Torah or the *haftarah* — during the lesser Friday evening service. That year, the Committee on Jewish Laws and Standards decided that women could count toward a minyan, but the question of whether women could be rabbis, they claimed, warranted further study.

Now, as she stood with what was left of her family and Gertie recited *Kel Maleh Rachamim* in Hebrew, something changed. A lock popped off; air rushed in, and with it a colossal tide of grief — or was it relief? — for the words she had heard since childhood. She could not recall each of their meanings, but she knew they connected the dead, Simon and Saul, to the living: Klara and Varya, Gertie and Daniel. In the words of the prayer, no one was missing. In the words of the prayer, the Golds gathered together.

Three months later, she returned to New York for the High Holy Days. It was agonizing to be with anyone at all, like rubbing sandpaper on a burn, but she still scrounged the money for a plane ticket: it was least agonizing to be with people who loved Simon, too. At first, they were gentle with one another. By midweek, though, that softness wiped off like dust. Daniel chopped apples at a fierce clip.

"I feel like I didn't even know him," he said.

Klara dropped the spoon she was using to scoop honey. "Why? Because he was a fag? Is that what you think of him — that he was just some fag?"

Her words ran together. Varya eyed her with distaste. Klara had filled a water bottle with clear liquor and hidden it beneath the bathroom sink, in a basket cluttered with body wash and old shampoo.

"Keep your voice down," Varya said. Gertie was in bed, where she stayed whenever they weren't at services.

"No," said Daniel, to Klara. "Because he cut us out. He didn't tell us *shit.* Do you know how many times we called, Klara? How many messages we left, begging him to talk to us, asking him why he just left? And you going along with it, keeping his secrets, not even calling us" — his voice breaking — "not even calling us when he got sick?"

"It wasn't my right," Klara said, but it came out feebly, for she burned constantly with guilt. She saw it now: her brother's departure was the bomb that blew them apart, even more than Saul's death. Varya and Daniel were sidelined by resentment,

187

Gertie by suffering. And if Klara hadn't urged Simon to go, would he still be alive? She was the one who believed in the prophecies; she was the one who managed his trajectory, nudging until it canted and turned left. And no matter how many times she recalled Simon's words in the hospital — how he squeezed her hand, how he thanked her — she couldn't help but feel that things would have been different if they'd gone to Boston or Chicago or Philadelphia, if she'd kept her goddamn beliefs to herself.

"I was trying to be loyal to him," she whispered.

"Yeah? And where was your loyalty to us?" Daniel looked at Varya. "V put her whole life on hold. You think she wants to be here? Twenty-five years old, still living with Ma?"

"Yeah, sometimes I do. Sometimes I think she likes to play it safe. Sometimes," Klara said, looking at Varya, "I think you're more comfortable that way."

"Screw you," Varya said. "You know nothing about what the past four years have been like. You know nothing about responsibility, or duty. And you probably never will."

If Daniel had filled out, Varya seemed to have shrunk. She was working as an administrative assistant at a pharmaceutical company, having put off graduate school to live with Gertie. One evening, Klara saw Varya bent over Gertie's bed at the waist. Gertie had her arms around Varya, and she was shuddering. Klara receded, ashamed. The privilege of their mother's touch, her confidence, was something Varya had earned.

Gertie spent the Days of Repentance in a fog of misery. After Saul's death, she had said: not again. She could not, once more, bear the consequences of love — so she bid Simon goodbye before he could do it to her. *I don't want you coming back.*

He hadn't. And now, he never would.

"Three books are opened in heaven on Rosh Hashanah," Rabbi Chaim said, on the first night of the High Holy Days. "One for the wicked, one for the virtuous, and one for those in-between. The wicked are inscribed in the book of death, the virtuous in the book of life, but the fate of the in-between is suspended until Yom Kippur — and let's be honest," he added, to smiles from the audience, "that's most of us."

Gertie could not smile. She knew she was wicked. All the prayer in the world would make no difference. But she must try, said Rabbi Chaim, when she went to see him privately. His eyes were kindly through his spectacles, his beard bobbing peaceably. She thought of his family — his dutiful wife, who rarely spoke, and his three healthy boys — and for seconds, she had hated him.

Another sin.

Rabbi Chaim put a hand on her shoulder. "None of us are free from sin, Gertie. But God turns no one away."

Then where was He? Since Saul's death, Gertie had committed anew to the temple and its promises, she had thrown herself at it like a lover — she had even enrolled in Hebrew lessons. And though she had cried enough tears to fill the Hudson, she felt no forgiveness, no change. God remained as distant as the sun.

On Yom Kippur, Gertie dreamed of visiting Greece. It was no place she'd ever been, though she had seen photos of it in a magazine at the dentist's office. In the dream, she stood on a cliff and clutched two ceramic pots, each of which held one set of ashes: those of her husband, and those of her son. From the cliff, Gertie could see the blue-capped churches and white houses that withdrew into the mountain, like a rescinded offer. When she tipped the pots toward the water, she felt dreadful freedom — an unbounded aloneness so dizzying she felt the pull of the water herself.

When she woke, she was nauseated that she had not buried Simon and Saul according to Jewish custom. Just as bad was the pull of the water, that dark slope of pity.

Her nightgown was heavy with sweat. She pulled on her pink bathrobe and knelt on the wood floor at the foot of the bed.

"Oh, Simon. Forgive me," she whispered. Her knees shook. Outside the window, the sun was just beginning to rise, and she wept for it, for all the suns that Simon, her bright one, would never see. "Forgive me, Simon. It's my fault, my fault, I know it. Forgive me, my son."

There was no relief. There would never be any relief. But the sun, slanting through the bedroom window, was warm on her back. She could hear the taxis honking on Rivington and the bodegas rustling to life.

She walked unsteadily to the living room, where the children — she would always call them that — had fallen asleep. Klara curled against Varya on the couch. Daniel's long legs hung over the arm of Saul's favorite chair. When she returned to the bedroom, she made the bed and whacked Saul's pillow until it fluffed. She dressed in a dark wool shift and flesh-colored stockings, fit her feet into the black heels she wore to work. She powdered her face and put hot

191

rollers in her hair. By the time she came out again, Varya was making coffee.

She looked up in surprise. "Mama."

"It's Tuesday," said Gertie. Her voice was scratchy from disuse. "I need to go to work."

The office: clacking of keys, central air. By 1982, Gertie had her own computer, a magical gray behemoth sent to do her bidding.

"Okay," said Varya, swallowing. "Good. Let's get you to work."

Four months later, in January of 1983, Klara noticed Eddie O'Donoghue in the audience at a club in the Haight. As she was being lifted for the Jaws of Life, his upturned face grew smaller and smaller, and his badge caught the glare of the spotlight. It took a moment for Klara to recognize him as the cop who had once harassed Simon; then her body grew hot. She stumbled when she landed, bowed gracelessly and exited the stage. She was thinking of all the times she'd slipped a hand into a man's back pocket and grabbed a twenty or two, more if she needed it. Was he tracking her? A vendetta, maybe, after she cursed at him on the station steps?

No. It didn't make sense. She was careful when she picked pockets, she had sharp eyes that took everything in. One month later, those eyes spotted Eddie again at a show in North Beach. This time, he wasn't wearing his uniform, just a white crew neck and Dockers jeans. It took all of Klara's focus to stay on script during her cup-and-ball routine, to ignore his crossed arms and closed smile, which she saw next at a Valencia Street nightclub. This time, she nearly dropped her steel rings. After the show, she strode toward Eddie, who sat on a round leather stool at the bar.

"What's wrong with you?"

"Wrong?" asked the cop, blinking.

"Yes, wrong." Klara sat down on the stool beside him, which wheezed. "This is the third show you've come to. So what's your problem?"

Eddie frowned. "I saw your brother's picture in the paper."

"Fuck you," she said, and it felt so good, like alcohol burning out a virus, that she said it again. "Fuck you. You know nothing about my brother."

Eddie flinched. He'd aged since she saw him outside the Mission Street police station. There were creases below his eyes and a fuzz of orange hair around his chin. His strawberry blond hair was mussed, as though he'd just woken up.

"Your brother was young. I was hard on him." Eddie met her eyes. "I'd like to apologize."

Klara stiffened. She wasn't expecting this. Still, she couldn't pardon him. She grabbed her duster and her duffel bag and walked out of the bar as quickly as she could without attracting the attention of the manager, a sleaze who never missed the opportunity to pressure her into a nightcap. Outside, it was shockingly cold, and hardcore punk streamed from the doorway of Valencia Tool & Die. Klara's eyes smarted. It seemed unfathomable that Eddie was alive while Simon was not, and yet he was — alive and presently jogging after her, his eyes sharp with new determination.

"Klara," he said. "I have to tell you something."

"You're sorry, I know. Thank you. You're absolved."

"No. Something else. About your show," said Eddie. "It's changed me."

"It's changed you." Klara chortled. "That's sweet. You like the dress I wear? You like the way my ass looks when I spin?"

He grimaced. "That's crass."

"It's honest. Do you really think I don't know why men come to my shows? You think I don't know what you get out of it?"

"No. I don't think you know." He was wounded but held her gaze with a stubbornness that surprised her.

"Okay, then. What do you get out of it?"

He opened his mouth just as the door to the Die expelled a clot of punks, who paused against the empty storefront to smoke. Their heads were shaved or garishly dyed, and chains hung from their belts. In comparison, Eddie looked painfully conventional, and he paused with discomfort. Years ago, Klara might have felt sympathy for him — for anyone at all — but by now her sympathy had been exhausted. She turned and walked swiftly toward Twentieth Street.

"When I was a kid," said Eddie, to her back, "I was a fiend for comic books. The Flash. The Atom. You name it. I'd see the Green Lantern when I looked at the sky. If I passed a fire, I knew it was Johnny Blaze. I thought my wristwatch was Jimmy Olsen's; hell, I thought *I* was Jimmy Olsen. 'Hallucinations,' my father said. 'That's what they are.' But they weren't. They were dreams."

Klara crossed her arms, hugging her jacket closer, but she stopped walking. She stared straight ahead as Eddie caught up and came around to face her.

"Of course, I couldn't say that to my

pops," he said. "We're talking real old-school Irish Catholic, labor union organizer, member of the Ancient Order of Hibernians. 'Do you hear me? Hallucinations,' he goes. 'And I don't wanna hear you say a word of it again.' 'All right,' I said. And I didn't. I went to Sacred Heart and I joined the force and I imagined I could still be like those guys. A hero, right? But I wasn't like those guys. I was a man, or less than — a pig. I hated the kids and the gays and the burnt-out hippies, all the people who hadn't worked as hard as I had and still had it better than I did. People, I thought, like your brother."

She was crying. It took nothing to make her cry. Next month, it would be one year since she lay in bed with Simon and watched him inhale for the last time.

"I was wrong," said Eddie. "When I watched you, making a card appear out of nowhere or working those steel rings, I remembered the comics. How it was possible to be more than you were — more than you started out being. I guess one way to put it is you gave me faith. Another is that I figured maybe I'm not too far gone yet."

For seconds, Klara could not speak. Finally, unbeknownst to her, she had reminded someone of magic. She had given Eddie faith.

"You're not screwing with me, are you?" she asked.

Eddie smiled, a childlike smile whose guilelessness made her cry harder.

"Why would I do that?" he said, and leaned forward, keeping his hands in his pockets, to kiss her.

She stilled at the shock of it. She'd been kissed plenty of times, but only now did she see how intimate the act really was. She had barely spoken to anyone since Simon's death; usually, it was too painful to even see Robert. Inside her, a flock stirred and flew toward Eddie, desperately. But when he pulled back to smile at her, a smile of delight and good fortune, her desperation turned to revulsion. What would Simon think?

"No," she said, quietly. Eddie's hand appeared behind her neck to draw her closer, because he had not heard her or because he had decided to pretend as much, and she allowed herself to be kissed by him for seconds more. In doing so, she could pretend to be a different kind of person: someone who kissed a man because she liked him, not because it made her forget the hard ledge of rock from which she hung, clawing.

"No," she repeated, and when Eddie still did not let go she shoved him in the sternum. He grunted and stumbled backward. A 26 trundled down Valencia, dispelling a haze of exhaust, and Klara started after it. By the time the gas cleared, Eddie stood alone beneath a street lamp, his mouth hanging open, and Klara was gone.

That fall, during the High Holy Days, she returned to New York for the third time. Klara and Varya chopped apples for kugel, Gertie cooking the noodles, while Daniel told stories of life in Chicago. Varya, twenty-seven, had finally moved into her own apartment. She had started graduate school at NYU, where she was studying molecular biology. Her focus was gene expression: she assisted a visiting professor in removing mutated genes from fast-growing organisms — bacteria and yeast, worms and fruit flies — to see if this altered their likelihood of disease. Eventually, she hoped to do the same in humans.

At night, Klara climbed into bed with Zoya, who had, in her old age, developed a queenly indisposition to walking anywhere. With the cat on her stomach and Varya in the opposite bunk, she asked to hear stories of Varya's work. It gave Klara hope: the match-strike of genetic expression and the infinite variables that could be used to adjust eye color, predisposition to disease, even death. She had not felt so close to her siblings in years, and everyone, even Gertie, seemed lighter. When Gertie suggested the Golds perform the *kaparot* before Yom Kippur, in which a live chicken is swung above the head while reciting from the *Mahzor* — "Children of man who sit in darkness and the shadow of death," she intoned, "bound in misery and chains of iron" — Klara burst into laughter; the *charoset* in her mouth splattered Daniel's shirt.

"That's the most depressing thing I've ever heard," she said.

"What about the poor chicken?" asked Daniel, flicking Klara's chewed apple off with two fingers. Gertie's indignation melted, and suddenly she was snorting, too — a miracle, it seemed to Klara, who had not heard her mother laugh in years.

Still, Klara could not explain to anyone what it meant for her to lose Simon. She'd lost both him and herself, the person she was in relation to him. She had lost time, too, whole chunks of life that only Simon had witnessed: Mastering her first coin trick at eight, pulling quarters from Simon's ears while he giggled. Nights when they crawled down the fire escape to go dancing in the hot, packed clubs of the Village — nights when she saw him looking at men, when he let her see him looking. The way his eyes shone when she said she'd go to San Francisco, like it was the greatest gift anyone had ever given him. Even at the end, when they argued about Adrian, he was her baby brother, her favorite person on earth. Drifting away from her.

At 72 Clinton, she lay in her old bed and closed her eyes until his presence was tangible. One hundred and thirty-five years ago, the Fox sisters heard rapping noises in their Hydesville bedroom. On a gray, blustery afternoon in September 1983, Simon knocked for Klara. It was more than a creak in the floorboards, more than the whine of a door: a low, sonorous pop that seemed to come from the bowels of 72 Clinton, as if the building were cracking its knuckles.

Klara's eyes flew open. She could feel her heartbeat in her ears. "Simon?" she ventured.

She held her breath. Nothing.

Klara shook her head. She was getting carried away.

She had all but forgotten the knock by June 21st, 1986, the fourth anniversary of

Simon's death. She'd spent previous anniversaries in bars, drinking vodka straight until she forgot what day it was, but this year, she forced herself to make coffee, tie her Doc Martens, and walk to the Castro. It was remarkable: many of the gay clubs had closed with the bathhouses, but Purp was still standing. It even looked freshly painted. She wished she could tell Simon, or Robert. Robert had never liked Purp, but Klara knew he would be glad to hear it survived.

Robert. She used to meet him downtown. In 1985, President Reagan still hadn't acknowledged AIDS, and two men chained themselves to a building at UN Plaza in protest. Klara and Robert brought food and copies of the *Bay Area Reporter* to a growing mass of volunteers. If Robert wasn't too sick, they slept outside. Klara begged a nurse who had cared for Simon to include Robert in the Suramin trial, and he received the last open spot. But the medication made him sick, so sick he couldn't dance, and he stopped taking it within days. Klara banged on the door of the Eureka Street apartment where Robert now lived alone. "You owe it to Simon," she shouted. "You can't quit now." By August, they weren't speaking. By October, every patient in the trial was dead.

When Klara read about it in the paper, it

felt like her whole body was on fire, like she could melt through the floor from the burn. She tried to call Robert, but his line had been disconnected. When she got to Academy, Fauzi told her that Robert had moved back to Los Angeles. *Just picked up and left.* That was seven months ago. She hadn't been able to find him since.

She found an orange nasturtium on the ground and hooked it through Purp's door handle. That night, she made Gertie's meat loaf, which Simon had loved, and undressed for a bath. Underwater, her hair spread like Medusa's. She could hear the echo of voices, muffled feet on the stairs. And then: a crack. She recognized it instantly as the noise she'd heard in New York.

She burst through the surface of the water, wetting the floor.

"If you're real," she said, "if it's you, do it again."

The noise came a second time, like a bat striking a ball.

"Jesus Christ." When she began to shake, tears hit the water. "Simon."

14.

June 1988: Raj stands onstage at Teatro Zin-Zanni as Klara paints her face in the dressing room. It's the nicest one she's ever been in, with a gold vanity and a TV screen that shows what's happening onstage.

"Life isn't just about defying death," Raj says, his voice coming through the speakers on either side of the television. "It's also about defying yourself, about *insisting* on transformation. As long as you can transform, my friends, you cannot die. What does Clark Kent have in common with the chameleon? Right when they're on the brink of destruction, they change. Where have they gone? Nowhere we can see. The chameleon has become a branch. Clark Kent has become Superman."

Klara sees the miniature Raj onscreen spread his arms. She lines her lips with bright red pencil.

Three months later, Klara flies to New York: her visits over the High Holidays have become a tradition. She is dizzy with happiness. Second Sight was a success, and though the collapsed birdcage poked like veins through Klara's jacket sleeve — they'll have the seamstress let it out — the audience didn't seem to notice. Teatro ZinZanni has booked them for ten more shows.

Klara wants Raj to meet her family, but they can't afford two tickets to New York. Soon, though, he says, they'll have the cash to go anywhere. On Rosh Hashanah, Klara pulls Varya into the bunk room. It feels like her body's all helium, like she could rise to the ceiling if she just took off her shoes.

She says, "I think we might get married."

"You started dating in March," says Varya. "It's been six months."

"February," says Klara. "Seven."

"But Daniel hasn't even proposed to Mira."

Mira is Daniel's girlfriend. They met one year ago, when Mira was studying for an art history degree, and she's already come to meet Varya and Gertie. As soon as Daniel gets a job, he plans to propose with a ruby ring Saul gave Gertie.

Klara tucks a lock of Varya's hair behind her ear. "You're jealous."

She's observing Varya, not accusing her, and it is this — the tenderness in Klara's voice — that makes Varya wince.

"Of course not," she says. "I'm happy for you."

Varya must think it's another one of Klara's acts, something she'll quit in a month or two. She doesn't know they've all but done it, that Klara has her dress and Raj has his suit, that they plan to go to City Hall as soon as Klara returns from New York. She certainly doesn't know about the baby.

It was an unsurprising surprise. Klara knows what happens when you're careless, but that doesn't mean she isn't. And it was more than that, it was the surge of it, dancing on the brink of causality — *if this, then* — with the man she loves. What is growing a baby if not making a flower appear from thin air, turning one scarf into two?

She's stopped drinking. By the third trimester, her mind is clear, never better — but that's the problem, it's too empty, miles and miles of space in which Klara sits and thinks. She distracts herself by imagining the baby. When he kicks, Klara sees his little boy feet. She's told Raj they have to name him Simon. During the last month, when she's so swollen her shoes don't fit, when she can't sleep more than thirty minutes at a time, she pictures Simon's face and doesn't resent the baby anymore. And so, when a doctor pulls the child from Klara's body on a stormy night in May and Raj cries, "It's a girl!" Klara knows that he must be mistaken.

"That's not right." She is delirious with pain; it feels as though a bomb exploded in her body, and she — the empty structure — is on the verge of collapse.

"Oh, Klara," Raj says. "It is."

They swaddle the child and bring her to Klara. The baby's face is florid, startled alive. Her eyes are dark as olive pits.

"You were so sure," Raj says. He's laughing.

They call the girl Ruby. Klara remembers a friend of Varya's by that name, a girl who lived above them at 72 Clinton. Rubina. It's Hindi, which Raj's mother would have appreciated. He moves into Klara's apartment and coos to Ruby, sings lullabies in rusty Hindi. *Soja baba Soja. Mackhan roti cheene.*

In June, Klara's family comes to visit. She shows them the Castro, Gertie clutching her pocketbook as they pass a gaggle of drag queens, and takes them to a Corps performance. Klara sits beside Daniel with her stomach flipping — she doesn't know how he'll respond to seeing men do ballet — but when the dancers bow, he claps louder than anyone else. That night, while Gertie's meat loaf is in the oven, Daniel tells Klara about Mira. They met in the university dining hall and have since spent long nights in Hyde Park's dive bars and all-night diners, debating Gorbachev and the NASA explosion and the merits of *E.T.*

"She challenges you," Klara observes. Ruby is sleeping, her warm cheek stuck to Klara's chest, and for once, Klara feels as though nothing is wrong in the world. "That's good."

In the past, Daniel would have made some retort — *Challenges me? What makes you think I need that?* — but now, he nods.

"That she does," he says, with a sigh so contented that Klara is almost embarrassed to have heard it.

Gertie adores the baby. She holds Ruby constantly, staring at her raspberry-sized nose, nibbling her miniature fingers. Klara searches for a resemblance between them and finds one: their ears! Petite and delicate, curling in like seashells. But when Gertie met Raj, she opened her mouth and closed it, silent as a fish. Klara watched her mother take inventory of Raj's dark skin and work boots, his secular slouch. She pulled Gertie into the bathroom.

"Ma," Klara hissed. "Don't be a bigot."

"A bigot?" asked Gertie, flushing. "Is it too much to ask for the child to be raised Jewish?"

"Yes," Klara said. "It is."

Varya is full of advice. "Have you tried warm milk?" she asks, when Ruby cries. "What about a walk in the stroller? Do you have an infant swing? Is she colicky? Where's her binky?"

Klara's brain spirals. "What's a binky?"

"What's a binky?" repeats Gertie.

"You can't be serious," Varya says. "She doesn't have a binky?"

"And this apartment," Gertie adds. "It's not child-proofed. You wait until she starts walking: she could split her head on this table, take a tumble down the stairs."

"She's fine," says Raj. "She has everything she needs."

He takes the baby from Varya, who holds on a moment too long. "Hand her over!" Daniel teases, prodding Varya in the ribs, which incites a smack of rebuttal and accompanying howl so loud that Klara nearly orders them to leave. But when they do, the next day — Gertie trundling into the front seat of a cab, Varya and Daniel waving through the back window — she misses them desperately. While they were here, it was easier to ignore the fact that Simon and Saul were not. Her father had loved babies. Klara still remembers visiting the hospital after Simon was born breech, his umbilical cord wrapped like a necklace. Saul stood in front of the ICU as if to guard this half-blue, backward boy, his last. At home, he could hold the baby for hours. When Simon twitched in his sleep or puckered his lips, Saul chuckled with disproportionate delight.

As children, the siblings believed Saul could answer any question they wished to know. But Klara and Simon grew to dislike his answers. They disdained his routine of work and Torah study, his uniform of gabardine slacks and trench and walking hat. Now, Klara has more sympathy for him. Saul came from immigrants, and Klara suspects he lived in fear of losing the life he'd been given. She understands, too, the loneliness of parenting, which is the loneliness of memory — to know that she connects a future unknowable to her parents with a past unknowable to her child. Ruby will come to Klara with questions. What will Klara tell her, with frantic and unheard insistence? To Ruby, Klara's past will seem like a story, Saul and Simon no more than her mother's ghosts.

By October, it's been months since Klara and Raj performed. Klara couldn't do the Jaws of Life while pregnant; now, nights awake with Ruby have turned her brain to fog, and she can't count properly during the mind-reading act. They haven't been able to recoup the costs of their materials. Their meager savings have gone to diapers and toys, clothes that Ruby outgrows by the hour. Raj walks from the Tenderloin to North Beach, pitching nightclubs and theaters, but most of them turn him away. The manager at Teatro ZinZanni can only give them four dates that fall.

"We need to leave," Raj says, at dinner. "Take this show on the road. San Francisco's burned out. The people here, they're robots, they're computers. Death to 'em, man." He boxes with an invisible computer.

"Wait," says Klara, raising a finger. "Did you hear that?"

She's pointed out Simon's knocks to Raj before, but he always claims not to hear them. This time, he can't have missed it. The knock was loud as a gunshot; even the baby yelped. She is five months old, with Raj's silky black hair and Klara's Cheshire cat grin.

Raj puts his fork down. "There's *nothing there.*"

It pleases Klara, that Ruby can hear the knocks. She bounces the baby, kisses her pointy new teeth.

"Ruby," she sings. "Ruby knows."

"Focus, Klara. I'm talking about moving. Making money. Breathing new life into this thing." Raj claps in front of her face. "The city's over, baby. It's dead. We've gotta hit it. Find gold somewhere else."

"Maybe we expanded too quickly," says Klara as Ruby begins to cry; the clapping has scared her. "Maybe we need to slow down."

"Slow down? That's the last thing we need to do." Raj begins to pace. "We've gotta move. We've gotta keep moving. You stay too long in one place, you'll burn out anywhere. That's the secret, Klara. We can't stop moving."

His face is lit up like a jack-o'-lantern. Raj has big ideas, just like Klara does; it's one of the things she loves about him. She thinks of Ilya's black box. *It's meant to be on the road,* Ilya said. Maybe she is, too.

"Where would we go?" she asks.

"Vegas," says Raj.

Klara laughs. "Absolutely not."

"Why?"

"It's gaudy," she says, counting off on her fingers. "It's over-the-top and overdone. It's cheap, but it's ridiculously expensive. And there are never any female headliners."

Vegas reminds her of the first and only magic convention she attended: a glitzy event in Atlantic City at which the line for the men's bathroom was longer than the women's.

"Most of all," she adds, "it's fake. There's nothing real about Vegas."

Raj raises his eyebrows. "You're a magician."

"Damn straight. I'm a magician who'll perform anywhere but Vegas."

"Anywhere but Vegas. It could be our new show title."

"Cute." Ruby whimpers, and Klara maneuvers awkwardly out of her T-shirt. She used to walk naked through the apartment, but now she's embarrassed by her body's utility. "I'd rather live like nomads."

"Okay," says Raj. "We'll live like nomads, then. Stay a few months in each town. See the world."

Ruby unlatches, distracted. Klara pulls her shirt down, and Raj scoops Ruby up by the armpits. "San Francisco's full of memories, Ruby-bean," he says. "You stick around here, you're messing with ghosts."

Does Klara imagine that he glances at her? His eyes are pencil points. But perhaps she's wrong; when she looks again, he's returned to the baby, blowing raspberries on her soft brown skin.

Klara stands to clear the dishes. "Where would we stay?"

"I know a guy," Raj says.

That night, Raj and Ruby fall asleep easily, but Klara can't. She climbs out of bed and walks past Ruby's cradle to the closet, where she keeps Ilya's black box. Inside it are her cards and steel rings, her balls and silk scarves. She doesn't use them very often anymore, the flashier acts having overtaken her sleight-of-hand tricks, but now she brings two scarves to the round table in the kitchen. Raj's old chili pepper lights are tacked around the window; to avoid his notice, she leaves them off. Before she sits down, she reaches for the bottle of vodka in the back of the freezer and pours herself a drink.

She used to work late like this. As a teenager, she'd wait until she heard Simon's steady breathing and Varya's muffled dream sounds, until Daniel began to snore, and then she collected her tools from underneath the bed and snuck out to the living room. She relished the unusual quiet and the feeling that the entire apartment was hers. She kept the lights off then, too, setting up on the floor beside the living room window so as to see by the street lamps on Clinton. For months, these sessions were her secret. But one night in winter, she padded into the living room to find that her father had beaten her to it.

For seconds, he did not notice her. He sat in his favorite armchair — tufted, upholstered in pea-colored velvet — and he was reading a book. There was a new fire in the hearth, the logs whole and glowing.

Klara nearly turned around, but stopped herself. If he could sit here at one in the morning, why couldn't she? She stepped out of the darkness of the hallway and over the threshold to the living room, where Saul noticed her at last.

"Couldn't sleep?" she asked.

"No," said Saul, and held up the book. He was learning, of course. Klara did not know how he had not become sick of it. By that time, he'd read it every which way: front to back, back to front, in tiny pieces chosen seemingly at random and in large chunks through which he worked his way over weeks. Sometimes, he stared at a single page for days.

"Which part are you reading?" asked Klara — a question she usually avoided so as to also avoid a lecture about Jephthah's sacrificial daughter, or the Babylonian men who refused to worship King Nebuchadnezzar's golden statue and thus survived when thrown into a furnace.

Saul hesitated. By then, he had mostly given up on family Torah study. Even Gertie fidgeted when he read from the books.

"The story of Rabbi Eliezer and the oven," he said. "He was the only sage to believe that an impure oven could be purified."

"Oh. That's a good one," said Klara, idiotically, as she did not recall the story at all. She expected Saul to continue, but instead he caught her eye and smiled in surprise, or in gladness at her reaction. She stepped farther into the room, holding a deck of cards in one hand. When she sat down by the window, Saul returned to the Talmud. They stayed like this until the log crumbled and both of them were yawning. When they walked back to their respective rooms, Klara slept better than she had in months.

Gertie never approved of Klara's magic. Surely, Gertie thought, Klara would outgrow it; surely she would go to college, like Varya, and get the degree that Gertie herself had never finished. But Saul was different. And this was why Klara could leave home weeks after his death, why she could do such a thing without hating herself: because it was not her mother who was gone but her father, who had stayed up with her on long nights in perfect quiet, and who, on the morning of his death, looked up from the Mishnah to see her turning a blue scarf into a red one.

"That's marvelous," he said as the silk slipped through her hands, and chuckled in an impish way that reminded her of Ilya. "Do it again, will you?" And so she did it again and again until he put the great book down to cross a leg and really watch her, not in the vague way he often looked at his children but with true interest and wonder, the way he had looked at Simon as a baby. So he would have understood, wouldn't he, her decision to leave? If nothing else, Judaism had taught her to keep running, no matter who tried to hold her hostage. It had taught her to create her own opportunities, to turn rock into water and water to blood. It had taught her that such things were possible.

By four in the morning, Klara is woozy, her hands beset by the satisfying muscular pain caused by hours of work. She thinks of

216

putting the scarves back in Ilya's box, but instead she stuffs them into her left fist and then into a right thumb tip; when she opens her hands, the scarves have disappeared. She is thinking about what it means to leave San Francisco, whether being on the road will ever feel like home, and what comes to her is one of Saul's stories. The year was 1948, the setting a kitchen in an apartment on Hester Street. A man and a boy sat on either side of a table, their heads touching over a Philco PT-44 radio. The boy was Saul Gold. The man was Lev, his father.

When they heard that the British Mandate had expired, Lev cupped his hands over his mouth. His eyes were closed, and salt water dribbled into his beard.

"For the first time, we the Jews will be in charge of our own destiny," he said, grasping Saul's narrow chin. "Do you know what that means? You will always have a place to go. Israel will always be your home."

In 1948, Saul was thirteen. Never before had he seen his father cry. Suddenly, he realized that what he took to be his home — a two-bedroom apartment in a newly renovated brick building above Gertel's bakery — was to his father no more than a prop on someone else's stage, which could at any moment be struck and carried into the wings. In its absence, home was in the rhythm of the halakhah: the daily prayer, the weekly Sabbath, the annual holy days. In time was their culture. In time, not in space, was their home.

Klara tucks Ilya's box back in the closet and climbs into bed. Propping herself up on one elbow, she reaches for the window blinds and creates a gap through which she sees a fingernail of moon. She's always thought of home as a physical destination, but perhaps Raj and Ruby are home enough. Perhaps home, like the moon, will follow wherever she goes.

15.

They buy a motor home from Raj's co-worker. Klara expected it to be depressing, but Raj refinishes the wood table in the kitchen booth, rips out the orange plastic countertops and replaces them with laminate that looks like marble. "Hit the road, Jack," he sings. He mounts shelves beside the bed, outfitting them with aluminum railings to prevent books from falling when the RV moves. During the day, their bed folds into a couch, revealing a wide swath of floor on which Ruby can play. Klara sews red velvet curtains and puts Ruby's crib beside the back window so she can watch the world go by. They load their equipment into a storage unit attached to the back of the RV.

On a cold, sunny morning in November, they head north.

Klara straps Ruby into her car seat. "Wave goodbye, Rubini," says Raj, reaching back to lift her hand. "Wave goodbye to all that."

I love you all, Klara thinks, looking at the Taoist temple, the bakery below her apartment, the old women carrying boxes of dim sum in pink plastic bags. *Goodbye to all that.*

They land two gigs at a casino in Santa Rosa, four at a resort in Lake Tahoe. The audiences smile at Raj — showman and family man — and at Ruby, large-eyed beneath a child-sized top hat, which Raj uses to collect tips after each show. He keeps the cash in a locked box beneath the driver's seat. In Tahoe, he buys a car phone to use for bookings. Klara wants to call family, but Raj swats her away. "Bill's enough as it is," he says.

When winter comes, they go south. LA is lousy with competition, but they do okay in the college towns and better at the desert casinos. But Klara hates the casinos. The managers always mistake her for Raj's assistant. People amble over from card tables and slot machines because they want to see a young woman spin in a tight dress or because they're too drunk to go home. They like Raj's Indian Needle Trick, but they boo during the Vanishing Birdcage. "It's up her sleeve!" someone bellows, as if the failure of the trick is a personal offense. Klara begins to look back at the small shows in San Francisco with nostalgia, remembering the dark battered stages but forgetting the hecklers, forgetting that nobody, there or here, has ever really wanted what she's selling.

During the day, while Raj is at pitch meetings, she reads to Ruby in the trailer. She admires the look of the desert, the blue mountains and sorbet sky, but she doesn't like the feel of it, both languid and restless, or the heat that presses down on her like hands. She keeps miniature bottles of vodka in her makeup case, which she prefers for their clarity and smarting punch, for the way they tear her throat. In the morning, when Raj leaves, she pours two fingers into her instant coffee. Sometimes she walks Ruby to a nearby convenience store and gets a bottle of Coke, which does a better job of disguising the smell. Raj knows she stopped drinking during her pregnancy, but he also thinks she never started back up. It's different now, though. The blackouts and retching have been replaced by something steadier, harder to detect: a low-grade but constant remove from the facts of her life. Before Raj comes home, she throws the bottles away. Back in the RV, she brushes her teeth and spits out the window.

"This," Raj says, counting checks. "This is the stuff."

"We can't stay here much longer," says Klara. They're parked illegally behind a boarded-up Burger King because Raj doesn't want to pay rent in an RV park.

"Nobody knows we're here, baby," he says. "We're invisible."

The seasons are all wrong. When she calls home during Hanukkah, huddled over the car phone while Raj is at Stop 'n Save, it's snowing in New York and eighty-six degrees in the RV.

"How are you doing?" Daniel asks, and it shocks her how much she misses him. When he visited San Francisco, she watched him play peekaboo with Ruby and imagined him for the first time as a father.

"I'm good," she says, faking sparkle, faking shine. "I'm fine."

Klara has kept two things from her siblings: the knocks, and the fact that Simon's death aligned with his prophecy. Simon never shared his date with Varya and Daniel, and they haven't discussed the woman on Hester Street since Saul's shiva. But the knowledge festers inside Klara. After shows, taking off her makeup while Raj collects tips, she calculates how long she'll live if the woman was right about her, too.

I'm not going to die, she told Simon. *I*

refuse to.

It was easier for her to adopt that swagger until the woman's first prediction came true. When Simon died, Klara careened back to the age of nine, back to the doorstep of the apartment on Hester Street. In truth, she hadn't wanted to know her date of death, not really. She'd only wanted to meet the woman.

She had never heard of a female magician. ("Why are there so few of us?" she asked Ilya once. "For one thing," he said, "the Inquisition. For two more, the Reformation and the Salem Witch Trials. What's more, the clothing. You ever try to hide a dove in an evening gown?") When Klara entered the apartment, the woman was standing against the window. She wore her hair in two long, brown braids, which made her face look symmetrical and complete. Years later, Klara cut class to wander through the Great Hall at the Metropolitan Museum of Art. There she saw a statue representing the head of Janus, on loan from the Vatican Museum, and thought of the fortune teller. The statue's faces stared in different directions, representing the past and the present, but this didn't make the figure look disjointed; instead, it had a circular coherence. Klara only resented that the statue portrayed Janus — god of beginnings as well as transitions and time — as a man.

"Wow." Klara gazed at the charts and calendars, the I Ching and fortune sticks, in the woman's apartment. "You know how to use all these things?"

To Klara's surprise, the woman shook her head.

"That stuff's for show," she said. "The people who come here? They like to think I know things for a reason. So I got props."

When she walked toward Klara, her body had the power and electricity of a moving vehicle. Klara nearly stepped aside, but no: she steeled herself, held her ground.

"The props make everybody feel better," said the woman. "But I don't need nothing like that."

"You just know," Klara whispered.

The gap between their bodies was as charged as the space between two magnets. Klara felt faint, as though she'd float into the woman's arms if she let herself relax.

"I just know," said the woman. She tucked her chin, cocked her head and looked at Klara, slant. "Like you."

Like you: it felt like proof of existence. Klara wanted more. She hadn't thought she cared to know her date of death, but now she was entranced. She wanted to linger longer in the woman's spell, a spell in which, like a mirror, Klara saw herself. She asked for her fortune.

When the woman replied, the spell broke. Klara felt as though she'd been smacked. She can't remember whether she thanked the woman or how she made her way into the alley. She was simply there, her face streaked and her palms caked brown by the dirt on the railing of the fire escape.

Thirteen years later, the woman was right about Simon, just as Klara had feared. But this is the problem: was the woman as powerful as she seemed, or did Klara take steps that made the prophecy come true? Which would be worse? If Simon's death was preventable, a fraud, then Klara is at fault — and perhaps she's a fraud, too. After all, if magic exists alongside reality — two faces gazing in different directions, like the head of Janus — then Klara can't be the only one able to access it. If she doubts the woman, then she has to doubt herself. And if she doubts herself, she must doubt every-thing she believes, including Simon's knocks.

What she needs is proof. In May 1990, on a warm night when Raj and Ruby are asleep, Klara sits up in bed.

She should time them, like she does in

Second Sight. One minute per letter.

She stands and walks to the kitchen booth on which she's left Simon's watch — a gift from Saul, leather banded with a small gold face. She sits in the cab, where there's enough moonlight to see the ticking of its slender second hand.

"Come on, Sy," she whispers.

When the first knock comes, she starts timing. Seven minutes pass, then eight — twelve when a knock sounds again.

M.

She stares at the watch like it's a key, like it's Simon's grinning face. The next knock comes five minutes later: *E.*

Ruby whimpers.

Not now, Klara thinks. *Please, not now.* But the whimper becomes a warble and then Ruby's cry breaks through like dawn. Klara hears Raj climb out of bed, hears him murmur until the baby's only sniffling, and then they appear in the cab.

"What are you doing?"

He holds Ruby high on his chest, so that her head is aligned with his. Their eyes loom in the dark.

"Nothing. I couldn't sleep."

Raj bounces Ruby. "Why not?"

"How should I know?"

He lifts his free hand — *just asking* — and

226

recedes into the darkness. She hears him set Ruby down in her crib.

"Raj." She faces forward to stare at the nailed-over door of the Burger King. "I'm not happy."

"I know." He comes to sit in the passenger seat and scoots the chair back until his legs can stretch forward. He wears his hair in a ponytail — it's been days since he washed it — and his eyes are watery with exhaustion.

"I never wanted this for us. I wanted something better. I still do. For her." Raj jerks his chin at Ruby's crib. "I want her to have a house. I want her to have neighbors. I want her to have a fucking puppy, if that's what she wants. But puppies aren't cheap. Neither are neighbors. I'm trying to save, Klara, but what we're making? It's better than it was, but it's not nearly enough."

"Maybe this is as far as we go." Klara's voice is uneven. "I'm tired. I know you are, too. Maybe it's time we both got real jobs."

Raj snorts. "I dropped out of high school. You never did college. You think Microsoft'll want us?"

"Not Microsoft. Someplace else. Or we could go back to school. I've always been good at math; I could do an accounting course. And you — as a mechanic, you were talented. You were brilliant."

"So were you!" bursts Raj. "*You* were talented. *You* were brilliant. First time I saw you, Klara, that little show in North Beach, I looked at you onstage and I thought: That woman. She's different. Your dreams were too big and your hair was too long, it kept getting tangled in the ropes, but you spun at the ceiling like nothing I'd seen and I thought you might never come down. I'm not ready to give up. And I don't think you are, either. You really want to settle down? Get a job shuffling papers or working with other people's money?"

His speech moves her in deep, buried ways. Klara has always known she's meant to be a bridge: between reality and illusion, the present and the past, this world and the next. She just has to figure out how.

"Okay," she says, slowly. "But we can't keep going on like this."

"No. We can't." Raj's eyes bore straight ahead. "We need to think bigger."

"Like what?"

"Like Vegas."

"Raj." Klara presses her palms into her eye sockets. "I told you."

"I know you did." Raj shifts in his seat and leans toward her over the armrest. "But you want an audience, you want impact — you want to be known, Klara, and you can't be known here. But people come from all over to visit Vegas, looking for something they can't get at home."

"Money."

"No — entertainment. They want to break the rules, turn the world on its head. And isn't that what you want? Isn't that what you do?" He grabs her hand. "Look. I never wanted to be the star. You never wanted to be the assistant. You've always felt you were meant to do something great, something better than this, right? And I've always believed in you."

"I'm not like that anymore. Something's gone. I'm weaker."

"You've been doing better since you stopped drinking. You're only weak when you get into your head, when you get stuck down there and can't climb out. You have to stay up here," he says, holding his hand flat under his chin. "Above water. Focus on what's real, like Ruby. And your career."

When Klara thinks of Ruby, it's like trying to hold on to a rock in the middle of a river, like trying to cling to something small and hard while everything is pulling her away.

"If we go to Vegas," she says, "and I can't do it. If we don't get hired. Or if I . . . if I just can't. What then?"

"I don't think that way," Raj says. "And neither should you."

"Vegas," says Gertie. "You're going to Vegas."

Klara hears her mother's hand muffling the receiver. Then she hears her shouting.

"Varya, did you hear me? Vegas. She's going to Vegas is what she said."

"Ma," says Klara. "I can hear you."

"What?"

"It's my choice."

"No one said it isn't. It certainly wouldn't be mine."

There is the click of another receiver being picked up.

"You're going to Vegas?" Varya asks. "For what? A vacation? Are you bringing Ruby?"

"Of course we're bringing Ruby. What else would we do with her? And not for a vacation — for good."

Klara looks out the window of the RV. Raj is pacing while he smokes. Every few seconds, he glances at Klara to see if she's still on the phone.

"Why?" asks Varya, aghast.

"Because I want to be a magician. And that's where you have to be if you want to be a magician — if you want to make money doing it. And besides, V, I have a kid; you

230

don't know how expensive that is. Ruby's food, her diapers, her clothes —"

"I raised four children," says Gertie. "And I never once went to Vegas."

"We know," says Klara. "I'm different."

"We know." Varya sighs. "If you're happy."

Raj is walking back to the car before she's put the phone back in its cradle.

"What'd they say?" he asks, swinging into the driver's seat, putting his key in the ignition. "Disapprove?"

"Yup."

"I know they're your family," he says, veering onto the road. "But if they weren't, you wouldn't like them, either."

They stop in a campground in Hesperia to sleep. Klara wakes to the sound of Raj's voice. She turns over and squints at Saul's watch: three fifteen in the morning and Raj is sitting next to Ruby's crib. He's peering at her through the bars, whispering about Dharavi.

Sheet metal painted bright blue. Women selling sugarcane. Houses with walls made of jute bags; enormous pipes that rise, like the backs of elephants, in the streets. He tells her about the electricity goons and the mangrove swamp, the shanty where he was born.

"That's Tata's house. Half of it was demolished when I was a kid. The other half is probably gone by now, too. But we can picture it that way. Picture the half still standing," he says. "Each floor is a business. On Tata's floor are glass bottles and plastic and metal parts. On the next floor up there are men building furniture; on the one above that, they're making leather briefcases and handbags. On the top floor are women stitching tiny blue jeans and T-shirts, clothing for children like you."

Ruby coos and waves a hand, bluish white in the moonlight. Raj takes it.

"They say that your people are untouchable, worse than the ones who came from beneath Brahma's feet. But your people are workers. Your people are shopkeepers and farmers and repairmen. In the villages, they aren't allowed to enter temples or shrines. But Dharavi is their temple," he says. "And America is ours."

Klara's head is turned toward the crib, but her body is rigid. Raj has never spoken of such things to her before. When she asks him about Dharavi, or the insurgency in Kashmir, he changes the subject.

"Your *tata* would be proud of you," Raj says. "And you should be proud of him."

232

Raj stands. Klara presses her cheek to the pillow.

"Don't forget it, Ruby," he says, pulling the blanket up to her chin. "Don't forget."

16.

In Vegas, they stop in an RV park called King's Row. It's fifteen minutes from the strip and costs two hundred dollars a month, which Raj hands over resentfully, because the pool has been drained and all the laundry machines except one are broken. "It's just for now," he tells Ruby, kissing her button mushroom nose. "We'll sell this thing soon." While he levels the rig with electric jacks and hooks up the utilities, Klara explores the grounds. There's a rec room with a ping-pong table and a half-empty vending machine. The RVs seem to have been anchored for months, with wooden decks on which residents have placed potted plants or American flags.

They get a long-term car rental, three months with an '82 Pontiac Sunbird, and drive to the Strip. Klara has never seen anything like it. Waterfalls that never dry. Tropical flowers in constant bloom. The resort hotels are metallic and angular as space stations. "Live hot girls," someone hisses, and a postcard materializes in Klara's hand. Gods parade in front of Caesars; a woman lies facedown on the side of the street, her head on a pink leather pocketbook. Showgirls and fake Elvises stand beside a live Chucky doll that waves to Klara with its knife-wielding hand.

The newest hotel rises up like an open book, two slender buildings connected at the binding. *The Mirage* is written on an electronic sign in curling, red capitals. It scrolls: *In our first ten hours we paid the largest single jackpot in Las Vegas history! 4.6 million! Enjoy the buffet!* Then the letters vanish, coy, and *The Mirage* reappears. A volcano in front of the hotel fires nightly, they're told, to the sound of the Grateful Dead and the Indian tabla player Zakir Hussain. There's an atrium with a manmade rainforest and an enclosure for real tigers. It's exactly what Klara's always never wanted, but she thinks of Ruby. There's money here. They walk into the lobby, which is hung with giant chandeliers and glass petals the size of car tires. Behind the front desk, stretching from floor to ceiling, is an aquarium fifty feet wide. She hears a shrill roar, which she thinks is the waterfall or the volcano before she recognizes it for a saw: the building is still under construction.

"Psst," says Raj. He points to a large banner above the front desk. It shows Siegfried and Roy, their faces pressed to either side of a white tiger. *Daily at 1 and 7 p.m.* It's 1:45. They follow the signs to the theater. Since the show has already begun, there's no ticketer. Raj slips through the door with Ruby on his hip and pulls Klara into two empty seats. Siegfried and Roy are dressed in unbuttoned silk shirts, cropped fur jackets, and leather pants with codpieces. They ride a fire-breathing mechanical dragon, whipping the ten-foot head while women in shell bikinis dance with crystal-headed staffs. At the end of the show, Roy sits on top of a white tiger that sits on top of a mirrored disco ball. Joined by Siegfried and twelve more exotic animals, they levitate into the rafters.

It's a garbled American dream, a dream of the American dream: forty years earlier, the pair met aboard an ocean liner and fled postwar Germany with a cheetah stowed in their trunk. Now their show has a cast and crew of two hundred and fifty people.

As the men bow, Raj puts his mouth to Klara's ear. "We just have to find a way in. Somebody's gotta know somebody," he says.

236

■ ■ ■ ■

Klara breast-feeds Ruby on the futon, keeping one eye on Simon's watch. The same two letters appear as before: *M,* then *E.* Five minutes later, there's a second *E.* The next span of time is so long — twenty minutes — that she's worried she missed something while burping Ruby. Then she hears the noise again.

T.

"Meet!"

Ruby shrieks. Klara's milk is running dry.

"What?" calls Raj from outside. He's belly-up under the RV, looking at the backboard.

"Nothing," Klara says. Raj won't want to hear what's just occurred to her, which is this: If Simon is communicating with her from beyond the lip of death, then who's to say Saul isn't, too?

Klara clasps her nursing bra and shushes the baby, but there's an ache in her sinuses like she might start crying. Ruby is alive, and Ruby needs her. Klara needs Simon, needs Saul, but they're —

Dead? Perhaps. But perhaps not completely.

Raj strikes out with his contacts at the

Southern California casinos, but the owner of the Lake Tahoe resort has a cousin whose wife's brother manages the Golden Nugget. Raj goes to meet the man in his nicest outfit at a steakhouse on the Strip. When he returns, he's jacked up, energy to burn and a wild look in his eyes like rapture.

"Baby," he says. "I got a phone number."

17.

Klara has never performed anywhere like the Mirage's proscenium theater. The battens stand thirty feet above the floor; there are two moving platforms, five stage lifts, twenty spotlights, and two thousand seats. The ascension rope has been set, and the Proteus cabinet waits on wheels backstage. Three Mirage executives sit in the front row.

During Raj's opening monologue, Klara stands in the wings, sweat shimmying down the sides of her sequined dress. For the first time, Ruby is in day care, a service on the seventeenth floor for the children of hotel employees. Klara's stomach is clenched. She tries to focus, for Ruby's sake. *Shake out your hands. Swallow. Smile, goddammit.* She steps, in gold heels, onstage.

Light. Heat. She can't tell the executives apart, with their untucked dress shirts and their faces in shadow. They fidget through the Proteus cabinet. One leaves during the

Vanishing Birdcage, citing a conference call. The remaining two perk up during Second Sight, but Klara times the Breakaway incorrectly and must lift her knees to avoid hitting the stage too soon. When she opens her eyes, one of the men is looking at his pager. The other clears his throat.

"That it?" he calls.

A stagehand flicks the house lights on, and Raj walks out from the wings. He's smiling his salesman smile, but anger comes off him like heat. For a fraction of a second, the enormity of this opportunity — the enormity of their failure — knocks the air out of Klara. In the RV refrigerator, there are three jars of Ruby's food. She and Raj have been eating fast food, and she can feel it in her body, the combination of glut and lack. They have sixty-four dollars in a locked box in the glove compartment. If they don't get another gig, what will they do?

Klara thinks of Ilya, her mentor. He was the one who taught her that magic tricks are created for men: the pockets in suit jackets are perfectly sized to hold steel cups, and palming is easier with large hands. Then he taught her how to reinvent them. Klara uses compression-friendly foam balls, and she learned to work seamlessly with the drawer in a card table. But there was no way to get around the size of her palms, and when it came to sleight-of-hand magic, she could only rely on technique. "You've gotta get as good as the best men in magic," Ilya told her, drilling her in one-handed cuts until her fingers throbbed with pain. "And then you've gotta get better."

Those sleight-of-hand tricks — they were her strength. They still are. But Klara and Raj have been trying to be Siegfried and Roy. In the process, Klara forgot the old, humble magic on which she was raised. She forgot herself.

"No," she says. "It isn't."

She walks into the wings to retrieve Ilya's black box, which she brought today for luck. She carries it across the stage and hops down into the audience, then turns the box into a table in front of the executives. Up close, the men don't look alike at all. One is compact and hygienically bald, his blue eyes alert behind silver-rimmed glasses. He wears a red silk shirt. The other, in a black-and-white pinstriped shirt, is tall and pear shaped, his dark hair combed into a pony-tail. Lavender glasses perch atop his nose, a delicate gold cross around his neck.

Raj walks to the edge of the stage and sits behind Klara. His body is stiff, but he's watching her. She pulls her favorite deck out of the table's hidden compartment and spreads the cards on Ilya's table.

"Pick three," she tells the bald man. "Turn them faceup."

He selects the ace of clubs, the queen of diamonds, and the seven of hearts. She puts them back in the deck. Then she claps.

The ace flies out, fluttering midair before landing on a chair. She claps again: the queen sticks out of the center. When she claps a third time, the seven of hearts appears in her hand.

"Ha!" says the man. "Very nice."

Klara doesn't allow herself the compliment. She has work to do — Raise Rise, to be exact. She pulls a permanent marker out of the drawer and passes it to the man in the lavender glasses.

"Cut the cards," she says. "Any place you like." He does, revealing the three of spades. "Excellent. Would you sign this card for me?"

"With the marker?"

"With the marker. You'll keep me honest. There may be another three of spades in this deck, but none that look like yours. We'll put it back in the middle of the deck, like this. But here's a funny thing. When I tap the card at the top of the deck" — she turns it over — "there's your three. Strange, isn't it? Now, let's put it where it belongs, in the center. But wait: if I tap the top card a second time, here's the three again. It's risen through the deck."

Raise Rise is one of the most difficult tricks Klara knows, and she hasn't practiced it in years. She shouldn't be able to do it — but something is helping her. Something is pulling her back to the person she's been all along.

"Now, I'll show you very carefully how I put it in the middle of the deck. I'll even leave it sticking out this time so you can be sure I'm not lying — you see it? So do I. So why," she says, turning the top card over, "is it on top for the *third* time? And now — let's see; I think I feel it moving — it's strange, but I could swear it's on the bottom. Would you remove the bottom card, please?"

He does. It's his. He chuckles. "Well done. I wouldn't have noticed the double lift if I hadn't been looking for it."

He still has one eye on his pager. Klara makes him her target. Her pinkie is cramping — it's been a year since she worked on her outjogging — but she doesn't have time to shake out her hands. She grabs a fistful of quarters when she puts the deck away and points at the metal coffee mug that sits at the bald man's feet.

"Mind if I use that? Thank you; you're very kind. I don't know if you've noticed — I don't know if you've looked — but this place is lousy with coins."

She holds the mug in her right hand and splays her left, to show them it's empty. When she snaps, a quarter appears between her left thumb and forefinger. She drops it into the mug, where it clinks. She pulls two coins from the bald man's shirt collar, one from each of his ears, and two from the larger man's shirt pocket.

"Now, this is your mug, not mine. There's no secret compartment, no storehouse of coins. So I bet you're wondering how I'm doing this. I bet you already have your predictions." Klara gestures to the dark-haired man's glasses. He hands them to her, and she tips them toward the coffee mug. One quarter slides over each lens. "It's a natural response: we give life logic all the time. You see me producing coins over and over. Well, you assume, they must be in my left hand. And when I show you my left hand, when you realize that I can't be holding them there, you change the logic. Now you're thinking they're all in my *right* hand. It would be useful, wouldn't it? So close to the mug. You can't see that I might" — she

passes the mug to her left hand — "be shift-
ing" — she reveals her right hand, empty —
"methods."

She coughs; two coins tumble out of her
mouth. The dark-haired man puts his pager
in his shirt pocket. Now she has his attention.

"You're a religious man," says Klara, eyeing the cross around his neck. "My father
was, too. Sometimes I thought he was my
opposite. His rules versus my rule-breaking.
His reality versus my fantasies. But what
I've realized — what I think he already knew
— is that we believed in the same thing. You
could call it a trapdoor, a hidden compartment, or you could call it God: a placeholder
for what we don't know. A space where the
impossible becomes possible. When he said
the kiddush or lit the candles on Shabbat,
he was doing magic tricks."

Raj coughs, to warn her. *Where are you
going?* But she knows where she's going.
She's known all along.

"We know something about reality, my
father and I. And I bet you know it, too. Is
it that reality is too much? Too painful, too
limited, too restrictive of joy or opportunity?
No," she says. "I think it's that reality is not
enough."

Klara sets the mug on the floor and retrieves a cup and ball from the drawer. She puts the empty cup facedown on the table and places the ball on top.

"It's not enough to explain what we don't understand." She lifts the ball and holds it tight in her fist. "It's not enough to account for the inconsistencies we see and hear and feel." When she opens her fist, the ball has vanished. "It's not enough on which to pin our hopes, our dreams — our faith." She raises the steel cup to reveal the ball beneath it. "Some magicians say that magic shatters your worldview. But I think magic holds the world together. It's dark matter; it's the glue of reality, the putty that fills the holes between everything we know to be true. And it takes magic to reveal how inadequate" — she puts the cup down — "reality" — she makes a fist — "is."

When she opens her first, the red ball isn't there. What's there is a full, perfect strawberry.

Silence stretches from the carpeted floor to the fifty-foot ceiling, from the back of the stage to the balcony. Then Raj begins to clap, and the bald man joins in. Only the man with the gold cross withholds applause. Instead, he says, "When can you start?"

Klara stares at the strawberry in her palm. It's damp. She can smell it. There's a roar in her ears like the waterfall she heard outside the Mirage — or was it a saw?

The bald man takes a leather-bound calendar from his pocket. "I'm thinking December, January — January? Put her right before Siegfried and Roy?"

The larger man has a voice like something moving underwater. "They'll eat her alive."

"Right, but as an opener. We'll give her a half hour, people are filtering in, they want something to look at; she's a good-looking girl — you're a good-looking girl — she gets their attention, asses in seats, and bam! Tigers, lions, explosions. Blast off."

"They'll need new costumes," says the other man.

"Oh, complete overhaul on the costumes. We'll get you a production team, cut the birdcage, cut the cabinet, amp up the rope hang, amp up the mind-reading trick — bring an audience member onstage, that kind of thing; we'll get you set up for it." Someone's pager beeps. Both men check their pockets. "Listen, we'll talk. You got four months before opening, you're gonna be fine."

"Jesus fucking Christ," says Raj as soon as the elevator doors close. "A strawberry." He's laughing, crumpled in the corner where two of the glass walls meet. "I'll never know how you pulled that off, but it was perfect."

"I don't know, either."

Raj's laughter stops, though his smile still hangs open.

"I'm serious," Klara says. "I'd never seen that strawberry before. I have no idea where it came from."

Her first thought is that the blackouts have come back: perhaps she drove to a market, bought a container, stuffed one in her pocket. But that doesn't make sense. Raj is the only one who drives the rental car, and there's no grocery store in walking distance from King's Row.

"What do you think you are?" Raj asks. There's something feral in his face, something wild, like a wolf guarding his kill. "A magician who believes in her own tricks?"

Months ago, she would have been wounded. This time, she isn't. She's noticed something.

The look in Raj's eyes. She mistook it for anger. But that's not what it is.

He's afraid of her.

18.

Raj works with the production team to rig the Jaws of Life and stage Second Sight. He designs a new set of props for the Indian Needle Trick: bigger needles, so they read from the stage, and red cord instead of thread. The Mirage's entertainment director asks Klara if she'll let Raj saw her in half — "Easy-peasy; won't hurt a bit" — but she refuses. He thinks she's afraid of the trick when the truth is that she could give him an hour-long tutorial on P. T. Selbit and his misogynistic inventions: Destroying a Girl, Stretching a Lady, Crushing a Woman, all of them perfectly timed to capitalize on postwar bloodthirst and women's suffrage.

Klara won't be a woman who is sawed in half or tied in chains — nor will she be rescued or liberated. She'll save herself. She'll be the saw.

But she knows they might lose the job if

she pushes back more. She lets the costumer raise her hemline by five inches and lower her neckline by two, fit the chest with padded cups. During rehearsals, Raj stands proudly, but Klara is shrinking. The radiance she felt during the audition is becoming dimmer every day — it's washed out by the five-hundred-watt spotlights, obscured by the fog of the smoke machines. She thought the Mirage wanted her as she was, but they want her cubed, larger than life. They want her Vegas. To them, she's as much a novelty as the pink volcano outside the hotel: their very own girl magician.

Ruby's cartilage is turning to bone, and her bones are fusing. Her body is seventy percent water, the same percentage of water on Earth. She has delicate canine fangs and one set of knobby molars. She can say *go* and *no* and *come me,* which means *come with me,* which turns Klara's heart to goop. She shrieks with delight at the sight of the pink lizards that crawl through King's Row and holds pebbles tight in her fists. When the show opens and they get their first big paycheck, Raj wants to sell the trailer and rent an apartment, look at preschools and pediatricians. But Klara is running out of time. If the woman on Hester Street was right, she'll die in two months.

She doesn't tell Raj. He'll think she's even crazier. Besides, she rarely sees him: between rehearsals, he stays at the theater. From a grid ninety feet above the stage, he rigs a system of customized lines and pulleys to steel pipe battens. He uses the stage's traps and sloats to devise a disappearance for Klara after her Breakaway bow. He builds a new card table with the construction crew and helps them carry props from the shop to the stage. The stage manager loves him, but some of the techs are resentful. Once, on her way to pick Ruby up from day care, Klara passes two stagehands. They're standing just inside the doors to the theater, watching Raj mark the stage with tape.

"You used to be the one to set the marks," one says. "You aren't careful, Gandhi'll take your job."

Klara walks to Vons, pushing Ruby in her red plastic stroller. She nicks eight cans of Gerber sweet potatoes from aisle four, which clink in her purse as she walks toward the exit. The sliding doors open, and she feels a rush of warm air. It's evening in late November, but the sky is still denim blue. She sits down beneath a street lamp, opens

251

one of the Gerber jars, and feeds Ruby with her index finger.

Two orbs of white light grow closer, larger, and a silver Oldsmobile rolls to a stop. Klara covers Ruby's eyes and squints, but the car doesn't keep moving: it pauses in front of her like she's blocking the way out of the lot. In the driver's seat, a man is staring at her. He has rumpled strawberry blond hair and pale gold eyes and a mouth hanging open. He looks exactly like Eddie O'Donoghue, the cop from San Francisco.

Klara scrambles to her feet and pulls Ruby onto one hip. In the process, she drops the jar of food, which cracks and spills orange mush, but she doesn't stop — she walks and then she starts running back to the anonymous crowds of the Strip. She's weaving through tourists, pushing the empty stroller crookedly with one hand and remembering the thrust of his tongue in her mouth, when she slams into the back of a heavyset woman with two long, brown braids.

Klara's blood freezes. It's the fortune teller. She grabs the woman's shoulder.

The woman turns. She's only a teenager. Beneath the dancing lights of the Stage Door Casino, her face turns red, then blue.

"What the fuck is wrong with you?" The girl's pupils are dilated, and there's a bullish thrust to her chin.

"I'm sorry," Klara whispers, withdrawing. "I thought you were someone else."

Ruby screams from her waist. Klara fumbles ahead, past Caesars Palace and the Hilton Suites, past Harrah's and Carnaval Court. She never thought she'd be so glad to see the Mirage volcano's stupid hot pink froth. Only when she enters the hotel does she realize she left Ruby's stroller in front of the Stage Door, empty.

She doesn't want to hear the knocks — she wants them to go back where they came from — but they're only getting louder. Simon is angry with her; he thinks she's forgetting him. An hour before their first dress rehearsal, Klara walks into the women's bathroom at the Mirage and sets Ruby on the counter next to a vase of fake flowers. She takes out her watch. *Meet* comes quickly, as before. Thirteen minutes later, she hears a fifth knock: another *M*. In five minutes, there's an *E*.

She thinks he's starting the same word over when she realizes what he's telling her. *Meet me.* After sixty-five minutes, she has another one.

Us.

Simon and Saul. *Us.* The bathroom seesaws. Klara puts her hands on the marble counter and drops her head to her chest. She's not sure how long it's been when she hears Ruby's voice. The baby isn't crying; she's not even babbling. What she says is clear as day: "Ma. Ma. Ma-ma."

Inside Klara, a long stalk keels and snaps. Always, it's like this: the family that created her and the family she created, pulling her in opposite directions. Someone's beating on the door.

"Klara?" Raj shouts, coming inside.

Instead of his usual outfit — a white T-shirt, smudged ashy, and an old pair of Carhartts — he wears his costume: a custom-made swallowtail coat and top hat, smooth and black as a penguin's pelt. Ruby sits on the other side of the counter. She's crawled into one of the Mirage's gaping gold sinks and is playing with the automatic soap dispenser. There's blue froth in her mouth, and she's wailing.

"What the fuck, Klara? What's wrong with you?" Raj takes Ruby in his arms and helps her spit, flushing out her mouth with his hands. He wets a paper towel and gently wipes her eyes and nose. Then he puts both hands against the counter and leans forward, resting his chin in the baby's dark hair. It takes Klara a moment to realize he's crying.

"You were talking to Simon," he says. "Weren't you?"

"The knocks. I've been timing them. I wasn't sure if they were real before, but I know it now: they are, they just spelled —"

Raj leans in as if to kiss her. But he pauses with his nose at her cheek before withdrawing.

"Klara." When he looks at her, there's something vivid in his face, something alive, something she thinks is love before she realizes it's fury. "I can smell it on you."

"Smell what?" asks Klara, buying time. She downed two mini bottles of Popov in the trailer; they were supposed to help her steady.

"You must be some kind of masochist, to do this to us now. Or do you just think I'll always be here to pick up the pieces?"

"It was one drink." She hates the way her voice shakes. "You're controlling."

"Is that what you tell yourself?" Raj's eyes widen. "Years ago. If I hadn't found you. Where do you think you'd be?"

"Better off." She'd be in San Francisco, doing gigs on her own. She'd be lonely, but in control.

"You'd be a drunk," says Raj. "A failure."

Ruby gazes at Klara from Raj's arms. Blood rushes to Klara's cheeks.

"The only reason you're still doing what you're doing," Raj says, "is because I met you. And the only reason you were getting by before you met me was because you were ripping people off. You stole, Klara. Shamelessly. And you think all you were doing was giving people a good show?"

"I was giving people a good show. I am," says Klara. "I'm trying to be a good mother. I want to be a success. But you don't know what it's like in my head. You don't know what I've lost."

"I don't know what you've lost? Do you know — do you have any idea — what happened in my country?" Raj wipes his eyes with the heel of his free hand. "Your dad had a business, a family. You still have a mom and a sister and a doctor big brother. My dad picked trash; my mom died so young I can't remember her. Amit died in '85 on a plane, minutes from Bombay, the first time he tried to go home. Your family had it good. They *have* it good."

"I know how difficult your life has been," Klara whispers. "I never meant to minimize that. But my brother died. My father died. They didn't have it good."

"Why? 'Cause they didn't live till ninety?

Think about what they had while they were here. People like me, on the other hand — we hang on by our teeth, and if we're really, really lucky, if we're fucking exceptional, we get somewhere. But you can always be airlifted out." Raj shakes his head. "Jesus, Klara. Why do you think I don't talk to you about my problems, real problems? It's 'cause you can't take it. You don't have space in your head for anyone's problems but yours."

"That's an awful thing to say."

"But is it true?"

Klara can't speak; her brain is tangled, wires crossed, the monitor shutting down. Raj checks Ruby's diaper and reties the laces on her tiny shoes. He takes the diaper bag from Klara's shoulder and walks to the bathroom door.

"I swear to God, Klara, I thought you were getting better. Soon as the health insurance comes through, soon as we get a day off, I'm taking you to see somebody. You can't lose it now," he says. "We're too close."

December 28th, 1990. If the woman is right, Klara has four days to live. If the woman is right, she'll die on opening night.

There must be a loophole, a secret trapdoor. She's a magician, goddammit. All she has to do is find the fucking trapdoor.

She takes a red ball to bed and plays with it under the covers. She's figured out how to turn it into a strawberry. A French drop from the right hand to the left makes the ball disappear. Then she moves her left hand over her right. When she does a shuttle pass and opens her left fist again, there's the cool, fragrant fruit. She eats each strawberry and tucks their green stems under the mattress. Then she slips out of the RV.

It's black, black night, but it must be over ninety degrees. She can hear people moving around in their campers: showering and cooking, eating and arguing, yelps from the teenage couple in the Gulf Stream who are constantly having sex. Everywhere, there's life: rattling in tin cans, trying to get out.

She walks to the pool. It's shaped like a kidney bean and glows an acid, unearthly blue. There are no pool chairs — the manager claims they only get stolen — so Klara stands at the deep end. She takes off her tank and shorts, letting them fall in a clump. Her stomach is still soft and creped from Ruby. When she removes her underwear, her pubic hair seems to bloom.

She jumps.

The water surrounds her like a membrane.

Klara's feet look nearer than they are, and her arms seem to bend. The pool appears shallower than eight feet, though she knows this is an illusion. Refraction, it's called: light bends when it enters a new medium. But the human brain is programmed to assume that light travels in straight lines. What she sees is different than what's there.

She's heard the same thing about stars: they appear to twinkle when light, viewed through earth's atmosphere, becomes bent. The human eye processes the movement as absence. But the light is always there.

Klara breaks through the water. She gasps.

Perhaps the point is not to resist death. Perhaps the point is that there's no such thing. If Simon and Saul are contacting Klara, then consciousness survives the death of the body. If consciousness survives the death of the body, then everything she's been told about death isn't true. And if everything she's been told about death isn't true, maybe death is not death at all.

She turns onto her back and floats. If the woman is right, if she could see Simon's death in 1969, then there's magic in the world: some strange, shimmering knowledge in the very heart of the unknowable. It doesn't matter whether or when Klara dies; she can communicate with Ruby just as she

does with Simon now. She can cross boundaries, like she always wanted to.

She can be the bridge.

19.

The billboard outside the hotel has changed. *Tonight,* it reads. *The Immortalist, with Raj Chapal.* The show won't begin until eleven o'clock — a New Year's Eve special — but the entrance is already overflowing with tourists. Raj parks the Sunbird in the employee lot. Usually, she carries their bags and he carries Ruby, but tonight Klara won't let go of the baby. She's put Ruby in a red party dress that Gertie sent for Ruby's first birthday, with thick white tights and black patent leather shoes.

They walk through the lobby. Fish glow and scuttle in the fifty-foot aquarium. The tiger habitat is swarmed, though the animals are sleeping, their downy chins flat on the concrete. Raj and Klara turn toward the elevators. This is where they'll part: Raj will bring their bags to the theater, and Klara will bring Ruby to day care.

Raj turns to her and puts his hand on her

cheek. His palm is warm, calloused from work in the shop. "You ready?"

Klara's heartbeat trips. She looks at his face. It's beautiful: the swan's neck of each cheekbone, the angular chin. His shoulder-length hair is in a ponytail, as usual; the makeup artist will blow it out and add silicone to make it shine.

"I want you to know that I'm proud of you," he says.

His eyes are glossy. Klara inhales in surprise.

"I know I've been hard on you. I know things have been tense. But I love you; I love us. And I have faith in you."

"But you don't believe in my tricks. You don't believe in the magic."

She smiles. She feels sorry for him, for how much he doesn't know.

"No," he says, frustrated, like he's talking to Ruby. "There's no such thing."

Families surge toward the elevators, moving around Klara and Raj, through them, and Raj drops his hand. When they're alone again, Raj puts it back where it was, but it's harder, now, his palm cupping her jaw.

"Listen. Just because I don't believe in your tricks doesn't mean I don't believe in you. I think you're great at what you do. I think you have the power to affect people.

You're an artist, Klara. An entertainer."

"I'm not a show pony. I'm not a clown."

"No," says Raj. "You're a star."

He drops his bags and reaches for her. With his arms around her back, he pulls her close and squeezes. Pressed to Klara's breast, Ruby squeaks. Their family of three. Already they feel like ghosts, like people she used to know. She thinks of the days — they feel so long ago — when she thought Raj could give her everything she wanted.

"I'm going upstairs," she says.

"Okay." Raj makes a fish face at Ruby, who giggles. "Wave goodbye, Ruby. Wave goodbye to your papa. Wish him good luck."

The woman who runs the day care cracks the door when Klara knocks. The suite behind her is filled with the children of stagehands and performers, receptionists and line cooks, managers and maids.

"Nuts tonight." She looks like a hostage, her face haggard behind the bolted chain. "Happy fucking New Year."

Klara hears the crash of glass and a series of whooping noises.

"Good God," shouts the woman, turning. Then she faces Klara again. "Mind if we make this quick? Hello, you."

She unbolts the door and wiggles a finger

at Ruby. Klara clutches the baby. Everything in her that is rational resists letting go.

"What, you're not dropping her off tonight? Don't you have a show?"

"I am," says Klara. "I do."

She smooths Ruby's cowlicky black hair, cups her soft fatty cheeks. She only wants the baby to look at her. But Ruby squirms: the other children have distracted her.

"Goodbye, my love." Klara puts her nose to Ruby's forehead and inhales the milky sweetness, the sour sweat — the essential humanness — of her skin. She drinks it in. "I'll see you soon."

When she gets in the elevator again, it's as though Simon's been waiting for her. She sees him in the glass, his face waving rainbow like an oil spill. She rides to the forty-fifth floor. She only wanted to see the view from the top, but luck's on her side: when she steps into the hall, a housekeeper comes out of the penthouse suite. As soon as the woman enters the elevator, Klara lunges for the door. She catches it with her pinky and steps inside.

The suite is bigger than any apartment Klara's ever seen. The living room and the dining room have cream leather chairs and glass tables; the bedroom sports a California

King as well as a TV. The bathroom is as large as the RV, with an extra-long Jacuzzi and two marble sinks. In the kitchen, there's a steel refrigerator with full-sized bottles of alcohol instead of minis. She takes a bottle of Bombay Sapphire and Johnnie Walker Black Label, a Veuve Clicquot. She rotates between them, coughing on the champagne before she starts the cycle again.

She's forgotten to look at the view. The thick, folded curtains, also cream, are closed. When she touches a round button on the wall, they slide open to reveal the Strip, glowing with electricity. Klara tries to imagine what it looked like sixty years ago — before twenty thousand men built the Hoover Dam, before the neon signs and the gambling, when Las Vegas was just a sleepy railroad town.

She walks to the phone and dials out. Gertie picks up on the fourth ring.

"Ma."

"Klara?"

"My show is tonight. My opening. I wanted to hear your voice."

"Your opening? That's marvelous." Gertie's breathless as a girl. Klara hears laughter in the background, a stray cry. "We're celebrating here. We're —"

"Daniel's engaged!" Varya's voice; she

must have picked up the other receiver.

"Engaged?" A moment before it registers. "Engaged to Mira?"

"Yes, silly," says Varya. "Who else?"

Warmth seeps through Klara like ink. A new member of the family. She knows why they're celebrating, why it means so much.

"That's wonderful," she says. "That's so, so wonderful."

When she hangs up, the suite feels cold and abandoned, like a party everyone has just vacated. But she won't be alone for long.

Magicians have never been very good at dying.

David Devant was fifty when tremors forced him off the stage. Howard Thurston collapsed on the floor after a performance. Houdini died of his own confidence: in 1926, he let an audience member punch him in the stomach, and the blow ruptured his appendix. And then there's Gran. Klara always assumed she died during the Jaws of Life in Times Square because she fell, but now she has her doubts. Gran had recently lost Otto, her husband. Klara knows what it's like to hang on to the world by her teeth. She knows what it's like to want to let go.

She opens her purse and retrieves the

rope, which is coiled like a snake. It's the first one she ever used for the Jaws of Life, back in San Francisco. Klara remembers its rough, strong weave, its sudden snap. She stands on the living room table and ties it around the neck of the massive light fixture above.

She's been waiting for something to prove that the woman's prophecies were right. But this is the trick: Klara must prove it herself. She's the answer to the riddle, the second half of the circle. Now, they work in tandem — back-to-back, head-to-head.

Not that she isn't terrified. The thought of Ruby in day care — toddling across the room on her plump legs, shrieking with glee — wrenches every cell in her body. She halts.

Perhaps she should wait for a sign. A knock — just one.

She's so sure the knock will come that she's startled when, after two minutes, it hasn't. She cracks her knuckles and remembers to breathe. Another minute passes, then five more.

Klara's arms begin to shake. Sixty more seconds and she'll give it up. Sixty more seconds and she'll pack her rope, return to Raj and perform.

And then it comes.

Her breath is uneven, her chest shuddering; she cries thick, sloppy tears. The knocks are insistent now, they're coming fast as hail. *Yes,* they tell her. *Yes, yes, yes.*

"Ma'am?"

Someone is at the door, but Klara doesn't pause. She hung a *Do Not Disturb* sign on the knob. If it's housekeeping, they'll see it.

The living room table looks expensive, all glass and sharp corners, but it's surprisingly light. She pushes it toward the wall and replaces it with a stool from the kitchen bar.

"Ma'am? Miss Gold?"

More knocking. Klara feels a flash of fear. She crosses to the kitchen and takes a swig of whiskey, then of gin. Dizziness comes on so suddenly that she has to bend over and drop her head to keep from vomiting.

"Miss Gold?" calls the voice, more loudly. "Klara?"

The rope hangs, waiting. Her old friend. She climbs onto the chair and ties her hair back.

One more look outside, at the stream of people and the lights. One more moment to hold Ruby and Raj in her mind; she'll speak to them soon.

"Klara?" shouts the voice.

January 1st, 1991, just like the woman promised. Klara takes her hands, and they

268

tumble through the dark, dark sky. They flutter crisply as leaves, so small in the infinite universe; they turn and flicker, turn again. Together, they illuminate the future, even from so far away.

Raj is right. She's a star.

■ ■ ■ ■

PART THREE:
THE INQUISITION

■ ■ ■ ■

1991–2006
Daniel

20.

Daniel saw Mira three times before they ever spoke: first in a study carrel at Regenstein Library, writing in a small red notebook, then at the student-run café in the basement of Cobb, striding out of the door with a coffee in hand. Her gait had an electricity that he felt as she brushed past him. He noticed it again a couple of weeks later, when he saw her running along the perimeter of Stagg Field, but it was not until May of 1987 that she approached him.

He sat in the dining commons, eating a pulled pork sandwich. (Gertie would have had a heart attack if she'd known he was eating pork. He'd even developed a taste for bacon, which he kept in the refrigerator of his Hyde Park apartment and which he swore she could smell on him whenever he returned to New York.) At three p.m., the space was nearly empty; Daniel ate at this time because his clerkship rotation ran from six a.m. to two thirty. He felt a gust of air as the front doors opened, another chill as he recognized the young woman in the frame. Her eyes whisked through the room, and then she began to walk toward Daniel. He pretended not to notice her until she stopped in front of his four-person table.

"Do you mind if I — ?" She had a sturdy leather tote bag on one shoulder and an armful of books.

"No," said Daniel, looking up as if he hadn't noticed her until now before leaping into action. He cleared a squashed can of Coke and the snakeskin of a straw wrapper, as well as a red plastic basket filled with the detritus of his sandwich: blobs of pork fat and maroon sauce. "Of course not."

"Thanks," said the woman, in a business-like tone. She sat down diagonally from Daniel, extracted a notebook and pencil case, and began to work.

Daniel was puzzled. It seemed she wanted nothing to do with him. Of course, she might have had other reasons for choosing this table: its distance from the buffet, or the fact that it was next to the windows, in a rare patch of Chicago sun.

He searched his backpack for a book and studied her out of the corner of his eye. She was petite but not thin, with a round face that tapered to a slender, shapely chin. She had elegant, furry brows and chestnut-colored eyes with surprisingly pale lashes. Her skin was olive toned and scattered with freckles. Straight brown hair hung to her collarbones.

The clock ticked toward three thirty, then four. At four fifteen, he cleared his throat. "What are you studying?"

The woman had a blue and silver Sony Walkman in her lap. She pulled off her headphones. "What's that?"

"I was just wondering what you study."

"Oh," she said. "Art history. Jewish art."

"Ah," said Daniel, raising his eyebrows and smiling in what he hoped was an interested-seeming way, though the subject did not interest him very much.

"Ah. You disapprove."

"Disapprove? God, no." Daniel flushed. "You're entitled to study whatever you like."

"Thank you," she said, deadpan.

Daniel reddened. "I'm sorry. That sounded patronizing. I didn't mean it like that. *I'm* Jewish," he added, in solidarity. The woman looked at the remainder of his sandwich. "Ancestrally."

"You're pardoned, then," said the woman, but she smiled. "I'm Mira."

"Daniel." Should he shake her hand? He

wasn't usually so awkward around women. He smiled back instead.

"So," said Mira. "You're no longer religious?"

"No," he admitted.

As a kid, Daniel was soothed by the synagogue: the bearded men with their silk shawls and rituals, the honeyed apples and bitter herbs, the praying. He developed a private prayer that he repeated each night with faithful exactitude, as though one botched phrase would cause something terrible to befall him. But terrible things *did* befall him: the death of his father, then of his brother. Shortly after Simon's passing, Daniel stopped praying entirely. He was not troubled by his abandonment of religion. After all, there had been no struggle. His belief went willingly, logically, the way the boogeyman disappeared once you looked under the bed. That was the problem with God: he didn't hold up to a critical analysis. He wouldn't stand for it. He disappeared.

"You're a man of few words," said Mira.

Something in her tone made him laugh. "It's just that — well, talk of religion . . . it can make people uncomfortable. Or defensive." In case Mira herself was becoming defensive, he added: "I do see a lot of value in religious tradition."

Her head was inclined with interest. "Like what?"

"My father was devout. I respect my father, and so I respect what he believed in." Daniel paused to collect his thoughts; he had never articulated them before. "In a way, I see religion as a pinnacle of human achievement. In inventing God, we've developed the ability to consider our own straits — and we've equipped Him with the kind of handy loopholes that enable us to believe we only have so much control. The truth is that most people enjoy a certain level of impotence. But I think we *do* have control — so much that it scares us to death. As a species, God might be the greatest gift we've ever given ourselves. The gift of sanity."

Mira's mouth made a little upside-down semicircle. Soon, that expression would become as familiar to Daniel as her small, cool hands or the mole on her left earlobe.

"I track pieces of Nazi-stolen art," she said, after a moment. "And what I've noticed is just how far each object travels. Take Van Gogh's *Portrait of Dr. Gachet.* It was painted in 1880 in Auvers-sur-Oise about a month before Van Gogh committed suicide. The work changed hands four times — from Van Gogh's brother to his brother's widow to two independent collectors — before it was acquired by the Städel in Frankfurt. When Nazis plundered the museum in 1937, it was seized by Hermann Göring, who auctioned it off to a German collector. But here's where things get interesting: that collector sold it to Siegfried Kramarsky, a Jewish banker who fled the Holocaust for New York in 1938. It's remarkable, isn't it? That the painting wound up, after all that, in Jewish hands, and directly from a Göring associate?" Mira fingered her headphones. She seemed suddenly shy. "I suppose I think we need God for the same reason we need art."

"Because it's nice to look at?"

"No." Mira smiled. "Because it shows us what's possible."

It was exactly the sort of comforting notion Daniel had long ago rejected, but he was drawn to Mira despite it. That weekend, they drank wine and listened to Paul Simon's *Graceland* on a boom box Mira wedged in the open window of her third-floor walk-up. When she put her hands in the back pockets of his jeans and pulled him close, Daniel felt such bliss that it almost embarrassed him. He had not realized how lonely he was, or how long he'd been lonely.

At his wedding, when he looked into the audience and saw only Gertie and Varya, something snapped in his heart like a branch. That Klara and Mira had never met remained one of the biggest regrets of his life. Mira was eminently practical and Klara was certainly not, but they shared an arch sense of humor and an air of playful — sometimes, not so playful — challenge. He didn't know how much he relied on his sister for this purpose until he met his wife. During the breaking of the glass, he imagined his life until now shattering, too: its ignorance and anguish, its great and petty losses. From the pieces, he would assemble something new with Mira. He looked into her bright, hazel eyes, shimmering beneath a layer of tears, and felt his soul relax as if into a warm bath. So long as he kept looking at her, that feeling of peace pulsed outward, pushing pain to the perimeter of his consciousness.

Later, lying naked with his bride — Mira snored, her forehead damp on his chest — Daniel began to tremble. He prayed. The words came forth as naturally, as necessarily, as urine. (A terrible analogy, he knew — Mira would have been horrified, had he shared it — and yet it still seemed to him more fitting than the inflated metaphors he'd heard in childhood.) *Please, God,* he thought. *Oh God, may this last.*

In the following weeks, when he remembered the prayer, Daniel felt bashful, but also, somehow, lighter; it was as though he'd cut a lock of hair. He had not thought religion could do this for him. Truthfully, the seeds of his atheism had been sown years before the deaths of Klara and Simon and Saul. It began with the woman on Hester Street. He had felt such shame at his paganism, his desire to know the unknowable, that his shame became repudiation. No one, he vowed, could have such power over him: no person, no deity.

But perhaps God was nothing like the dreadful, lurid fascination that brought him to the fortune teller, nothing like her preposterous claims. For Saul, God had meant order and tradition, culture and history. Daniel still believed in choice, but perhaps that did not foreclose belief in God. He imagined a new God, one who nudged him when he was going the wrong way but never strong-armed him, one who advised but did not insist — one who guided him, like a father. A Father.

Several years later, when they were married and living in Kingston, New York, he asked Mira if she'd intentionally sat beside him in the dining hall all those years before.

"Of course," said Mira. When she laughed, a beam of light from the kitchen window turned her eyes to gold coins. "The cafeteria was empty. Why else would I have picked your table?"

"I don't know," said Daniel, embarrassed for having asked, or for having doubted her. "You might have wanted company. Or sun. It was sunny, I recall."

Mira kissed him. He could feel the cool strip of her wedding ring, a gold band that matched his own, on the back of his neck.

"I knew exactly what I was doing," she said.

21.

Ten days before Thanksgiving, 2006, Daniel sits in the office of Albany MEPS Commander Colonel Bertram. In his four years with the Military Entrance Processing Station, Daniel has only visited the colonel's office a handful of times — usually to discuss an unusual case, once to receive a promotion from physician to chief medical officer — and today, he hopes for a raise.

Colonel Bertram sits in a leather chair behind a glossy, wide desk. He is younger than Daniel, with a clean shell of blond hair, shaved at the sides, and a tight, wiry frame. He looks scarcely older than the eager ROTC graduates who arrive by the carload for assessment.

"You've had a good run," he says.

"Pardon?"

"You've had a good run," he repeats. "You've served your country well. But I'm going to be blunt, Major. Some of us think it's time you took a break."

Daniel commissioned after medical school. For the first ten years of his career, he worked at Keller Army Community Hospital in West Point. This was the kind of work he had always imagined doing, high-stakes and unpredictable, but he was depleted by the hours and the relentless suffering. When a job opened up at MEPS, Mira encouraged him to apply. The position wasn't glamorous, but Daniel came to enjoy its stability, and now he can hardly imagine a return to the hospital — or, worse, a deployment.

Sometimes, he fears his preference for routine is cowardly. The paradox of his job — confirming that young people are healthy enough to go to war — is not lost on him. On the other hand, he also sees himself as a guardian. It's his job to act as a sieve, separating those who are ready for war from those who are not. Applicants look at him with anxious hopefulness, as if he can give them permission to live, not license to die. Of course, there are some whose faces show pure terror, and in them Daniel sees the military fathers or dead-end poverty that brought them to the armed forces in the first place. He always asks them if they're sure they want to go to war. They always say yes.

"Sir." For a moment, Daniel's mind goes dark. "Is this about Douglas?"

The colonel inclines his head. "Douglas was fit. He should have been cleared."

Daniel remembers the boy's papers: Douglas's spirometry and peak flow tests were far below normal. "Douglas had asthma."

"Douglas is from Detroit." Colonel Bertram's smile is gone. "Everyone from Detroit has asthma. You think we should stop letting kids in from Detroit?"

"Of course not." For the first time, the gravity of the situation becomes clear to Daniel. He knows that enlistment is down by ten percent. He knows that the military has lowered standards for the mental aptitude exam — they haven't admitted so many Category IV applicants since the seventies. He's heard that certain commanding officers have written waivers for misconduct convictions: petty theft, assault, even vehicular manslaughter and homicide.

"This isn't just about Douglas," he says.

"Major." Colonel Bertram leans forward, and his commander's pin — a wreathed star — catches the light. Daniel pictures the colonel hunched over his desk with the pin in his hand, scrubbing it with a cotton ball doused in silver polish. "You're well-intentioned; we all know that. But you come from a different generation. You're conservative, and that's fair: you don't want to see anyone go down who doesn't have to. Some of these kids aren't right, I'll grant you that. We screen for a reason. But there's a time to be conservative, Major, and this isn't it. We need guys, we need numbers, for God and country, and sometimes we get a guy come in here with a bad knee or a little cough, but his heart's in the right place, he's good enough — and right now, Dr. Gold, we need heart. We need good enough. We" — the colonel picks up a stack of forms — "need waivers."

"I write waivers when they're merited."

"You write waivers when you think they're merited."

"I thought that was my job description."

"You work for me. I give you your job description. And I'm sure you don't want an Article 15 sitting in your file, stinking like shit."

"For what?" Daniel's mouth turns to chalk. "I've never gone against the code."

An Article 15 would end his career in the military. He'd never get a promotion; he could even be discharged. Regardless, he'd be disgraced. The humiliation would burn him alive.

But his pride is not the only issue. Mira works at a public university. When Daniel left his job at the hospital, they had more money than they needed, but since then, he and Mira have taken on Gertie's living expenses. Mira's mother was diagnosed with cancer, too, and her father with dementia. After her mother died, they moved her father into an assisted living facility whose annual payments have swallowed much of their savings and will continue to do so: her father is sixty-eight and otherwise healthy.

"For insubordination." A wedge of egg white quivers below the colonel's lower lip. He lifts the tinfoil in which his sandwich was wrapped and folds it in half. "For a failure to comply with military standards."

"That's a lie."

"I'm a liar?" asks the colonel, quietly. He still holds the piece of tinfoil, folding it over and over again.

Daniel knows he's been given an opportunity to correct himself. But the thought of the Article 15 blazes inside him. He is riled by the threat of it, the injustice.

"Either that or a sheep," he says. "Doing whatever leadership tells you."

The colonel stops. He puts the piece of

foil, now the size of a business card, in his pocket. Then he rises from his chair and leans over the desk toward Daniel, his palms flat.

"Your duty is suspended. Two weeks."

"Who will do my job?"

"I've got three other guys who can do exactly what you do. That'll be all."

Daniel stands. If he salutes, Colonel Bertram will see that his hands are shaking, and so he doesn't, though he knows this will make his situation much worse.

"You must think you're a special fucking snowflake," the colonel says as Daniel turns toward the door. "A real American hero."

Daniel walks to the parking lot with his ears ringing. He lets the car warm up and stares at the Leo W. O'Brien Federal Building, a tall glass square that has housed the Albany MEPS since 1974. After a renovation in 1997, Daniel was given an expansive new office on the third floor. Downtown Albany isn't much to look at, but when Daniel first sat in that office, he was filled with purpose and surety — the sense that his life had been leading up to this moment from the beginning, and that he had arrived here by making a series of smart, strategic choices.

Daniel reverses out of the parking lot and

begins the fifty-minute commute to Kingston. What will he tell Mira? Before today, men sought his counsel, asked for his consent: he was an oracle himself. Now, he's indistinguishable from any other man, like a priest divested of robes.

"Bastard," says Mira, when he slumps into her arms and tells her. "I've never liked that guy — Bertram? Bertrand? *Bastard.*" She rises onto her tiptoes and puts her palms to Daniel's cheeks. "Where are the ethics? Where are the goddamned ethics?"

Outside, the garage light illuminates the woods that border their garden. A deer sniffs at sticks beyond the first scrim of trees. The landscape has turned brown so quickly this year.

"Use it to your advantage," Mira says. "We'll spend the next two weeks building your case. In the meantime, you'll have a break; think about what you'd like to get out of it."

Scrolling through Daniel's mind, as if across a television screen: the list of disqualifying conditions. *Ulceration, varices, fistula, achalasia, or other dysmotility disorders. Atresia or severe microtia. Meniere's syndrome. Dorsiflexion to ten degrees. Absence of great toe(s).* On and on — thousands of regulations in all. For women, it's even more restrictive. *Ovarian cysts. Abnormal bleeding.* It's a wonder anyone gets through at all, but then again, it's also a wonder that most people, despite rising rates of cancer and diabetes and cardiovascular disease, still live to the age of seventy-eight.

"What are things you've been meaning to do?" Mira continues. She's trying to be strong, for his sake, but her anxiety is obvious: she always tries to keep busy when she's worried. "You could rebuild the shed. Or get in touch with your family."

Many years ago, Mira asked, with characteristic straightforwardness, why Daniel wasn't closer to his siblings.

"We're not *not* close," he said.

"Well, you're not close," said Mira.

"Sometimes we are," said Daniel, though the truth was muddier. There were times he thought of his siblings and felt love sing from him like a shofar, rich with joy and agony and eternal recognition: those three made from the same star stuff as he, those he'd known from the beginning of the beginning. But when he was with them, the smallest infraction made him irreversibly resentful. Sometimes, it was easier to think of them as characters — straitlaced Varya; Klara, dreamy and heedless — than to confront them in all of their off-putting, fully bloomed adulthood: their morning breath and foolish choices, their lives snaking into unfamiliar underbrush.

That night, he drifts into wooziness, then out again. He is thinking of his siblings and of waves, the process of falling asleep not unlike the ocean lapping shore. During one of their New Jersey vacations, Saul took Daniel's siblings to a movie, but Daniel wanted to swim. He was seven. He and Gertie brought slotted plastic chairs to the beach, and Gertie read a novel while Daniel pretended to be Don Schollander, who had won four medals in Tokyo the year before. When the tide carried Daniel toward the horizon, he let it, electrified by the growing distance between himself and his mother. By the time he grew tired of treading water, he had drifted fifty yards from shore.

The ocean sloshed in his nose, in his mouth. His legs were long and useless. He spat and tried to yell, but Gertie couldn't hear him. Only because a sudden wind blew her sun hat into the sand did she stand and, in retrieving it, see Daniel's dropping head.

She let go of the hat and ran to Daniel in what felt like slow motion, though it was the fastest she had ever moved. She wore a diaphanous muumuu over her bathing suit whose hem she had to carry; then, with a roar of consternation, she pulled the whole thing off and left it shriveled on the ground. Underneath was a black one-piece with a skirted hem that revealed her stout and dimpled thighs. She sloshed through the shallow water before inhaling deeply and plunging into the waves. *Hurry,* thought Daniel, gargling salt water. *Hurry, Mama.* He had not called her that since he was a toddler. At last, her hands appeared beneath his armpits. She dragged him out of the water and together they collapsed in the sand. Her entire body was red, her hair slicked to her head like an aviator's helmet. She was heaving great breaths that Daniel thought were from exertion before he realized she was sobbing.

At dinner that evening, he told the story of the near-drowning with pomp, but inside, he glowed with renewed attachment to his family. For the rest of the vacation, he forgave Varya her most sustained sleep-babbling. He let Klara take the first shower when they returned from the beach, even though her showers took so long that Gertie once banged on the door to ask why, if she needed this much water, Klara did not bring a bar of soap into the ocean. Years later, when Simon and Klara left home —

and after that, when even Varya pulled away from him — Daniel could not understand why they didn't feel what he had: the regret of separation, and the bliss of being returned. He waited. After all, what could he say? *Don't drift too far. You'll miss us.* But as the years passed and they did not, he became wounded and despairing, then bitter.

At two a.m., he walks downstairs to the study. He leaves the overhead light off — the bluish glow of the computer screen is light enough — and enters the address for Raj and Ruby's website. When it loads, large red words appear on the screen.

Experience the WONDERS OF INDIA without leaving your seat! Let RAJ AND RUBY take you on a MAGIC CARPET RIDE of otherworldly delights, from the Indian Needle Trick to the Great Rope Mystery, which famously confounded HOWARD THURSTON — the greatest AMERICAN MAGICIAN of the TWENTIETH CENTURY!

The capitalized letters dance and blink. Below them, Raj's and Ruby's faces loom, bindis on their foreheads. There's a rotating slideshow in the center of the webpage. In one image, Raj is trapped in a basket that Ruby has stabbed with two long swords. In another, Raj holds a snake as thick as Daniel's neck.

It's gaudy, Daniel thinks. Exploitative. Then again, it's Vegas: clearly, gaudy is a selling point. He's been twice — first for a friend's bachelor party, then for a medical conference. Both times, it struck him as a uniquely American monstrosity, everything a blown-up cartoon version of itself. Restaurants called Margaritaville and Cabo Wabo. Volcanoes spewing pink smoke. The Forum Shops, a mall built to look like ancient Rome. Who could feel, living there, like they were in the real world? At least Raj and Ruby travel: their show is based at the Mirage, but a link marked Touring & Schedule shows that they're performing at Boston's Mystery Lounge this weekend. In two weeks, they'll begin a monthlong run in New York City.

Daniel wonders where they plan to spend Thanksgiving. Raj has largely kept Ruby from the Golds, reappearing and disappearing her every couple of years like a rabbit in a hat. Daniel saw her as a passionate three-year-old, then a somber, observant child of five and nine, last as a sullen preteen. That visit ended with an explosive argument about the Jaws of Life, Klara's signature act. Raj was teaching it to Ruby, which sickened Daniel. He could not fathom why Raj would want to re-create the image of Klara hanging from a rope via her daughter.

"I'm keeping her memory alive," Raj had roared. "Can you say the same?"

They haven't spoken since, though this isn't just Raj's fault. There have been plenty of times when Daniel could have reached out — certainly before that falling-out, and even after. But being in the presence of Raj and Ruby has always given Daniel a disturbing feeling of regret. When Ruby was young, she looked like Raj, but in her teens, she assumed Klara's full, dimpled cheeks and Cheshire cat smile. Long, curly hair fell to her waist like Klara's, except that Ruby's was brown — Klara's natural color — instead of red. Sometimes, when she was moody, Daniel experienced a phantasmagoric sense of déjà vu. With holographic ease, Ruby became her mother, and Klara stared at Daniel with accusation. He had not been close enough to her, had not known how sick she was. He had initiated their visit to the fortune teller, too, which affected all of his siblings, but perhaps Klara most of all. He still remembers the way she looked in the alley afterward: wet-cheeked and raw-nosed, her eyes both alert and strangely vacant.

The only phone number Daniel has is

Raj's landline. Since they're traveling, he clicks on Contact. E-mail addresses are listed for Raj and Ruby's manager, publicist, and agent above a box that reads, Write to the Chapals! Who knows if they even check it — the box seems designed for fan mail — but he decides to try.

Raj:

Daniel Gold here. It's been quite some time, so I thought I'd write. I noticed that you'll be traveling to New York in the coming weeks. Any Thanksgiving plans? We'd be happy to host you. It seems a shame to go so long without seeing family.

Best,
DG

Daniel rereads the e-mail and worries it's too casual. He puts *dear* before *Raj,* then deletes it (Raj isn't dear to him, and neither Daniel nor Raj tolerate phoniness; it's one of the few things they have in common). Daniel writes, *Do you have* before *any Thanksgiving plans?* and substitutes *really like* for *be happy* before *to host you.* He deletes the last line — are they family, really? — and then rewrites it. They're close enough. He hits Send.

He figured he'd be up at 6:30 the next morning, despite his suspension — at forty-eight years old, he's nothing if not predictable — but when his cell phone rings, the sun is high in the sky. He squints at the clock, shakes his head, squints again: it's eleven. He fumbles around his bedside table with one hand, finds his glasses and flip phone, puts the first on and opens the second. Could Raj be calling already?

" 'Lo?"

He's greeted by static. "Daniel," says a voice. ". . . t's . . . Dee . . ."

"I'm sorry," says Daniel. "You're breaking up. What was that?"

"It's . . . Dee . . . here in the . . . son . . . ley . . . service . . ."

"Dee?"

". . . Dee," says the voice, insistently. "Eddie O . . . hue . . ."

"Eddie O'Donoghue?" Even in its garbled form, something about the name jogs Daniel's memory. He sits up, stuffing a pillow behind him.

". . . 'es . . . Cop . . . we met . . . cisco . . . your . . . 'ter . . . FBI . . ."

"Oh my God," Daniel says. "Of course."

Eddie O'Donoghue was the FBI agent assigned to Klara's case. He attended her memorial service in San Francisco, and afterward, Daniel ran into him at a pub on Geary. The following day, Daniel woke with a splitting migraine and could not imagine why he'd shared so much with Eddie, but he hoped the agent had been drunk enough to forget it.

". . . pull over," says Eddie, and suddenly, his voice becomes clear. "There we go. Mother of God, the service here is shit. I don't know how you stand it."

"We have a landline," says Daniel. "It's much more reliable."

"Listen, I can't talk long — I'm on the side of the highway — but would that work for you? Four, five o'clock? Some place in town? There's a few things I want to share with you."

Daniel blinks. The phone call — the entire morning — feels surreal.

"Okay," he says. "Let's meet at the Hoffman House. Four thirty."

Not until he hangs up does he notice the wide shadow in the bedroom doorway: his mother.

"Jesus, Ma," Daniel says, pulling the covers up. She still has the power to make him feel like a twelve-year-old. "I didn't see you."

"Who were you talking to?" Gertie is

wearing her quilted pink bathrobe — how many decades she's owned it, Daniel doesn't want to calculate — and her thick gray hair looks like Beethoven's.

"No one," he says. "Mira."

"Like hell it was Mira. I'm not an imbecile."

"No." Daniel gets out of bed, pulls on a SUNY Binghamton sweatshirt and steps into his sheepskin slippers. Then he walks to the doorway and kisses his mother's cheek. "But you are a busybody. Have you eaten?"

"Have I eaten? Of course I've eaten. It's almost noon. And here's you sleeping in like a teenager."

"I've been suspended."

"I know. Mira told me."

"So go easy on me."

"Why do you think I didn't wake you?"

"Oh, I don't know," says Daniel, walking downstairs. "Maybe because I'm no longer a child?"

"Wrong." Gertie sneaks out from behind him and takes the lead, sweeping magisterially into the kitchen. "Because I go easy on you. No one goes easier on you than me. Now sit down if you want me to make you coffee."

■ ■ ■

Gertie moved to Kingston three years ago, in the fall of 2003. Until then, she insisted on remaining at Clinton Street. Usually, Daniel visited monthly, but that year, he had skipped March and April: work was chaotic due to the Iraq invasion, and Gertie assured him that she would spend Passover with a friend.

When he arrived on the first of May, she was in bed, wearing her bathrobe and reading Kafka's *The Trial.* The windows were covered in brown packing paper. Where the wooden-framed mirror above her dresser once hung, there was now a lone nail. She had pried the bathroom mirror, which doubled as the door of the medicine cabinet, off by its hinges, exposing a cluttered pharmacy of prescription pill bottles.

"Ma," said Daniel. His throat was dry. "Who's been prescribing this stuff?"

Gertie walked into the bathroom. Her eyes had a stubborn *Who, me?* quality.

"Doctors."

"Which doctors? How many doctors?"

"Well, I'm not sure I can say. I see a man for my gut problems and a man for my bones. There's the primary physician, the eye doctor, the dentist, the allergy doctor, although I haven't seen her in months, the women's doctor, the physical therapist who thinks I have scoliosis, which nobody once diagnosed even though all my life I've had back pain; there's a little bone in my rib cage that I swear to you pops out when I do what Dr. Kurtzburg calls 'heavy twisting' " — she held up a palm as Daniel began to protest — "and you should be glad I'm being treated, cared for, looked after, an old woman alone, needing what care she can get in this world, and getting it. You," she repeats, keeping her palm aloft, "should be glad."

"You don't have scoliosis."

"You're not my doctor."

"I'm better than that. I'm your son."

"I just remembered the dermatologist. She's keeping an eye on my moles. People think they're just beauty marks, but beauty can kill you. Did you ever consider whether Marilyn Monroe died of a mole? That one on her face she was famous for?"

"Marilyn Monroe committed suicide. She took a bunch of barbiturates."

"Maybe," said Gertie, conspiratorially.

"Why did you take down the mirrors?"

"That's for your brother and your sister and your father," Gertie said. Daniel walked into the kitchen. A tall glass of wine, rimmed by fruit flies, sat on the counter. "And that's for Elijah. Don't touch it."

When Daniel poured the reeking Manischewitz down the drain, a haze of flies rose and dispersed. Gertie huffed. On the other side of the sink was an aluminum tray of store-bought kugel, left uncovered: the noodles were shiny and hard as plastic. Here, as in the bedroom, the windows were covered with paper.

"Why did you black out the windows?"

"There's reflections in there, too," Gertie said, her pupils dilating, and Daniel knew something had to be done.

Initially, Gertie refused, but she was flattered to think Daniel wanted her close and relieved by the end of her solitude. They moved her out of Manhattan in August. Varya had relocated to California to take a job at the Drake Institute for Research on Aging, but she flew east to assist. By evening, the apartment was so denuded that Daniel felt sorrow at having done it. Once they carried out Saul's pea-green velvet chair, a hideous piece of furniture that the entire family adored, the only remaining task was to dismantle the bunk beds.

"I won't watch," said Gertie — half-threatening, half-despondent. The bunk beds had been purchased at Sears forty years earlier, but even after Klara and Simon were gone, she wouldn't take them down. At first she claimed that everyone would need a place to sleep, should Daniel and Mira and Varya all visit at once, but when Daniel suggested that at least one of the pairs could be taken apart, Gertie became so agitated that he knew not to raise the issue again. Before Mira ushered her down to the car, Gertie insisted on having her picture taken with the bunks. She stood holding her pocketbook and smiling gaily, like a tourist in front of the Taj Mahal, before she trundled quickly out of the bedroom, turning her face toward the wall so that they could not see it.

Daniel closed the front door behind her and returned to the bedroom. At first, he didn't see Varya. But snuffling noises came from her old top bunk, and when Daniel peered upward, he saw her right foot listing over the edge. Tears rolled sideways out of each eye, creating two wet circles on the mattress.

"Oh, V," he said. He began to reach for her, then thought better of it: he knew she didn't like to be touched. For years, he was hurt by her habit of ducking hugs, and by her general distance. They were the only two left, and sometimes it took weeks for her to return his calls. But what could he do? It was too late for either of them to change very much.

"I was just thinking about," Varya said, and inhaled. "When I used to sleep here."

"What, when we were kids?"

"No. When we were older. When I was" — she hiccupped — "visiting."

The word seemed freighted with meaning, but Daniel had no idea what that meaning was. This was the way it went with her: the landscape she saw was different, certain things portentous or ominous, Varya veering around what seemed to him an unblemished piece of sidewalk. Sometimes he thought of asking her, but then whatever channel had opened up between them closed, as it did now: Varya wiped her face hurriedly with one hand and swung her legs around to the ladder.

But she couldn't climb down. The ladder was attached to the top bunk with screws so old that the sudden force of Varya's weight caused them to pull out of the wood. The ladder keeled to the floor; Varya cried out, one foot dangling. The jump from the top bunk to the floor was far from dangerous, but she clung to the railing, looking dubiously over the edge.

Daniel held his arms out. "Come here, you old bird," he said.

Varya paused. Then she gasped her laughter and reached for him. He put his hands under her armpits, and she held on to his shoulders as he lowered her to the ground.

22.

Fifteen years ago, Klara's memorial took place at the San Francisco Columbarium. Raj planned to have her body sent to the Gold family plot in Queens, but Gertie initially forbade it. When Daniel confronted his mother, she cited the Jewish law that prohibits those who commit suicide from being buried within six feet of other Jewish dead, as though only the strictest adherence could protect the Golds who remained. Daniel raged at Gertie until she cowered; he could have hit her. He had never felt capable of such a thing before.

Daniel and Mira had just moved to Kingston. Mira had secured an assistant professorship at SUNY New Paltz in art history and Jewish studies, Daniel an overnight position at the hospital. His job would begin in one month, his wedding would take place in six, and he had never felt more incapacitated. Simon's death had been shattering enough; how was it possible to lose Klara, too? How could the family sustain it? After the memorial, Daniel stumbled into an Irish pub on Geary, lay his head on the bar, and wept. He was scarcely aware of how he looked, or what he was saying — *Oh God, oh God; everyone's dying* — until someone responded.

"Yes," said the man on the next barstool. "But that never makes it any easier."

Daniel looked up. The man was roughly his age, with strawberry blond hair and thick sideburns. His eyes — a queer color, more gold than brown — were threaded with red. A scruff of stubble extended from his cheeks to the bottom of his neck.

He raised his Guinness. "Eddie O'Donoghue."

"Daniel Gold."

Eddie nodded. "I saw you at the service. I investigated your sister's passing." He reached into the pocket of his black pants and pulled out an FBI ID. *Special Agent,* it read, beside an unintelligible signature.

"Oh," Daniel managed. "Thank you."

Was that what one said, under the circumstances? Daniel was glad, very glad, that Klara's death was being investigated — he had his own suspicions — but he was alarmed that the feds were involved.

"If you don't mind my asking," he said, "why did the FBI take the case? Why not the local police?"

Eddie put his ID away and looked at Daniel. Despite the bloodshot eyes and the scruff, he looked like a boy. "I was in love with her."

Daniel nearly choked on his own saliva. "What?"

"I was in love with her," repeated Eddie.

"With — my sister? She was unfaithful to Raj?"

"No, no. I doubt she knew him back then. Anyway, it wasn't returned."

The bartender appeared. "Get you boys anything?"

"I'll have another. And so will he. On me." Eddie nodded at Daniel's glass of bourbon, a bourbon Daniel only just realized he'd been drinking.

"Thank you," said Daniel. When the bartender left, he turned to Eddie. "How did you meet her?"

"I was on duty in San Francisco. Your mother called us — she said your brother was a runaway, and she asked us to pick him up. This was, what, a dozen years ago? He couldn't have been older than sixteen. I roughed him up; I shouldn't have. I don't think your sister ever forgave me. Even so, she woke me up. When I saw her outside the station, with her hair blowing back and those boots on, I thought she was the most gorgeous woman I'd ever seen. Not just because she was beautiful, but because she was powerful. So I remembered her."

Eddie finished his beer, wiped the froth off his mouth.

"Couple years later I came across a flier with her face on it," he said, "and I started to go see her perform. The first time must have been early '83; I'd had a god-awful day, bunch of junkies killed each other in the Tenderloin, and when I sat down to watch her I felt — transported. One night, I told her so. How she'd helped me. How her show had made me different. It took months to work up the courage. But she wanted nothing to do with me."

The bartender returned with their drinks. Daniel gulped. He had no idea how to respond to Eddie's revelations, which were intimate enough to make him uncomfortable. All the same, they numbed his despair: as long as Eddie talked, his sister was suspended in the room.

"I'll be honest with you," Eddie said. "I was not in good shape. My dad had just passed, and I was drinking too much. I knew I had to get out of San Francisco, so I applied for the bureau. Straight out of Quantico, they had me in Vegas working on mortgage fraud. When I passed the Mirage and saw Klara's face on the sign, I just about thought I'd gone crazy. Next day, I see her in the parking lot at Vons. I'm driving an Oldsmobile, and she's on the curb with a baby."

"Ruby."

"That her name? Cute kid, even when she was screaming. Your sister ran; I must've scared her. I didn't mean to. Soon as I saw her, I wanted to talk to her. So I decided I'd go to her opening. I'd stay afterward, I figured, and make sure we were clear. No hard feelings. Nothing for her to be nervous about."

They stared straight ahead. It was the gift of parallel bar seating, Daniel thought: that you could have a conversation without ever looking the other person in the eye.

"Night before, I couldn't sleep. I get to the Mirage early. I'm pacing outside the theater when I see the three of them come in, Klara and her man and the baby," said Eddie. "She's arguing with the guy — I can see it from a mile away. When he goes into the theater, she takes the baby in the elevator. The elevators are glass, so I get in the one beside her: keep my head down, watch to see where she gets off. She dropped the baby at a day care on seventeen before she rode up to forty-five. She didn't seem to know where she was going until a maid came out of the penthouse suite. When the maid left, Klara slipped in."

Daniel was grateful for the dimness of the bar and the liquor, grateful that there were places one could go at one in the afternoon for darkness. The beard he'd just started to grow was salty with tears.

"Friday night," Eddie said, "and everyone was out. I'd never heard Vegas so quiet. And here's what you learn, being a cop: peaceful is nice, so's quiet, but if it goes on too long it's not peace and quiet. I ran down the hall and I knocked on the door. 'Ma'am,' I shout. 'Miss Gold.' But there's no answer. So I got a key from the front desk and I went back up." He drank until his beer was finished. "I shouldn't say any more."

"It's all right," said Daniel. He had already lost her. What he heard now would make little difference.

"At first, I didn't know what I was seeing. I thought she was practicing. She was strung up on the rope, like in her show; she was spinning, just barely; but the bit hung off beside her jaw. I laid my hands on her. I wanted to heal her. I tried to breathe into

310

her mouth."

Daniel was wrong. What he heard did make a difference. "That's enough."

"I'm sorry." In the dark, Eddie's pupils were oversized, gleaming. "She didn't deserve it."

Elvis's "Love Me Tender" came on the jukebox. Daniel gripped his glass.

"So how did you get the case?" he asked.

"I was the one who found her. That counted for something. And then I argued. Major murder cases, crimes that cross state boundaries, kidnappings — those are all under the jurisdiction of the FBI, not the police. Sure, it looked like a suicide, but my radar was up and something was off. I knew they'd crossed state lines. I knew she'd been stealing. And I knew I had a funny feeling about Chapal."

"Raj," said Daniel, startled. "You suspect him?"

"I'm an agent. I suspect everyone. Do you?"

Daniel paused. "I barely knew him. I do think he was controlling. He didn't like for her to stay in touch with us." He squeezed his eyes shut. It was horrible, this use of the past tense.

"I'll look into it," Eddie said. "You have any other suspicions?"

Daniel wished he had other suspicions. He wanted a reason, but all he had was a coincidence. When Simon died, Daniel had not thought of the woman on Hester Street. His death was so shocking as to erase all other thoughts from Daniel's mind, and after all, Simon had never shared his prophecy. But Daniel remembered Klara's: the woman had said she'd die at thirty-one. And that was exactly the age she had been.

"There's only one thing I can think of," he said. "It's horseshit. But it's strange."

Eddie lifted his hands. "No judgment."

Pain ricocheted in Daniel's skull. He wasn't sure whether it was the alcohol or the impending disclosure, which he had not even made to Mira. When he finished telling Eddie about the woman on Hester Street — her reputation and their visit, the timing of Klara's death — Eddie frowned. He'd look into it, he said, but Daniel didn't have much hope. He sensed he'd disappointed the agent — that Eddie wanted secrets or conflict, not the childhood memory of a traveling psychic.

Six months later, when Klara's death was ruled a suicide, Daniel was not surprised. It was the simplest hypothesis, and the simplest hypothesis, he'd learned, was usually right. His advisor in medical school had been a student of Dr. Theodore Woodward and liked to quote what Woodward told his medical interns: "When you hear hoof beats, think horses, not zebras."

Fourteen years later and ten states east, Daniel enters the Hoffman House to meet Eddie again. The Hoffman was a fortification and lookout during the Revolutionary War; now it serves burgers and beer. Aside from its architecture — Dutch rubble construction, white shutters, low ceilings, and wide-planked wood floors — the only reminder of the Hoffman's history is the annual arrival of war enthusiasts, who come to reenact the British Burning of Kingston.

At first, Daniel was intrigued by the reenactors. He was certainly impressed by their attention to detail. They make their costumes by hand, based on original documents and paintings, and carry their weapons in white linen haversacks. But they grate on him now: the women bustling around in petticoats and white bonnets, the men scrambling with fake muskets like actors run amok from a community theater. The cannons still make him jump. What's more, the premise annoys him. Why rehearse the drama of a war long past when there's one in the present? The reenactors' determination to live in a different time unnerves him. It reminds him of Klara.

Today, at the Hoffman, there is only Eddie O'Donoghue. He sits in a wooden booth beside the fireplace, nursing a beer. Across from him is a glass of untouched bourbon.

"Woodford Reserve," Eddie says. "Hope that's all right."

Daniel clasps Eddie's hand. "Good memory."

"That's what they pay me for. It's good to see you."

They look at each other: Daniel and Eddie, Eddie and Daniel. Like Eddie, Daniel is at least twenty pounds heavier than he was in 1991. Like Daniel, Eddie must be nearly fifty, if he isn't fifty already. Daniel's eyebrows sprawl like intrepid explorers, so fast growing that Mira bought him an industrial trimmer for Hanukkah; Eddie's face has softened and swelled, like a hang-dog, around the jaw. But his eyes, like Daniel's, are bright with recognition. Daniel is nervous — he can only imagine that something new has emerged in Klara's case — but he's glad to see Eddie, who feels like a friend.

"Appreciate you taking off work to meet with me," Eddie says, and Daniel does not correct him. "I won't keep you waiting."

Daniel is conscious of his worn jeans and sweater, the latter a decade-old gift from Mira. Eddie wears a dress shirt and slacks, a sport coat thrown over the back of the booth. He lifts a black briefcase from the bench, sets it on the table, and unlatches it. Out comes a notebook and folder, also black. Eddie removes a sheet of paper and turns it toward Daniel.

"Any of these people look familiar to you?"

On the page are at least twelve photo-copied photos. Daniel reaches into his jacket pocket for his glasses. Most are mug shots, small squares within which a variety of dark-haired, dark-eyed people scowl or glare, though a couple of teenagers grin, and one young man flashes the peace sign. Below the mug shots are three photos of a heavy-set, white-haired woman. They look like security shots taken in the vestibule of a building.

"I don't think so. Who are they?"

"The Costellos," says Eddie. "This woman here?" He points to the first mug shot, which shows a woman perhaps in her seventies. Her hair is waved like that of a 1940s movie star, her eyes heavy lidded and cool. "That's Rosa. She's the matriarch. This is her husband, Donnie; these two are her sisters. This row is her children — she's got five — and below are *their* children: that's nine more. Eighteen people in all. Eighteen people running the most sophisticated fortune-telling fraud in U.S. history."

"Fortune-telling fraud?"

"That's right." Eddie folds his hands and leans back for effect. "Now, fortune-telling is notoriously difficult to prosecute. It's banned in some parts of the country, but those bans are rarely enforced. After all, we've got people who predict what the stock market is going to do. We've got people who predict the weather and get paid for it. Hell, there are horoscopes in every newspaper. What's more, it's a cultural issue. These people, they're what's called the Rom, the Romani; you might know them as Gypsies. They ran from the Mongols and the Europeans and the Nazis. Historically, they're poor, they're underserved. They don't go to school — they're bred for fortune-telling since birth. So when you nab someone on fraud charges, what's the first thing the defense is gonna do? They're gonna frame it as a free speech issue. They're gonna frame it as discrimination. So how'd we do it? How'd we convict the Costellos of fourteen federal crimes?"

Something sour rises to the base of Daniel's throat. Eddie doesn't have information about Klara, he realizes. Eddie has information about the woman on Hester Street.

"I don't know," he says. "How?"

"I'll tell you a story about a man we'll call Jim." Eddie lowers his voice. "This man Jim had lost a child to cancer. His wife divorced him. His anxiety was through the roof, and he was in constant muscular pain. So you have a really sick guy, a guy who no one in the mainstream medical establishment will deal with because he's so off-putting, such a pain in the ass, that his relationships with conventional doctors deteriorate — you get a guy like that, it's no wonder he winds up on the doorstep of someone different, someone who says, 'I can help you; I can do you good.' Someone like Rosa Costello."

Rosa Costello. Daniel looks at her picture. He knows she isn't the woman he met in 1969. Her lips are too plump; her face is heart shaped. In a word, she's prettier. And yet, in his mind, she morphs. Her face assumes the woman's bullish chin and flat, unaccommodating eyes.

"So this is how it starts," Eddie says. "This reader, this Rosa Costello, she goes, 'I'm gonna sell you a candle for fifty dollars, and I'm gonna burn it for you and say this prayer, and you're gonna notice a difference in your nerves.' And when Jim doesn't notice a difference, she goes, 'Okay, so we gotta do more. Let me sell you these leaves, spiritual leaves, and we're gonna burn these and say a different prayer.' Fast-forward two years and this man has undergone several healing rituals and two very dramatic sacrifices the sum total of which is somewhere in the vicinity of forty thousand dollars. Finally, Rosa says, 'It's your money that's the problem, it's cursed and it's trouble, so you have to bring me ten thousand more, and we'll get the hex removed.' The sum was termed a donation; this family was termed a church. The Church of the Free Spirit, they called themselves."

Daniel hadn't thought he was hungry, but when a waiter appears beside them, he's ravenous. Eddie orders the tavern wings. Daniel picks the calamari.

"What you have to understand about these cases," Eddie continues, once they're alone, "is that they make prosecutors run like hell. But the Costellos were different. The Costellos were thumbing their noses. When we seized their assets, we found cars, motorcycles, boats, gold jewelry. We found homes on the Intracoastal Waterway. We found fifty million dollars."

"Jesus Christ."

"Hang on," says Eddie, raising a hand. "Before the pleas are entered, their defense attorney files a twenty-four-page request for dismissal on the grounds of freedom of religion. They're their own church, remember? The Church of the goddamn Free Spirit! What's more, he claims, this is nothing but the most recent example in a long line of Romani persecution. Now, am I saying that all Gypsies are swindlers and crooks? Absolutely not. But we got nine of these ones on grand larceny, false income returns, mail fraud, wire fraud, money laundering. We subpoenaed birth records — we wanted to get everyone involved in this thing. There was just one person we couldn't find."

Eddie points to the security shots of the woman in the vestibule. She wears a long brown coat and gray shoes that close with Velcro. Her hands rest on the railing of a revolving door, and her white hair hangs in two long, slender braids.

"Oh my God," Daniel says.

"That your woman?"

Daniel nods. He sees it now. The broad forehead. The pinched, unfriendly mouth. He remembers watching her mouth as she spelled out his future. He remembers the part of her lips, the wet pink tongue.

"I want you to look carefully," Eddie says. "I want you to be sure."

"I'm sure." Daniel exhales. "Who is she?"

"She's Rosa's sister. It could be she's involved; it could be she isn't. What we do know is that she seems to be estranged from the rest of the family. You find the Rom living in groups, which is why it's unusual that your woman works alone. Here's how she's typical, though: she's always traveling. And she's savvy. She works under a number of aliases. She's not licensed, which is illegal in most parts of the country, but it also keeps her out of the system."

"This family," says Daniel. "Do they not accept payment in the beginning? Because that's how it was with us. She didn't ask, or my brother didn't give it to her. And I've always found that strange."

Eddie laughs. "Do they accept payment? They accepted all the payment they could get. Maybe this woman went easy on you 'cause you were kids."

"But if that were true, then why would she have said such hideous things? Klara was nine. I was eleven, and she still scared me shitless. The only thing I've been able to come up with is that she used fear to hook her customers — like the worse she scares them, the more likely they are to come back.

To become dependent."

When he was a medical resident in Chicago, Daniel shadowed a doctor who used similar techniques: insisting that someone's depression could not be managed without regular visits, or telling an obese patient he'd die without surgery.

"Or it doesn't matter what she says, because she's already cornered the market. Romani fortune-telling is usually very formulaic: they talk about your love life, your money, your job. Giving you a date of death? That's ballsy. It's shrewd. The Rom do a couple other things — the men lay pavement, sell used cars, they do body and fender work — but even if the world stops producing pavement, even if we stop using cars, what's the one thing that'll be around as long as human beings? Our desire to know. And we'll pay anything for it. The Rom have been telling fortunes for hundreds of years with an equal amount of economic success. But your woman goes a step further. If she's telling you when you'll die, she's offering a service that even the other Rom don't. She has no competition."

The fireplace is making Daniel sweat. He pulls off his sweater, tugging down the polo shirt beneath. It occurs to him that he hasn't told Mira where he is, and that he's supposed to meet her at temple at six. But he can't leave, not now, not even to write her one of the text messages he's finally figured out how to send.

"What else do you know about them?" he asks as the waiter arrives with their food.

Eddie drags a wing through a glop of electric-orange sauce, then dunks it in thick ranch dressing. "About the Costellos? They came to Florida from Italy in the thirties. Probably they were running from Hitler. Like all of the Rom, they're very private. When they're not with customers, they speak their own language; they don't even try to assimilate. They need the *gazhe* for money — that's the non-Rom, like us — but they also think we're polluted." He wipes his mouth. "It's the women who tell fortunes. They see it as a gift from God. But because the women interact with the *gazhe,* the Rom think the women are polluted, too. They're very obsessive about cleanliness, purity. You go into a Romani house, it's gonna be spotless."

"But the woman I saw — her place was cluttered. I'd almost call it filthy." Daniel frowns. "Did you ask the family about her?"

"Of course we did. But they wouldn't talk. Which is why I'm talking to you."

"What do you want to know?"

Eddie pauses. "What I'm about to ask you — I'm aware it's sensitive. I'm aware you might not want to discuss it. But I'm asking you to try. Like I said: we haven't found much. Sure, this woman isn't registered, but we're not gonna charge her for that. What we're interested in is the fact that we've linked her to a number of deaths. Suicides."

It's so simple, so instantaneous, the body's response: Daniel's hunger is gone. He could vomit.

"Now, we've found no direct, causal relationship," says Eddie. "These are people who've gone to see her two, ten, sometimes twenty years earlier. But there are several of them — five, including your sister. Which is enough to make you wonder." He folds his hands and leans toward Daniel. "So here's what I want to know. I want to know if she said anything — did anything — to push you in that direction. Or if she did it to Klara."

"Not to me. I told her what I wanted from her, and she gave it to me. It was transactional. I didn't get the sense she cared what I did with the information once I left." There's a crawling feeling on his neck, many-legged and swift, like a centipede, though when Daniel uses his index finger to probe beneath his shirt collar, he feels nothing. It occurs to him that Eddie has not mentioned whether this is a conversation or an interview. "As for Klara, I'm not sure. She never told me she felt pressured. But she was different to begin with."

"Different how?"

"She was vulnerable. A little unstable. Susceptible, I guess. Which may have been something she was born with — or maybe it developed over time." Daniel pushes his food away. He doesn't want to look at the squid's mantle, sliced in perfect rings, or the arms curling inward. "I know what I told you after the memorial: I thought it was a very strange coincidence, the fact that this fortune teller predicted Klara's death. But I was distraught. I wasn't thinking clearly. Yes, the fortune teller was right, but only because Klara chose to believe her. There's no mystery in that."

Daniel pauses. He feels deeply uneasy, though it takes him a moment to identify why.

"On the other hand," Daniel adds, "if you *do* think this woman had something to do with it — if we entertain the thought of that very slim chance — then frankly, I blame myself. I was the one who heard about her. I was the one who dragged my siblings to that apartment."

"Daniel. You can't blame yourself." Eddie's hand is poised above the notebook, but his brow softens with compassion. "You doing that is like blaming our man Jim for going to see Rosa. You doing that, it's blaming the victim. It can't have been easy on you, either, going to this woman at such a young age. Hearing when she says you're gonna die."

Daniel has not forgotten his date — the twenty-fourth of November, this year — but neither has he given it credence. Most of the people he knows who died young were the unlucky recipients of hellish diagnoses: AIDS, like Simon, or an untreatable cancer. Just two weeks ago, Daniel had his annual physical. On the way there, he felt rattled, but afterward he was embarrassed for having let the superstition of it get to him. Apart from a bit of weight gain and borderline elevated cholesterol, he was in excellent health.

"Sure," he says. "I was a kid; it was an unpleasant experience. But I shook it off a long time ago."

"And what if Klara couldn't?" asks Eddie, jabbing his index finger in emphasis. "This is what scammers do: they go after whoever's most vulnerable. Look — this susceptibility you're talking about? Think of it like a gene. The fortune teller may have been the environmental factor that triggered it. Or maybe she noticed it in Klara. Maybe she preyed on it."

"Maybe," echoes Daniel, but he bristles. He realizes that Eddie likely invoked a medical metaphor to appeal to Daniel's expertise, but the idea sounds pseudoscientific and the effort feels condescending. What does Eddie know about gene expression, much less Klara's phenotype? Eddie is better off sticking to what he does best. Daniel would not tell him how to run an interrogation.

"And what about your brother?" Eddie glances down at his notes. "He died in '82, didn't he? Did the fortune teller predict that?"

Something about Eddie's gesture — the brief peek at the open folder, enough to suggest he had to look to find the date but too short to actually do it — irritates Daniel more. He has no doubt that Eddie knows the year of Simon's death, as well as a host of other things about Simon — things Daniel surely doesn't.

"I don't have any idea. He never told us what she said to him. But my brother was always going to do exactly what he wanted.

He was a gay man who lived in San Francisco in the eighties and contracted AIDS. To me, that seems pretty damn clear."

"All right." Eddie keeps his wrists on the table but lifts his fingers and palms. A gesture of appeasement: the edge in Daniel's voice was not lost on him. "I appreciate what you've given me. And if anything else comes to mind" — he passes a business card across the table — "you have my number."

Eddie stands and closes his folder, tapping it once on the table to level the papers inside. He tucks the folder into his briefcase and slings his jacket over one shoulder.

"Hey, I looked you up," he says. "Saw you're still working with our troops."

"That's right," says Daniel, but then his throat becomes plugged, and he finds himself unable to go on.

"Good stuff," says Eddie on his way out, clapping Daniel on the back with the genial encouragement of a Little League coach. "Keep it up."

Daniel walks briskly to his car and departs with a lurch. He feels both wired and drained; he didn't realize how disturbing it would be to revisit the story of the woman in such detail, or to hear the scope of her family's transgressions. It's so painful to contemplate the deaths of his siblings that Daniel has done it only in isolation: lying awake while Mira sleeps or driving home from work in winter, the road lit by headlights, the radio rattling in the background.

What he told Eddie is true: he doesn't buy the fortune teller's claims. He believes in bad choices; he believes in bad luck. And yet the memory of the woman on Hester Street is like a miniscule needle in his stomach, something he swallowed long ago and which floats, undetectable, except for moments when he moves a certain way and feels a prick.

He's never told Mira. She grew up in Berkeley, the studious child of musicians — her father Christian, her mother Jewish — who produced interfaith songs for children. Mira loves her parents, but she can't bear to listen to "Oy to the World" or "Little Drummer Mensch," and she has little patience for New Age institutions. It's no wonder she gravitated toward Judaism: she likes its intellectualism and morality, its lawfulness.

Before they married, Daniel thought she would find the story of the fortune teller childish. He didn't want to drive her away. After Klara's death, he longed to share it, but again, he did not. This time, he feared Mira's brow would furrow with concern — a tiny, delicate *v*, like a goose sure of its direction. He feared she would see in him an alignment with Klara: her eccentricity, her lack of reason. Even her illness. And he was not aligned with Klara — this much Daniel knew. There was no reason to make Mira think so.

23

Raj and Ruby are coming for Thanksgiving. On Friday, Raj e-mailed Daniel and agreed.

They'll arrive on Tuesday, two days before the holiday, so Daniel and Mira spend the weekend preparing. They wash the linens in the guest room and set up the fold-out in Daniel's study. They clean the house: Mira the kitchen and living room, Daniel the bedrooms and bathrooms, Gertie the dining room. They go to Rhinebeck to buy produce at Breezy Hill Orchard and cheeses at Grand Cru. Before they drive back across the river to Kingston, they stop at Bella Vita for a centerpiece with tulips and pomegranates and apricot-colored roses. Daniel carries it back to the car. Against the dim November sky, the flowers seem to glow.

The doorbell rings two hours early, while Mira is teaching and Gertie is taking a nap. Daniel scrambles downstairs, still in his

Binghamton T-shirt and furry moccasins, cursing himself for not having changed. Through the peephole: a man and a girl, or not a girl — a teenager, nearly as tall as her father. Daniel pulls the door open. It's drizzling outside; a stream of droplets rests on Ruby's lustrous, copper-black mane.

"Raj," Daniel says. "And Rubina."

Instantly, he feels self-conscious for resorting to her full name, a name listed on her birth certificate and rarely, to his knowledge, used since. But she appears so changed, looking not like the child he remembers but like an adult he's never met, that what came to him was the equally adult, never-met name: Rubina.

"Hi," says Ruby. She wears a fuchsia velour sweat suit tucked into knee-high Ugg boots. When she smiles, she looks so much like Klara that Daniel nearly winces.

"Daniel," says Raj, stepping forward to shake his hand. "It's good to see you."

When Daniel last saw Raj, he looked anemically handsome, like a street dog: sharp chin, sharp cheekbones, slant of nose. Now he is trim and healthy, his upper body toned beneath a hooded cashmere sweater. His hair is neatly clipped. There's a comb of gray at his temples, but his face has fewer wrinkles than Daniel's. He holds a juice of

331

an unappealing, green-brown color.

"And you," says Daniel. "Come on in. Gertie's sleeping and Mira's teaching, but they'll both be here soon. Can I get you something to drink?"

"I'd love a glass of water," Raj says.

He pulls a silver Tumi suitcase through the doorway. Ruby has a Louis Vuitton duffel bag. She turns to hitch it onto one shoulder. Across the back of her sweatpants are two words, encrusted in rhinestones: *Juicy,* in elaborate capitals, and in smaller, less-eye-catching capitals, *Couture.*

"You sure?" asks Daniel, closing the door. "I have a great Barolo in the garage."

Why is he trying to impress Raj? To make up for his schlubby T-shirt and moccasins? He's already thinking of what he'll cook for breakfast tomorrow morning: a frittata, perhaps, with fontina and what's left of the heirloom tomatoes.

"Oh," says Raj. "No need. But thank you."

"It's no hassle." Suddenly, Daniel is desperate for a drink. "It's just languishing down there, waiting for a time like this."

"Really," says Raj. "I'm fine. But feel free."

A pause as their eyes meet, and Daniel understands: Raj doesn't drink. A large silver watch slides down on Raj's wrist.

"Of course," says Daniel. "Water, then.

And let's get you settled. The guest room has a queen bed, and there's a fold-out in my office. We've set up both."

Ruby has been typing something on a skinny, pink flip phone — that Motorola Razr all the teenagers have — but now she snaps it shut. "Dad'll take the fold-out."

"Incorrect," says Raj.

"And I'll have a glass of the Barolo," she adds.

"Wrong again," Raj says.

Ruby slits her eyes and smirks, but when Raj raises his eyebrows, Ruby's smirk becomes a real smile.

"Silly old Dad," she says, following Daniel to the office. "Spoilsport old Dad. Spoilsport Daddy longlegs."

The next morning, a Wednesday, Daniel wakes at ten. He curses. He hears the shower in the master bathroom — Mira — and hopes Raj and Ruby have slept in, too. Shocking to Daniel, how late they were up, even more shocking how well it went — a leisurely, two-hour dinner with his mother, his wife, his brother-in-law, and his niece, as if such a thing were normal for them, followed by chocolates and tea in the living room. Daniel broke out the Barolo after all, and even Gertie trundled to bed after eleven.

Daniel stayed up even later. His desktop computer is in the office, where Ruby was sleeping. Mira was in bed, too, so Daniel took the opportunity to retrieve her laptop from the bedside table and carry it into the master bathroom.

The Louis Vuitton suitcase sparked his curiosity. Most designer brands mean nothing to him, but he recognized those iconic brown and tan letters. Raj's watch, too, was clearly expensive. And the cashmere hoodie: who wears such a thing? So Daniel investigated. He knew they were doing well — in 2003, when Roy Horn was mauled by one of the duo's white tigers, Ruby and Raj replaced Siegfried and Roy as the Mirage's main act — but what he learned via Google astounded him. Their home, a gated, all-white estate, has been profiled in *Luxury Las Vegas* and *Architectural Digest.* The gates are marked with an ornate *RC* and open onto a mile-long driveway that leads to thirty acres of interconnected mansions and walkways. There's a meditation center, a movie theater, and an animal habitat where black swans and ostriches can be visited for a hefty entrance fee. For Ruby's thirteenth birthday, Raj bought her a Shetland pony, a rather overfed specimen named Krystal with whom Ruby posed for the teen magazine *Bossy* — Ruby's arms slung around the pony's neck, her dark mane lying atop Krystal's blond one. In the article, a pdf of which Daniel found online, *Bossy* identifies Ruby as the youngest millionaire in Las Vegas.

Why didn't Daniel know all this? Is it that he didn't want to? He's avoided reading about Ruby and Raj's act, mostly because it makes him think about the disaster of their last meeting and the guilt he feels about his distance from them. Now he couldn't help but rethink the previous night. Daniel and Mira purchased their house in 1990, when they couldn't afford Cornwall-on-Hudson or Rhinebeck and still believed Kingston was up-and-coming. Daniel imagined Raj and Ruby driving into town, expecting a historical site — Kingston was once the capital of New York — and finding a city still struggling to right itself after the closure of the IBM factory that employed seven thousand residents. He saw them pass the abandoned technology center and Main Street, fallen into shabby disrepair. How must they have regarded the fold-out cot in Daniel's office and the expensive cheese — the former an embarrassment, the latter an attempt to make up for it?

He could not bear to contemplate his return to work on Monday, and what might happen if he holds his ground when it comes to the waivers. Days earlier, he submitted a request to review his case with the local Area Defense Counsel, a military attorney who provides representation for accused service members. He knows that Mira is right — it's best to be aware of what options he has to defend himself — but the request alone was humiliating. Without a job, who would he be? Someone who sat on a bath mat with his back against the toilet, reading about his brother-in-law's solarium, he thought — an image terrible enough to force him to bed, so that he could fall asleep and stop seeing it.

Now he dresses nicely and hurries downstairs. Raj and Ruby sit at the kitchen counter, sipping orange juice and eating omelets.

"Crap," says Daniel. "I'm sorry. I wanted to cook for you."

"Nothing to apologize for." Raj is freshly showered, wearing another expensive-looking sweater — sage green this time — and a pair of dark jeans. "We rattled around."

"We always get up early," says Ruby.

"Ruby's school starts at seven thirty," Raj says.

"Except on performance days," Ruby says. "On performance days, we sleep late."

"Oh?" says Daniel. Coffee will help. Mira usually has it ready for him, but today, the pot is empty. "Why's that?"

"Because we're out so late. Till one, sometimes. Or later," Ruby says. "On those days, we homeschool."

She's still in her pajamas: SpongeBob SquarePants scrubs and a white tank top with a pink bra underneath. The effect is disconcerting — the childish pants and the tank, which isn't tight, exactly, but still shows more than Daniel expected to see.

"Oh," he says again. "That sounds complicated."

"See?" asks Ruby, turning to Raj.

"It's not complicated," Raj says. "School days, early. Performance days, late."

"Have you seen my mother?" asks Daniel.

"Yup," says Ruby. "She was up early, too. We had coffee together. Then she went to Tai Chi." She puts her fork down with a clatter. "Hey, do you have a juicer?"

"A juicer?" asks Daniel.

"Yeah. Dad and I found this in the fridge" — Ruby lifts her glass; orange juice sloshes precariously close to the rim — "but we prefer to make our own."

"I'm afraid we don't," says Daniel. "Have a juicer."

"That's okay," Ruby chirps. She spears a folded corner of omelet. "So, what kind of stuff do you guys like to have for breakfast?"

She's only making conversation, Daniel knows, but he's having trouble keeping up. What's more, the coffee machine isn't turning on. He's filled the filter with grounds, poured the water in, and flicked the switch that starts the brewing process, but the little red light remains off.

"I'm not much for breakfast, actually," he says. "Usually, I just bring a mug of coffee to work."

Soft padding of feet on the stairwell, and Mira sweeps into the kitchen. Her hair, shiny and freshly blown out, lifts like a wing.

"Good morning," she says.

"Morning," says Raj.

"Morning," says Ruby. She turns back to Daniel. "Why aren't you at work today?"

"The plug, sweetheart," says Mira. She crosses behind him, touching the small of his back, and plugs the machine into the wall. The red light comes on immediately.

"It's the day before Thanksgiving, Roo," says Raj. "No one's at work."

"Oh," says Ruby. "Right." Another corner

of omelet. She's eating her way in, leaving a thick, stacked blob of central toppings. "You're a doctor, aren't you?"

"I am." The humiliation of it — his career so long established, now precarious — is exacerbated by Raj's mansion, his cashmere, his juicer. It takes monumental effort for Daniel to remember Ruby's question. "I work for a military entrance processing station. I make sure that soldiers are healthy enough to go to war."

Raj laughs. "Well, if that ain't an oxymoron. How do you like it?"

"Very much," says Daniel. "I've been with the military for over fifteen years."

He still feels proud to say it. Coffee drips thinly into the pot.

"Okay," says Raj, as if agreeing to a stalemate.

"And you?" asks Mira. "How are you two enjoying work?"

Raj smiles. "We love it."

Mira leans forward with her elbows on the counter. "It's so exciting — such a different world from ours. We'd love the opportunity to see you perform. You're welcome anytime at the Ulster Performing Arts Center, though I'm afraid it might not be up to your standards."

"And you're welcome to come to Vegas,"

says Raj. "We're on every week, Thursday through Sunday."

"Four nights in a row," says Mira. "It must be exhausting."

"I don't think so." Raj's voice is mild, but his smile is pasted on. "Rubina, on the other hand —"

"Dad," says Ruby. "Don't call me that."

"But it's your name."

"Yeah, it's like" — Ruby scrunches her nose — "my *God*-given name, but it's not my *name.*"

"Oops," says Daniel, smiling. "I called you Rubina yesterday."

"Oh, that's okay," says Ruby. "I mean, you're a stranger."

The word hangs in the room for seconds before her face drops.

"Oh, gosh," she says. "I'm sorry. I didn't mean — you're not a *stranger.*"

She looks pleadingly at Raj. Daniel is touched by the gesture: the teenager running back to a parent's legs to cling, to hide.

"That's okay, sweetheart." Raj ruffles her hair. "Everyone understands."

They pile into Daniel's car, all five of them, everyone offering the front seat to Gertie and acquiescing when she demurs to sit beside Ruby in the back. They drive to the maritime museum and the historic district and take a brief hike through Mohonk Preserve. Daniel races Ruby across a field, mud flying up to streak their jackets. The air in his lungs is gloriously cold, and he gasps with pleasure. When it begins to snow, he expects Ruby to complain, but she claps. "It's like Narnia!" she exclaims, and everyone laughs as they walk back to the car.

She surprises him in other ways, too. At dinner, for instance, when Gertie recounts her ailments — a topic favored by Gertie herself and dreaded by Daniel and Mira, who share a panicked look as she begins.

"I had a corn on my foot that didn't heal for a year," she says. "That's part of the story. Then, because of the infection, I got something called lymphadenitis. The lymph nodes in my legs were inflamed, I had pockets of pus the size of golf balls. The hair on my legs stopped growing — utterly. And before long it spread to my groin."

"Ma," hisses Daniel. "We're eating."

"Forgive me," Gertie says. "But I wasn't responding to the antibiotics. So the doctor took a look and said that if I came in for surgery they'd drain all of my nodes, and that might be enough to fix the problem. There were two of them working on me, an older doctor and a younger, and the younger says, 'Mrs. Gold, you wouldn't believe the gunk we found.' Afterward they hooked me up to a drainage tube and I had to stay in the hospital until all the blood and the fluids oozed out."

"Ma," Daniel says. Raj has put his fork down and Daniel's mortified; he'd like to slap duct tape across his mother's mouth, but Ruby is leaning forward with interest.

"So what was it?" she asks. "What was causing all that stuff?"

"Well," says Gertie. "Given we're eating I'm not sure I should say. But seeing as you're interested —"

"We are not," says Daniel firmly, "not now," and the peculiar thing is that Ruby looks just as disappointed as Gertie. When Mira asks Raj about their tour schedule, Ruby leans toward her grandmother. "Tell me at home," she whispers, and Gertie flushes with a pleasure so rare that Daniel nearly reaches for Ruby to thank her.

That night, while brushing his teeth, Daniel thinks of Eddie. Eddie's question about Simon — whether the fortune teller predicted his death — is troubling him.

Daniel doesn't know when the fortune teller claimed Simon would die. Simon only said it was *young* — this in the attic of 72

342

Clinton Street on that drunken, befuddled night seven days after their father's death. But young could have been thirty-five. Young could have been fifty. The detail was so vague that Daniel discarded it. It seemed more likely that Simon's death was the consequence of his own actions. Not because he was gay — whatever mild discomfort Daniel has with Simon's sexuality is far from moralizing homophobia — but because Simon was careless, selfish. He thought only of his own pleasure. One could not go on that way forever.

But Daniel's resentment of Simon masks something deeper, darker: he is just as angry with himself. For his failure to know Simon — truly know him — while Simon was alive. For his failure to understand Simon, even in death. Simon was his only brother, and Daniel had not protected him. Yes, they spoke after Simon's arrival in San Francisco, and Daniel had tried to convince him to return to New York. But when Simon hung up, Daniel became so incensed that he threw the phone on the ground, where it cracked against the linoleum, and thought that perhaps Gertie's life would be easier without Simon, anyway. Of course, that thought was as temporary as it was cruel, but could Daniel not have tried harder?

Could he not have gotten the next Greyhound to San Francisco instead of stewing in his own resentment and waiting to be proven right?

They look at who's vulnerable, Eddie said of the fortune teller. *They can see straight through to the point.*

It's true, Daniel thinks, that Simon was vulnerable. He was seven years old, but that wasn't the only reason. Just as there was something different about Klara, there was something different about him. Impossible to say whether he knew at that age he was gay, but he was elusive regardless, difficult to parse. He was not as verbal as his siblings. He had few friends in school. He loved to run, but he ran alone. Maybe the prophecy did plant inside him like a germ. Maybe it incited him to be rash — to live dangerously.

Daniel spits in the sink and reconsiders Eddie's theory: that what innate vulnerability Klara had may have been triggered, or compounded, by her visit to the fortune teller. There are certainly situations in which the marriage of psychology and physiology are undeniable, if not fully understood — the fact that pain originates not in the muscles or nerves but in the brain, for instance. Or that patients whose outlooks are positive are more likely to beat disease. When he was a student, Daniel served as a research assistant for a study that explored the placebo effect. The study's authors hypothesized that the effect was caused by patient expectations — and indeed, patients who were told the tablet of starch they'd consumed was a stimulant soon showed an increase in heart rate, blood pressure, and reaction time. A second patient group, told the placebo was a sleeping pill, fell asleep within an average of twenty minutes.

Of course, the placebo effect was not new to Daniel, but it was another thing when witnessed firsthand. He saw that a thought could move molecules in the body, that the body races to actualize the reality of the brain. By this logic, Eddie's theory makes perfect sense: Klara and Simon believed they had taken pills with the power to change their lives, not knowing they had taken a placebo — not knowing that the consequences originated in their own minds.

A tall column in Daniel tips over. Sorrow floods out, as well as something else: an empathy for Simon, unbearably tender, that he has kept sealed for years. Daniel rests the heels of his hands on the marble countertop and leans forward until it passes. He needs to call Eddie.

Eddie's business card is in the study. Ruby is inside with the door closed, but the light is on. When Daniel knocks, there's no answer. He knocks a second time before cracking the door with concern.

"Ruby?"

She's sitting under the covers with a pair of oversized headphones over her ears and a book, *Darkly Dreaming Dexter,* in her lap. When she sees Daniel, she twitches.

"Shit," she says, pulling the headphones off. "You scared me."

"I'm sorry," says Daniel, holding a hand up. "I was just hoping to grab something. I can come back in the morning."

"That's okay." She turns the book over. "I'm not doing anything."

During the day, she wore makeup — eyeliner and some sort of sparkly goop on her lips — but now she's barefaced and looks younger. Her skin is a shade lighter than Raj's, and though her eyes are dark like his, she has Klara's full cheeks. Klara's smile, too, of course. Daniel crosses to the desk, finds Eddie's card in the top drawer, and slips it in his pocket. He's about to leave when Ruby speaks again.

"Do you have any pictures of my mom?"

Daniel's heart compresses. He pauses, facing the wall. *My mom.* He's never heard anyone refer to Klara this way before.

"I do." When he turns, Ruby has pulled her knees to her chest. She's wearing the SpongeBob SquarePants pajama bottoms and a baggy sweatshirt, hair elastics stacked on her wrist like bracelets. "Would you like to see them?"

"We have some, too," she says, quickly. "At home. But they're all the same ones I've seen a million times. So yeah. I would."

He walks to the living room to dig out the old albums. How strange it is, to have Ruby here. His niece. Daniel and Mira, of course, are not parents. When he asked Mira to marry him, she told him about her endometriosis — stage four. "I can't have children," she said.

"That's okay," said Daniel. "There are other options. Adoption —"

But Mira explained that she didn't want to adopt. She was diagnosed, unusually, at seventeen, so she'd had years to consider it. She would find other satisfaction in life, she'd decided; she didn't need to be a parent. Daniel found he couldn't say goodbye to her. Privately, though, he mourned. He had always imagined himself as a parent. When he watched a sleeping child being carried out of the restaurant by her father,

her head limp against his neck, Daniel thought of his own siblings. But fatherhood frightened him, too. He had only Saul — rigid, distant — for comparison. It was impossible to know how he'd fare. Back then, he thought he would do better than Saul, but perhaps that was a fallacy. It was equally possible that he would do worse.

He returns to the office with two photo albums. Ruby is sitting cross-legged on the bed now, her back against the wall. She pats the empty space beside her, and Daniel climbs up. He isn't flexible enough to cross his legs, so they dangle off the edge of the futon as he opens the first album.

"I haven't looked at these in years," he says. He thought it would be painful, but what grips him, when he sees the first photo — all four of the Gold children on the steps of 72 Clinton Street, Varya a leggy adolescent, Simon a towheaded toddler — is joy. The way it floods him, warm: he could cry.

"That's Mom." Ruby points at Klara. She's four or five, in a green plaid party dress.

"It sure is." Daniel laughs. "She loved that dress; she'd scream when your grandmother washed it. She pretended to be Clara from the *Nutcracker* whenever she wore it. And we were Jewish! It drove my father nuts."

348

Ruby smiled. "She was strong willed, wasn't she?"

"Very."

"I am, too. I think it's one of my best qualities," Ruby says. Daniel is amused, but when he looks at her, he sees she's serious. "Otherwise, people will push you around. Especially if you're a woman. Especially if you're in the entertainment business. Dad taught me that. But I think Mom would've agreed."

Daniel is sobered — has Ruby been pushed around? How? — but she turns the page to reveal photos from the same day of the siblings in pairs.

"That's Aunt Varya and Uncle Simon. He died before I was born, of AIDS." She looks to Daniel for confirmation.

"That's right. He was very young. Much too young."

Ruby nods. "There's going to be a pill for that soon — Truvada. Did you know? It doesn't cure HIV, but it prevents you from getting it. I read an article about it in the *New York Times*. I wish it'd been around back then. For Uncle Simon."

"I did hear that. It's incredible."

Miraculous, even, and unthinkable at the height of the epidemic, when tens of thousands were dying each year in the U.S.

alone. In the nineties, when AIDS medications were introduced, patients had to take up to thirty-six pills per day, and in the early eighties, there were no options at all. Daniel pictures Simon, just twenty, dying of a disease unknown and unnamed. Had the hospital been able to do anything to make him more comfortable? He has the same feeling he did moments ago, in the bathroom — that unbearable empathy, so much more intrusive than resentment.

"Look at Grandma," says Ruby, pointing. "She's so happy."

Grandma. Another word Daniel's never heard, and he's profoundly touched by it, by the fact that Ruby thinks of the Golds as her family. "She was happy. That's her with your grandfather, Saul. They must have been in their twenties."

"He died before Uncle Simon, right? How old was he?"

"Forty-five."

Ruby crosses her legs. "What's one thing about him?"

"One thing?"

"Yeah. One cool thing. Something interesting that I wouldn't know."

Daniel pauses. He could tell her about Gold's, but instead he thinks of a jar with green lettering and a white lid.

"You know those miniature pickles? Saul was obsessed with them. Very particular, too: he worked his way through Cains and Heinz and Vlasic before he discovered a brand called Milwaukee's, which my mother had to order from Wisconsin because they weren't in many New York stores. He could eat a whole jar in one sitting."

"That's so weird." Ruby giggles. "You know what's funny? I like to eat pickles on peanut butter sandwiches."

"You do not." Daniel makes a fake-retching sound.

"I do! I cut them up and put them on top. They're good, I swear — there's this sort of, like, sweet-sour crunch, and then the peanut butter's sweet and crunchy, too —"

"I don't buy it," says Daniel, and now they're both laughing. The sound is remarkable. "I don't buy it at all."

At midnight, he leaves Ruby with the stack of photo albums and climbs to the house's main level. In the kitchen, he pauses. He was so contented, sitting with Ruby, and the feeling trails him: it seems foolish, or unnecessary, to do anything but get into bed with Mira. But when he retrieves Eddie's business card from the pocket of his sweatpants, his contentment morphs, and he feels a wistfulness that borders on mourning. He could have had more of that connection — over the years, with Ruby, or with a child of his own. Maybe, he thinks, there's another reason he did not urge Mira to reconsider adoption. Maybe he felt that he did not deserve it. After all, with Saul so often at work, Daniel had tried to be a leader for his siblings. He'd tried to face down danger, unpredictability, chaos. And look how that had turned out.

You doing that, Eddie said, *it's blaming the victim.* But it's too late: Daniel did do it, he *did* think that way. He spent decades punishing himself for something that had never been his fault. As Daniel's compassion for himself swells, his anger toward the fortune teller hardens. He wants her to be caught — not just for Simon and Klara, but for himself, now, too.

He walks to the front door and opens it gently. There's a suctioning noise and an affront of frigid November air, but he steps outside and closes the door behind him. Then he opens his cell phone and enters Eddie's number.

"Daniel? Something wrong?"

Daniel pictures the agent in a Hudson Valley hotel room. Perhaps Eddie is working through the night, a cup of cheap coffee at his elbow. Perhaps he's thinking of the fortune teller as fixedly as Daniel, this shared thought connecting them like cord.

"I've remembered something," Daniel says. It must be thirty-five degrees outside, but his body is warm. "You asked about Simon — whether the fortune teller predicted his death — and I said I didn't know. But he did tell us she said he'd die young. So let's say he knew he was gay. He's sixteen, our father's gone, and he's rattled by the prophecy; he feels like this is his only chance to live the life he wants. So he disregards sense, disregards safety."

"All right," Eddie says, slowly. "Simon wasn't any more specific?"

"No, he wasn't any more specific. I told you: we were kids, it was one conversation, but it gives credence, doesn't it, to what you said before? That she pushed him, too?"

"It might," Eddie says, but he sounds detached. Now Daniel imagines him differently: rolling to one side, holding the phone in place with his shoulder. A hand skittering across the bedside table to turn the light back off, Daniel's revelation having disappointed him. "Anything else?"

The heat is leaving Daniel, depression setting in. Then something occurs to him. If Eddie is unmoved by this information —

perhaps even disillusioned with the case —
then maybe Daniel should do his own dig-
ging.

"Yes. One question." As he breathes, puffs
of white air hover like parachutes. "What's
her name?"

"What's knowing her name going to do
for you?"

"It'll give me something to call her," Daniel says, thinking fast. He keeps his tone
jocular, to put Eddie at ease. "Something
that isn't 'the fortune teller,' or worse, 'the
woman.' "

Eddie pauses. He clears his throat. "Bruna
Costello," he says, finally.

"What?" There is a rushing noise in Daniel's ears, a flood of adrenaline.

"Bruna," says Eddie. "Bruna Costello."

"Bruna Costello." Daniel savors the
words, each one a fact. "And where is she?"

"That's two questions," Eddie says.
"When it's over, I'll call you. When it's all
said and done."

24.

On Thanksgiving morning, Daniel wakes earlier than Raj and Ruby. It's six forty-five, milky pink light and the rustling of squirrels, a deer nibbling at the brown lawn. He makes a pot of strong coffee and sits in the rocking chair beside the living room window with Mira's laptop.

When he Googles Bruna Costello's name, the first link that appears is the FBI's Most Wanted website. *Protect your family, your local community, and the nation by helping the FBI catch wanted terrorists and fugitives,* the webpage reads. *Rewards are offered in some cases.* She is categorized under "Seeking Information," a black-and-white thumbnail in the fourth row. It's fuzzy, a close-up from security footage. When Daniel clicks on her name, the photo enlarges, and he sees it's the same one Eddie showed him at the Hoffman House.

The Federal Bureau of Investigation (FBI) is

seeking the public's assistance to identify the alleged victims of Bruna Costello, suspected for fraud in connection with a fortune-telling ring in Florida. Other members of the Costello family have been convicted of federal crimes including grand larceny, false income returns, mail fraud, wire fraud, and money laundering. To date, Costello remains the only suspect who has evaded questioning.

Costello travels in a 1989 Gulf Stream Regatta motor home (see More Photos). She has previously lived in Coral Springs and Fort Lauderdale, Florida, and is known to have traveled extensively throughout the continental United States. Currently, she is thought to be based outside of Dayton, Ohio, in the village of West Milton.

Daniel clicks on More Photos. There's a picture of the trailer, wide and blunt-nosed, painted a dingy cream — or perhaps it was originally white — with a thick stripe of brown. Below More Photos is another link titled Aliases.

Drina Demeter
Cora Wheeler
Nuri Gargano
Bruna Galletti

A half dozen more. Abruptly, Daniel closes the computer. Eddie must have known her location. So why didn't he say so? He must think Daniel is unsteady, intent on revenge.

Is he? It's true that Daniel feels motivated for the first time since his suspension. He feels the woman's presence like a song sung in the next room or a hair-raising waft of wind, daring him to come closer.

Mira and Raj work on the vegetables while Gertie makes her famous stuffing. Daniel and Ruby tend to the bird, an eighteen-pound beast slathered in butter and garlic and thyme. In early afternoon, while most of the food is roasting or waiting to roast and Mira is wiping the counters down, Raj takes a business call in the guest room. Gertie naps. Ruby and Daniel sit in the living room: Daniel in the rocking chair with the laptop, Ruby on the couch with a book of sudoku puzzles. Snow drifts outside the window, melting as soon as it touches the glass.

Daniel is researching the Rom: how they originated in India, how they left to escape religious persecution and slavery. They traveled west, into Europe and the Balkans, and began to tell fortunes as refugees. Half a million were killed in the Holocaust. It reminds him of the story of the Jews. Exodus and wandering, resilience and adaptation. Even the famous Romani prov-erb, *Amari čhib s'amari zor* — *"Our language is our strength"* — sounds like something his father would have said. Daniel takes a dry-cleaning receipt from his pocket and writes the phrase down, along with a second proverb: *Thoughts have wings.*

Lately, he has struggled to sustain a con-nection with God. One year ago, he decided to explore Jewish theology. He thought of it as a tribute to Saul, and he hoped for solace about the deaths of his siblings. But he found little: on the topics of death and im-mortality, Judaism has little to say. While other religions are concerned with dying, Jews are most concerned with living. The Torah focuses on *olam ha-ze:* "this world."

"Are you working?" Ruby asks.

Daniel looks up. The sun is nestled just above the Catskills, the mountains a mellow wash of periwinkle and peach. Ruby is curled against the arm of the couch.

"Not really." Daniel shuts the lid of the laptop. "You?"

Ruby shrugs. "Not really." She closes her sudoku book.

"I don't know how you do those puzzles," Daniel says. "They look like Greek to me."

"You have a lot of downtime, doing a show. If you don't find something else you're good at, you'll go crazy. I like solving things."

Ruby tucks her legs to one side, clad today in a different pair of Juicy sweatpants. Her hair is a bulbous bird's nest of a bun. Daniel realizes that he'll miss her when she goes.

"You'd be a good doctor," he says.

"I hope so." When she lifts her head to look at him, her face is vulnerable. A surprise: she cares what he thinks. "I want to be one."

"You do? What about your show?"

"I won't do that forever."

She speaks in a flat, matter-of-fact tone that Daniel can't quite parse. Does Raj know about this? He would never be able to have a relationship with another assistant like the one he has with Ruby. Daniel thinks of the conversation they had the previous morning, the tension when Ruby and Raj discussed their schedule. Raj claimed it was simple. *Rubina,* he said, *on the other hand* —

Ruby flicks her hair over one shoulder. She isn't matter-of-fact, he sees. She's annoyed.

"I mean, Jesus," she says, "I want to go to *college,* I want to be a real *person.* I want to do something that matters."

"Your mother didn't want to be a real person."

The words are out before Daniel can stop them. His voice is low and he's smiling, for somehow, when he thinks of Klara, this is what comes to mind first: her gall, her daring. Not what happened later.

"So?" Ruby's cheeks flush. There's a sheen to her eyes that flashes in the light from the living room lamp. "So what about my mom?"

"I'm so sorry." Daniel feels ill. "I don't know what's wrong with me."

Ruby opens her mouth, closes it. He's losing her already, she's leaving for that foreign, teenage-girl place: mountains of resentment, potholes he can't see.

"Your mother. She was special," Daniel says. It feels urgent, that he convince her of this. "That doesn't mean you have to be like her. I just want you to know."

"I know that," says Ruby dully. "Everyone tells me that."

She leaves to take a walk in the snow. Daniel watches her clomp through the slush in her Ugg boots and hooded sweatshirt, dark tendrils of hair floating next to her face, before she disappears into the trees.

25.

" 'Hallelujah. Praise God in his sanctuary. Praise him in the firmament of his power. Praise him for his mighty acts. Praise him according to his abundant greatness. Praise him with the blast of the horn. Praise him with the psaltery' " — here Gertie pauses — " 'and harp.' "

"What's a psaltery?" asks Ruby.

When she returned from her walk, she was chipper again. Now she sits between Raj and Gertie on one side of the table. Mira and Daniel hold hands on the other.

"I don't know," says Gertie, frowning at the Tehillim.

"Hang on. I'll look it up on Wikipedia." Ruby pulls her flip phone out of a pocket and types efficiently on the tiny keys. "Okay. 'The bowed psaltery is a type of psaltery or zither that is played with a bow. In contrast to the centuries-old plucked psaltery, the bowed psaltery appears to be a twentieth-century invention.' " She shuts the phone. "Well, that was helpful. As you were, Grandma."

Gertie returns to the book. " 'Praise him with the timbrel and dance. Praise him with the loud-sounding cymbals. Let every thing that hath breath praise HaShem. Hallelujah.' "

"Amen," says Mira, quietly. She squeezes Daniel's hand. "Let's eat."

Daniel squeezes her back, but he feels unsettled. That afternoon, he learned of an explosion in the Sadr City district of Baghdad. Five car bombs and a mortar shell killed more than two hundred people, largely Shiites. He takes a long sip of wine, a Malbec. He had a glass or two of a white Mira uncorked while they were cooking, but he's still waiting for the pleasant fog that comes over him when he drinks.

Gertie looks at Ruby and Raj. "What time are you leaving tomorrow?"

"Early," says Raj.

"Unfortunately," says Ruby.

"We have a show in the city at seven," Raj says. "We should be there before noon to meet the crew."

"I wish you didn't have to," Gertie says. "I wish you'd stay a little longer."

"Me, too," says Ruby. "But you can come

362

visit us in Vegas. You'd have your own suite. And I can introduce you to Krystal. She's a Shetland and a total chub. She probably eats an acre of grass a day."

"My goodness," says Mira, laughing. She cuts a group of green beans in half with her fork. "Now, I have a personal request. I didn't want to bring it up, because I'm sure people ask this sort of thing all the time, the way our friends are always trying to get Daniel to diagnose them — but we have two magicians in the house, and I can't let you leave without trying."

Raj raises his eyebrows. It's nearly silent in the dining room — a result of this wooded area of Kingston.

Mira sets down her fork; she's blushing. "When I was young, a street magician did a card trick for me. He asked me to pick a card as he flipped through the deck, which couldn't have taken more than a second. I picked the nine of hearts. And that was what he guessed. I made him do the trick another time to make sure the deck wasn't filled with nines of hearts. I've never been able to figure out how he did it."

Raj and Ruby share a glance.

"Forcing," says Ruby. "When a magician manipulates your decisions."

"But that's just it," Mira says. "There was

nothing he said or did to influence me. The decision was entirely mine."

"So you thought," says Raj. "There are two kinds of forcing. In psychological forcing, a magician uses language to steer you toward a particular choice. But physical forcing is likely what he used — that's when a particular object is made to stand out from the rest. He would have paused at the nine of hearts for just a millisecond more than any of the other cards."

"Increased exposure," adds Ruby. "It's a classic technique."

"Fascinating." Mira leans back in her chair. "Though I confess I almost feel — disappointed? I suppose I didn't expect the solution to be so rational."

"Most magicians are incredibly rational." Raj is slicing meat from a turkey leg, placing it in neat strips on one side of his plate. "They're analysts. You have to be, to develop illusions. To trick people."

Something about the phrase needles Daniel. It reminds him of what he's always resented about Raj: his pragmatism, his obsession with business. Before Klara met Raj, magic was her passion, her greatest love. Now Raj lives in a gated mansion, and Klara is dead.

"I'm not sure my sister saw it that way,"

Daniel says.

Raj spears a pearl onion. "How do you mean?"

"Klara knew that magic can be used to deceive people. But she tried to do the opposite — to reveal some greater truth. To pull the wool off."

The candelabra in the center of the table throws the lower half of Raj's face into shadow, but his eyes are lit. "If you're asking me whether I believe in what I do, whether I feel I'm providing some kind of essential service — well, I could ask you the same thing. This is my career. And it means as much to me as yours does to you."

The food in Daniel's mouth becomes difficult to chew. He has the terrible thought that Raj has known about his suspension from the beginning and has played along out of generosity, or pity.

"What do you mean by that?"

"You feel it's noble to send young men into deadly combat?" asks Raj. "You're motivated by some greater truth?"

Gertie and Ruby look from Raj to Daniel. Daniel clears his throat.

"I have a deep-seated belief in the importance of the military, yes. Whether what I do is noble is not up to me to judge. But what the soldiers do? That's nobility, yes."

He sounds convincing enough, but Mira has noticed the tightness in his voice. She tilts her head toward her plate. Daniel knows she is avoiding him out of courtesy, so that whatever is in her gaze does not reveal him, but this only makes him feel like more of a fraud.

"Even now?" asks Raj.

"Especially now."

Daniel remembers well the horror of 9/11. His childhood best friend, Eli, worked in the South Tower. After the second plane hit, Eli stood in the stairwell to the seventy-eighth floor, ushering people toward the express elevator. *Okay,* he shouted. *Everybody out.* Before that, some people had been paralyzed by fear. Later, a colleague who had been in the towers during the 1993 bombing referred to him as the wake-up voice. Eli made it to the roof, a rescue location in 1993, and called his wife. *I love you, darling,* he said. *I might be home late.* He fell with the tower at ten in the morning.

"Especially now?" asks Raj. "When the infrastructure of Iraq has been decimated? When innocent men are being abused by sadists at Abu Ghraib? When WMDs are nowhere to be found?"

Raj meet Daniel's eyes. This Vegas celebrity, this magician in expensive clothes —

Daniel has underestimated him.

"Dad," says Ruby.

"Beans?" asks Mira, holding the platter aloft.

"And you would have us let a brutal tyrant continue the murder and oppression of hundreds of thousands?" asks Daniel. "What of Saddam's genocide against the Kurds and the violence in Kuwait? The Barzani abductions? The chemical warfare, the mass graves?"

The wine is hitting him now. He feels unclear and hazy and is glad, therefore, to have been able to articulate Hussein's crimes on demand.

"The U.S. has never been guided by a moral compass when choosing political alliances. They run military operations out of Pakistan. They supported Hussein during the height of his atrocities. And now they're hunting something that doesn't exist. Iraq's WMD program ended in 1991. There's nothing there — nothing but oil."

What Daniel refuses to admit is that he fears Raj is right. He saw the horrific photos from Abu Ghraib: the men hooded and naked, beaten and shocked. There are rumors that Hussein will be hung in December during Eid al-Adha, the Muslim holy day — a perversion of religion, and not by the enemy.

"You don't know that," he says.

"No?" Raj wipes his mouth with a napkin. "There's a reason no country in the world is enthusiastic about the war in Iraq. Except Israel."

He says it like an afterthought, as if he has, for once, forgotten his audience. Or was it calculated? The Golds seize, pulling together instantly, atomically. Daniel has his own reservations about Zionism, but now his jaw is rigid and his heart beats wildly, as though someone insulted his mother.

Mira puts her silverware down. "Excuse me?"

For the first time since his arrival, Raj's confidence slips back like a hood.

"I don't have to tell you that Israel is a strategic ally, or that the invasion of Baghdad aimed to strengthen their regional security as much as our own," he says, quietly. "That's all I meant."

"Is it?" Mira's shoulders are angular, her voice constricted. "Frankly, Raj, it sounded more like the scapegoating of the Jews."

"But the Jews are no longer the underdog. They're one of America's most important constituencies. The Arab world opposes an American war in Iraq, but American Arabs will never have the power of American

Jews." Raj pauses. He must know the entire table is against him. But because he is threatened or because he has decided not to be, he advances. "Meanwhile, the Jews act as though they're still the victims of terrible oppression. It's a mind-set that comes in handy when they want to oppress others."

"That's enough," says Gertie.

She has dressed up for this dinner: a maroon shift dress with pantyhose and leather mules. A glass brooch from Saul is pinned to her breast. It pains Daniel to see the grief on her face. Even worse is the look on Ruby's. Daniel's niece is facing her plate, scraped empty of food. Even in the candlelight, he can see that her eyes are beginning to smart.

Raj looks at his daughter. For a moment, he looks stricken, almost confused. Then he pushes his chair back with a screech.

"Daniel," he says. "Let's take a walk."

Raj leads Daniel past the first line of maples — flaming weeks ago, now bare — to the clearing beyond: a pond rimmed by cattails and birch trees. He's shorter than Daniel, perhaps five nine to Daniel's six feet, but Daniel is struck by Raj's confidence — how he strode out of the house and into the clearing, as if he's as comfortable on Daniel's property as he is at home. It's enough to make Daniel strike first.

"You talk about the war like you know just who to blame, but it's damn easy to make allegations when you're sitting in a gated mansion doing coin tricks. Maybe you should try doing something that matters." Where has he heard the phrase before? From Ruby. *I want to go to college,* she told him. *I want to be a real person. I want to do something that matters.* Daniel can feel the heat in his cheeks, feel his pulse in his throat, and suddenly, he knows exactly what will hurt Raj most. "Even your own daughter thinks you're nothing but a Vegas showman. She told me she wants to be a doctor."

The pond reflects the light of the moon, and Raj's face tightens like a fist. Daniel sees Raj's weakness as surely as he knows his own: Raj is afraid of losing Ruby. He's kept her from the Golds not just because he doesn't like them, but because of the threat they pose. An alternate family — an alternate life.

But Raj holds Daniel's gaze. "You're right. I'm not a doctor. I don't have a college degree, and I wasn't born in New York. But I raised an incredible kid. I have a successful career."

Daniel fumbles, for suddenly, he sees Colonel Bertram's face. *You must think you're a special fucking snowflake,* the colonel said, his grin looming over the wreathed pin. *A real American hero.*

"No," he says. "You stole one. You stole Klara's act." He has wanted to make this allegation for years, and it revives him to finally say it.

Raj's voice becomes lower, slower. "I was her *partner,*" he says, the effect not of calm but terrible restraint.

"Bullshit. You were cocky. You cared more about the show than you did about her."

With each word, Daniel feels a rush of conviction, and of something initially hazy before it grows clearer in shape: the echo of another story — the story of Bruna Costello.

"Klara trusted you," Daniel says. "And you took advantage of her."

"Are you kidding me, man?" Raj tips his head back a fraction of an inch, and the whites of his eyes flash with moonlight. In them, Daniel sees possessiveness, yearning, and something else: love. "I took care of her. Do you know how fucked up she was? Did any of you know? She blacked out. Her memory was in pieces. She wouldn't have gotten *dressed* in the morning if it wasn't for me. Besides, she was your sister. What did you do to help her? You met Ruby once? You talked on Hanukkah?"

Daniel's stomach rises and turns. "You should have told us."

"I barely knew you. No one in your family had welcomed me. You treated me like I was trespassing, like I'd never be good enough for Klara. For the *Golds* — the precious, entitled, long-suffering Golds."

The scorn in Raj's voice stuns Daniel, and for a moment, he cannot speak. "You know nothing about what we've been through," he says, finally.

"That!" says Raj, pointing, and his eyes are so alive, his arm so electric, that Daniel has the impression — absurd — that Raj is about to do a magic trick. "That is exactly the problem. So you've been through tragedy. No one's denying it. But *that is not the life you're living now.* The aura is stale. The story, Daniel, is stale. You can't let go of it, because if you did, you wouldn't be a victim anymore. But there are millions of people still living in oppression. I come from them. And those people can't live in the past. They can't live in their heads. They don't have the luxury."

Daniel recedes, stepping into the dark of the trees as if for cover. Raj doesn't wait for his reply: he turns and walks back around the pond. But he pauses at the path to the house.

"One more thing." Raj's voice carries easily, but his body is shadowed. "You claim you're doing something important. Something that matters. But you're deceiving yourself. All you do is watch other people do your dirty work from thousands of miles away. You're a cog, an enabler. And my God, you're afraid. You're afraid that you could never do what your sister did — stand onstage by yourself, night after night, and bare your fucking soul without knowing whether you'll be applauded or booed. Klara may have killed herself. But she was still braver than you."

26.

Raj and Ruby leave before eight in the morning. It rained overnight, and their rental car sits in the driveway, wet. Raj and Daniel load the trunk without speaking. Drizzle clings to the yellow velour of Ruby's latest sweat suit. She hugs Daniel stiffly. She's just as frosty with Raj, but Raj is Ruby's father: she'll have to forgive him eventually. Not so with Daniel, who feels a visceral despair as Ruby climbs into the passenger seat and shuts the door. When they reverse out of the driveway, he waves, but Ruby has already ducked her head to look at her phone, and all he sees is a mass of hair.

Mira drives to New Paltz for a department meeting. Daniel walks to the refrigerator and begins to unload yesterday's leftovers. The turkey skin, formerly crisp, has become shriveled and damp. The pan drippings are opaque, beige puddles.

He reheats a full plate in the microwave and eats at the kitchen counter until he feels sick. He can't bear to sit at the dining room table, where the Chapals and the Golds ate dinner what seems like years ago. For the first time, Daniel felt bonded to Ruby — felt that he *could* be close to her, that he need not be ashamed of his role in her mother's death. And now he's lost her. Maybe Ruby will visit when she's eighteen and can make her own decisions, but Raj won't bring her back and will never encourage it. Daniel could reach out to Ruby, but who knows whether she would respond? The wreck of Thanksgiving was not just Raj's fault.

After his last blowup with Raj, years ago, Daniel found solace in work. But he can do that no longer: this time, when he thinks of the office, he feels strangled. He will only be able to keep his job if he relinquishes his power, which lies in his ability to make decisions. And if he does that — if he chooses job over integrity, security over free will — he'll be just as much a pawn as Raj claimed.

His cell phone rings from the bedroom. Daniel walks upstairs. When he sees the number on the screen, he yanks the phone so abruptly that the charger comes out of the socket.

"Eddie?" he asks.

"Daniel. I'm calling with an update on the case. You wanted me to keep you appraised."

"Yes?"

Eddie's voice is heavy, strained. "We've cleared her of charges."

Daniel drops down onto the bed. He presses the phone to his ear, the cord trailing like a tail. "You can't do that."

"Look, it's" — Eddie exhales — "it's a very gray area. How can you prove she killed these people when she never touched them, never even urged them, not in so many words? I've spent the past six months trying to pin this woman down. When I came to you, we'd almost closed the case. But I thought there might be one thing I was missing: some shred of evidence only you knew. And you did what you could. You were honest. It just wasn't enough."

"What's enough? Five more suicides? Twenty?" Daniel's voice splits on the last syllable, something that hasn't happened since boyhood. "I thought you said she isn't registered. Can't you get her that way?"

"Yeah, she's not registered. But she's barely making any money. The bureau thinks it's a waste of time. Besides, she's an old lady. She won't be around much longer."

"What does that matter? You look at people who have done horrible things, despicable things, it doesn't matter how late you get justice. The point is you get justice."

"Easy, Daniel," Eddie says, and Daniel's ears become hot. "I wanted this as badly as you. But you have to let it go."

"Eddie," says Daniel. "Today is my day."

"Your day?"

"The date she gave me. The date she said I would die."

This is Daniel's last card. He never thought he would share it with Eddie, but he is desperate to make the agent reconsider.

"Oh, Daniel." Eddie sighs. "Don't go there. You'll only torture yourself, and for what?"

Daniel is silent. Outside the window, he sees a delicate, crystalline flurry. The snowflakes are so weightless he can't tell whether they're drifting toward the sky or the ground.

"Take care of yourself, okay?" Eddie presses. "The best thing you can do today is take care of yourself."

"You're right," says Daniel, wooden. "I understand. And I appreciate everything you've done."

When they hang up, Daniel hurls the phone at the wall. It breaks into two pieces with a dull crack. He leaves them on the floor and walks downstairs to the study. Mira has already stripped Ruby's bed, put the linens in the laundry machine, and turned the futon back into a couch. She even vacuumed the floor — a thoughtful gesture, but one that makes it feel even more like Ruby was never here.

Daniel sits down at his desk and pulls up the FBI's Most Wanted. Bruna Costello has been removed from the Seeking Information page. When he plugs her name into the Search bar, a short line of text appears: *Your search did not match any documents.*

Daniel leans back in the desk chair and spins, bringing his hands to his face. He returns to the same memory he has many times before — the last time he spoke to Simon. Simon called from the hospital, though Daniel didn't know that at the time. "I'm sick," he said. Daniel was stunned; it took a moment for him to identify Simon's voice, which was both more mature and more fragile than it had ever been before. Though he didn't let on, Daniel felt as much relief as he did resentment. In Simon's voice, he heard the siren song of family — how it pulls you despite all sense; how it forces you to discard your convictions, your righteous selfhood, in favor of profound dependence.

If Simon had made the slightest apology, Daniel would have forgiven him. But Simon didn't. He did not, in fact, say very much at all. He asked how Daniel was doing, as though this were a casual phone call between brothers who had not been estranged for years. Daniel didn't know whether something was truly wrong or whether Simon was simply being Simon: self-centered, evasive. Perhaps he decided to call Daniel as thoughtlessly as he'd decided to go to San Francisco.

"Simon?" Daniel asked. "Is there anything I can do?"

But he knew that his voice was cold, and Simon soon hung up.

Is there anything I can do?

He can't save Simon and Klara. They belong to the past. But perhaps he can change the future. The irony is impeccable: on the very day that Bruna Costello prophesied his death, he can find her and force her to confess how she took advantage of them. And then he'll make sure she never does it again.

Daniel stops spinning. He removes his hands from his face, blinking in the study's artificial light. Then he hunches over the keyboard and tries to remember phrases from the FBI posting. There was a photo of a cream and brown trailer, a string of aliases. And the name of a village in Ohio — something Milton — he read *Paradise Lost* in college and was struck by the word when he read it. East Milton? No: West Milton. He Googles the phrase. Links to an elementary school and a library appear, as well as a map, West Milton outlined in red and shaped like Italy without the heel. He clicks on Images and sees a quaint down-town, storefronts hung with the American flag. One picture shows a small waterfall beside a set of stairs. When Daniel clicks on it, he's routed to a message board.

West Milton Cascades and Stairway, some-one has posted. *This place is not well taken care of. People are throwing junk and the stairs and railing are not too safe.*

It seems a better place to hide than the main drag. Daniel navigates back to the map. West Milton is a ten-hour drive from Kingston. The thought makes his pulse speed. He knows nothing about Bruna's precise location, but the cascades seem promising, and the entire village is barely more than three square miles. How hard could it be to spot a rundown RV?

He hears a shrill ringing from the kitchen. These days, they use the landline so infrequently that it takes him a moment to place it. The only people who even have the number are telemarketers and family members, the odd neighbor. This time, he doesn't have to check the caller ID to know it's Varya.

"V," he says.

"Daniel." She was unable to come for Thanksgiving, having committed to a conference in Amsterdam. "Your cell phone was off. I just thought I'd check in."

Eddie's voice crackled from the highway, but Varya's comes through the receiver from four thousand miles away with such clarity she could be standing in front of him. She speaks with a cool self-control for which Daniel has no patience.

"I know why you're calling," he says.

"Well." She laughs, brittle. "Sue me." There is a pause that Daniel makes no effort to fill. "What are you doing today?"

"I'm going to find the fortune teller. I'm going to hunt her down, and I'm going to force her to apologize for what she did to our family."

"That isn't funny."

"It would have been nice to have you here yesterday."

"I had to give a presentation."

"Over Thanksgiving?"

"Turns out the Dutch don't celebrate it." Her tone has tightened, and Daniel's resentment plumes again. "How did it go?"

"Fine." He'll give her nothing. "How was the conference?"

"Fine."

It enrages him, that Varya cares enough to call him now but not on any other day, and certainly not enough to come see him. Instead she watches from above as he scurries around, never coming down to intervene.

"So how do you keep track of these things?" he asks, pressing the phone to his ear. "A spreadsheet? Or do you have it all memorized?"

"Don't be nasty," she says, and Daniel falters.

"I'm fine, Varya." He leans against the counter and uses his free hand to rub the bridge of his nose. "Everything is going to be fine."

He feels regretful as soon as they hang up. Varya is not the enemy. But there will be plenty of time to smooth things over. He walks to the counter and grabs his keys from a wicker basket.

"Daniel," says Gertie. "What are you doing?"

His mother stands in the doorway. She wears the old pink bathrobe, her legs bare. The skin around her eyes is damp and strangely lavender.

"I'm going for a drive," he says.

"Where to?"

"The office. There're a few things I want to get done before Monday."

"It's Shabbat. You shouldn't work."

"Shabbat's tomorrow."

"It starts tonight."

"Then I have six hours," Daniel says.

But he knows he won't be back by then. He won't be back before morning. Then, he'll tell Gertie and Mira everything. He'll tell them how he caught Bruna, how she confessed. He'll tell Eddie, too. Perhaps Eddie will reopen the case.

"Daniel." Gertie blocks his exit. "I'm worried about you."

"Don't be."

"You're drinking too much."

"I'm not."

"And you're keeping something from me." She stares at him: curious, pained. "What are you keeping, my love?"

"Nothing." God, she makes him feel like a child. If only she'd move out of the doorway.

"You're paranoid."

"I don't think you should go. It's not right, on Shabbat."

"Shabbat means nothing," says Daniel, viciously. "God doesn't care. God doesn't give a rat's ass."

Suddenly, the notion of God feels as enraging and useless as Varya's phone call. God did not watch over Simon and Klara, and he certainly has not brought justice. But what did Daniel expect? When he married Mira, he chose to return to Judaism. He imagined — he chose — a God to believe in, and this was the problem. Of course, people choose things to believe in all the time: relationships, political ideology, lotto tickets. But God, Daniel sees now, is different. God should not be designed based on personal preference, like a custom pair of gloves. He should not be a product of human longing, which is powerful enough to pull a deity from thin air.

"Daniel," says Gertie. If she doesn't stop repeating his name, he'll scream. "You don't mean that."

"You don't believe in God, either, Ma," he says. "You just want to."

Gertie blinks, her lips pursed, though she keeps very still. Daniel puts a hand on her shoulder and leans down to kiss her cheek.

She's still standing in the kitchen when he leaves.

He walks behind the house to the shed. Inside are Mira's gardening tools: the half-empty packets of seeds, the leather gloves and silver watering can. He moves the green hose from the bottom shelf in order to reach the shoe box behind it. Within the shoe box is a small handgun. When he joined the military, he received firearm training. It seemed reasonable to have a weapon. Besides an annual trip to the firing range in Saugerties, he hasn't used it, but he renewed his permit in March. He loads the gun and carries it to the car inside his jacket. He may need to intimidate Bruna to make her talk.

It's just after noon when he pulls onto the highway. By the time he realizes he forgot to clear his browser history, he's already in Pennsylvania.

27.

He passes Scranton in early afternoon. When he hits Columbus, it's nearly nine. His shoulders are tight and his head pounds, but he rattles with cheap coffee and expectation. The cities become more rural: Huber Heights, Vandalia, Tipp City. West Milton is denoted by a small green and beige sign. It takes less than five minutes to drive through the town. Flat houses with aluminum siding, then soft hills and farmland. There's no trailer or trailer park to be seen, but Daniel is undeterred. If he wanted to hide, he'd go to the woods.

He checks the clock: ten thirty-two and there are no other cars on the road. The waterfall from the message board is at the corner of Routes 571 and 48, behind a furniture store. Daniel parks and walks to the overlook. He sees nothing except the staircase, which is as rickety as reported. The steps are slick with wet leaves, the railing scabbed with rust.

What if Bruna has left West Milton entirely? But it's too soon to give up, he tells himself, walking back to the car. The forest extends unbroken to the next town over. If she has left, she might not have gone far.

He continues north, following the Stillwater River into Ludlow Falls, population 209. Beyond a field on Covington Avenue, he can see the bridge that carries Route 48 over another waterfall, the most impressive one yet. He parks at the edge of the grass, pulls on his wool coat, and tucks the gun in his pocket. Then he walks downhill, under the bridge.

The Ludlow Falls are almost two stories tall, roaring. An old stairway leads at least thirty feet into the gorge, to a pathway skirting the river and lit only by moonlight.

He descends slowly at first, then faster as he adjusts to the width and tempo of the steps.

The gorge is jagged, more difficult to navigate. His coat keeps catching on branches, and he trips twice over gnarled roots. Why did he think this was a good idea? The gorge is too narrow to accommodate a motor home, the entrance too steep. He keeps walking, hoping to find another staircase or a trail that leads to higher ground, but his anticipation soon turns to fatigue. At one point, he slips on a slick ledge of sheet rock and has to drop to all fours to avoid falling into the river.

His hands scrabble over moss and stone. The knees of his slacks are soaked through; his heartbeat has dropped to his stomach and settled there, wrongly. There's still time for him to turn around. He could rent a motel room, clean up, and arrive home by morning, telling Mira he fell asleep at the office. She might be perturbed, but she would believe him. Above all, he is loyal.

Instead, he peels himself carefully off of the rock, rising to his knees and then to stand. He finds better traction farther from the water, where the underbrush is dry. As the gorge narrows, it begins to rise. He's not sure how much time has passed when he notices that the falls have become distant. He must have walked around them, to the south side.

Daniel sees flatter land above. He stumbles more quickly, grabbing tree trunks and low branches to help pull himself out of the gorge. As he climbs, straining his eyes in the dark, he notices that part of the clearing is blocked by something angular. Rectangular.

A motor home is parked in a patch of flat land beneath dense trees. By the time he reaches the upper lip of the gorge, he's out of breath, but he feels like he could do the climb twice over. The trailer is speckled with mud. Snow clumps on the roof. The windows are covered, and the word *Regatta* is written in slanting script across the side.

He's surprised to find the door unlocked. He mounts the stairs and steps inside.

A moment before his eyes adjust to the dark. It's difficult to see with the windows covered, but the basic layout is discernible. He stands in a cramped living area, his left knee touching a dingy couch in a terrible abstract pattern. There's a table across from the couch, or barely a table — a surface that folds out from the wall, currently stacked with boxes. Two metal folding chairs are wedged between the table and the front seats, also covered with boxes. To the left of the table is a sink and another strip of counter space with an assortment of candles and figurines.

He walks farther into the trailer, passing a spare, cramped bathroom before he comes to a closed door. In the center of the door, at eye level, a wooden cross hangs from two thumbtacks. He turns the doorknob.

A twin bed has been pushed up next to the wall. Beside it is a crate with a bible on top, as well as a plate, empty except for a plastic wrapper. Above that is a small, square window. The bed is covered with plaid flannel sheets and a navy blue comforter between which extends a single foot.

Daniel clears his throat. "Get up."

The body stirs. Its face is turned to one side and hidden beneath long tendrils of hair. Slowly, a woman shifts onto her back and opens one eye, then the other. For a moment, she looks at him blankly. Then she inhales sharply and pushes herself to a seated position. She wears a cotton nightgown printed with tiny yellow flowers.

"I have a gun," says Daniel. "Get dressed." Already, he's disgusted by her. Her foot is bare, the heel rough and cracked. "We're going to talk."

He brings her into the living area and tells her to sit on the couch. She carries the navy comforter from the bedroom and keeps it wrapped around her shoulders. Daniel removes the black shades from the windows, so that he can see her better in the moonlight.

She's still heavy, though perhaps she looks larger this way, swaddled in the comforter. Her hair is white and unkempt and hangs down to her breasts; her face is covered with

390

delicate, capillary wrinkles, so precise they could be drawn by pencil. The flesh beneath her eyes is a sallow pink.

"I know you." Her voice is rusty. "I remember you. You came to see me in New York. You had your siblings, they were there. Two girls and a little boy."

"They're dead. The boy, and one of the girls."

The woman's mouth is pursed. She shifts beneath the comforter.

"I know your name," Daniel says. "It's Bruna Costello. I know your family, and what they've done. But I want to know about you. I want to know why you do what you do, and why you did what you did to us."

The woman's mouth is set. "I don't got nothing to say to you."

Daniel takes the gun out from inside his jacket and fires two bullets into the aluminum floor. The woman shrieks and covers her ears; the comforter falls to one side. There's a scar, white and shiny like dried glue, beneath her collarbone.

"That's my home," she says. "You got no right to do that."

"I'll do worse." He points the gun at her face, its barrel level with her nose. "So let's start with the basics. You come from criminals."

"I don't talk about my family."

He points upward, fires again. The bullet explodes through the roof and whistles in the air outside. Bruna screams. With one hand, she pulls the comforter up over her shoulders again; she holds the other out straight, her palm facing Daniel like a stop sign.

"*Drabarimos,* it's a gift from God. My family wasn't using it right. They're backward, they're dishonest, they hit and run. I don't do nothing like that. I talk about life, and God's blessings."

"You know they're locked up, don't you? You know they've been caught?"

"I heard. But I don't talk to them. I got nothing to do with it."

"Bullshit. You stick together, you people, like rats."

"Not me," says Bruna. "Not me."

When Daniel lowers his gun, she drops her hand. In her eyes, Daniel sees a gloss of tears. Perhaps she's telling the truth. Perhaps her family feels as remote to her as Klara and Simon and Saul do to Daniel — like part of another lifetime.

But he can't become soft. "Is that why you left home?"

"That's part."

"Why else?"

" 'Cause I was a girl. 'Cause I didn't wanna be nobody's wife, nobody's mother. Starting seven years old, you're cleaning the house. Eleven, twelve, you're working; fourteen, married. Me, I wanted to go to school, be a nurse, but I didn't have no education. All it was was *'Shai drabarel, shai drabarel?'* Can she tell fortunes. So I ran. I did what I knew, I gave readings. But I says to myself, I'll be different. No charge if I don't have to. No witchcrap. There was a client I had for years, I didn't ask her once to pay me. I says to her, 'Teach me. Teach me how to read.' She's laughing: 'Palms?' 'No,' I tell her. 'The newspaper.' "

Bruna's mouth quivers. "I'm fifteen," she says, "living in a motel. I can't write an advertisement. I can't read a contract. I'm learning, but I look at what you got to do to be a nurse, college and like that, and here's me leaving school at seven. I know I can't do it; I know it's too late. So I says to myself, Okay, I have the gift — I still have that. Maybe it's all how I use it."

At the end of this monologue, she deflates. He can tell how miserable she is, forced to share it with him.

"Keep going," he says.

Bruna inhales with a wheeze. "I wanted to do something good. So I think, Okay: What do nurses do? They help people, people who suffer. Why do they suffer? 'Cause they don't know what's gonna happen to them. So what if I can take that away? If they have answers, they'll be free, is what I thought. If they know when they'll die, they can live."

"What do you want from the people who come to you? Not money — so what?"

"Nothing." Her eyes bulge.

"Bullshit. You wanted power. We were kids, and you had us eating out of the palm of your hand."

"I didn't make you come."

"You advertised your services."

"I did not. You found me."

Her face is animated and indignant. Daniel tries to remember if this is true. How did he hear of her? Two boys in a deli. But how did *they* hear of her? The trail must lead back to Bruna.

"Even if that were true, you should have turned us away. We were children, and you told us things no child should hear."

"Kids, they all think about death. Everyone thinks about it! And the ones that make their way to me — they got their reasons, every one of 'em, so I give 'em what they came for. Children are pure in their wishes

— they got courage; they want knowledge, they're not afraid of it. You were a bold little boy, I remember you. But you didn't like what you heard. So don't believe me, then — don't believe me! Live like you don't believe me."

"I do live like that. I do." He's veering off track. It's the fatigue and the cold — how does Bruna stand it? — the drive, the thought of Mira finding his cell phone on the floor. "Do you know your own future? Your own death?"

Bruna appears to be shuddering until he realizes she's shaking her head. "No, I don't know it. I can't see myself."

"You can't see yourself." A cruel pleasure blooms in Daniel. "That must drive you insane."

She's his mother's age, his mother's size. But Gertie is robust. Somehow, Bruna looks both bloated and frail.

He aims his gun. "What if it's now?"

The woman gasps. She puts her hands over her ears, and the comforter falls to the floor, revealing her nightgown and bare legs. Her feet are crossed at the ankle and pressed together for warmth.

"Answer me," says Daniel.

She speaks thinly, from the upper register of her throat. "If it's now, it's now."

"It doesn't have to be now, though," he says, fingering the gun. "I could do it any time. Show up at your door, you'd never know when I was coming. Which would you rather? Going now, or never knowing when? Waiting, waiting, walking on tiptoes — looking over your shoulder every fucking day, sticking around while everyone around you dies and you wonder whether it should've been you, and hating yourself because —"

"It's your day!" shouts Bruna, and Daniel is startled by the change in her voice, how it becomes lower and more confident. "Your day, it's today. *That's* why you're here."

"You think I don't know that? You think I didn't do this intentionally?" he says, but Bruna is looking at him with a dubiousness that suggests another narrative: one in which he did not come intentionally at all but was compelled by the very same factors as Simon and Klara. One in which his decision was rigged from the start, because the woman has some foresight he can't understand, or because he is weak enough to believe this.

No. Simon and Klara were pulled magnetically, unconsciously; Daniel is in full possession of his faculties. Still, the two narratives float like an optical illusion — a vase or two faces? — each as convincing as the other, one perspective sliding out of prominence as soon as he relaxes his hold on it.

But there is one way he can make his own interpretation become permanent, the other fading into what was before, or might have been. He isn't sure whether the idea just occurred to him or whether it's been inside him since he saw her photograph.

The woman's eyes flick to the left, and Daniel goes still. At first, he only hears the rush of the waterfall, but then another noise becomes apparent: the slow, padded crunch of feet in the gorge.

"Don't move," he says.

He walks to the cab. When his eyes adjust to the dark, he sees a black mass moving quickly through the narrow passage.

"Get out," says Bruna. "Go."

The footsteps are becoming closer now, faster, and his pulse begins to speed.

"Daniel?" calls a voice.

The map to West Milton on his computer screen. The business card by the mouse pad. Mira must have found them. She must have called Eddie.

"Daniel!" Eddie shouts.

Daniel moans.

"I told you get out," Bruna says.

But Eddie is too close. Daniel sees a figure scrambling up over the edge of the gorge and into the clearing. His stomach rises and turns. He slams Bruna's folding table up toward the wall so that the boxes fall to the floor. The metal folding chairs collapse on top of them.

"All right," snaps Bruna. "That's enough."

But Daniel can't stop. He is alarmed by his own fear, by the deep unstoppable rush of it. It is not him, it is not his: he must cut it out at the root. He walks to the counter beside the sink and uses the barrel of his gun to knock the religious icons to the floor. He empties the boxes in the front seats, dumping their contents — newspapers and canned food, playing cards and tarot cards, old papers and photographs — on the ground. Bruna is shouting now, rising heavily from the couch, but he moves past her to the bedroom door. He rips the wooden cross from its peg and slams it into the wall of the trailer.

"You got no right to do that," Bruna cries, unsteady on her feet. "This is my home." The whites of her eyes are threaded red, and the bags beneath them gleam. "I been here for years, and I'm not going nowhere. You got no right. I'm an American, same as you."

Daniel grabs her wrist. It feels like a chicken bone.

"You are not," he says, "the same as me."

The door of the Regatta swings open, and Eddie appears in the frame. He's off duty, wearing a leather jacket and jeans, but his badge is out and his gun drawn.

"Daniel," he says. "Drop your weapon."

Daniel shakes his head. He has so rarely acted with courage. So now he will — for Simon, his sexuality hidden in life, understood only in death. For Klara, wild-eyed, tied to a light on the ceiling. For Saul, who worked twelve-hour days so that his children might not, and for Gertie, who lost them all.

It is, for him, an act of faith. Faith not in God, but in his own agency. Faith not in fate, but in choice. He would live. He will live. Faith in life.

He still holds Bruna's delicate wrist. He raises the gun to her temple, and she cringes.

"Daniel," roars Eddie. "I'll shoot."

But Daniel barely hears him. The freedom, the expansiveness, of thinking he is innocent: it fills and lifts him like helium. He looks down at Bruna Costello. Once he believed that responsibility flowed between them like air. Now he can't remember what he thought they had in common.

"*Akana mukav tut le Devlesa.*" Bruna

399

speaks under her breath, a strained mutter. "*Akana mukav tut le Devlesa.* I now leave you to God."

"Listen to me, Daniel," Eddie says. "After this, I can't help you."

Daniel's hands are damp. He cocks the gun.

"*Akana mukav tut le Devlesa,*" says Bruna. "I now leave you to —"

■ ■ ■ ■

Part Four:
Place of Life

■ ■ ■ ■

2006–2010
Varya

28.

Frida is hungry.

Varya enters the vivarium at seven thirty and already the monkey is standing up in her cage, holding on to the bars. Most of the animals warble and chirp, knowing that Varya's arrival portends breakfast, but Frida releases the same rapid bark she has for weeks. "Shh-shh," says Varya. "Shh-shh." Each monkey receives a puzzle feeder that forces them to work for their food as they would in the wild: they use their fingers to guide a pellet from the top of a yellow plastic maze to a hole at the bottom. Frida's neighbors scrabble at the feeders, but Frida leaves hers on the cage floor. The puzzle is easy for her; she could have the pellet in seconds. Instead she stares at Varya and calls in alarm, her mouth wide enough to hold an orange.

A flash of dark hair, a hand on the doorway, and Annie Kim pokes her head into the room.

"He's here," she says.

"Early." Varya wears blue scrubs and two pairs of heavy, elbow-length gloves. Her short hair is protected by a shower cap, her face by a mask and plastic shield. Still, the odor of urine and musk is overpowering. She detects it in her condo as well as the lab. She isn't sure whether her own body has begun to take on the scent or whether it's now so familiar that she imagines it everywhere.

"Only by five minutes. Look," Annie says. "The sooner you get going, the sooner it'll be over. Like pulling a tooth."

Some of the monkeys have finished their puzzles and call for more food. Varya uses her elbow to scratch an itch on her waist. "A weeklong dentist appointment."

"Most grant applications take longer," says Annie, and Varya laughs. "Remember: when you look at him, see dollar signs."

She holds the door open for Varya with her foot. As soon as it closes behind them, the screeching is almost undetectable, as if it comes from a distant TV. The building is concrete, with few windows, and all the rooms are soundproof. Varya follows Annie through the hallway to their shared office.

"Frida's still on her hunger strike," Varya says.

"She won't hold out much longer."

"I don't like it. She makes me uneasy."

"Don't you think she knows that?" Annie asks.

The office is a long rectangle. Varya's desk is tucked into the short western wall; Annie's rests against the long southern one, to the left of the door. Between their desks, opposite the door, is a steel laboratory sink. Annie sits and swivels to face her computer. Varya removes her mask and shield, scrubs and gloves, hair and shoe covers. She washes her hands, soaping and rinsing three times in the hottest water she can stand. Then she adjusts her street clothes: a pair of black slacks and a blue oxford shirt with a black cardigan buttoned on top.

"Well, go on." Annie squints at the computer with one hand on the mouse, the other holding a half-eaten Luna bar. "Don't leave him alone too long with the marmosets. He'll start to think all our monkeys are that cute."

Varya squeezes her temples. "Why can't I send you?"

"Mr. Van Galder was very clear." Annie doesn't take her eyes off the computer screen, but she grins. "You're the lead.

You're the one with the fancy findings. He doesn't want me."

When Varya gets out of the elevator, she finds the man facing the marmoset pen. The pen is the lab's only public exhibit. It's nine feet tall by eight wide, with walls made of stiff mesh and encased in glass. The man does not immediately turn around, which gives Varya the opportunity to observe him from behind. He's perhaps six feet, with a dense shrubbery of blond curls, and wears clothes better suited to hiking than to a laboratory tour: some sort of nylon technical pant with a windbreaker and a complicated-looking backpack.

The marmosets crowd against the mesh. There are nine: two parents and their children, all but one of the latter fraternal twins. Fully grown, they measure roughly seven inches long, sixteen if you include their striped, expressive tails. The monkeys' faces are the size of walnut shells but extraordinarily detailed, as if designed on a larger scale and perfectly shrunk: their nostrils the size of pinheads, their black eyes slanted teardrops. One squats on a length of cardboard tubing at a forty-five-degree angle. Its feet are turned out and its round thighs cloaked in hair, which give it the impression of a genie. It emits a piercing whistle that is only slightly blunted by the glass. Ten years ago, when Varya began work at the lab, she mistook the marmosets' calls for alarms sounding in some hallway deep inside the building.

"They do that," she says, stepping forward. "It isn't what it sounds like."

"Abject terror?"

When the man turns, she is surprised by how young he looks. He's lean as a whippet, with a face that lags behind a large and probing nose. But his lips are full, and when he smiles, his face splits into expected handsomeness. There's a slight, boyish gap between his front teeth. Behind silver-rimmed glasses his eyes are a hazel color that reminds her of Frida's.

"It's a contact call," she says. "The marmosets use it to communicate across long distances and greet newcomers. Rhesus monkeys, you don't want to stare at them. They're territorial and they become threatened. But marmosets are curious, and more submissive."

It's true that marmosets are less aggressive than the other monkeys, but this open-mouthed whistle is a call of distress. Varya is not sure what possessed her to lie so immediately, and about something of such little consequence. Perhaps it was the intensity of the man's gaze, an intensity he now applies to her.

"You must be Dr. Gold," he says.

"Mr. Van Galder." Varya does not reach for his hand in the hope he won't hers, but he does and so she brings herself to shake. Immediately she marks the hand in her mind, her right.

"Please. Luke is fine."

Varya nods. "Until your TB results come through I won't be able to take you into the lab. So I thought today I'd show you the main campus."

"You don't waste time," Luke says.

His teasing makes Varya anxious. This is what journalists do: they create a false sense of intimacy, ingratiating themselves until you become comfortable enough to tell them things you'd otherwise have the good sense not to. The last journalist they allowed in the lab was a TV reporter whose footage caused such a frenzy among donors that the Drake built a new play area for the monkeys to placate them. Of course, that reporter elected to include only the most damning B-roll, the rhesus monkeys shaking the cage bars and barking as if they had not just been fed.

Varya leads Luke to the entrance vestibule,

where a heavyset man sits behind a security desk, reading the paper. "You'll have met Clyde."

"Sure. We're old friends. I was just hearing about his mother's birthday."

"She turned a hundred and one last month," Clyde says, setting the paper down. "So my brothers and me, we went to Daly City and threw her a party. She can't leave the house, so we paid the choir from her old church to come sing to her. She still knows all the words."

Varya has not exchanged more than daily greetings with Clyde in the ten years she's worked at the lab. She reaches for the heavy steel door and punches Annie's latest code into the keypad beside it. "Your mother's one hundred and one?"

"You bet," Clyde says. "You should really be pricking her instead of those monkeys."

The Drake Institute for Research on Aging is a series of angular, white buildings nestled within the perpetually green slopes of Mount Burdell. Its property — nearly five hundred acres — lies two miles south of Olompali State Historic Park and two miles north of Skywalker Ranch, almost all of it untouched countryside. The campus is confined to a plateau halfway down the mountain where great hulks of limestone sit amidst the bay trees and chaparral like an alien encampment. To Varya, the mountainside has always seemed unsightly in its lack of grooming — the shrubs tangled and thorny, the bays drooping like overgrown beards — but Luke Van Galder reaches his arms above his head and sighs.

"My God," he says. "To work in such a place. Seventy degrees in March. You can hike in a state park during lunch."

Varya reaches for her sunglasses. "I'm afraid that doesn't ever happen. I'm at work by seven in the morning. Very often I have no idea what the weather is like until I leave that evening. See that building?" she says, pointing. "That's the main research facility. It was designed by Leoh Chen. He's known for his geometric elements — you must have parked in the visitor's lot, so you'll have seen that the building is a semicircle. There are windows on all sides. From here they look small, but they're really floor-to-ceiling." She halts, fifty paces from the primate lab and a quarter mile from the main facility. "Do you have a notebook?"

"I'm listening. I can fact-check later."

"If that seems to you the best sequence of events."

"I'm getting my bearings. I'll be here all

week." Luke raises his eyebrows and smiles. "I figured we might sit down."

"Certainly, we'll sit down," says Varya, "at some point. But I don't usually meet with journalists and I trust you'll understand if certain pieces of information are relayed in transit. Given the study design, it's important that I spend as little time away from the lab as possible."

At five ten, she stands almost at eye level with Luke. His face, as seen through her sunglasses, is subdued in color and dimension, but she can still see surprise play across it. Why? Because she is brisk, impersonal? Surely Luke would not be surprised if the lab were run by a man who displayed these qualities. What guilt she feels at her terseness is replaced by self-assurance. She is, in the world of primate research, establishing dominance.

Luke swings his backpack around to the front and retrieves a black tape recorder. "Okay?"

"Fine," says Varya. Luke depresses the Record button, and she begins to walk again. "How long have you worked at the *Chronicle*?"

A peace offering, this bit of dreaded small chat, as they transition to the wider, paved paths that surround the main facility. The path to the primate lab is no more than a repurposed dirt trail. "They like to keep us tucked away," said Annie once, "the savages," and Varya laughed, though she didn't know whether Annie was referring to the monkeys or the two of them.

"I don't," Luke says. "I'm a freelancer. This is the first piece I've done for them. I work out of Chicago; usually I write for the *Tribune.* You didn't see my pitch?"

Varya shakes her head. "Dr. Kim deals with those things."

Though Annie is a researcher, not a public information officer, she has taken on the latter role with ease. Varya is constantly grateful for Annie's media savvy, so she consented when Annie suggested they take this week's interview, which will be published in the *San Francisco Chronicle.* The primate lab is ten years into a twenty-year study. This year, they'll apply for a second round of competitive funding. Officially, publicity has no bearing on research grants. Unofficially, the foundations that support the Drake like to feel they're enabling something important, something that has garnered both public excitement and — in the case of primate research — public approval.

"Have you worked in a newsroom before?"

she asks.

"In college. I was the paper's editor in chief."

Varya nearly laughs. Annie knew exactly what she was doing. Luke Van Galder is a kid.

"It must be an exciting job. Lots of travel. No two assignments the same," she says, though in truth these things do not excite her at all. "What did you study in college?"

"Biology."

"So did I. Where at?"

"St. Olaf. Small liberal arts college outside of Minneapolis. I'm from a farming town in Wisconsin. It was close enough to home."

Varya's outfit is appropriate for the lab, which is devoid of natural light and always cold, but not for the outdoors. The heat is making her sweat, so she's relieved when they reach the main facility, where the grass is manicured and the trees newly planted. Varya leads Luke across a circular driveway and through a revolving door.

"Holy crap," Luke says when they emerge indoors.

The lobby of the Drake is palatial, with two-story ceilings and limestone tree planters the size of kiddie pools. Its floors are made of imported white marble and stretch as wide as a high school cafeteria. One tour group huddles around the western wall, where videos and interactive exhibits play on flat screens. A second group is being led toward the elevators. The elevators are spectacular — modern glass and chrome cubes that look out over the San Pablo Bay — but the only staff member who uses them is a seventy-two-year-old researcher, wheelchair-bound due to rheumatoid arthritis, who studies the nematode worm *C. elegans.* Everyone else takes the stairs unless ill or injured, even those who work on the eighth floor.

"This way," says Varya. "We can talk in the atrium."

Luke lags behind her, staring. The atrium, modeled after the Louvre, is a glass triangle that faces the Pacific Ocean and Mount Tamalpais. It also functions as a café, with round tables and a juice bar whose line is already ten tourists long. Varya stops at the farthest table and sits, hooking her purse over one of the chair's arms.

"It isn't always this crowded," she says. "We hold tours for the public on Monday mornings."

She keels slightly forward so that only her lower back touches the fabric: a balancing act, threat offset by constant vigilance, as though discomfort is the price she pays for safety. There was a time, as a child, that she lay in her top bunk and propped one dirty foot on the ceiling, just to see how it felt. Her sole left a dark impression on the paint. That night, she feared that tiny particles of dirt would drift down onto her face as she slept, so she stayed awake, watching. She never saw the dirt fall, which meant it hadn't. If she had fallen asleep — if she hadn't kept watch — it might have.

"There must be intense public interest in this place," says Luke, sitting, too. He peels off his windbreaker, which is bright orange, like that of a crossing guard, and tosses it over the back of the chair. "How many people work here?"

"There are twenty-two labs. Each one is run by a faculty lead and has at least three additional members, sometimes up to ten: staff scientists, professors, research associates, lab and animal techs, postdocs and masters students and fellows. The larger ones have administrative assistants, like the Dunham lab — she's studying nerve cell signaling in Alzheimer's. Of course, that's not to mention the facilities and janitorial staff. Total? About one hundred and seventy employees, most of them scientists."

"And all of you are doing antiaging research?"

"We prefer the term *longevity.*" Varya squints: though she chose a shaded portion of the atrium, the sun has moved, and the surface of their metal table beams. "You say antiaging and people think of science fiction, cryonics and whole-brain emulation. But the Holy Grail, for us, is not just to enhance life span. It's to enhance health span — the quality of late life. Dr. Bhattacharya is developing a new drug for Parkinson's, for example. Dr. Cabrillo is attempting to prove that age is the single greatest risk factor for developing cancer. And Dr. Zhang has been able to reverse heart disease in elderly mice."

"You must have your detractors — people who think the human life span is already long enough. People who point to the inevitability of food shortages, overpopulation, disease. Which is not to mention the economics of increased life span, or the politics of who is most likely to benefit from it."

Varya is prepared for this line of questioning, for there have always been detractors. Once, at a dinner party, an environmental lawyer asked why, if Varya was so concerned about the preservation of life, she did not work in conservation. In this day and age, he argued, countless ecosystems, vegetation, and animal species are on the brink of extinction. Was it not more pressing to reduce carbon dioxide emissions or save the blue whale than it was to tack another ten years on to the human life span? Besides, his wife added — she was an economist — increased life expectancy would cause Social Security and Medicare costs to balloon, putting the country even deeper in dept. What did Varya think about that?

"Of course," she says to Luke. "And that's exactly why it's so important for the Drake to be transparent. It's why we host tours every week, why we allow journalists like you in our labs — because the public keeps us honest. But the fact is this: any decision you make, any study you do, there are going to be certain groups that benefit from it and certain groups that don't. You have to choose your allegiance. And my allegiance lies with human beings."

"Some would say that's self-interested."

"Some would. But let's follow that argument to its logical conclusion. Should we stop searching for cancer cures? Should we not treat HIV? Should we cut off access to health care for the elderly, dooming them to whatever comes their way? Your points are valid in theory, but everybody who's lost a father to heart disease or a spouse to Alzheimer's — you ask any of those people, before and after, whether they would support our research, and I guarantee you that what they would say afterward is yes."

"Ah." Luke leans forward and clasps his hands, resting them on the table. One of his jacket sleeves droops to brush the floor. "So it's personal."

"We aim to reduce human suffering. Is that not as much a moral imperative as saving the whales?" This is her trump card, the line that silences acquaintances at cocktail parties and the inevitable argumentative question asker at each public lecture. "Your jacket," she says, flinching.

"What?"

"Your jacket is on the floor."

"Oh," says Luke, and shrugs, leaving it right where it is.

29.

The sky is powdery with dusk by the time Varya leaves the lab. When she is halfway across the Golden Gate Bridge, the main cable lights prick to life. She arcs through Land's End, past the Legion of Honor and the mansions of Seacliff, and pulls into visitor parking on Geary. Then she signs in at reception and walks the outdoor path to Gertie's building.

Gertie has been a resident at Helping Hands for two years. In the months after Daniel's death, she stayed in Kingston while Mira and Varya discussed options. But in May of 2007, Mira returned from work to find Gertie facedown in the backyard, having collapsed on her way from the garden. Gertie's left cheek was pressed to the dirt, a glassy circle of drool beside her chin. There was blood on her right arm from where she'd scraped the chicken wire fence. Mira screamed, but she soon discovered Gertie could stand on her own and even walk. After a CT scan and a blood test, doctors labeled the incident a stroke.

Varya was furious. There was no other word for it; there was barely even sadness — just rage so blinding she felt dizzy as soon as she finally heard Gertie's voice.

"Why," Varya demanded, "didn't you call Mira? You could stand. You could walk. So why didn't you go inside and call Mira — and if not Mira, then me?"

She pressed her cell phone to her ear. She was dragging her suitcase through SFO, soon to board the plane that would take her to Kingston.

"I thought I was dying," Gertie said.

"You must have soon realized you weren't."

Silence stretched on, and in it Varya heard what she already knew to be true, the source of her rage in the first place. *I hoped I was. I wanted to.* Gertie didn't have to say it. Varya knew. She also knew why — of course, she knew why — and yet it seemed unbearably cruel to think of Gertie leaving her now, of her own volition, when they were the only two left.

Within weeks, Gertie experienced complications. She became easily confused. Her left arm went numb, and her balance was worse. For six months, she lived in Varya's condo, but a series of dangerous falls convinced Varya she needed round-the-clock care. They toured three different facilities before deciding on Helping Hands, which Gertie liked because the building — painted cream and robin's egg blue, with yellow awnings over each balcony — reminded her of the beach house the Golds used to rent in New Jersey. Also, it has a library.

When Varya enters her mother's room, Gertie stands from a faded armchair and wobbles to the door on her soft ankles. The staff at Helping Hands suggested she use a wheelchair at all times, but Gertie detests the contraption and finds any excuse to get rid of it, like a teenager leaving her parents behind in a crowd.

She clasps Varya's upper arms. "You look different."

Varya leans down to kiss her mother's delicate, velvety cheek. For most of her life, Varya hid her nose by keeping her hair long. But now her hair has gone silver, and last week, she had it cropped close to her skull.

"Why the black clothing?" Gertie asks. "Why the hair like *Rosie's Baby?*"

"*Rosemary's Baby?*" Varya frowns. "She was blond."

A light knock on the door, and a nurse enters to bring Gertie dinner: chopped salad; a chicken breast in a gelatinous yellow membrane; a small roll of bread with a pat of butter, the latter wrapped in gold foil.

Gertie climbs in bed to eat, activating a robotic arm that unfolds to become a small table. In the beginning, she hated the facility. She called it that — "the facility," instead of Varya's preferred term, "the home" — and weekly she tried to escape from it. Eighteen months ago — after she called Don Dorfman's Auto Emporium and set in motion plans to purchase a Volvo S40, giving Don Dorfman the number of a long-defunct credit card once owned by Saul — Gertie was prescribed an antidepressant, and her circumstances improved. Now she attends continuing education classes on subjects like Battles of the Second World War and the popular Presidential Affairs (Not of State). She plays mah-jongg with a group of boisterous widows. She makes use of the library and even the pool, where she bobs atop an inflatable lounger like a celebrity on a parade float, calling to whomever is in shouting distance.

"I don't know why you won't come to the dining hall," she tells Varya when the nurse leaves. "We could sit at the table and socialize. Maybe you'd even eat something."

But Gertie's new friends make Varya uncomfortable. They gossip constantly about whose son is due to visit, whose granddaughter has just given birth. They responded with shock, then pity, after learning that Varya is both childless and unmarried. And they showed little interest in her longevity research, which aims, after all, to help people like them.

"But no children?" they persisted, as if Varya might have lied the first time. "No one to share your life with? What a shame."

Now Varya pauses at Gertie's bedside, standing. "I come here to see you. I don't need to socialize with anyone else. And I've told you, Ma, that I never eat this early. Not before —"

"— seven thirty. I know."

Gertie's face is both defiant and doleful. She knows Varya better than anyone else, knows her deepest secret and has probably guessed plenty of others, and lately Varya's visits have provoked these power struggles — times when Gertie pushes against Varya's carefully assembled exterior and Varya pushes the wooden thing back, insisting on its legitimacy.

"I brought you something," Varya says.

She walks to a small, square table by the

window and begins to unload a care package from a brown paper bag. There is a book of poems by Elizabeth Bishop, which she found at a library sale; a jar of Milwaukee's dill pickles, in honor of Saul; and lilacs, which she brings into Gertie's small bathroom. She cuts the stems over a trash can, fills a tall glass with tap water, and carries them back to the table by the window.

"If you'd stop walking back and forth like that," Gertie says.

"I brought you flowers."

"So stop and look at them."

Varya does. The glass is too short. One flower keels dumbly over the side. They won't be alive much longer.

"Very pretty," says Gertie. "Thank you."

And when Varya takes in the bland plastic table and the window felted with dust, the hospital-like bed across which Gertie has laid a faded afghan Saul's mother crocheted, she can see why Gertie thinks so. In these surroundings, the flowers stand out, so colorful they almost look neon.

Varya pulls a metal folding chair from the card table at the window to Gertie's bedside. The armchair is closer to the bed, but its fabric is nubby and stained and Varya has no way of knowing who's sat on it.

Gertie peels back the foil around the butter and digs inside with a plastic knife. "Did you bring me a photo?"

Varya has, though every week she hopes Gertie will forget to ask. Ten years ago, she made the mistake of photographing Frida with the camera on her new cell phone. Frida had just arrived at the Drake after a three-day journey from a primate lab in Georgia. She was two weeks old: her pink face wrinkled and pear shaped, her thumbs in her mouth. That year, Gertie was still living alone, and the thought of her isolation compelled Varya to send a photo by e-mail. Immediately she realized her error. She had joined the Drake one month before, at which point she signed an uncompromising confidentiality policy. But Gertie responded to the photo with such glee that Varya soon found herself sending another — this one of Frida wrapped in a teal blanket while being fed by bottle.

Why didn't she stop? For two reasons: because the photos were a way to share her research with Gertie, who had never fully understood it — previously, Varya had worked with yeast and drosophila, organisms so small and uncharismatic that Gertie could not fathom how Varya might discover anything of use to human beings — and because they brought Gertie delight; because *Varya* brought Gertie delight.

"Better," says Varya now. "A video."

Gertie's face is a mask of anticipation. Her hands, thickened and gnarled by arthritis, reach for the cell phone, as if Varya has brought news of a grandchild. Varya helps Gertie hold the phone and press Play. In the video, Frida is grooming herself while looking into the mirror that hangs outside of her cage. The mirror is a source of enrichment, like the puzzle feeders and the classical music played in the vivarium each afternoon. By reaching their fingers through the bars, the monkeys can manipulate the mirrors, using them to look at themselves as well as the rest of the cages.

"Oh!" said Gertie, holding the screen close to her face. "Look at that."

The video is two years old. Varya has taken to recycling old material during these visits, for Frida looks very different now. She smiles, remembering Frida at this age, but Gertie's face is darkening. In the three years since her stroke, these moments have become more frequent. Varya knows what will happen before the transformation has finished: a vacancy in the eyes, a slackness of the mouth, as Gertie's new disorientation asserts itself.

Now she looks from the phone to Varya

with accusation. "But why do you keep her in a cage?"

30.

"There are two major theories about how to stop aging," Varya says. "The first is that you should suppress the reproductive system."

"The reproductive system," repeats Luke. His head is bowed over a small black notebook, which he brought today in addition to the tape recorder.

Varya nods. She met Luke in the atrium this morning, and now he follows her down the dirt trail to the primate lab. "A biologist named Thomas Kirkwood suggested that we sacrifice ourselves in order to pass genes along to our offspring, and that tissues with no role in reproduction — the brain, for example; the heart — endure damage in order to protect the reproductive organs. This has been proven in the lab: there are two cells in worms that give rise to its entire reproductive system, and when you use a laser to destroy them, the worm lives sixty percent longer."

A pause before she hears Luke's voice behind her. "And the second theory?"

"The second theory is that you should suppress caloric intake." She punches a new key code — Annie changed it last night — into the pad beside the door with the knuckle of her right pointer finger. "Which is what I'm doing."

The light turns green, and Varya opens the door as it beeps. Inside, she nods hello to Clyde and glances at the marmosets — today, all nine of them lie in the same hammock, indistinguishable except for their small metal tags — while using her elbow to press the elevator button for the second floor.

"And that works how?" asks Luke.

"We think it has to do with a gene called DAF-16, which is involved in the molecular signaling pathway initiated by the insulin receptor." The door opens, and out walks an animal technician in blue scrubs; Varya and Luke take her place. "When you block this pathway in *C. elegans,* for instance, you can more than double its life span."

Luke looks at her. "In English?"

Rarely does Varya discuss her work with non-scientists. All the more reason to take this interview, said Annie: to bring their work to the *Chronicle*'s wide audience.

"I'll give you an example," she says as the elevator door opens. "The people of Okinawa have the highest life expectancy in the world. I studied the Okinawan diet in graduate school and what's clear is that while it's very nutritious, it's also very low in calories." She turns left, into a long hallway. "We eat food to produce energy. But energy production also creates chemicals that harm the body, because they cause cells to become stressed. Now, here's the interesting part: when you're on a restricted diet, like the Okinawans, you're actually causing the system *more* stress. But this is what allows the body to live longer: it's continuously dealing with a low level of stress, and this teaches it how to deal with stress in the long-term."

"It doesn't sound very enjoyable." Luke wears a pair of technical pants with a zip-up hoodie. A pair of sunglasses is stuck in his hair, held in place by the curls.

Varya fits her key in the office door and pushes it open with her hip. "Hedonists don't tend to live very long."

"But they have fun while they're doing it." Luke follows her into the office. Her side is immaculate, while Annie's is littered with PowerBar wrappers and water bottles and disheveled stacks of academic journals. "It sounds like you're saying we can choose to live. Or we can choose to survive."

Varya hands him a stack of facility clothing. "Protective gear."

He takes the bundle in his arms and sets his backpack down. The pants are almost too short; Luke's legs are long and thin, and without warning Varya sees Daniel's legs, Daniel's face. She turns away from him to steady herself. For years after his death, she had no episodes at all. But one Monday, four months ago, her coffeemaker broke, so she went to Peet's and stood in a long line of customers. The music was hideous — a jazzy Christmas compilation, though it was barely Thanksgiving — and something about this and the crowds and the dense, suppressive smell of coffee grinding and the accompanying screech made Varya feel as though she were choking. By the time she reached the cashier, she could see that the employee's mouth was moving but she could not hear what it said. She stared, watching the mouth as if from one end of a telescope, until it spoke more sharply — *"Ma'am? Are you all right?"* — and the telescope clattered to the ground.

When she turns around, Luke is already suited up, and he is staring at her.

"How long have you been working here?" he asks, which is different than what she thought he would say — *Are you all right?* — and for this she is grateful.

"Ten years."

"And before that?"

Varya crouches to slip on her shoe covers. "I'm sure you've done your research."

"You graduated from Vassar with your BS in 1978. By 1983 you were in graduate school at NYU, which you finished in '88. You stayed on as a research assistant for another two years, and then you took a fellowship at Columbia. In '93 you published a study on yeast — 'Extreme life span extension in yeast mutants: age-dependent mutations increase at slower pace in organisms with CR-activated Sir2,' if I'm not mistaken — which was groundbreaking enough to be covered by some of the popular science magazines, and then the *Times.*"

Varya stands, surprised. The information he's cited is available on the Drake's website, but she had not given him so much credit as to expect he had it memorized.

"I wanted to make sure I had my facts straight," Luke adds. His voice is muffled by the mask, but his eyes, as seen through the face shield, look slightly sheepish.

"You do."

"So why the leap to primates?" He holds the office door open for her, and she locks it from the outside.

She had been used to organisms so tiny they could only be properly viewed through a microscope: laboratory yeast, shipped in vacuum-sealed containers from a supply company in North Carolina, and fruit flies bred for human study, with miniature wings too small for flight. Varya was forty-four when the Drake's CEO — then a stern older woman who warned Varya that an opportunity like this would not come her way again — invited her to run a caloric-restriction study in primates. When they hung up, Varya laughed in fear. She had enough trouble going to the doctor's office; to spend her days in close proximity to rhesus monkeys, from which she could catch tuberculosis and herpes B, was inconceivable.

What's more, she was baffled. She hadn't worked with primates, or even with mice, but this, said the CEO, was the source of their interest: the Drake wanted not to promote a low-calorie lifestyle for human beings — "Imagine how successful that would be," the woman said, wryly — but to develop a drug that would have the same effect. They needed someone who was well

433

versed in genetics, someone who could analyze their findings on a molecular level. And she was quick to assure Varya that her daily tasks would have little to do with the animals. They had technicians and a veterinarian for that. Most of Varya's time would be spent on conference calls, in meetings, or at her desk: reading and reviewing papers, writing grants, assessing data, preparing presentations. Really, if she preferred, she could have no contact with the animals at all.

Now Varya leads Luke toward a large steel door. "We share about ninety-three percent of our genes with rhesus monkeys. I was more comfortable working with yeast. But I realized that what I was doing with yeast would never matter as much to human beings — could never matter as much, biologically speaking — as a study in primates."

What she does not say is that the year 2000, when she was approached by the Drake, was almost ten years after Klara's death and twenty after Simon's. "Think about it," the CEO said, and Varya said she would, while calculating how much time would reasonably pass if she were to do such a thing so that she knew how long to wait before declining. But when she returned to her lab at Columbia, where she was running a new study on yeast, she felt not satisfaction or pride but worthlessness. When Varya was in graduate school, her research had been groundbreaking, but these days, any postdoc knew how to extend the life span of a fly or a worm. In five years, what would she have to show for herself? Likely no partner, certainly no children, but this, ideally: a major finding. A different sort of contribution to the world.

She took the job for another reason, too. Varya had always told herself that she did her research out of love — love for life, for science, and for her siblings, who hadn't lived long enough to reach old age — but at heart, she worried that her primary motivation was fear. Fear that she had no control, that life slipped through one's fingers no matter what. Fear that Simon and Klara and Daniel had, at least, lived in the world, while Varya lived in her research, in her books, in her head. The job at the Drake felt like her last chance. If she could push herself to do this, in spite of what misery it would cause her, she could chip away at her guilt, that debt her survival had engendered.

"Your gloves," she says, stopping outside the door to the vivarium. "Don't take them off, either pair."

Luke holds up his hands. His camera

hangs around his neck from a strap; he's left his notebook and tape recorder in the office. Varya opens the rubber-sealed door of Vivarium 1, another door opened only by a key code that Annie changes each month, and leads Luke into the blinding midday roar.

Vivarium, in Latin, means "place of life." In science it refers to an enclosure where living animals are kept in conditions that simulate their natural environment. What is the natural environment of the rhesus monkey? Human beings are the only primate more broadly distributed across the globe than the rhesus macaque, these nomads who have traveled across land and over water, who can live as well on a four-thousand-foot mountain as in a tropical forest or a mangrove swamp. From Puerto Rico to Afghanistan the monkey thrives, making homes of temples and canal banks and railway stations. They eat insects and leaves along with what food they can scavenge from humans: fried bread, peanuts, bananas, ice cream. Every day, they travel miles.

None of this is easy to simulate in the lab, but the Drake has tried. Because macaques are social creatures, they are caged in pairs, and each cage has the ability to open up into the next, creating a column the width of the vivarium. Enrichment activities ensure that the monkeys are stimulated: psychologically, via the puzzle feeders and mirrors as well as plastic balls and videos viewed on iPads (though recently the iPads were removed because the monkeys so frequently broke the screens) and jungle sounds played through overhead speakers. The lab is visited annually by a representative from the federal Department of Agriculture, who ensures their compliance with the Animal Welfare Act, and last year this person recommended that staff occasionally enter the vivarium wearing different clothing — hats or gloves in exciting patterns — to intrigue and entertain the animals, which they now do as well.

Varya is not deluded. Of course, the monkeys would rather be outdoors. Behind the vivarium is a larger caged area where the monkeys can play with tires or ropes and swing on netting, though in truth it should be larger, and each monkey receives only a couple of hours there each week. But the point is that her study seeks not to test new drugs or research SIV but to keep the animals alive for as long as possible. Where is the fault in that?

She turns to Luke and shares the talking points that Annie prepared. Without primate research, countless viruses would not have been discovered. Countless vaccines would not have been developed, and countless therapies would not have been proven safe for Alzheimer's, Parkinson's, and AIDS. Then there is the fact that life in the outside world is no picnic, full of predators and potential starvation. Nobody but a sadist, and perhaps Harry Harlow, likes the sight of a monkey in a cage, but at least, at the Drake, they are cared for and protected.

Still, she can see how a visitor could get the wrong impression. The cages are stacked against the walls, leaving a narrow center aisle for Varya and Luke. The animals face them, splayed against the mesh like geckos. Their pink bellies are stretched long, fingers hooked through the open squares. The dominant monkeys stare silently with their mouths open and their long, yellow teeth bared; the less dominant ones grimace and scream. They do the same thing to the Drake's new CEO, a man who visits the lab once or twice a year for as little time as possible.

In her first year, the monkeys also reacted this way to Varya. It took all her self-control not to flee. But she did not flee, and though the former CEO had been right — most of Varya's time is spent at her desk — she forces herself to visit the vivarium once daily, usually to administer breakfast. She does not touch the animals, but she likes to know how they are doing, likes to see the evidence of her success. She brings Luke's attention to the calorie-restricted monkeys and then to the control monkeys, who eat as much as they please. Luke takes photos of each group. The flash makes them scream louder. Some of the monkeys have begun to shake the bars of their cages, so Varya shouts to explain that the controls are more prone to early-onset diabetes and that their risk of disease is almost three times higher than that of the restricted group. The restricted group even looks younger: their oldest members have lush, auburn fur while the controls are wrinkled and balding, their red rumps showing through.

This is the midpoint of the study, so it's too soon to assess total life span. Still, it's clear that the results are promising, that they suggest Varya's thesis is likely to be proven, and in sharing this she feels such pride that she can ignore the screaming, the scrabbling, the scent, and face the monkeys, her subjects, with pleasure.

When Luke has left, she retrieves Frida.

Earlier today, she asked Annie to move her into the isolation chamber. Frida is her favorite monkey, but Frida is bad PR — Frida of the broad, flat brow, her golden eyes rimmed in black as if by kohl. As a baby, her ears were overlarge, her fingers long and pink. She arrived in California one week after Varya herself. That morning, Annie had received a shipment of new monkeys, but there was one held up due to a snowstorm, a baby who had been bred at a research center in Georgia. Annie had to leave, so Varya stayed. At nine thirty p.m. an unmarked white van trundled up the hill and stopped outside of the primate lab. Out climbed an unshaven boy who couldn't have been more than twenty and who had Varya sign a receipt, as if for a pizza. He seemed to have no interest in his cargo, or perhaps he had grown sick of it: when he retrieved the cage, which was covered by a blanket, it emitted such horrible screeching that Varya instinctively backed away.

But the animal was her responsibility now. She wore full protective clothing, though this did nothing to dim the sounds that came from the cage as the driver handed it over. He wiped his face with relief and jogged back to the van. Then he drove down the hill far faster than he had driven up, leaving Varya and the screaming cage alone.

The cage was the size of a microwave. They would not introduce Frida to the other animals until tomorrow, so Varya brought the cage to an isolated room the size of a janitor's closet, and set it down. Her arms were already aching and her heartbeat flapped with terror. Why had she ever agreed to this? She had not even done the hardest part, which was the physical transition from old cage to new, and which required Varya to touch the animal inside.

The cage was still covered by what Varya now saw was a baby blanket, patterned with yellow rattles. She peeled back a corner of the blanket, and the animal's cries grew louder. Varya sat back on her heels. Her anxiety was ballooning — she knew she had to do the transition now or she would not be able to do it at all — so she hefted the small transport cage until its opening aligned with the door of the lab cage. Inhaling, she removed the blanket. The carrier was barely bigger than the monkey itself, but the animal began to revolve, turning circles while grasping the bars. Varya reached for the lock as Annie had shown her, but her hands shook — the monkey's confusion and fear were unbearable — and before she could steady herself, the carrier slid to one side.

Out shot the baby, as if from a cannon. It did not land in the larger cage but on Varya's chest. She could not help it: she screamed, too, and fell back from her knees to her rear. She thought the monkey meant to hurt her, but it wrapped its slender arms around her back and clung, pressing its face to her breast.

Who was more terrified? Varya had images of amebiasis and hepatitis B, all the diseases of which she dreamed nightly and feared she would die, all the reasons she had not wanted to take this job in the first place. But pressing back against that fear was another living creature. The baby's body was heavy, so much denser than a human baby's that it made the latter seem hollow. She did not know how long they stayed that way, Varya rocking back on her heels as the monkey cried. It was three weeks old. Varya knew it had been taken from its mother at two weeks, that it was the mother's first child, and that the mother, whose name was Songlin — she had been transported from a breeding center in Guangxi,

China — had been so distressed that she was tranquilized in the midst of that process.

At one point she looked up and saw their reflection in the mirror mounted to the outside of the cage. What came to her then was Frida Kahlo's *Self-Portrait with Monkey*. Varya did not look like Kahlo — she was not as strong, she was not as defiant — and the lab, with its beige concrete walls, could not be further from Kahlo's yucca and large, glossy leaves. But there was the monkey in Varya's arms, her eyes dark and enormous as blackberries; there were the two of them, equally fearful, equally alone, staring into the mirror together.

31.

Three and a half years ago, when Varya arrived in Kingston after Daniel's death, Mira brought her into the guest room and shut the door.

"There's something I need to show you," she said.

Mira sat on the edge of the bed, a laptop on her thighs. With her legs taut and her toes grasping the carpet, she showed Varya a series of cached webpages: Google searches about the Rom, a screenshot of Bruna Costello on the FBI's Most Wanted site. Varya recognized the woman immediately. At once, she felt a head rush: dizzying, silver confetti. She nearly slid to the floor.

"This is the woman Daniel decided to pursue. He took our gun from the shed and drove to West Milton, where she was living. And I called the agent who shot him," said Mira; her voice bent like a reed. "Why,

444

Varya? Why did Daniel do it?"

So Varya told Mira the story of the woman. Her voice was raspy, the words flaking like rust, but she forced them until they ran faster, clearer. She was desperate to help Mira understand. When she finished, though, Mira looked even more bewildered.

"But that was so long ago," she said. "So deep in the past."

"It wasn't, for him." Varya's tears ran freely; she wiped her cheeks with her fingers.

"But it should have been. It should be." Mira's eyes were bloodshot, her throat scarlet. "Goddammit, Varya. My God! If only he had let it go."

They strategized about what to tell Gertie. Varya wanted to say that Daniel had become fixated on a local woman's crimes after his suspension — that the notion of justice gave him something to work for, to believe in. Mira wanted to be honest.

"What does it matter whether we tell her the truth?" she asked. "The story isn't going to bring Daniel back. It won't change how he died."

But Varya disagreed. She knew that stories did have the power to change things: the past and the future, even the present. She had been an agnostic since graduate school, but if there was one tenant of Judaism with

445

which she agreed, it was this: the power of words. They weaseled under door cracks and through keyholes. They hooked into individuals and wormed through generations. The truth might change Gertie's perception of her children, children who weren't alive to defend themselves. It would almost certainly cause her more pain.

That night, while Mira and Gertie slept, Varya climbed out of the guest bed and walked to the study. Specks of Daniel were everywhere — comforting in their familiarity, agonizing in their superficiality. Beside the computer was a paperweight in the shape of the Golden Gate Bridge, which Varya purchased at SFO when she was a harried postdoc, en route to Kingston for Hanukkah, and realized she'd forgotten gifts. She'd hoped Daniel would mistake it for a piece of art. He didn't. "An airport tchotchke?" he hooted, swatting her. Now, the gold plating had turned a coppery green; she had not known he'd kept it all these years.

She sat in his chair and tipped her head back. She had not gone to Amsterdam over Thanksgiving, as she'd told him; there was no conference. She had defrosted a bag of chopped vegetables, sautéed them in olive oil, and ate the sloppy pile at the kitchen table by herself. That fall, her anxiety about Daniel's date had become acute. She did not know what would happen that day, did not think she could stand to witness it — or perhaps it was that, if she were there, she would feel responsible. She still feared she might catch or transmit something terrible, as though her luck was both bad and contagious. The best thing she could do for Daniel was stay away.

But by nine in the morning on the day after Thanksgiving, her heart had begun to palpitate. She was sweating so profusely that a cold shower provided only a temporary reprieve. Varya did what she'd sworn she wouldn't and called him. He made some remark about finding the fortune teller, something she thought was flip and hadn't believed. Then came the old guilt trip, Daniel's voice becoming gnawing and childlike — *It would have been nice to have you here yesterday* — and she felt an irritation suffused with self-hatred. There were times she deleted his voice mails without listening to them so that she did not have to hear this tone of voice, a maddening and indefatigable woundedness, as if he was content to be let down over and over again. Why did he keep trying? He had Mira, after all. The sooner he realized that Varya had nothing to offer, that she would only continue to fail him, the sooner he would be happy, free of her, and the sooner Varya would be released by him.

A dry-cleaning receipt, previously pinned down by the paperweight, fluttered next to the computer. Daniel's neat, boxy handwriting bled through from the other side.

Varya turned it over. *Our language is our strength,* he'd written. Beneath that was a second phrase, one Daniel had traced over so many times that it seemed to rise, three-dimensionally, from the page: *Thoughts have wings.*

She knew exactly what it meant. Once, in graduate school, she tried to explain this phenomenon to her first therapist.

"It's not a question of *seeing* something is clean," she said. "It's a question of *feeling* it's clean."

"And what if you don't?" the therapist asked. "Feel something's clean?"

Varya paused. The truth was that she did not know exactly what would happen; she simply felt a constant foreboding, the sense that ruin loomed behind her like a shadow, and that the rituals could continue to forestall it.

"Then something bad will happen," she said.

When did it begin? She had always been anxious, but something changed after her visit to the woman on Hester Street. Sitting in the rishika's apartment, Varya was sure she was a fraud, but when she went home the prophecy worked inside her like a virus. She saw it do the same thing to her siblings: it was evident in Simon's sprints, in Daniel's tendency toward anger, in the way Klara unlatched and drifted away from them.

Perhaps they had always been like this. Or perhaps they would have developed in these ways regardless. But no: Varya would have already seen them, her siblings' inevitable, future selves. She would have known.

She was thirteen and a half when it occurred to her that avoiding cracks in the sidewalk could prevent the woman's prediction from coming true for Klara. At her fourteenth birthday, it felt imperative to blow out all her candles as quickly as possible, because something awful would happen to Simon if she didn't. She missed three candles and Simon, eight years old, blew out the rest. Varya yelled at him, knowing it made her seem selfish, but that wasn't the problem. The problem was that Simon's act had ruined her attempt to protect him.

She was not diagnosed until the age of thirty. These days, every child has an acronym to explain what's wrong with them, but when Varya was young, the compulsions seemed like nothing but her own secret burden. They became worse after Simon's death. Still, not until graduate school did it occur to her that she might want to try therapy, and not until her therapist mentioned OCD did it occur to her that there was a name for the constant hand-washing, the toothbrushing, the avoidance of public restrooms and Laundromats and hospitals and touching doors and subway seats and other people's hands, all the rituals that safeguarded every hour, every day, every month, every year.

Years later, a different therapist asked her exactly what she was afraid of. Varya was initially stumped, not because she didn't know what she was afraid of but because it was harder to think of what she wasn't.

"So give me some examples," said the therapist, and that night Varya made a list.

Cancer. Climate change. Being the victim of a car crash. Being the cause of a car cash. (There was a period when the thought of killing a bicyclist while making a right turn caused Varya to follow any bicyclist for

450

blocks, checking again and again to make sure she hadn't.) Gunmen. Plane crashes — sudden doom! People wearing Band-Aids. AIDS — really, all types of viruses and bacteria and disease. Infecting someone else. Dirty surfaces, soiled linens, bodily secretions. Drugstores and pharmacies. Ticks and bedbugs and lice. Chemicals. The homeless. Crowds. Uncertainty and risk and open-ended endings. Responsibility and guilt. She is even afraid of her own mind. She is afraid of its power, of what it does to her.

At her next appointment, Varya read the list aloud. When she finished, the therapist leaned back in her chair.

"Okay," she said. "But what are you really afraid of?"

Varya laughed at the purity of the question. It was loss, of course. Loss of life; loss of the people she loved.

"But you've already been through that," the therapist said. "You lost your father and all your siblings — more familial loss than some people ever endure by middle age. And you're still standing. Sitting," she added, smiling at the couch.

Yes, Varya was still sitting, but it wasn't that simple. She *had* lost parts of herself as she lost her siblings. It was like watching the power incrementally turning off throughout a neighborhood: certain parts of her went dark, then others. Certain modes of bravery — emotional bravery — and desire. The cost of loneliness is high, she knows, but the cost of loss is higher.

There was a time before she understood this. She was twenty-seven years old and taking a graduate course in the physics department. The course was taught by a visiting professor from Edinburgh who had studied with a researcher named Peter Higgs.

"Plenty of people don't believe Dr. Higgs," he told Varya. "But they're wrong."

They sat in an Italian restaurant in Midtown. The professor said that Dr. Higgs had postulated the existence of something called the Higgs boson, which imbues particles with mass. He said it could be the key to our understanding of the universe, that it was a linchpin of modern physics even though no one had ever seen it. He said it pointed to a universe ruled by symmetry but in which the most exciting developments — like human beings — are aberrations, products of the brief moments when symmetry fails.

Some of Varya's friends were shocked by their own missed periods, but Varya knew instantly: she woke up one morning no longer herself. Three days before, she had slept with the professor on a twin bed in his campus apartment. When he nestled his face between her legs and moved his tongue, she orgasmed for the first time. Soon after, he became civil and distant, and she did not hear from him again. Now she imagined the new cells in her body and thought: You will undo me. You'll ground me forever. You will make the world so vivid, so real, that I won't be able to forget my pain for an instant. She was afraid of aberration, which could not be controlled; she preferred the safe consistency of symmetry. When she made an appointment to have her uterus emptied at the Bleecker Street Planned Parenthood, she saw the aberration disappear as if between two elevator doors, so cleanly it might never have been there.

Other people speak of the ecstasy to be found in sex and the more complicated joy of parenthood, but for Varya, there is no greater pleasure than relief — the relief of realizing that what she fears does not exist. Even so, it's temporary: a blustery, windswept pleasure, hysterical as laughter — *What was I thinking?* — followed by the slow erosion of that certainty, the creeping in of doubt, which requires another check in the rearview mirror, another shower, another doorknob cleaned.

Varya has had enough therapy to know that she's telling herself stories. She knows her faith — that rituals have power, that thoughts can change outcomes or ward off misfortune — is a magic trick: fiction, perhaps, but necessary for survival. And yet, and yet: Is it a story if you believe it? Her deeper secret, the reason she doesn't think she'll ever be rid of the disorder, is that on some days she doesn't think it's a disorder. On some days, she doesn't think it's absurd to believe that a thought can make something come true.

In May of 2007, six months after Daniel's death, Mira called Varya in hysterics.

"They've cleared Eddie O'Donoghue," she said: an internal review had found no evidence of wrongdoing.

Varya did not cry. She felt fury enter her body and settle there, like a child. She no longer believed that Daniel died of a bullet meant for the pelvis but which entered his thigh, rupturing the femoral artery, so that all his blood was lost in less than ten minutes. His death did not point to the failure of the body. It pointed to the power of the human mind, an entirely different adversary — to the fact that thoughts have wings.

32

On Friday morning, while driving to work, Varya pulls to the side of the road, wrenches the car into park, and drops her head between her knees. She is thinking of Luke. For the past two days, he has met her at the lab at seven thirty and followed her into the vivarium. There he's been useful — helping her weigh pellets for feedings, transferring heavy cages to the storage room for cleaning — and the animals have taken to him. On Wednesday he developed a game with one of their older males, Gus, a beautiful rhesus with a full orange coat and an ego to match. Gus came to the front of his cage and presented his belly to ask for a scratch. Then he either jumped back in an attempt to startle Luke, who laughed and played along, or sat there for as long as Luke scratched his exposed, salmon-colored stomach, smacking his lips in affection.

When Varya expressed surprise at his skill

with the monkeys and his desire to help, Luke explained that he grew up on a farm, that physical labor and working with animals are familiar to him, and that this is what his editor at the *Chronicle* wanted, anyway: to get a sense of daily life at the Drake, so that the researchers come alive as real people, and the monkeys as individuals, too. On Thursday, while eating lunch in the office — Varya with her Tupperware of broccoli and black beans, Luke with a chicken wrap from the atrium — he asked her about this, whether she thought of the monkeys as individuals, and whether it troubled her to see them in cages. If he had done so on Monday, she would have been wary, but the days since have passed so easily, without crisis or judgment, that by Thursday she was relaxed enough to answer honestly.

Before she came to the Drake, she had never been around organisms of such size and flesh. The monkeys' bodies were meaty and impossible to ignore: they smelled and screeched, they were covered in hair, they suffered from diabetes and endometriosis. Their nipples were pink as bubblegum and distended, their faces startlingly emotive. It was impossible to look into their eyes and not see — or think you saw — just what they were thinking. They were not passive subjects to be acted upon but opinionated participants. She was conscious of not anthropomorphizing them, and yet, in those early years, she was struck by the familiarity of their faces and especially by their eyes. When they gathered together and stared at her with those bottomless eyes they looked to her like humans in monkey suits, peering through cutouts in masks.

"Which was obviously unsustainable," she tells Luke, "that kind of thinking."

She sat at her desk, Luke at Annie's. He had propped his right ankle up on his left knee, his long legs bent with the spider awkwardness of tall young men. Put at ease by the gentleness of his attention, Varya continued.

"One Thanksgiving — this would have been my second or third year at the Drake — I visited my brother, who worked as a military doctor, and I shared all of this. He told me about a patient he'd seen that day, a twenty-three-year-old soldier with an infected amputation who cursed the Afghans every time Daniel touched his skin. Daniel remembered him from a medical screening a couple of years earlier, when the soldier expressed so much anxiety about the state of Afghanistan — so much concern for its people — that Daniel almost ordered a psychiatric evaluation. He was worried the boy was too soft."

Daniel had sat much like Luke did on Thursday — one leg cast over the other, his large eyes intent — but the skin beneath his eyes was dark and his formerly thick hair sparse. In that moment Varya remembered him as a boy, her younger brother, whose idealism had been replaced by something more realistic but just as simple, something she recognized in herself.

"His point," Varya said, "was that it's impossible to survive without dehumanizing the enemy, without creating an enemy in the first place. He said that compassion was the purview of civilians, not those whose job was to act. Acting requires you to choose one thing over another. And it's better to help one side than neither."

She fit the lid of the Tupperware on the bowl and thought of Frida, who was part of the restricted-calorie group. In the beginning, she called and called for more food. At home, Varya was haunted by those calls. There was something in the monkey's shameless hunger that made her feel both guilty and repulsed. So clear was Frida's desire for life, so visible the accusation in her eyes, that Varya nearly expected her to trade her rough, staccato shrieks for English.

"I do grow attached to the monkeys," she added. "I shouldn't say that — not very scientific. But I've known them for ten years. And I remind myself that the study benefits them, too. I'm protecting them, the restricted ones especially. They'll live longer this way." Luke was quiet; he'd put his tape recorder away, and though his notebook sat on Annie's desk, he didn't touch it. "Still, you have to draw a line in the sand that says: 'This research is worth it. This animal's life is simply not as valuable as whatever medical advances that life can serve.' You have to."

That night, Varya lay awake for hours. She wondered why she had shared all of this with Luke, and how it might reflect on her if Luke were to include it in his article. She could ask him to omit the conversation, but that would indicate a degree of doubt about her work, and the thinking required to accomplish it, that she did not want to project. Now she sits in her car, nauseated. She has the overwhelming feeling that she has not only put herself at risk but that she has also betrayed Daniel. When she thinks of meeting Luke at the lab, she sees her brother. It makes no sense. Their only similarity is their height, and yet the visual remains, Daniel waiting for her in Luke's windbreaker and

460

backpack, Daniel's face transposed on Luke's younger, expectant one. The image morphs, then: she sees Daniel in the trailer, a bullet in his leg and the floor a red pool, and she knows that if she had not been so withdrawn, he would have come to her about Bruna, and she could have saved him.

By the time the nausea is gone and her hands have stopped trembling enough to hold the steering wheel, an hour has passed. She's never been late to work before, and Annie, to her relief, has brought Luke to the kitchen, where he is helping her weigh what food the monkeys have not eaten and separate next week's pellets into puzzle feeders. Varya avoids him, working on a grant in the office with the door closed. At one point, someone knocks, and because Annie would not bother her, Varya knows it can only be Luke.

"I thought I'd see if you'd like to go to dinner," he says when she opens the door. He has his hands in his pockets and, seeing her confusion, he smiles. "It's already six o'clock."

"Not hungry, I'm afraid." She walks back to her desk to shut down the computer.

"A drink? There's resveratrol in red wine. You can't say I haven't done my research."

Varya exhales. "Would this be on the

461

record or off?"

"Your choice. I thought off."

"If it's off the record," she says, swiveling, "what would be the point?"

"Networking? Human connection?" Luke stares at her peculiarly, as if he can't tell whether she's joking. "I don't bite. Or at least, I bite less than your monkeys."

She turns off the light in the office, and Luke's face drops into half shadow, lit only by the hallway fluorescents. She's hurt him.

"My treat," he adds. "To thank you."

Later, she will wonder what made her agree to go when nothing in her wanted to, and what would have happened if she hadn't. Was it guilt, or fatigue? She was so tired of guilt, which shrank only when she was working, and when she washed her hands, letting the tap run until it was so hot that the sensation was no longer one of water but fire or ice. It shrank, too, when she was hungry, which she so often was — there were times when she felt light enough to drift toward the sky, light enough to drift toward her siblings. And she was hungry now, but still, something made her go; something made her say yes.

They sit in a wine bar on Grant Avenue and share a bottle of red, a Cabernet that was grown and bottled seven miles south and which works in Varya immediately. She realizes how long it's been since she's eaten, but she does not eat at restaurants, so she drinks and listens as Luke tells her about his upbringing: how his family owns a cherry farm in Door County, Wisconsin, a combination of islands and shoreline that extends into Lake Michigan. He says that it reminds him of Marin, the land having belonged to Native Americans — in Door County, the Potawatomi; in Marin, the Coast Miwoks — before the arrival of Europeans, who took that land and used it for farming and lumber. He describes the limestone and the dunes and the hemlock trees, with their long fingers of green, and the yellow birch trees, which in late fall lay astonishing gold blankets on the ground.

During the off-season the population is less than thirty thousand, he says, but in the summer and early fall it grows by almost ten times that much. In July, the farm becomes frenzied, the rush to pick and dry and can and freeze the cherries a kind of madness. They have four kinds of cherries, and when Luke was young, each family member was assigned to collect one with a mechanical harvester. Luke's father took the large, juicy Balatons. Because Luke was the youngest, he and his mother paired up to pick the Montmorency cherries, with their translucent yellow flesh. Luke's older brother harvested the sweet cherries, firm and black and most precious of all.

Varya finds herself drifting as he speaks. She sees the cherries, their yellow and black and red, with the soft focus of a dream. He uses his phone to show her a photo of his family. It's early fall, the trees a fuzz of mustard and sage. Luke's parents have his thick blond hair, though theirs is lighter than Luke's. His brother — "Asher," he says — is a young teen, his face pimpled but grinning openly, his hands on Luke's shoulders. Luke can't be more than six. His shoulders rise into Asher's hands, and his smile is so wide it's nearly a grimace.

"What about you?" he asks, putting the phone back in his pocket. "What's your family like?"

"My older brother was a doctor, as I mentioned. My younger brother was a dancer. And my sister was a magician."

"No shit. With a black hat and a rabbit?"

"Neither." Around them, the lighting is dim, so Varya can't pick out things to worry her. "She was fantastic with cards, and she was a mentalist — her partner would pick an item from the audience, a hat or a wallet, and she would guess it without verbal cues, blindfolded and facing the wall."

"What are they doing now?" asks Luke, and she startles. He watches her. "I'm sorry. It's just that you used the past tense. I thought they must have —"

"Retired?" asks Varya, and shakes her head. "No. They're gone." She doesn't know what makes her say what she does next; perhaps it's that Luke is leaving, and there is something that feels so unusual, so relieving, about sharing with another person these things she's only told a therapist. "My youngest brother died of AIDS; he was twenty. My sister — took her life. Looking back, I've wondered if she was bipolar or schizophrenic, not that there's anything I can do about it now." She finishes her glass and pours another; she rarely drinks, and the wine makes her feel lazy, dulled, open. "Daniel got caught up in something he shouldn't have. He was shot."

Luke is quiet, gazing at her, and for a ridiculous moment she fears he will reach out and squeeze her hand. But he doesn't — why would he? — and she exhales.

"I'm so sorry," he says. "Is that why you do the work you do?" She does not answer, and he pushes on, hesitantly at first and then with deliberateness. "The medications we have now — well, they would have saved your brother's life, if they'd been available back then. And genetic testing could make it possible to detect an individual's risk of mental illness, even to diagnose them. That might have saved Klara, right?"

"What is your article about?" Varya asks. "My work, or me?"

She tries to keep her voice light. Inside her is a vein of fear, though she isn't sure why.

"It's difficult to separate the two, isn't it?" When Luke leans forward, his eyes loom, and something deep in Varya lurches. She realizes it now, what frightened her: she never told him Klara's name.

"I should leave," she mumbles, pressing her hands to the table to stand. Immediately the floor seesaws upward, the walls sway, and she sits — she falls — down again.

"Don't," says Luke, and now he does place his hand on hers.

A bubble of panic climbs her throat and bursts. "Please don't touch me," she says, and Luke lets go. His face is sorrowful; he finds her pathetic, and this is more than she can tolerate. She stands again and this time is successful.

"You shouldn't drive," Luke says, standing, too. She sees panic in his face, the same panic she feels, and this alarms her even more. "Please — I'm sorry."

She fumbles with her wallet, drawing out a thin stack of twenties, which she deposits on the table. "I'm fine."

"Let me drive you," he presses as she makes her way to the door. "Where do you live?"

"Where do I live?" she hisses, and Luke drops back; even in the dark of the bar she can see him redden. "What's wrong with you?" and she is now at the door, she is outside of it. After checking behind to make sure Luke is not following her, she sees her car and runs.

33.

She wakes on Saturday to a crunch of pain in the center of her back and a hammer in her skull. Her clothes are wet with sweat and stink. She kicked off her shoes in the night, and her sweater as well, but her blouse sticks to her stomach and her socks are so damp that when she peels them off they drop heavily to the floor of the car. She sits up in the backseat. Outside, it is morning, and Grant Street is thick with rain.

She brings the heels of her hands to her eyes. She remembers the wine bar, Luke's face coming toward her, his voice low but insistent — *It's difficult to separate the two, isn't it?* — and his hand on hers, which was hot. She remembers running to the car, and curling in the backseat like a child.

She is starving. She crawls from the backseat to the front and scrabbles around in the passenger seat for yesterday's leftovers. The apples have turned spongy and brown, but she eats them anyway, as well as the warm, puckered grapes. She avoids the car mirror but catches sight of herself, accidentally, in the passenger side window — her hair like Einstein's, her mouth drooping open — before she looks away and finds her keys.

At her condo, she strips off her clothes, depositing everything directly in the washing machine, and showers for so long the water turns cool. She pulls on her bathrobe — pink and ridiculously fluffy, a gift from Gertie, something Varya never would have bought for herself — and takes as much Advil as she thinks her body can stand. Then she climbs into bed and sleeps again.

It's mid-afternoon when she wakes up. Now that she is no longer purely exhausted, she feels a bolt of panic and knows she cannot spend the rest of the day at home. She dresses quickly. Her face is pale and birdlike and her silver hair sticks up in tufts. She wets her hands and smooths it down, then wonders why: the only people at the lab on Saturdays are the animal techs, and anyway, Varya will put a hair cover on as soon as she arrives. She doesn't usually eat lunch, but today she grabs another baggie from the refrigerator and eats the hardboiled eggs as she drives.

As soon as she enters the lab, she feels calmer. She pulls on her scrubs and walks into the vivarium.

She wants to check on the monkeys. It still makes her nervous to be close to them, but she is sometimes beset by the fear that something will happen to them while she is gone. Nothing has, of course. Josie uses her mirror to look at the doorway and, when she sees Varya, lets the mirror drop. The infants skitter anxiously in their communal enclosure. Gus sits in the back of his cage. But the last cage — Frida's cage — is empty.

"Frida?" Varya asks, absurdly; there is no proof that the monkeys understand their names, and yet she says it again. She leaves the vivarium and walks down the hallway, calling, until an animal technician named Johanna steps out of the kitchen.

"She's in isolation," Johanna says.

"Why?"

"She was plucking," says Johanna, rapidly. "I thought, in isolation, she might —"

But she does not finish, because Varya has already turned around.

The second floor of the lab is a square. Varya and Annie's office is on the western side, the vivarium north. The kitchen is south, along with the procedure rooms, and the isolation chamber — as well as the janitor's closet and the laundry room — is east. At six feet wide by eight tall, the isolation chamber is actually bigger than the monkeys' normal cages. But it is devoid of enrichment, a place where disobedient animals are sent to be punished. Of course, there is nothing threatening about it, nothing overtly frightening. There is merely nothing interesting about it, either: it is a stainless steel cage with a small, square door for entry, which locks from the outside. It's equipped with a food box and a water bottle. There are four inches between the floor and the bottom of the chamber, which has been drilled with holes to allow urine and waste to drop into a retractable pan.

"Frida," says Varya. She looks into the chamber, the same place she brought Frida on the night of her arrival, when the monkey was only days old.

Now Frida faces the rear of the cage and rocks in place, hunching. Her back is bald in fist-sized areas where she pulled the hair out. Six months ago, she stopped grooming what fur she has, and the other animals keep away, sensing her weakness, repelled by it. She sits in a thin layer of rust-colored urine that has not yet drained into the pan.

"Frida," repeats Varya, louder now, but soothingly. "Stop, Frida — please."

When the monkey hears Varya's voice, she turns her face to one side. In profile, her eyelid is glossy and lavender, her mouth an open half-moon. Then she grimaces. Slowly, she turns, but when she comes to face Varya, she does not stop: she continues to rotate, favoring her right limb, dragging the left. Two weeks ago, she bit her left thigh so badly it required stitches.

How did it happen? When Frida was young, she had more zest than any of the other monkeys. She could be Machiavellian in her social behavior, forging strategic alliances and stealing the more submissive animals' food, but she was also charming and impossibly curious. She loved to be held: she reached through the bars for Varya's waist, and Varya would occasionally let Frida out and carry her around the vivarium on one hip. The experience of being so close to her made Varya feel both frightened and ecstatic — frightened because of the fact of Frida's contamination, and ecstatic because Varya could briefly, through layers of protective clothing, feel what it was like to be close to another animal, to be an animal herself.

A knock on the door. Johanna, Varya

thinks, or Annie, though Annie rarely comes to the lab on weekends. Like Varya, she is both childless and unmarried. At thirty-seven, it's hardly too late, but Annie does not want these things. "I lack for nothing," she said once, and Varya believed her. Annie's populous Korean American family lives just over the bridge. She seems always to have a lover — sometimes male, sometimes female — and she executes these liaisons with the same confidence she does her research. Varya feels a motherly appreciation for Annie, as well as a motherly envy. Annie is the kind of woman Varya hoped to be: the kind who makes unconventional choices, and who is satisfied by them.

The knock comes again. "Johanna?" calls Varya, rising to open the door.

But the person who faces her is Luke. His hair is tangled, dark with grease. His lips are chapped, and his face has a strange yellow cast. He wears the same clothes he did the day before. He must have slept in them, too. The sheet of calm Varya assembled this afternoon cracks down the center and falls.

"What," she says, "are you doing here?"

"Clyde let me in." Luke blinks. One of his hands is still on the doorknob, and the other, she sees, is trembling. "I need to talk to you."

Frida has turned to face the wall and resumed her rocking. Varya hates her rocking, and she hates that Luke is here to see it. She turns away from him to lock the door of the isolation chamber. The process takes no more than two seconds, but before she is finished she hears a dull click and seizes. By the time she whips back to face him, he is stuffing his camera back in his bag.

"Give that to me," she says, savagely.

"No," says Luke, but his voice is small, like a young boy with a treasured belonging.

"No? You weren't authorized to take that photo. I'll sue you."

Luke's face is filled not with the professional glee she expected but with fear. He clutches the backpack.

"You're not a journalist," Varya says. Her dread is acute, it is ringing. She thinks of the marmosets' alarm calls. "Who are you?"

But he does not answer. He is fixed in the doorway, his body so still it would be statuesque if not for the still-quaking left hand.

"I'll call the police," she says.

"Don't," says Luke. "I —"

But he does not finish, and in that pause a thought rises in Varya unbidden. *Let it be benign,* she thinks, *let it be benign,* as if she is staring at the X-ray of a tumor and not into the face of an utter stranger.

"You named me Solomon," he says.

And the pitch into darkness. At first she feels confusion: *How? It isn't possible. I would have known.* Then the full impact, the flattening. Her vision smears.

For she stopped outside the Bleecker Street Planned Parenthood, those twenty-six years ago, and stood rooted to the ground as if by lightning. It was early February, dark and freezing at three thirty, but Varya's body seared. Inside her was an unfamiliar flutter. She looked at the flat-iron building in which the clinic was housed and wondered what would happen if she did not quash that flutter. She could make the choice she had planned to make; her life could continue on as it had been before the aberration and so remain symmetrical. Instead, she unbuttoned her coat to a flush of cold air. And then she turned around.

475

34.

She stumbles out of the vivarium and takes the stairs to the first floor. Through the lobby she runs, past Clyde, who stands to ask if she's all right, and out onto the mountain. She does not care that Luke is inside unsupervised; she wants only to get away from him. The rain has cleared to reveal sun so bright her eyes burn. She walks toward the parking lot as fast as she can without attracting attention, not wanting to waste the time it would take to grab her sunglasses, because she can hear that Luke is following her.

"Varya," he calls, but she does not stop. "Varya!"

Because he has shouted, she turns. "Keep your voice down. This is my workplace."

"I'm sorry," says Luke, panting.

"How dare you. How dare you trick me. How dare you do it in the lab, my lab."

"You would never have talked with me

otherwise." Luke's voice is strangely high in pitch, and Varya sees that he is trying not to cry.

She laughs, a bark. "I won't talk with you now."

"You will." A cloud passes across the sun, and in the new, steely light, he steadies. "Or I'll sell the photos."

"To whom?"

"To PETA."

Varya stares. She thinks of the notion of having the wind knocked out of you, but that isn't right: it has not been knocked but suctioned.

"But Annie," she says. "Annie checked your references."

"I had my roommate pose as a *Chronicle* editor. She knew how badly I wanted to meet you."

"We adhere to the strictest ethical standards," says Varya. Her voice is brittle with useless rage.

"Maybe so. But Frida wasn't doing very well."

They stand halfway down the mountain. Behind them, two postdocs walk toward the main facility, eating forkfuls of takeout.

"You're blackmailing me," says Varya, when she is able to speak again.

"I didn't want to. But it took years to

figure out who you were. The agency was no help at all, they knew you didn't want to be found, and all my records were sealed. I spent everything I had on a trip to New York and I pored over the birth certificates at the county courthouse for — for weeks. I knew my birthday but not which hospital you'd gone to, and when I found you, when I finally found you, I couldn't —"

It comes out in a rush and now he inhales deeply. Then he sees her face. He swings his backpack around to reach inside and emerges with a folded piece of white cloth.

"Hanky," he says. "You're crying."

She had not noticed. "You carry a handkerchief?"

"It was my brother's, and our dad's before that. Their initials are the same." He shows her the tiny embroidered lettering, and then he sees her pause. "It's clean. I haven't used it since the last time I washed it, and I always wash it in hot water."

His voice is confidential. She knows then that he has seen her as she is, in the way she does not want to be seen, and she swells with shame.

"The thing is I have it, too," Luke says. "I noticed it in you right away. Mine doesn't have to do with contamination, though. I'm afraid I'll hurt someone — that I'll kill them accidentally."

Varya takes the handkerchief and wipes her face, and when she emerges she thinks of what Luke said — *that I'll kill them accidentally* — and laughs until he joins in and she begins to cry again, because she understands exactly what he means.

She drives to her condominium in silence while Luke follows behind. As she climbs the stairs, she hears his footsteps behind her, feels the weight of his body, and her stomach wedges in her throat. She rarely brings anyone into her condo, and if she'd known he was coming she would have readied it. But there is no time for that now, so she flicks on the lights and watches as he takes it in.

The condo is small. Its decoration is a balancing act that aims to reduce her anxiety as much as possible. She chose pieces that both enhance and obstruct visibility: her couch is leather, for example, dark enough that she can't see every speck of fuzz or dirt, but smooth enough that — unlike a nubbly, patterned fabric — she can easily skim it for anything egregious before sitting down. Her sheets are a dull charcoal for the same reason; the white sheets in hotels are so bare a canvas that she nears hysterics every time she checks the beds. The walls are devoid of artwork, the tables without linens and so easier to clean. The drapes are drawn, as they always are, even during the day.

Not until she sees the condo through Luke's eyes does she remember how dark it is, and how ugly. The furniture is not aesthetically pleasing, because she does not choose it for aesthetic reasons. And if she did? She hardly knows what her taste would be, though once she passed a shop in Mill Valley that specialized in Scandinavian décor and saw a dove-gray sofa with rectangular pillows and slender, walnut legs. She stared for thirty seconds, a minute, before she remembered that the fabric would be terrible to clean, that she would be able to see every hair and stain, and that, most of all, it would be grossly painful to get rid of it if she ever became convinced of its filth.

"Can I get you something?" she asks. "Tea?"

Tea is fine, Luke tells her, and sits on the couch to wait for her, dropping his backpack at his feet. When she returns with two mugs and a ceramic pot of Genmaicha, he has his knees pressed together and the tape recorder in his lap.

"Can I record us?" he asks. "So I can

remember this. I don't think I'll see you again."

He knows the trade-off he has made; so he accepts it. He has caught her and will make her speak but has earned her resentment in return. Still, she has made a bargain, too: she chose to be his mother, and so she'll answer him.

"Okay." Her face is dry and the fury she felt at the lab has been replaced, for the moment, by resignation. She is reminded of the monkeys, the ones who have screamed themselves hoarse and give their bodies over to be studied with vacant acceptance.

"Thank you." Luke's gratitude is genuine: she can feel it reaching for her, and looks away. "Where and when was I born?"

"Mount Sinai Beth Israel; August 11th, 1984. It was eleven thirty-two in the morning. You didn't know that?"

"I did. Just checking your memory."

She brings the mug to her mouth, but the tea is scalding, and her eyes water.

"No more tricks," she says. "You've asked for my honesty. I deserve yours in return. You don't have to be suspicious of me; you don't have to try to catch me in a lie. I could not forget this — any of this — if I spent my life trying."

"Fair enough." Luke's gaze drops. "I

won't, anymore. Forgive me." When he looks at her again, his cockiness has been peeled away. What remains is sheepish, shy. "What was it like, that day?"

"The day you were born? It was sweltering. The window of my room looked out over Stuyvesant Square, and I could see women walking by, women my age, in cutoffs and crop tops, like it was still the seventies. I was enormous. I had a rash down my front and sweat in every possible crevice. My feet had swelled so much I wore slippers in the cab to the airport."

"Was anyone with you?"

"My mother. She was the only one I told."

Gertie by her side, murmuring. Gertie with a washcloth and a bucket of ice water; Gertie who bellowed at the nurses every time the air conditioner stopped working. Gertie, who has kept her secret all these years. "Mama," said Varya, wildly, after she gave the baby over. "I can't talk about this again, not ever," and since that day Gertie has not raised the subject. All the same, they talk about it constantly: for years, it was the lining to every conversation, it was a weight they carried heavily in tandem.

"What about the father?"

She notices that he says "the father" instead of "my father," which relieves her.

She does not want him to think of the professor that way.

"He never knew." She blows on her tea. "He was a visiting professor at NYU. I was in my first year of graduate school, and that fall, I took his class. We slept together a couple of times before he said he thought we shouldn't. By the time I realized I was pregnant it was early January, the winter holiday, and he'd flown back to the UK, though I didn't know that then. I called him over and over — first at the department and then at the number they gave me for his office in Edinburgh. In the beginning I left messages, and then I tried not leaving them. It wasn't that I was in love with him. I wasn't, not anymore. But I wanted to give him a chance to raise you, if he wanted to. Finally I understood he didn't deserve it, and that was when I stopped calling."

Luke's face is constricted, his throat ridged with veins. How did she not recognize him? She has imagined it — coming face-to-face with a strange but familiar man in an airport or a grocery store — and thought an animal awareness would rise within her, some sense memory of the nine months they shared a body and the breathtaking, anguished forty-eight hours that followed. She would not have been surprised to hear her pelvis shattered during the birth, but it had not: her experience was utterly normal, the birth so routine a nurse said it boded well for Varya's second. But Varya knew there would not be a second and so she clutched the tiny human, her biological son, and said goodbye not just to him but to the part of her that had been brave enough to love a man who thought so little of her and carry a child she knew she would not keep.

Luke takes off his shoes and brings his socked feet to the sofa. Then he wraps his arms around them, letting his chin rest on his knees. "What was I like?"

"You had a shiny pelt of black hair, like an otter, or a punk kid. Your eyes were blue, but the nurses said they might turn brown — which, of course, they did." Varya kept this in mind when she scanned sidewalks and subway cars and the background faces in other people's photos, looking for the blue- or brown-eyed child that had been hers. "You were sensitive. When you got overstimulated, you shut your eyes and pressed your hands together. We thought you looked like a monk, my mother and I, annoyed and trying very hard to pray."

"Black hair." Luke smiles. "And blue eyes. It's no wonder you didn't how who I was."

Outside the window, it is six o'clock and drizzling, the sky a luminous periwinkle. "Did your mom want you to give me up?"

"God, no. We fought about it. Our family had been through a lot of loss. My father died, very suddenly, when I was in college. And two years before you were born, Simon died of AIDS. She wanted me to keep you."

Varya had her own apartment by then, a studio near the university, but during the pregnancy, she often slept at 72 Clinton. Sometimes she argued with Gertie past midnight, but she still went to bed in her old top bunk. Ten minutes or two hours later, Gertie joined her, taking the bottom bunk that Daniel used to occupy instead of her own bed down the hall. In the mornings she stood on the bottom rung of the ladder to brush the hair away from Varya's face and kiss her fatly on the forehead.

"So why didn't you?" asked Luke.

Once, while driving through Wisconsin in the depth of summer — she was en route from a conference in Chicago to a second conference in Madison — Varya stopped to stand knee-high in Devil's Lake. She was desperate to cool off, but the water was warm, and dozens of tiny minnows began to peck at her ankles and feet. For a moment, she could not move; she stood in the

485

sand, so full of feeling she thought she might burst. Of what feeling, exactly? The unbearable ecstasy of proximity, of symbiotic exchange.

"I was afraid," she says. "Of all the things that can go wrong when people are attached to each other."

Luke pauses. "You could have gotten an abortion."

"I could have. I made an appointment. But I couldn't do it."

"For religious reasons?"

"No. I felt —" But here her voice becomes rough and drops off. She picks up her mug and drinks until her throat relaxes. "It's as though I was trying to compensate — for the fact that I was inward. For the fact that I didn't engage in life, not fully. I thought — I hoped — you would."

How had she been able to do it? Because she thought of them: Simon and Saul, Klara and Daniel and Gertie. She thought of them in her second trimester, when she was often disabled by panic, and during her third, when she felt huge as a walrus and peed more than she slept. She thought of them with every push. She held them in her mind so that she could feel nothing else — she loved them and loved them until they disarmed her, made her strong and broke her open, gave her powers she did not normally have.

But she could not sustain it. As she rode home from the hospital with her arms folded over her stomach, she wondered what kind of a person she was to give up a child for no better reason than her own fearfulness. The answer came to her immediately: the kind of person who did not deserve that child. Her body, which had been full to bursting with life, which *had* burst with life, was now hollow, the way it had been before — the way it had always been. At this she felt sorrow but also relief, and the relief inspired such self-loathing that she knew she was right. She could not bear that kind of life: dangerous, fleshy, full of love so painful it took her breath away.

"So what's happened since then?" asks Luke.

"What do you mean?"

"Did you have another kid? Did you ever get married?"

Varya shakes her head.

He frowns, puzzled. "Are you gay?"

"No. I've simply never — not since then, I haven't —"

She inhales sharply, a soundless hiccup. When Luke grasps her meaning, he startles. "You haven't had a relationship since the professor? You've had nothing?"

"Not *nothing*. But a relationship? No."

She prepares herself for his pity. Instead, he looks indignant, as if Varya has deprived herself of something essential.

"Aren't you lonely?"

"Sometimes. Isn't everyone?" she says, and smiles.

Abruptly, Luke stands. She thinks he's going to the bathroom, but he walks into the kitchen and stands at the sink. He presses his palms to the counter; his shoulders are hunched like Frida's. In front of the sink, on the windowsill, is her father's watch. After Klara's death, Daniel went to the trailer in which Klara and Raj had been living. Raj had collected items that he thought the Gold family would want: an early business card; Saul's gold watch; an old burlesque program, which showed Klara Sr. dragging a group of men on leashes. It wasn't much, but Daniel was grateful for the gesture. He called Varya from the airport.

"The trailer, on the other hand. It's not that it was filthy — it was fairly nice, as trailers go. But the fact of the trailer itself." Daniel's voice was furtive, almost muffled. "This seventies-era Gulf Stream, and Klara lived there for over a year" — much of that while docked at a trailer park called King's Row, he added, as if to add insult to injury. Under Klara's side of the bed, he'd found a small group of strawberry stems. At first he mistook it for a clump of grass, brought inside on somebody's shoe. They were feathery with mold; he threw them away in the rec room. But he would send Varya the watch, which had been Simon's before it was Klara's and Saul's before it was Simon's.

"It's a man's watch," Varya told him. "You should keep it."

"No," said Daniel, in the same, covert tone, and she understood that he had seen something that unsettled him, something he did not want to carry home.

"Luke?" she calls now.

He coughs and reaches for the handle of the fridge. "Mind if I — ?"

Stop, she thinks, but he's already there, he has pulled the door open and seen it.

"You keep the monkeys' food in here?" he calls, though when he turns to her, his bewilderment is already giving way to understanding.

The door hangs open. From the living room, Varya can see the rows of prepacked meals inside. On the top shelf are her breakfasts, mixed fruit in plastic bags with two tablespoons of high-fiber cereal. On the lower shelf are her lunches: nuts with beans or, on weekends, a slab of tofu or tuna. Her dinners are in the freezer, cooked weekly and then divided into foil-wrapped portions. Taped to the side of the refrigerator, the side that faces Luke, is an Excel spreadsheet with each meal's caloric count, as well as its vitamin and mineral content.

In the first year of her restriction, she lost fifteen percent of her body weight. Her clothes became baggy, and her face took on the narrow insistence of a greyhound's. She observed these changes with curious detachment: she was proud to be able to resist the temptation of sweets, carbs, fat.

"Why do you do this?" Luke asks.

"Why do you think?" she says, but she balks when she sees him coming toward her. "Why are you angry? Is it not my right to decide how to live?"

"Because I'm sad," says Luke, thickly. "Because to see you like this breaks my fucking heart. You cleared the decks: you had no husband, no kids. You could have done anything. But you're just like your monkeys, locked up and underfed. The point is that you have to live a lesser life in order to live a longer one. Don't you see that? The point is that you're willing to

490

make that bargain, you *have* made that bargain, but to what end? At what cost? Of course, your monkeys never had the choice."

It is impossible to convey the pleasure of routine to someone who does not find routine pleasurable, so Varya does not try. The pleasure is not that of sex or love but of certainty. If she were more religious, and Christian, she could have been a nun: what safety, to know what prayer or chore you'll be doing in forty years at two o'clock on a Tuesday.

"I'm making them healthier," she says. "They'll live longer lives because of me."

"But not better ones." Luke comes to stand over her, and she presses back against the couch. "They don't want cages and food pellets. They want light, play, heat, texture — danger! All this bullshit about choosing survival over life, as if we ever have control over either one. It's no wonder you feel nothing when you see them in their cages. You feel nothing for yourself."

"And how should I go about my life? Should I live like Simon, who cared for no one but himself? Should I live in a fantasy world, like Klara?"

She peels away from the couch, careful not to touch him, and strides into the kitchen. There she reopens the door of the refrigerator and begins to restack the bags of food that jostled when Luke closed the door.

"You blame them," he says, following her, and Varya turns toward him the anger she feels for her siblings, the anger that simmers constantly inside her. If they had only been smarter, more cautious. If they had shown self-awareness, shown humility — if they had shown patience! If they had not lived as though life were a mad dash toward some unearned climax; if they had walked instead of fucking run.

They began together: before any of them were people, they were eggs, four out of their mother's millions. Astonishing, that they could diverge so dramatically in their temperaments, their fatal flaws — like strangers caught for seconds in the same elevator.

"No," she says. "I love them. I do my work in tribute to them."

"You don't think any part of it is selfishness?"

"What?"

"There are two major theories about how to stop aging," Luke parrots. "The first is that you should suppress the reproductive system. And the second theory is that you should suppress caloric intake."

"I should never have told you anything. You're too young to understand; you're a child."

"I'm a child? I am?" Luke laughs sharply, and Varya recoils. "You're the one trying to convince yourself the world is rational, like there's anything you can do to put a dent in death. You're telling yourself that they died because of *x,* and you lived because of *y,* and that those things are mutually exclusive. That way you can believe you're smarter; that way you can believe you're different. But you're just as irrational as the rest of them. You call yourself a scientist, you use words like *longevity* and *healthful aging,* but you know the most basic story of existence — *everything that lives must die* — and you want to rewrite it."

He leans closer still, until their faces are inches apart. She cannot look at him. He is too near, he wants too much from her — she can smell his breath, a bacterial fudge cut by the Genmaicha's roasted grain.

"What do you want from your life?" he asks, and when she is silent, he grabs her wrist and squeezes. "You want to continue on like this forever? Like this?"

"And what do you want? To save me? Does it make you feel good, to be the savior? Make you feel like a man?" She's struck him: his hand drops, and his eyes shine. "Don't lecture me; you don't have the right, and you certainly don't have the experience."

"How would you know?"

"You're twenty-six years old. You grew up on a goddamn cherry farm. You had two healthy parents and a big brother who loved you so much he let you have his precious hanky."

She edges out from behind the door of the refrigerator and walks to the front door. Later she'll try to sort out what happened — later she'll turn the conversation over and over in her mind, wondering how she might have saved it before it plummeted for good — but now she wants him gone. If he stays any longer, she'll do something terrible.

But Luke doesn't leave. "He didn't let me have it. He died."

"I'm sorry," says Varya, tightly.

"Don't you want to know how? Or do you only care about your own tragedies?"

The truth is that she does not want to know; the truth is that she has no room for anyone else's pain. But Luke, framed in the arched doorway between the living room and the kitchen, has already begun to speak.

"The thing you have to know about my

brother is that he looked out for me. My parents had always wanted another child, but they couldn't have one, and so they got me. Asher was ten when I was adopted. He could have been jealous. But he wasn't jealous: he was kind, and generous, and he took care of me. We lived in New York at the time, upstate. When we moved to Wisconsin we had more land but a smaller house, and we had to share a room. Asher was thirteen; I was a toddler. What middle schooler wants to share a room with a three-year-old? But he never complained.

"I was the difficult one. I was the brat. I wanted to see how far I could push them: Are you still glad you got me? If I do this, will you want to send me back? Once I ran out of the house and wriggled under the porch and stayed there for hours, because I wanted to hear them looking for me. Another time I went with Asher to the trees and hid right when it was time to leave with the harvester. This became a game we did, me hiding at exactly the wrong time, the most annoying time, and Asher always put down what he was doing and looked for me and then when he found me we'd start working."

She puts a hand out, as if to stop him. She does not want to hear what comes next, she can't stand it — her body is already crawling with dread — but Luke ignores her, continuing on.

"One day we went to the grain bins. At that time we had chickens and cows, and in April, the grain had to be checked for clumps. Asher lowered himself into the bin. I was supposed to stand on a platform at the top and watch him so I could call for help if anything went wrong. Once he was inside he looked up at me and smiled. He was crouched on the top of the crust; it was yellow, it looked like sand. 'Don't you dare,' he said. And I smiled back at him and climbed down the ladder and ran.

"I hid between the tractors, because that's where he knew to come looking for me. But he didn't come. After a couple of minutes I knew there was something wrong, that I'd done something bad, but I was scared. So I stayed there. Asher had brought two picks into the grain bin; he used them to break up the clumps. When I left he'd tried to use them to climb out. But they made too many holes. He sank within the first five minutes. But it took longer for him to be crushed, and then suffocated. They found pieces of corn in his lungs."

For seconds, Varya is silent. She stares at Luke and he at her. The air feels charged and weighty, as though only the force of their gaze is keeping something aloft between them. Then Varya falters.

"Please go," she says. Her hand on the door is slick; she'll have to wipe it down when he leaves.

"Are you kidding me? That's all you have to say?" he asks, his voice cracking. "Unbelievable." He walks to the couch and retrieves his shoes, shoving his feet — his floppy-eared, gray-toed socks — inside them. Varya opens the door. It's all she can do not to scream at him, scream after him, when he shoves past her and down the stairs.

She watches from the window as he walks to his car and speeds out of the lot with a jolt. Then she grabs her keys and does the same. She tracks him for two lights before she loses her nerve. What could she possibly say? At the next stop sign, she does a U-turn and goes the opposite way, to the lab.

Annie isn't there. Neither is Johanna, or any of the other techs. Even Clyde has left for the night. Varya walks to the vivarium — indignant screeching from the monkeys, who are frightened by the suddenness of her entrance — and finds Frida's cage.

She thinks Frida is sleeping before she

sees that the monkey's eyes are open. She lies on her side with her left forearm in her mouth.

Frida has engaged in self-mutilation before — the bite on her thigh, for example — but she has always hidden the behavior. Now she scrabbles shamelessly at her own bone, the flesh around it a mangled gash of blood and tissue.

"Come on," barks Varya, "come here," and opens the door of the cage. Frida looks up but does not move, so Varya crosses to the opposite wall and retrieves a leash, which she hooks around Frida's neck and uses to pull the monkey out onto the floor. The other animals scream, and Frida turns to look at them, wild with sudden awareness. She sits and hugs her arms around her knees, rocking, so Varya has no choice but to tug and tug until she is dragging Frida's body across the floor. She is nauseated by Frida's frailty. Formerly eleven pounds, the monkey is now only seven and barely able to hold herself erect. At the next yank, she keels over, onto her back, and the leash begins to choke her. The other monkeys increase their pitch — they sense Frida's weakness, they are excited by it — and Varya, frenzied, reaches down to lift the creature in her arms.

Frida drops her head to Varya's shoulder and rests her arm on Varya's breast. Varya gasps. She wears no protective gear, and the wound, which releases a foul odor of decay, sticks to her sweater. She begins to jog, Frida's forehead bouncing into her clavicle, and enters the kitchen. The puzzle feeders are stacked against the wall, but Varya wants the loose pellets, the huge bins of open food, and the treats that are given to the unrestricted monkeys: apples and bananas and oranges, grapes, raisins, peanuts, broccoli, shaved coconut, each in their own bucket. She pulls out the buckets and bins and sets them on the floor with Frida on her waist. Then she puts Frida down before the troughs.

"Go," she snaps. "Eat!" but Frida stares blankly at the feast. Varya urges more loudly, pointing, and Frida unfurls her left hand. Her legs are splayed on the floor like a toddler's, her knees bent; the soles of her feet are soft and gray. Varya watches greedily as Frida reaches for the raisins, but before her hand enters the bin, she changes course and brings her forearm to her face. She opens her mouth, finds the wound, and chews.

Varya reaches down to pull Frida's hand away and sobs. The wound is matted with hair but very deep. Frida may have cracked the bone.

"Eat," cries Varya. She crouches to reach into the bin of raisins and brings her hand to Frida's lips. Frida snuffles. Slowly, slowly, she takes the first raisin in her mouth. Varya uses both hands to scoop again. Soon her fingers are covered in flecks of food and flesh, but she continues, reaching now into the bin of coconut, the peanuts, the grapes. "Oh, good," says Varya; "Oh, my baby," words she has not used in decades, words she used only once — Luke crowning, her body splitting to accommodate his sudden life.

When Frida turns away from Varya's hand, Varya tempts her with another kind of fruit or a differently shaped pellet. Frida eats these, too, and then she vomits: clear mucus, bile, a river of raisins. Varya keens. She wipes Frida's mouth, her patchy scalp, and her salmon-colored, translucent ears, for the animal is sweating. Vomit flows hotly over Varya's pants. She must call the veterinarian. But at the thought of calling the veterinarian — what Dr. Mitchell will ask Varya, what Varya will have to explain — she cries harder.

So she will hold Frida, until Dr. Mitchell comes; she will comfort her, she will make

Frida feel better. She drags the animal onto her lap. Frida's eyes are glassy and unfocused, but she wriggles, she wants to be left alone. Varya squeezes more tightly. "Shh-shh," she whispers. "Shh-shh." Still Frida struggles to get away, and still Varya clings. She is over, she is done for. What does it matter? She wants to hold something, she wants to be held. She does not let go until Frida brings her face to Varya's, her lips soft against Varya's chin, and bites down.

35.

Varya did not call the vet. The next morning, Annie found her and Frida asleep in the kitchen — Varya with her back against a stack of boxes, Frida on a top shelf — and screamed.

In the hospital, Varya thought she would die: first from something contracted during the bite, and then, when the doctor told her that Frida had neither hepatitis B nor tuberculosis, from something she would contract in the isolation unit. She was astounded when she lived. It had seemed, in her panic, that the only outcome was the one she most feared. As soon as this fear was proven invalid, it was replaced by distress far more concrete: the knowledge that what she had done was so destructive as to be irreparable.

With each day she ate the hospital food, she grew more alert. She had not inhabited her body so wholly since childhood. Now the world rushed toward her in all its texture and sensation. She felt the acid misery of each wound-cleaning and the papery brush of the hospital sheets, which she was too depleted to inspect. When the nurse drew close, Varya smelled a shampoo she's sure Klara once used. Occasionally she saw Annie sleeping on a chair pulled up to her bed, and once, in a moment of coherence, she asked Annie not to tell Gertie what had happened. Annie looked grim and disapproving, but she nodded. Varya would tell Gertie someday, but telling her about the bite meant telling her about everything else, and she could not do that yet.

Frida had been flown to an animal hospital in Davis. Her bone had cracked, as Varya feared. A surgeon amputated her arm at the shoulder. But the only way to know whether Frida had rabies was to cut off her head and test the brain. Varya pleaded for leniency: she herself had no symptoms, and if Frida did have rabies, the monkey would die within days.

Two weeks later, Varya meets Annie at a café on Redwood Boulevard. Upon entering, Annie smiles — she wears street clothes, slim black pants with a striped tee and clogs, her hair loose — but her discomfort is obvious. Varya orders a vegetarian wrap.

Ordinarily, she would not eat, but her experiment was undone in the hospital, and she hasn't found the conviction to start over.

"I talked to Bob," Annie says when the waiter leaves. "He'll let you resign voluntarily."

Bob is Drake's CEO. Varya does not want to know how he reacted when told that she put a twenty-year experiment in jeopardy. Frida was in the restricted group. In feeding her, Varya nullified Frida's data and compromised the analysis as a whole: with Frida's results omitted, the number of restricted monkeys to controls will be skewed. All this is not to mention the publicity disaster that will arise should word get out that a high-ranking Drake researcher suffered a breakdown, endangering staff and animals in the process. When Varya thinks of how hard Annie must have pushed for Bob to allow a voluntary resignation, she fills with shame.

"It'll be easier that way," says Annie, haltingly. "To continue your career."

"Are you kidding?" Varya uses a napkin to blow her nose. "There's no way to keep this quiet."

Annie is silent, conceding this. "Still," she says. "It's a better way to go."

Annie has kept the bulk of her anger from

Varya, if only because, unlike Bob, she knows Varya's story: in the hospital, Varya confessed the truth about Luke as Annie's expression moved from fury to disbelief to pity.

"Goddammit," she said. "I wanted to hate you."

"You still can."

"Yes," said Annie. "But it's harder now."

Now Varya swallows a bite of her wrap. She is not used to restaurant portions, which seem comically huge. "What will happen to Frida?"

"You know as well as I do."

Varya nods. If Frida is very lucky, she'll be moved to a primate sanctuary, where former research animals live with minimal human intervention. Varya has campaigned for this, making daily calls to the hospital and to a sanctuary in Kentucky where primates roam thirty acres of outdoor enclosures. But the sanctuary's capacity is limited. More likely, Frida will be shipped to another research center and used for a different experiment.

That evening, Varya falls asleep at seven and wakes just after midnight. She crawls out of bed in her nightgown and stands at the window, opening the blinds for the first time in months. The moon is bright enough

505

for Varya to see the rest of the condominium complex; across the way, somebody's kitchen light is on. She has a curious feeling of purgatory, or perhaps it is afterlife. She has lost her work, which was meant to be her contribution to the world — her repayment. The worst has happened, and amidst the hollowing loss is the thought that now there is much less to fear.

She retrieves her cell phone from the bedside table and sits on top of the covers. The other line rings and rings. Just when she is resigned that it will go to voice mail, someone answers.

"Hello?" asks the voice, uncertainly.

"Luke." She is overcome by two emotions: relief that he has picked up, and fear that whatever window he'll give her will not be long enough for her to earn his forgiveness. "I'm so sorry. I'm sorry for what happened to your brother, and I'm sorry for what happened to you. You should never have had to experience that, never; I wish you hadn't, I wish I could take it away from you."

Silence on the other end. Varya presses the phone to her ear, breathing shallowly.

"How did you get my number?" he asks, finally.

"It was in your e-mail to Annie — when you asked for the interview." He is quiet again, and Varya continues. "Listen to me, Luke. You can't go through life convinced it was your fault. You have to forgive yourself. You won't survive otherwise — not in any comprehensive way. Not in the way you deserve to."

"I'll be like you."

"Yes," she says, and wills herself not to cry again. These words apply to her, too, of course. But she's never let herself believe them before.

"Are you really going to Jewish-mother me now? Because I'm pretty sure the statute of limitations ran out on that one twenty-six years ago."

"That's fair," she says, though she coughs out a laugh. "That's true."

She transmits a plea: that he will extend to her the gift of empathy, however undeserved. She looks across the condominium complex, at the one lit kitchen.

"I have to go to bed," says Luke. "You woke me up, you know."

"I'm sorry," says Varya. Her chin — stitched, still bandaged — trembles.

"Can you call me tomorrow? I get off work at five."

"Yes," Varya says, closing her eyes. "Thank you. Where do you work?"

"Sports Basement. It's an outlet for outdoor gear."

"I thought, the day I met you — I thought you looked ready to go hiking."

"I usually do. We get a huge employee discount."

How little she knows of him. She feels a bolt of disappointment that her son is not a biologist or a journalist but a retail employee, and then she rebukes herself. He is being honest now, and she holds his honesty inside her: one more thing she knows of him that's real.

Three months later, Varya sits in a French bakery in Hayes Valley. When the man she has come to meet enters the café, she recognizes him immediately. They've never met in person, but she's seen promotional photos of him online. Of course, he is featured too in older snapshots with Simon and Klara. The one Varya likes best was taken in the Collingwood Street apartment Klara and Simon once shared. A black man sits on the floor, leaning against the window, one arm slung up on the frame. His other arm rests on Simon, who lies with his head in the first man's lap.

"Robert," says Varya, standing.

Robert turns. She can see the handsome, muscular man he used to be — he is tall and arresting, his expression alert — though he is now sixty and thinner, his hair half-gray.

Varya has wondered about him for years, but she wasn't brave enough to search for him in any serious way until this summer. She found an article about two men who run a contemporary dance company in Chicago. When she wrote by e-mail, he told her he would be in San Francisco this week for a dance festival at Stern Grove. Now they chat about her research, his choreography, and the South Side flat where he and his husband, Billy, live with two Maine Coon cats. "Ewoks," Robert says. He's laughing, showing her photos on his cell phone, and Varya is laughing, too, until she's suddenly close to tears.

"What is it?" asks Robert. He pockets the phone.

Varya wipes her eyes. "I'm so happy to meet you. My sister, Klara — she talked about you frequently. She would have loved . . ." The conditional: a tense she still hates. "She would have loved to know you're —"

"Alive?" Robert smiles. "It's all right; you can say it. It was never guaranteed. Not that it's guaranteed for any of us." He adjusts an engraved, silver bracelet, which he and Billy wear instead of wedding rings. "I do have the virus. I never thought I'd live to be an old man. Hell, I thought I'd die by thirty-five. But I made it until the cocktail became available. And Billy has energy enough for both of us. He's young — too young to have gone through what we did. When Simon died, he was ten."

Robert meets her eyes. It's the first time either of them have said Simon's name.

"I've never been able to let go of the fact that I didn't see him after he left home," says Varya. "Four years he lived in San Francisco, and I never came. I was so angry at him. And I thought he'd . . . grow up."

The words hover. Varya swallows. Klara was with Simon and even Daniel spoke to him, a brief phone call he described after the funeral, but Varya was rock, was ice, so remote he could not have reached her if he'd wanted to. And why would he want to? He must have known that Varya resented him more than she did Klara. At least Klara had made it clear she was leaving; at least she had the decency, once in San Francisco, to pick up the phone. Varya gave up on Simon. It was no surprise that he also gave up on her.

Robert puts his hand on top of hers, and she tries not to flinch. His palm is broad and warm. "You couldn't have known."

"No. But I should have forgiven him."

"You were a kid. We all were. Look — before Simon died, I was cautious. Too cautious, maybe. But when he died I did some stupid, reckless things. Things that should've gotten me killed."

"The thought that you could die from sex," Varya says, haltingly. "You weren't terrified?"

"No, not then. Because it didn't feel that way. When doctors said we should be celibate, it didn't feel like they were telling us to choose between sex and death. It felt like they were asking us to choose between death and life. And no one who worked that hard to live life authentically, to have sex authentically, was willing to give it up."

Varya nods. Beside them, a little bell on the door of the café jingles as a young family enters. When they walk by her table, Varya forces herself not to lean away from them. She's seeing a new therapist, one who practices cognitive behavioral therapy and encourages her to withstand these moments of exposure.

"I've always wondered what drew you to Simon," she says. "Klara said you were so mature, so accomplished. But Simon was such a kid, and proud. Don't get me wrong

— I adored him. But I could never have dated him."

"That sounds about right." Robert grinned. "What did I love about him? He was fearless. He wanted to move to San Francisco, so he did. He wanted to become a dancer, so he became one. I'm sure he didn't always *feel* fearless. But he acted with fearlessness. That's something he taught me. When Billy and I started our company, we took out a loan we thought we might never repay. The first three years, man — we were all in the trenches. But then we did a show in New York, and we were reviewed in the *Times.* When we got back to Chicago, we turned a profit. Now we can afford to give our dancers health insurance." He takes a bite of his croissant; buttery flakes land on his leather jacket. "I never planned for retirement. I'm still afraid to look too far ahead. But that's okay; I love my work. I don't want it to end."

"I wish I felt that way. I've left my job. I've never felt so adrift."

"No more of that." Robert raises his croissant and points at her with an expression of exaggerated admonishment. "Think like Simon. Be fearless!"

She's trying, even if her definition of the word is laughably small when compared to anyone else's. She has begun to sit back against chairs, and take walks through the city. Ten years ago, when she moved to California, she visited the Castro for the first time since Ruby was born. She tried to envision Simon there, but she could only see him on their walks to Congregation Tifereth Israel, running away from her. Now she imagines him again, but this time, he does not stay within the bounds of the person she knew. As she hikes from the Cliff House to the old military hospital near Mountain Lake Park, she sees Simon pose by the remains of the Sutro Baths, where there was once enough space for ten thousand people to swim. She has no idea whether he walked these bluffs; the Richmond is at least forty-five minutes from the Castro by bus. It doesn't matter. He's there amidst the scrub and lilac, his hair whipped by the wind off the water, clearing a trail as Varya follows behind him.

When she returns to the condo, there is an e-mail from Mira.

Dearest V:
Will the eleventh of December work for you? Turns out Eli has a commitment on the fourth, and Jonathan still likes

513

the idea of dragging everyone to Florida in the winter, crazy man. (It will be nice, I think. I just have to get over the embarrassment of telling everyone I'm actually getting married in Miami.) Let me know.

Love — M.

Jonathan is a fellow professor at SUNY New Paltz who lost his wife to pancreatic cancer four years before Daniel's death. He was not someone Mira had ever considered romantically. After Daniel died, he brought Mira meals — "It's brisket," he said, "but store-bought; my wife was the one who cooked" — and stayed with her through the panic attacks she began to suffer before teaching. It was two years before she fell in love with him.

"Though I didn't fall. The pace was glacial," said Mira, during one of her Sunday night Skype sessions with Varya. "I had to surrender."

Mira put her plate on the coffee table and tucked her feet beneath her. She was still petite, but more muscular: after Daniel's death, she took up cycling, riding from New Paltz to Bear Mountain as the world rushed past, looking like the blur it felt.

"Surrender what?" Varya asked.

"Well, that's what I kept asking myself,

and I realized that what I had to surrender wasn't my pain, or my trust. I had to surrender Daniel."

Six months ago, Jonathan proposed. He has an eleven-year-old son, Eli, whom Mira is learning to parent. Varya is to be her maid of honor.

What do you want? Luke asked her, and if Varya had answered him honestly, she would have said this: To go back to the beginning. She would tell her thirteen-year-old self not to visit the woman. To her twenty-five-year-old self: Find Simon, forgive him. She would tell herself to take care of Klara, to sign up for JDate, to stop the nurse before she took the baby out of Varya's arms. She'd tell herself she would die, she would die, they all would. She would tell herself to pay attention to the smell of Klara's hair, the feel of Daniel's arms as he reached down to hug her, Simon's stubby thumbs — my God, their hands, all of them, Klara's hummingbird-quick, Daniel's slender and restless. She'd tell herself that what she really wanted was not to live forever, but to stop worrying.

What if I change? she asked the fortune teller, all those years ago, sure that knowledge could save her from bad luck and tragedy. *Most people don't,* the woman said.

It is seven o'clock, the sky a neon smear. Varya leans back in her chair. Perhaps she chose science because it was rational, believing it would set her apart from the woman on Hester Street and her predictions. But Varya's belief in science was rebellion, too. She feared that fate was fixed, but she hoped — God, she hoped — that it was not too late for life to surprise her. She hoped it was not too late for her to surprise herself.

Now she remembers what Mira told her after Daniel's burial. They hunched beneath a tree, snow filtering through the branches, as attendees made their way to the parking lot. "I never met Klara," Mira said. "But right now, I almost feel I understand her, because suicide does not seem irrational. What's irrational is continuing on, day after day, as if forward momentum is natural."

But Mira has done it. The impossibility of moving beyond loss, faced against the likelihood you will: it's as absurd, as seemingly miraculous, as survival always is. Varya thinks of her colleagues, with their test tubes and microscopes, all of them attempting to replicate the processes that already exist in nature. *Turritopsis dohrnii,* a jellyfish the size of a sequin, ages in reverse when under threat. In winter, the wood frog turns to ice: its heart stops beating, its blood freezes, and yet, months later, when spring arrives, it thaws and hops away.

The periodical cicada hibernates underground in broods, feeding on fluids from tree roots. It would be easy to think them dead; perhaps, in some way — sedentary and silent, nestled two feet below the soil — they are. One night, seventeen years later, they break through the surface in astounding numbers. They climb the nearest vertical object; the husks of their nymphal skins drop crisply to the ground. Their bodies are pale and not yet hardened. In the darkness, they sing.

36.

On the first week of July, Varya drives into the city for her weekly visit with Gertie. Gertie is buoyant: Ruby is visiting. Varya has never understood why a college student would spend two weeks every summer at a retirement home of her own volition, but Ruby suggested this plan as a freshman and hasn't wavered. Helping Hands is an eight-hour drive from UCLA, where Ruby will soon begin her senior year. Each summer, she arrives in a flurry of sunglasses and stacked bracelets, sundresses and platform heels, as well as a brutish white Range Rover. She plays mah-jongg with the widows and reads to Gertie from the books in her literature courses. On the last night of her visit, she does a magic show in the dining hall, which has become so well attended that the staff bring extra chairs in from the library. The residents are rapt as children. Afterward, they wait for Ruby in long lines, eager to tell her about the time they met Houdini's brother or saw a woman slide across Times Square from a rope held in her teeth.

"What are you going to do now?" Gertie asks Varya. "If you aren't going back to work?"

She sits in her armchair, a bowl of pickles in her lap. Ruby lies on Gertie's bed. She's playing a game on her cell phone called Bloody Mary. When she reaches the fifth level, she passes the phone to Varya, who takes particular satisfaction in smashing the spry, hopping tomato that guards a bag of celery sticks.

"It isn't that I'm not going back to work," Varya says. "I'm just not going back to the Drake."

She has told her mother that she made a critical mistake, something that compromised the integrity of the experiment. Soon — when Ruby leaves, perhaps — she'll tell Gertie about Frida, and, most of all, about Luke. Their relationship has been too fragile to share, and though it is less fragile now, Varya still fears she'll lose him as suddenly as he appeared. They've begun to exchange snail mail, photos and postcards and other small things. In May, Luke sent a picture of him with his new girlfriend, Yuko. Yuko is at least a foot and a half shorter than he, with an asymmetrical haircut dyed pink at the ends. In the photo, she is pretending to pick Luke up, one of his long legs slung over her arm as they squint with laughter. Another month passes before Luke admits that Yuko is his roommate, the one who posed as a *Chronicle* editor — though it wasn't romantic then, he hastens to add — and that he kept this a secret because he did not want Varya to resent her.

Varya flushed with pleasure, both to see his happiness and to think he cared what she thought. That week, she passed a farm stand advertising homemade fruit preserves. She pulled to the side of the road and picked through the glass jars, their contents jewel-like in the afternoon light. When she found cherries, she bought two jars, keeping one and mailing the second to Luke. Ten days later, his reply came:

Not exceptional, but steady. Solid. The almond extract is a nice touch, and brings out the muskiness of the cherries, so they're more than just sweet.

Varya grinned at the postcard and read it twice more. Unexceptional but steady and solid was not the worst thing one could be, she thought, and she went to the pantry to retrieve her own jar, which she had waited for his reply to open.

"Where, then?" says Gertie now, looking at her own lap. "You can't sit around all day, like me. Eating pickles."

Immediately, Varya hears her siblings. *As if you really have to worry about that,* Klara would say. Then Daniel: *Yeah — Varya, sitting around, eating pickles? I don't think she's capable of such a thing.* Lately, Varya sees them everywhere. A teenage boy, running past her apartment after dusk, will remind her of Simon, racing around 72 Clinton on cool summer nights. She sees Klara's smile — sparkling, sharp — on the face of a woman at a bar. She imagines herself going to Daniel for advice. He was always right behind her: in age, in his ambitions, in his support of the family. She knew she could count on him to care for Gertie or to try to bring Simon home.

For so long, she stifled these memories. But now, when she calls them up in these sensory ways, so that they feel more like people than ghosts, something unexpected happens. Some of the lights inside her — the neighborhood that went dark years ago — turn on.

"I think I might like to teach," she says. In

graduate school, she taught undergrads in exchange for tuition remission. She hadn't thought she could do such a thing — before her first class, she vomited in a sink in the women's restroom, unable to reach the toilet — but she soon found it invigorating: all those upturned faces, waiting to see what she had up her sleeve. Of course, some of the faces were not upturned but sleeping, and secretly, those were the ones she liked best. She was determined to wake them up.

On the last night of Ruby's visit, Varya comes for the magic show. While Ruby is setting up in the dining hall, Varya and Gertie eat dinner in Gertie's room. Varya is thinking of the Golds, what her siblings and Saul would think to see Ruby onstage, and then, in the strange half-light of dusk, she begins to share something she thought she never would: she tells Gertie about the woman on Hester Street. She describes the blanketing heat of that July day, her anxiety while climbing the stairs, the fact that each sibling entered the room alone. She shares the conversation they had on the last night of Saul's shiva, which she realized in hindsight was the last time the four of them were ever together.

As Varya talks, Gertie doesn't look up. She

stares at her yogurt, bringing each spoonful to her mouth with such bland focus that Varya wonders if this is a bad day, if her mother is absent. When Varya has finished, Gertie wipes her spoon with a napkin and sets it down on her dinner tray. Carefully, she closes the yogurt container with its aluminum foil lid.

"How could you believe that junk?" she asks, quietly.

Varya opens her mouth. Gertie puts the yogurt container beside the spoon and folds her hands in her lap, looking at Varya with owlish indignation.

"We were kids," says Varya. "She frightened us. And anyway, my point is that it isn't —"

"Junk!" says Gertie, decisive now, leaning back in her chair. "So you went to see a Gypsy. No one's stupid enough to believe them."

"You believe in that kind of junk. You spit when a funeral goes by. After Dad died, you wanted to do that thing with the chicken, swinging a live one around in the air while reciting —"

"That's a religious ritual."

"And the funeral spitting?"

"What about it?"

"What's your excuse?"

"Ignorance. What's yours? You don't have one," she says when Varya pauses. "After everything I gave you: education, opportunity — modernity! How could you turn out like me?"

Gertie was nine when German forces took Hungary. Her mother's parents and three siblings in Hajdú were sent to Auschwitz. If the Shoah had solidified Saul's faith, it had only diminished hers. By the time she was six, even her own parents were dead. God must have seemed less likely than chance, goodness less likely than evil — so Gertie knocked on wood and crossed fingers, tossed coins into fountains and rice over shoulders. When she prayed, she bargained.

What she gave her children, Varya sees: the freedom of uncertainty. The freedom of an unsure fate. Saul would have agreed. As the only child of immigrants, her father had few options. To look forward or back must have felt ungrateful, like testing fate — the free present a vision that might vanish if he took his eyes away from it. But Varya and her siblings had choices, and the luxury of self-examination. They wanted to measure time, to plot and control it. In their pursuit of the future, though, they only drew closer to the fortune teller's prophecies.

"I'm sorry," says Varya. Her eyes swell.

"Don't apologize," Gertie says, reaching out to swat Varya's arm. "Be different." But when she's finished swatting, she grasps Varya's forearm and holds on, as Bruna Costello did in 1969. This time, Varya doesn't pull away. They sit in silence until Gertie fidgets.

"So what'd she tell you?" she asks. "When are you gonna die?"

"Eighty-eight." It now seems very far away, an almost embarrassing luxury.

"Then what are you so worried about?"

Varya bites her cheek to keep from smiling. "I thought you said you don't believe in it."

"I don't," Gertie sniffs. "But if I did, I wouldn't be complaining. If I did, I'd think eighty-eight was just fine."

At seven thirty, they walk into the dining hall for the magic show. A raised platform acts as the stage; two lamps, set on either side, are spotlights. One of the nurses has hung red sheets over a clothing rack for curtains. Gertie and her friends have dressed up for the occasion, and the dining hall is teeming. An electric anticipation binds everyone in the room, invisible as dark matter. It pulls them together and toward the stage, toward Ruby.

Then the curtain parts, and she appears.

In Ruby's hands, the stage transforms. The curtain becomes a real curtain, and the lamps become spotlights. Klara excelled at rapid-fire patter, but Ruby has an unexpected gift for physical comedy and a way of including everyone in the room. There is something else, too, that sets her apart from her mother. She has an easy grin, and her voice never wavers. When she drops a ball she was meant to catch, she spends a moment in self-deprecating pantomime before recovering her even keel. It's confidence, Varya sees. Ruby looks more comfortable — in her skills, in herself — than her mother ever did.

Oh, Klara, Varya thinks. *If you could see your child.*

All night, Gertie looks at Ruby like a movie she never wants to stop watching. It's nearly eleven by the time the last residents filter out of the dining hall. Though Gertie agreed to ride in the detested wheelchair, her chest is puffed like a turkey's. Varya knows that stopping aging is as improbable as the idea that a compulsion can keep something bad from happening. But she still wants to shout: *Don't go.*

Ruby wheels Gertie back to her room.

Soon, she'll turn her attention to other miracles: how to suture a wound, to tap a spine, to deliver a child. Tonight, though, there was a bond that linked her to everyone in the room, a network of emotion, and Ruby didn't let go. When she stood onstage and looked out and felt that feeling, it made her think of the preschool children she sometimes sees walking past her apartment in Los Angeles. To make sure they don't stray, the children walk in a line with the rope in their hands. Tonight was like that, Ruby thinks. One by one, they came to the rope. One by one, they held on.

"Why would you want to be a doctor when you could keep doing this?" her father still asks. "You bring people so much joy."

But Ruby knows that magic is only one tool among many for keeping one another alive. When she was a child, Raj told her the four words Klara always said before a show. Ruby has recited the very same ones ever since. Tonight she stood behind the curtain with her hands clasped. On the other side, she could hear the audience whispering and fidgeting and rustling their cheap printed programs in anticipation.

"I love you all," she whispered. "I love you all, I love you all, I love you all."

Then she stepped through the curtain to join them.

ACKNOWLEDGMENTS

I am profoundly grateful for the many people who helped bring *The Immortalists* to life.

This book would not have been possible without the belief, labor, and advocacy of two incredible women. To my rock star and soul sister of an agent, Margaret Riley King: thank you for your faith, your loyalty, and your biweekly therapy sessions. Every time, it starts with you. To my editor, Sally Kim: your brilliance, passion, and integrity shine so brightly. Working with you has been one of the great honors, and pleasures, of my life.

I couldn't have dreamed of more superb teams at WME and Putnam. It's a privilege to work with Tracy Fisher, Erin Conroy, Erika Niven, Haley Heidemann, and Chelsea Drake at the former, and with Ivan Held, Danielle Dieterich, Christine Ball, Alexis Welby, Ashley McClay, Emily Ollis, and Katie McKee at Putnam, as well as the full Penguin team. My thanks, too, to Gail Berman, Dani Gorin, Joe Earley, and Rory Koslow at Jackal for their work in the TV arena.

I am indebted to the many writers, filmmakers, scientists, and other professionals whose work was pivotal to my research process. Essential sources include *A subtle craft in several worlds: Performance and participation in Romani fortune-telling* (Ruth Elaine Andersen); David Weissman's documentary *I Was Here; Hiding the Elephant: How Magicians Invented the Impossible and Learned to Disappear* (Jim Steinmeyer); and the life of Tiny Kline, a ground-breaking circus performer who originated the Jaws of Life and inspired the character of Klara Sr. (*Circus Queen and Tinker Bell: The Memoir of Tiny Kline,* Janet M. David). Lt. Scott Gregory served as a crucial advisor for Daniel's military career; Erika Fleury, Deborah Robbins, and Bob Ingersoll kindly shared their experiences with primates. The Drake was inspired by the Buck Institute for Research on Aging in Novato, California, though my version is, besides building features and general mission, entirely fictionalized. Finally, I couldn't have written Varya's section were it not for the many scientists whose longevity research informed her own, and who were so generous as to speak with me, including Drs. Ricki Colman, Stefano Piraino, and Daniel Martinez, as well as staff from the Wisconsin National Primate Research Center. Varya's research emerged from this background but is, like the Drake, fictionalized and not meant as commentary on specific existing work.

Eternal love for, and thanks to, the family members and dear friends who served as early readers and offered assistance. My parents are my fiercest and most faithful supporters; I am so grateful, and so lucky, to be your child. My beloved grandmother and guiding light, Lee Krug, was the first person to read this novel. Among my brilliant friends, I am thankful for Alexandra Goldstein's editing genius and lifelong devotion; Rebecca Dunham's intellectual companionship; Brittany Cavallaro's passionate solidarity; and Piyali Bhattacharya's wise, beating heart, as well as the sisterhood of Alexandra Demet and the brotherhood of Andrew Kay. Marge Warren and Bob Benjamin gave me the gift of insight into immigrant and mid-twentieth-century life in New York City. Judy Mitchell continues to be a mentor and dear friend.

To Jordan and Gabriel, my siblings: this

book is for you, too.

And, my God, what is there to say for Nathan? It isn't easy to be the partner of a writer, but I would think you do it effortlessly if I didn't know how much mind-bending conversation, editorial work, and emotional support it requires. You have the most abiding heart and the quickest brain and the kind of panoramic perspective that steadies even fluttery birds like me. Forever, thank you.

ABOUT THE AUTHOR

Chloe Benjamin is the author of the novel *The Anatomy of Dreams,* which received the Edna Ferber Fiction Book Award and was longlisted for the Center for Fiction First Novel Prize. A San Francisco native, Benjamin is a graduate of Vassar College and of the University of Wisconsin, where she received an MFA in fiction. She lives with her husband in Madison, Wisconsin. She is twenty-eight years old.

The employees of Thorndike Press hope you have enjoyed this Large Print book. All our Thorndike, Wheeler, and Kennebec Large Print titles are designed for easy reading, and all our books are made to last. Other Thorndike Press Large Print books are available at your library, through selected bookstores, or directly from us.

For information about titles, please call:
(800) 223-1244

or visit our website at:
gale.com/thorndike

To share your comments, please write:
Publisher
Thorndike Press
10 Water St., Suite 310
Waterville, ME 04901